AN INDECENT PROPOSITION

STEPHANIE JULIAN

One woman. Two men. Half a million dollars. One night...

One night. That's all Erik and Keegan want with Julianne. And they've come up with the perfect plan: Offer Julianne a half-million dollars. Julianne is in debt up to her eyeballs due to her mother's illness. Five-hundred-thousand dollars would pay off her bills and give her a start on a new life. All she needs to do is have sex with a man she's never met.

An explosion left Erik with scars, physical and psychological. Work is his only refuge. Until he sees Julianne through a surveillance camera. And he discovers a desire he thought had been burned out of him.

Keegan has watched his best friend retreat from the world for too long. If his desire for Julianne brings him back to life, Keegan will bring her to him, whatever it takes.

Julianne is young, adventurous and not afraid to take what she wants. And she wants these men...

Want to know more? Join Stephanie in her private Reader Salon on Facebook.

And don't miss updates about new books and sales! Join here.

Don't miss any of the books in the Indecent series:

An Indecent Proposition

An Indecent Affair

An Indecent Arrangement

An Indecent Longing

An Indecent Desire

ONE

"Do you honestly think she's going to show up? What woman in her right mind would?"

"She'll show. The money will get her here but it'll be up to you to get her to stay."

"Sure. Thanks for laying that all on me."

"Hey, you know what happens when women see me. They freak."

Keegan Malone set his Seven & Seven aside and rubbed a hand over his aching forehead.

Why the hell did he allow Erik to get him involved in these damn schemes?

The fact that they'd been best friends since boarding school probably had something to do with it.

Erik Riley, second son of the blueblood billionaire Boston Rileys, had always been the one goading Keegan to bigger and better, whether it was pranks or grades or sports. They'd been each other's perfect foil. Erik had pushed Keegan and Keegan had reined in Erik. Together they'd become unstoppable.

The world had been theirs to conquer until Erik had been seriously fucked up in that fire three years ago.

After five reconstructive surgeries, Erik had had enough. Why go through the agony if he'd never look the same? He hadn't gotten over that yet. Maybe he never would. But this...

"Don't you think you're taking this too far? I know you've been infatuated with the girl since the party but why not just introduce yourself in some normal way? You know, call her and ask her to dinner. Or 'accidentally' bump into her on the street and introduce yourself. Oh, wait." He let sarcasm bleed into his words. "You never go out so that won't work, will it?"

Erik gave him the finger, using his uninjured left hand. He could do it perfectly well with his right but that hand was scarred from elbow to fingertips.

"This will work out best for all of us. She needs the money for her mom—"

"And you have the hots for her so you'll use the money to get her here and you'll use me to..."

"Fuck her so I can watch. Yeah, I will."

Sighing, Keegan shook his head.

He and Erik had shared women for years, since one drunken night at Princeton had ended with them waking up in the same bed with a blissfully sated co-ed between them.

Afterward, the girl had sung their praises to her friends and a campus legend had been born. They'd never been without willing bed partners.

They didn't only work well together in bed. TinMan Biometrics was proof of that. After eight years, they'd taken the company from startup to global player. They had played their roles well and grown the company until they'd believed there was nothing they couldn't handle.

Then Erik had nearly died in the explosion and the world had shifted under their feet.

That it should've been Keegan in the lab at the time of the

explosion and subsequent fire probably had a lot to do with the fact that he couldn't refuse Erik anything.

Including this incredibly ridiculous scheme.

When Erik had suggested it, Keegan had laughed in his face. Until he'd realized Erik hadn't been kidding.

And you didn't try very hard to talk him out of it, did you?

No, he hadn't. Because when he'd seen Julianne Carter at the cocktail party their company had held for potential clients a month ago, he'd wanted her. Desperately.

And because of the earpiece he wore to keep in contact with Erik during these events—which Keegan loathed but Erik refused to attend personally—he'd known Erik had noticed her too.

It'd been the first time in a long time that they'd agreed on a woman. And the first time Erik had shown any interest in a woman since the explosion.

Keegan hadn't gotten a chance to talk to her that night but, by the next day, Erik had her entire history.

And this crazy-ass scheme.

Keegan had never thought she'd agree. Had expected her to refuse the offer flat out.

If she had, Keegan would've arranged a meeting. Or manipulated one.

Before the accident, Erik had been the master of the straight-forward approach and Keegan the one who worked behind the scenes. After, their roles had reversed. Neither of them was comfortable in their new world order.

But this—

The distant but distinct sound of a car pulling to a stop in front of the house snapped both of them to attention.

Erik grinned at him, the first time Keegan had seen him smile in—well hell, he couldn't remember the last time he'd seen Erik smile.

Holy shit.

She was here.

JULIANNE HAD BEEN TOLD to expect creepy, but this was beyond strange.

If she didn't have such utter faith in her friend, Carol, she would've turned around and headed home after getting a look at the house.

Hell, if you were smart you wouldn't be here at all.

Sighing, she shook her head. There was one huge reason she was here.

No. Actually, there were five-hundred-thousand good reasons.

And she needed every last one of them.

Steeling her backbone, she turned off the car, listening to it wheeze and moan. Her nearly fifteen-year-old Toyota needed new brakes to pass inspection. Hell, it needed a lot more than that but she didn't have the money for the brakes much less a complete overhaul.

But she would...*if* she went through with this very indecent proposition.

She'd have the money for a car and be able to pay off her mom's medical bills *and* have money left over to start her own business. Or go back to school.

But first she had to get out of the car.

Turning, she looked at the house. If this were a movie, she'd get out of the car and a guy in a mask made of other women's flesh would jump from behind one of the huge trees surrounding the place. He'd drag her off to hang her on a meat hook at the back of the house and skin her.

The house... Well, in the daylight, it probably looked a hell of a lot better.

Now, just after nine on the night before Christmas Eve, it looked pretty damn depressing.

No holiday lights hung from the rafters of the Victorian mansion. The building wouldn't look out of place in Cape May. But stuck out here in the middle-of-nowhere Berks County, Pennsylvania, it looked...

Sad. Lonely. And more than a little creepy. One tiny light shone on the porch, barely enough illumination to make out the front door. At least the house had no broken windows or unhinged shutters. And no sign that said "Beware!"

A new coat of paint would go a long way toward a new lease on life for the place. Which was exactly what Julianne needed. A new lease on life.

And this...whatever the hell this was would be the start of that. Half a million dollars would go a long way toward canceling her and her mom's debt and setting them up in a new life.

Far away from small towns and small-minded people.

Resolve stiffened her spine and she got out of the car. Her heels sank into the gravel driveway but she'd been wearing stilettos since she was fifteen. She could probably run a seven-minute mile in them and not break her ankle.

And her high school guidance counselor had told her she had no life skills.

So there, Mr. Clark.

A cold wind whipped through the trees, making them moan and shake. Gathering the lapels of her coat closer together, she shivered as the wind bit at her naked legs.

Hurrying up the front steps, she walked to the door and knocked before she had second thoughts. Or third or fourth. Or fiftieth.

It's not that she didn't enjoy sex. Some people in this one-stoplight town thought she enjoyed it a little too much.

And even if those same people figured she'd probably sold herself before, it would be a lie.

Sure, she enjoyed sex. Hell, she loved it. And if she met a guy she liked and took him home with her for the night, whose business was it but hers and his?

It wasn't like she went out of her way to find married men to tempt away from their wives. Was it her fault she didn't do background checks on every man she was attracted to?

No, goddammit, it wasn't.

But she'd found out the hard way that, even if the man lied and said he was single and had no kids, she was still the bitch who'd ruined his marriage.

She and her mom really needed to get out of here. Start over. Make her dream of owning her own catering business a reality.

The man inside this house would give her the means. According to Carol, she'd be doing this guy a favor. Her friend had implied that he'd been in an accident and had some "issues" from that.

As long as he didn't want to hurt her or, oh, say, hang her on a meat hook and skin her alive, she'd be on board. Five-hundred-thousand dollars was a great motivator.

But she still had to be attracted to him. And she had to like a guy to take him to bed. But she was no princess in an ivory tower either, waiting for Prince Charming to rescue her. If she really couldn't stand him, she was out. Money be damned.

"Think of this as a blind date," Carol had said. "If you hit it off, that's great. If you decide to spend the night, you'll be five-hundred-thousand bucks richer. If you want to leave, all you have to do is say the word and you'll be out the door. I give you my word."

She still wasn't sure why the man had gone through Carol to approach her with this unusual request. Carol was an event planner. She didn't typically set up reclusive rich guys with minimum-wage catering employees.

No more stalling. Knock on the damn door.

She reached for the old-fashioned brass knocker before she managed to talk herself out of it.

Seconds later, a lock clicked and the door swung open. She almost expected it to creak. Instead, it barely made a sound.

"Come in, please."

The voice was low, cultured and totally fit the man who opened the door. Had to be in his mid-seventies, at least. He was still handsome even though he had a bit of a paunch and not much hair. What little hair he did have was trimmed neatly around his head. He wore khaki pants and a blue, button-down shirt and...

Jesus, the guy reminded her of her grandfather.

This is so not going to happen.

There was no way in *hell* she could make herself go to bed with him. "You know—"

"Mr. Smith will see you in the drawing room." The man waved his hand down a dark hall to her left. "It's the last door. Can I take your coat?"

So she wasn't here to see him? She almost breathed a sigh of relief.

But really...Mr. Smith. Gee, how original. "No, I think I'll keep my coat, thank you."

If she wanted to make a fast escape, she wanted to have it close. Besides, she didn't want the grandfather look-a-like to see what she had on underneath.

She'd dressed for the occasion.

The man's slight smile appeared understanding. "Then I'll make myself scarce." He held out a little black disk that looked like a car remote. She took it without thinking. "When you're ready to leave or should you need anything, press this. Have a good night."

He nodded, turned on his heel, and disappeared down a hallway on the opposite side of the house.

A panic button? Seriously?

She couldn't decide if she should be relieved or amused.

Okay, girl. It's now or never.

Debt free with enough left over to finance her dream, all for one night in a man's bed?

Or back to working for minimum wage and trying to dig out from a mountain of bills for the rest of her life?

She turned and headed down the hall.

TWO

The strong knock made Erik smile, which pulled at the tight skin of his jaw. The pain was negligible but a reminder of why he'd come up with this plan to get Julianne into bed.

From the first moment he'd seen her, dressed in the buttoned-up, black-and-white uniform of a catering waitress, he'd wanted her.

Julianne Carter had long, dark hair, deep brown eyes, curves that wouldn't quit and a frail mother with a mountain of debt. She could have any man she wanted. And she'd never want him.

As beautiful as she was, she'd take one look at him and run the other way. This was the only way he'd ever get close to her.

He'd gotten used to seeing the shock on a person's face. He didn't want to see it on hers. He'd had so much taken away from him over the past two years. But he wanted her, or at least as much pleasure as he could get from watching Keegan fuck her.

And damn it, he was going to get it, even if it took deception and money. Everyone had their price. He'd learned that the hard way.

Anyway, it wasn't like she wouldn't get something out of the bargain. She needed the money. And she'd get Keegan.

If things worked the way he planned, she'd never even see him. And if they went better than planned... Well, then she wouldn't see much of him.

Getting up, he retreated to the far side of the room, where the shadows would hide him, but where he could see everything in the firelight.

"Go ahead. Let her in."

Keegan scowled at him, his normally easy-going expression nowhere in sight. God damn it, Keegan would screw the whole deal by scaring her off before she ever got in the room.

But Erik would frighten her more. Hell, he frightened his own parents. Keegan was the only one who didn't look at him with horror and pity.

The horror he could take. The pity...not at all.

Keegan knew that, which was why he took a deep breath and let the tension bleed away before he opened the door. The man was a damn good actor. He could've had a huge career on the screen.

Dim light from the hallway spilled into the room, though it didn't reach far enough to expose him.

And then she walked through the door.

Holy hell, she was fucking gorgeous.

He clamped down on the urge to groan. His cock hardened in his jeans, his lust for her so fucking hot, he swore he could taste it.

She made him wanted to walk out of the shadows, throw her naked on a bed and fuck her until she was so sated she couldn't see straight. Scars be damned.

But he couldn't take the chance of scaring her away.

She'd been curious enough to open the proposal he'd sent through Carol, their friend and business manager. When Carol had said Julianne had accepted the offer, he hadn't let himself hope she'd actually show up. And now that she was here, he didn't think he'd be able to keep his hands to himself.

He'd told Keegan he only wanted to watch.

He'd been lying. He wanted to do so much more.

JULIANNE RECOGNIZED the handsome man who opened the door, though she couldn't place the face.

He nodded, no hint of a smile on his face. "Come in. I'm... glad to see you made it."

Wow, nice voice with the hint of an accent. Irish? Scottish? She wasn't sure. Whatever it was, it sounded amazing.

The nervous energy gathering in her gut began to dissipate as her sensual, adventurous side responded to him.

"I wasn't sure I was going to come," she admitted. "But when you offer a girl five-hundred-thousand dollars to have sex with you, it certainly grabs her attention."

She swore she saw the faintest hint of a blush color his cheeks. What the hell? This was his deal. Why would he be embarrassed?

Still, it boosted her confidence. She *would* carry this off. She needed that damn money.

And this guy certainly wasn't hard on the eyes. His dark brown hair glinted red in the firelight and was a little longer than business casual, with waves that made her want to sink her fingers in them. Blue, blue eyes, a strong nose and beautifully curved mouth. And cheeks covered with absolutely adorable freckles.

He looked about ten years older than her so that made him early thirties. Didn't make a difference. Age meant little to her.

Unless he was old enough to be her grandfather. Then, yes, that obviously was a problem.

But why would a guy who looked like him need to bribe a girl to sleep with him?

Waving her into the room, he closed the door behind her. She almost expected to hear the click of a lock. She was surprised when he left the door cracked just enough that she could see it.

Had he done that for her?

"Would you like a drink?" He motioned toward a fully stocked bar on the other side of the room from the roaring fireplace. "And can I take your coat?"

Did she hear a hint of nerves in his voice? Was he afraid she'd leave?

Surprisingly, she really wanted to stay.

"I'll take some white wine if you have it."

As for the coat... Maybe it'd be best just to get this part over with. She'd worn her warmest, a down stadium jacket that covered her from neck to knees. Not only because the temperature outside hovered close to zero but because she wasn't wearing all that much underneath.

As he nodded and turned toward the bar, she unzipped. While he had his back to her, she took a deep breath and let it fall to the floor.

And swore she heard the distinct sound of a man drawing in a sharp breath. But she was pretty sure it hadn't come from the man standing at the bar.

Her gaze searched the darkened corners of the room, which was bigger than she'd first realized. Much bigger. Someone could hide in that darkness and she'd never know they were there. Unless they made a sound.

Was there someone else in the room with them?

"You're beautiful."

Her attention returned to the man she could see. He'd turned back to her and now she saw lust in every line of his face.

His desire emboldened her and she walked toward him with her head high and her gaze pinning him in place.

"Thank you for the wine." She accepted the glass and took a sip before touching her hand to the bare curves of her breasts revealed by the slinky corset. "Do you like? I've had it for a few years. Saw it online and knew I had to have it. I just never had the right occasion. I thought tonight might be time for its debut."

He took a gulp of his drink, his eyes closing for a brief moment before he took a deep breath. "I'm honored you wore it for me."

Honored? Okay, what was wrong with his man that he had to offer women a small fortune to sleep with him?

The mass of conflicting thoughts and emotions running through her made her head spin. This evening was becoming more surreal than it already had been. And she was so turned on right now, her panties were soaking through.

What decent girl would be so aroused under these circumstances?

No, she didn't believe sex between consenting adults was a bad thing. And yes, she was consenting.

For five-hundred-thousand reasons.

But the money... Did taking money to have sex with this man make her a whore?

Did it matter?

She took money for performing a service where people looked through her like she was invisible. Why should it be different to take money for a service she actually enjoyed?

"Obviously you know my name, so I'm at a disadvantage. What's yours?"

He didn't hesitate, like he was trying to decide if he should lie. "Keegan."

Unusual. She liked it. "Have we met before, Keegan?"

His gaze never left hers. "Not formally, no."

"But I do recognize you, don't I?"

There was that hint of a blush again. The one she really liked.

"Probably, yes. You catered an event I...attended a few weeks ago."

She thought for a minute, staring into those blue eyes. "TinMan Biometrics. The reception at their offices."

Finally, the guy smiled. And her doubts melted like chocolate in the sun.

Was she being too trusting? Taken in by a sweet face and her own greed?

Maybe. But was it really greed when the money wasn't all for her? When most of it would go to pay her mom's doctor's bills?

Sure, he could still knock her out cold, drag her into his basement and dismember her for kicks and giggles. And even though the agreement she'd signed had included a non-disclosure clause as well as one that ensured her safety, she'd left a note for her mom just the same.

That same agreement had assured her that her partner for the evening had a clean bill of health. Yes, she was on the pill but she'd still brought condoms.

"So tell me—Oh!"

He wrapped one hand around her neck and kissed the hell out of her.

The shock made her freeze for several seconds before her mouth began to soften.

She stood on her toes to make them fit together better. Even though she was wearing heels, he still had a good three inches on her.

She liked that he was taller. Liked the feel of his hand on her neck, the way his lips felt against hers.

Her eyes had snapped shut when their lips touched and she let herself fall headlong into the kiss. Holding her steady with one hand on the back of her neck and the other on her hip, he plastered her body against his.

And damn but the guy could kiss. She felt like she was being devoured. In the best possible way. His mouth sealed over hers, his tongue pressing between her lips, sliding against her tongue and demanding she give herself over to him.

Her pussy went wet, a tight ache building low in her body. A void that needed to be filled.

God, she wanted him to lay her out and fuck her until she screamed. And then to continue until she couldn't scream anymore.

Obviously, it'd been too long since she'd gotten laid.

Her arms slid around his waist, head tilting so she could get a better angle. She sought to assert some dominance, to control some part of this—to control him—but he wasn't going to allow it.

Sliding his hands into her hair, he tugged. It wasn't painful but he wasn't letting go either. She let him direct her movement and his mouth moved. He spread kisses along her jaw to her ear, worrying the lobe between his teeth before he bit his way down her neck. Each sharp nip at her skin made her shiver, made her nipples tighten into points as hard as diamonds. Her breasts were crushed against his chest but she wanted to rub herself against bare male flesh.

His bare male flesh.

She gasped as he lifted her off the ground just as he bit the curve of her neck and shoulder.

"Wrap your legs around my waist. Do it now."

My God, that voice. That accent did things to her that

should be illegal. Shouldn't be possible. Every nerve ending in her body tingled with anticipation.

Her clit swelled, her sex tightened into a hot, throbbing ache.

Had he put something in her drink? She didn't feel drugged. She felt...overheated. Overwhelmed. Like a vast pit of sexual need had been tapped deep within her and she needed to be fucked. Now. Right now. Hard and fast. Forced to submit. Forced to give over control.

No.

"Yes, that's right." He spoke as if he'd read her mind. But he was only praising her for following his orders, which she hadn't realized she'd done. "Fucking hell, you're beautiful."

Other men had said the same words to her. She'd believed it from some of them.

Now, as this stranger walked with her toward the fireplace, she wanted to believe him.

When he laid her out on a chaise lounge big enough for two people, she almost did.

"No. Stay there." His voice held a note of command as she moved to sit up, to reach for him.

She stilled, though she couldn't seem to catch her breath and her chest rose and fell so fast she thought she might hyperventilate.

Standing beside the chaise, his groin was just above her eye level and the bulge there made her mouth water.

Big and bold and she couldn't wait to uncover it.

She reached for him—

He grabbed her hand, stopping her short of her prize. "No touching. Not yet. I'll let you know when. Right now, I want you to do exactly what I say. Can you do that for me, Jules?"

She liked the nickname. It sounded exotic, intimate coming from his mouth.

She nodded, not sure she could form a coherent reply. Not even one word.

How the hell had he done this to her in such a short time?

Probably because when he smiled at her like that, lust pulsed through her body and short-circuited every one of her rational brain cells.

"I want you to play with your breasts. Pull your top down and stroke your nipples."

A flush suddenly burned her cheeks, which was ridiculous. Why should her own hands on her breasts make her embarrassed?

Maybe because it was almost too intimate. And this was not a lover she'd chosen for herself.

He'd bought her.

But she'd had to give her consent so technically, this *was* her choice.

She shrugged and the corset's spaghetti straps dropped off her shoulders, causing the front to dip.

She reached for the middle and pulled the material beneath her breasts, plumping them into overflowing mounds. She had great tits, full and firm. Men liked them, fixated on them. And she appreciated their appreciation.

Watching Keegan, she saw his chest rise and fall in a faster rhythm, saw his gaze narrow as he followed her hands.

Slowly, she cupped her breasts, massaging them. They felt heavy, sensitive. And when she pinched the nipples between her thumbs and forefingers, she groaned from the pleasure.

As she worked them into even harder points, that pleasure sank through her body.

Straight to her clit.

The heat in Keegan's eyes made that tiny organ between her legs throb. She let one hand fall from her breast to trail down her stomach—

"No. I didn't say you could touch your pussy. Not yet."

Keegan's voice sounded almost an octave deeper now and it resonated through her, causing her thighs to clench. She moved her hand back to her breast. Her lungs labored for air, her heart pounded against her ribs.

Could she make herself come with just her hands on her breasts? She wouldn't have thought it was possible but now...

Her eyes closed as she fondled her nipples harder, pinching the tips with more force. Eliciting more of a response.

She could smell her response, smell the scent of her arousal as it coated her pussy and slicked her thighs.

Did he notice?

He'd retreated to a chair not far from where she lay. He had full view of her.

And so would anyone sitting in the farthest corners of the room, where the shadows hid everything.

Was there someone else in the room? She swore she felt another pair of eyes on her from somewhere.

"Jules, look at me. I don't want you to take your eyes off of me, Beautiful. Good. Now take off your panties."

The panties were actually tap pants but she wouldn't expect a man to know that. She almost didn't want to leave her breasts but, right now, she wanted whatever he wanted.

She disobeyed for several seconds before she dragged her hands down her body to the elastic waistband of the pants. Lifting her ass off the chaise, she shimmied them down her thighs then lowered her ass back down and rolled her torso just enough so she could push the pants past her knees.

When they hung around her ankles, she leaned back into the cushion and worked the pants off with her feet.

Then she tossed them at him.

He caught them in one hand and held them, staring at her for several seconds, before he brought them close to his face and took a deep breath. He didn't actually rub them against his nose but he made sure she knew that he liked what he had in his hand.

After a few seconds, he dropped the pants into his lap, where it draped over the bulge of his erection.

Her mouth dried at the thought of what was beneath.

"Now show me how you get yourself off, Jules. Make yourself come."

"Is that all this will be? You and..." she let her pause drag for a second, wanted him to know she suspected there was other person in the room, but he showed no outward response, "me and no contact between us?"

His mouth pulled up at one corner. Sexy as hell. "Oh, I definitely plan to have contact, Jules. But not yet. Not until you show me what I want to see."

"And what's that?"

"I want to watch you come."

Damn, she wanted that too but she wasn't sure she could do it like this. Usually she needed a vibrator. "I don't know that..."

His eyes narrowed. "What?"

"I need a vibrator."

He didn't respond right away. She thought she might have lost him. Then he leaned forward. "Internal or external?"

"External."

Nodding, he rose and walked into the shadows behind his chair. As her eyes became more adjusted to the light level, she followed him farther into the shadows but then she lost him.

The room was *much* bigger than she realized.

Seconds later, he returned holding something in his hands.

"Will this work?"

He held out a palm-sized piece of green silicon, shaped like a curved leaf with a circular handle on one end and a rounded tip on the other.

She smiled into his eyes. "Yes."

His gaze held hers for several seconds before he let it wander. Down to her breasts, still naked and heaving from before, to her stomach and, finally, between her legs.

She kept the hair on her mound trimmed close and her pussy waxed bare. The lack of hair made her skin that much more sensitive.

He startled a quick gasp out of her when he reached down to stroke his fingertips over that hair. Her sex clenched, aching to be filled, and heat rolled over her like a wave, searing her from the tips of her toes to the top of her head.

"Use the vibrator, Jules. I want to see you come."

If he stood there the entire time, it wouldn't take her long. She couldn't believe how much she was turned on by all of this.

It didn't make any sense. She'd never been an exhibitionist or a hedonist. She loved sex, loved how it made her feel when she was with the right person. But this...

She didn't know Keegan and yet this was turning into the most intense sexual experience of her life.

And he hadn't done more than watch and let his fingertips brush over her.

Dragging her gaze away from his for a moment, she located the button that activated the vibrator then looked back at him. His gaze had transferred to the toy.

Pressing the button, she felt the subtle buzz ricochet through her body. The sound pricked at her ears and made her chest feel like a two-ton weight lay on it.

His fingers froze for a second before continuing up her leg. Curling his hand around her thigh, he pulled her leg out, opening her.

Slightly cooler air brushed against her exposed pussy, teasing and tormenting. She automatically tried to close her legs, ease the ache, but he held her open.

"Put it on your clit." Keegan voice sounded almost like a growl.

Her hand moved before her brain made sense of his words and she moaned as the vibrating tip made contact. Sensation ripped through her, sending pulses of ecstasy to her womb. Her eyes closed as she absorbed the sensation, let it course through her body.

Her orgasm gathered strength with each second. She knew it wouldn't be long before it broke and she welcomed it.

Opening her eyes, she saw Keegan's had narrowed to slits, his lips parted and his chest heaving.

His erection straining.

She wanted him to fill her with that thick shaft. From this angle, she could tell the guy was well hung, and damn if she didn't appreciate a man with a huge cock as much as the next girl.

Deliberately backing off the vibrator just a bit, she placed her free hand directly over that bulge.

And smiled when he bit back a groan.

She stroked him through the jeans, squeezed and fondled. Through slitted eyes, she watched his expression tighten into a mask of pure lust. His free hand, the one not gripping her thigh hard enough to leave marks, grabbed her and smashed her palm against his groin.

He ground his cock against her until she thought it had to hurt. And he did look to be in pain. But not the kind that made him want her to stop.

"Ah, fuck me. That's fucking—Christ almighty."

He ripped her hand away, startling her into pulling the vibrator away. Her body missed the stimulation and wanted to curl into a ball in denied lust.

She moaned, already reaching for him again when she realized what he was doing.

Ripping at the top button of his jeans, he dragged the zipper down then shoved his jeans and underwear down his hips, freeing his cock. It was just as wonderful as she'd imagined. Thick and long and standing at attention. The head was a ruddy red nearly two shades darker than the shaft. It pulsed with blood and one pearly drop of liquid sat on the tip.

"Suck me while you get yourself off, Jules. I can't wait any longer. I promise to return the favor."

Hell, yes.

She sat up and wrapped her free hand around the vividly hot shaft. So silky soft. And iron stiff.

Rubbing her thumb against the tip, she spread that little bit of moisture around the head, her mouth watering to taste him.

She repositioned the vibrator, catching her clit at an angle that kept her stimulated but didn't push her over the edge. Then she slid her hand back and forth on his dick.

"Yeah, that's right. Jerk me off."

Using every bit of skill she had, she brought him right to the brink but backed off every time she felt him get too close to coming.

His balls were drawn up so tight, she took pity on them and transferred her attention for several minutes. Rolling them in her hands, stroking one finger between them before dragging the tip back along his perineum.

He groaned, one hand reaching for her. But when she thought he'd pull her close so he could fuck her mouth, he only wove his fingers through her hair and cupped the back of her head. He used his other hand to stroke himself as she played with his balls.

She didn't know how long she watched him, holding onto the edge of her own orgasm by a slim margin.

Finally his eyes reopened. "Suck me now, baby. I want to come in your mouth."

She didn't hesitate. She shot to a seated position on the edge of the chaise. Keeping her legs spread, she repositioned the vibrator as she opened her mouth and let his cock slip between her lips. Sucking him deep, she held him there, letting her tongue rasp against the slickness of his skin. He stilled for several seconds, head thrown back, the sound of his rough breathing scraping the air around them.

But she couldn't wait that long. She moved, pulling back until only the head rested behind her lips, swirling the tip of her tongue over the slit.

He smelled like clean male, tasted salty and hot. She let herself work him with abandon, shoving all reservations aside. She didn't want to rush, she wanted to savor.

She didn't feel like she had to perform. Instead, she let herself revel in the sensations.

And between the vibrator and the powerful sense that she controlled his desire, a raging orgasm built low in her body.

Increasing the action of her mouth on his cock, she sucked him hard, her cheeks hollowing. She shivered as he groaned, his fingers curling into her hair. The slight burn on her scalp heightened her desire.

She wanted him to come harder than he ever had before. He was in her power.

She dipped down on him again, relaxing her throat so she could take him even deeper. Then she swallowed and heard him swear in a guttural tone that tugged low in her pussy.

She tried to smile but couldn't, her mouth stretched around his cock. As she returned to the tip, she used her teeth to scrape against the skin, making his shaft jerk.

His hips began to move, shallow thrusts as he held her head steady. She let him fuck her mouth, content for now to know he enjoyed this. She concentrated on pleasuring herself, teasing her clit until she teetered on the edge but pulling the vibrator away just before she hit completion.

They did that dance for countless minutes, lost in a sexual haze.

Was it the sheer decadence of the situation that made this so much more exciting? And did it matter?

No. All that mattered was the pleasure. Giving. Taking. Making this man come. The power in that.

With a groan, he began to thrust harder, his heightened sense of urgency infecting her, as well.

When he growled low in his throat, she swore it reverberated in his cock, against her tongue. Then his hands stilled, holding her steady as his cock jerked in her mouth and he came.

His fluid hit her tongue and she swallowed the salty essence as she tilted the vibrator at just the right angle and let herself explode.

THREE

Holy Christ.

Erik had to bite his tongue so he didn't make a sound as he came in his hand.

Warm, sticky fluid spurted over his fingers and spattered against the leg of his jeans. His cock twitched for at least a minute, as he tried not to breathe too heavily and give away his presence.

He'd never come that hard by himself before.

But you're not alone, are you?

What he wouldn't give to get out of the shadows and join them.

She ticked off every item on his fantasy girl list. Beautiful. Stacked. Adventurous. So very sexy.

Before the accident, he wouldn't have hesitated to introduce himself before seducing her into his bed, would've had no problem inviting Keegan along for the ride if she'd been willing.

Together, he and Keegan made for one outstanding fucking experience, one they'd perfected after years of practice.

Since the accident... Well, he didn't get out much. Or at all.

And certainly not to meet women. His libido had taken a nosedive since the fire.

Until he'd seen Julianne, he hadn't much cared. She'd reawakened something inside him that he'd been content to live without since the accident.

Now... Content sucked. Content should be a four-letter word.

And it was all her fault.

He wanted to curse, wanted to scream obscenities until he was hoarse.

He wanted out of the damn shadows.

But he wasn't sure the beautiful woman who'd just sucked off his best friend wouldn't run for the front door the second she saw him.

———

KEEGAN FELL BACK into the chair across from the chaise, his lungs working overtime.

Holy hell. She'd made his fucking knees weak.

Jules had stretched back out on the chaise, eyes closed, one arm over her head, the other palm-up by her side. Her dark hair looked like an ink stain spreading across the pale fabric of the cushion, the vibrator abandoned by her side.

Had she come as hard as he had? She looked worn out but satisfied if the curve of her lips was anything to go by.

That mouth... Just looking at her made his blood flow south again. He wanted to join her on the chaise, kneel between her thighs and shove himself deep inside her. Then he wanted to take her ass while Erik fucked her pussy.

No chance of that happening, now, is there?

Shit.

At least a minute passed as they both caught their breath. Finally, her eyes opened and stared straight into his.

"Are you going to introduce me to the other person in the room now or are we going to continue to pretend he's not there?"

He didn't feign surprise. From what he'd learned from Carol, Jules was smart. Intelligent, perceptive and sexually adventurous. Fucking perfect in his book.

She didn't seem shocked or morally outraged. She looked curious.

"Why do you think there's another man here?"

"Because I can feel him watching."

He thought about his response, considered simply outing Erik and letting him deal with the consequences. But he wouldn't do that to his friend. Still, he wasn't going to lie to the woman when she'd asked him a straightforward question.

"I'm not going to introduce you. He has to do that himself. But I don't think he will."

Would that taunt be enough to pull Erik out of the shadows? The challenge had been thrown. She knew he was here.

He didn't think Jules would turn out to be one of those women who flinched at the sight of Erik. If she did... well, then she wasn't the person he thought she was.

Sure, she'd be shocked. But he thought she'd be able to see beyond the scars. Maybe even to the person Erik had been before the fire. The one who'd actually enjoyed life. It pissed Keegan off to know Erik had lost not only his looks but also a shitload of confidence.

And that was the hardest part of all of this—for both of them.

Jules' gaze narrowed on his just before she looked out into the shadows on the other side of the room. Where Erik sat.

She couldn't see him. Keegan knew that because he knew where Erik was and he couldn't see him either.

Jules sat up, no hint of embarrassment about her partial nudity. "Are you going to join us or are you going to hide there are all night?"

Silence.

Damn it, Erik. Just fucking—

"Maybe you won't like what you see."

Erik's terse reply made Keegan's mouth drop open in shock. Maybe there was hope after all. And it all depended on Jules.

Keegan watched her consider her next move. She took her time before her attention returned to him. "Can I have my panties back? I'm feeling a little chilly."

"Of course."

He didn't want to give up the silky bit of fabric but he understood why she wouldn't want to sit here with her pussy on full display. After he'd handed them over, he reached for the chenille blanket lying over the back of his chair and draped it around her shoulders.

She gave him a grateful smile then stood, holding the blanket together between her breasts. Walking forward a few steps, she paused at the side of Keegan's chair.

"Maybe you should let me make that determination."

She spoke again to the shadows, responding to Erik's earlier statement.

Another silence held for several long seconds.

Keegan couldn't sit still any longer. He stood beside Jules and stared into the darkness.

Come on, Erik. Take that first step.

"I'm not a pretty sight for a pretty woman." Erik's voice held a hard edge of self-loathing. "You'll probably be happier if I stay back here while you and Keegan get to know each other better."

"While you watch?"

"Yes." He paused. "Unless you want me to leave."

She didn't hesitate. "I don't want you to leave. I want to see the man who's watching me fuck his friend. At least," she looked at Keegan, "I'm assuming you're friends?"

Keegan couldn't keep his smart-ass comment to himself. "Only if the bastard manages to grow a set and get out here."

A longer silence this time and Keegan's jaw tightened. Son-of-a-bitch. Erik wasn't going to—

The shadows began to move until they solidified into the form of a man.

FOUR

Erik almost couldn't help himself.

He wanted to join Keegan and Jules so bad, he swore he could taste it. Still, he knew there was a high probability his scars would prove too much for her and she'd run.

He wouldn't blame her. He couldn't. There were days he couldn't bear to look in the mirror.

But the need to touch her, to actually participate in fucking her... He couldn't pass it up. With steady strides, he made his way into the dim circle of light from the fireplace. Gaze glued to her face, breath frozen in his chest, he watched her response.

Her head tilted to the side as he came into view, her eyes narrowing as if she couldn't quite make sense of what she was seeing, then widening as she did.

He stopped as her shock became evident, her mouth parting to draw in a sharp breath. He wanted to keep walking straight out of the room.

Fucking hell, he should've stayed in the shadows where he belonged—

Jules stepped forward, hands reaching out to him. She

stopped before she touched him but her gaze held his steadily. "May I?"

She wanted to touch his face? Most women couldn't even look at it. The only people who had touched his face since the fire had been doctors and nurses. No one else had asked or even considered it.

"Why?" His voice emerged like a rough bark, revealing way too much about his mental state.

She didn't appear to be put off by his tone. "Because you need to see I'm not afraid of you. Are you in pain?"

Seriously? "The only pain I feel right now is between my legs. But, no, my scars don't hurt."

If he'd thought she'd stammer or be embarrassed by his crude statement, he'd thought wrong. Her expression never changed.

"How long ago were you hurt?"

"It's been two years. When they wanted to do a sixth reconstructive surgery, I said no. I'd had enough."

He was never going to look like he had before the surgery. Why put himself through the agony? The men and women who worked with him had gotten used to his appearance. Well, they no longer stared, at least.

Large crowds were a different story. He hated that everyone seemed to be looking at him, even if they tried not to. The few women he'd met the very few times he'd ventured out into society had practically run screaming. They couldn't look him in the eyes because all they saw were the scars on the right side of his face.

And those who actually *could* look at him stared with morbid curiosity instead. They wanted to prod at him, ask questions, dig into his psyche. He felt like a damn sideshow freak.

But he didn't get that vibe from Jules—and the lust pumping

through his veins had to be ten times as strong because he hadn't felt it in ages.

Except for the night he'd seen her.

"I understand recovery from reconstructive surgery can be brutal."

Her voice held no pity, which would've turned him off more than if she'd gasped at his hideousness and run for the door.

"It had its moments."

"Is your body scarred too?"

"Yes. My right arm and hand, my right leg and down my right side." He paused, another thought occurring to him. "Are you asking if everything still functions correctly?"

She didn't respond, just continued to look at them.

He held out his left hand. "I have an easy way to prove that to you."

She didn't reach for him right away but kept staring into his eyes as if searching for answers to questions she hadn't asked. He didn't know what else she could possibly want to know. This wasn't a date. It was more of a business transaction than anything else.

Since he was the one paying, he refused to answer any more questions. If she wanted to walk, now was the time. He opened his mouth to say that but before he could get the words out, she reached for him.

She didn't go for his hand, though. She reached for his cock, already hard again and straining against the zipper of his jeans.

"I guess that answers the question then, doesn't it?"

The sexual innuendo infused in her voice made his lungs tighten until he thought he wasn't going to be able to breathe. It'd been ages since a woman had looked at him like Jules was—with passion in her eyes.

Then she squeezed him, not hard, not to hurt, and he had to restrain the urge to grab her like Keegan had before and kiss her.

Instead, he held himself still and let her explore him. With her gaze glued to his, she found his shaft and rubbed her palm against it. A slow steady tease that made his breath rasp in his lungs.

"How long has it been?" she asked. "Have you had sex since the accident? Or will this be your first time?"

Shock made him silent. He hadn't believed anyone could do that to him anymore. A flush rose in his cheeks.

God damn, he refused to be embarrassed here but he couldn't get his brain to come up with a reply. Why the hell would she want to know that?

"I only ask because if the first round is...brief...I can plan for a second. Wouldn't want anyone to be left disappointed."

Seriously? He didn't think she could disappoint him if she tried. Especially not when she reached between his legs to fondle his balls, rolling them with her fingers and making his dick throb.

"Then make your plans," he managed to say. "I think seconds are definitely on the menu."

JULIANNE WOULD'VE BEEN LYING if she'd said she hadn't been shocked when this man first revealed himself.

But she'd taken care of her mom after her surgeries and she'd learned outward appearances didn't matter as much as most people thought.

Or, more specifically, men like her father. He hadn't been able to look at her mom after the double mastectomy. He'd only seen a woman no longer worthy of his time.

Fucking prick bastard. She'd called him that to his face after he'd blown through most their savings, spending the money on prostitutes and blaming his need for them on her mom's inability to see to his needs.

She'd had *cancer*, had barely made it through chemo and he wanted her to perform in bed.

Luckily, he'd left or someone would've had to call the cops to save his worthless ass from the Taser she kept in her pocketbook. The Taser she would have used on his pride and joy—his dick.

Her mom had survived. She'd beaten the cancer. She'd even managed to get back to work and attempt to pay off her bills. She'd gone through hell and come back.

This man had been through hell but was still stuck there.

Yes, his scars were ugly but *he* wasn't ugly. At least she didn't think so.

Or maybe that was the money talking.

Still, if she hadn't forced him out of the shadows, she could've fucked Keegan and taken the money. But her mom always told her she was like a dog with a bone. When she got hold of a puzzle or riddle or mystery, she couldn't let it rest until she'd figured it out.

She'd *known* someone else was in the room with them. She couldn't ignore it. She'd had to know. And now that she'd met Erik, she wasn't going to allow him to sneak back into the dark. She was baring herself in ways she'd never thought possible tonight. It was only fair that he and Keegan do the same.

"Do you and Keegan do this a lot?"

"What? Pay women to come to the house and fuck us? No. You're the first."

Her first instinct was to take offense at the sneer in his voice. She had a kneejerk reaction to slap him. But he was only answering the question she'd asked. And she heard the soul-deep hurt behind the sneer.

Keegan obviously didn't because he shoved Erik so hard, he stumbled backward.

"You utter, fucking bastard! What the fuck are you doing?"

"Keegan, no!"

She grabbed his arm, pulled him away from Erik, who'd held his ground.

Glaring at Keegan, Erik let his hands curl into fists at his side but didn't raise them. "She asked the question. I told her the truth."

"You son-of-a-bitch." Keegan's voice had dropped to a vicious, angry growl, his accent thickening even more. "Do you really want me to tell her why you felt you had to pay her?"

Erik's jaw tightened until she thought it might snap and his mouth drew into a thin line.

"Nothing to say?" Keegan taunted when Erik didn't respond. "No, you don't because you're too much of a damn cow—"

"Stop! Now." If Keegan said anything else, she was afraid it would break something between the men. "I already know why I'm here."

Both men turned to look at her, Keegan still furious, Erik with the wariness of a trapped animal.

"You think the only reason I would even *consider* sleeping with you is for the money, don't you?"

Silence fell until the only sound in the room was the crackling fire and the men's heavy breathing.

Erik blinked first, his throat moving as he swallowed. When he turned away from her, she saw the muscles on the undamaged side of his face jump.

He must have been a gorgeous man before the accident. Women had probably fallen at his feet.

Now... he wasn't hideous. Yes, he was scarred but that didn't make him a monster. It didn't make him a charity case either.

"I think we should start over."

Both men looked at her as if they had no idea what she was saying.

Maybe they didn't.

If Keegan had tried to pick her up in the traditional way—without paying her hundreds of thousands of dollars to do it—she probably would've let him.

He seemed sweet and, though that didn't usually do it for her, he also made her want to get him dirty. Or at least try.

Erik... Erik had an edge.

She'd always gravitated toward guys with an edge. Guys who didn't always watch what they said around women and rode motorcycles that tore through the streets with ear-splitting roars and worked with their hands. Guys who drank beer and didn't say "Pardon my French" every time they dropped the f-bomb around a woman.

She wanted to see what happened when she pushed Erik past that edge. According to, well, everyone who knew her, she was good at pushing people past their limits.

Crossing her arms under her breasts so they pushed over the top of the corset, she was impressed as hell when neither man's eyes dropped to her chest.

"Start over how?" Erik finally said. "Do you want me to stick out my hand and introduce myself and say how nice it is to meet you when I've already watched you get yourself off?"

If he wanted to make her blush, he was going to have to work a lot harder than that. "Did you enjoy watching? Did you come too?"

Erik's gaze narrowed. "I did. All over my hand."

Smiling at the surly tone of his voice, she took a step closer. He didn't back away, didn't move a muscle. "Next time I want to watch *you*."

The corners of his mouth curled into the slightest bit of a smile. The sight made her heart beat faster. "Next time, I want to be inside you when I come."

She lifted a challenging brow at him. "Then you're going to

have to change your attitude or you'll be relegated to the shadows for the rest of the night."

Erik's chin lifted. "So you're staying?"

She paused and she swore she heard Keegan draw in a deep breath and hold it. Erik flat-out refused to give her the satisfaction.

"I'll stay. For now. But I expect you both to make it worth my while."

"You mean—"

"Shut up, Erik. Just...shut up."

Keegan shoved at Erik's shoulder but Erik didn't budge. He didn't finish the thought either.

"Jules, would you like another drink?"

She gave Keegan a smile and watched him return it slowly.

Heat bloomed again between her legs, already so turned on she wanted to wrap her body around Erik and see how all that aggression translated into sex. And how the two of them would feel taking her at the same time.

And that had nothing at all to do with money.

AS KEEGAN MOVED toward the bar in the corner, Erik threw himself on the couch by the fireplace.

He tried not to stare as Julianne walked back to the fireplace, hips swaying with mouth-watering grace. He knew she was exaggerating for him. Jesus, the woman could convince the pope to give up his vows.

She had a world-class ass that he wanted to smack while he knelt behind her and fucked her so hard she passed out. Lust boiled through his veins like lava and he forced himself not to squirm like a teenager with a hard-on in the hot teacher's class.

He needed a drink. Maybe more than one.

His cock already at attention, it thickened even more as she sank onto the chaise and laid herself out on her side, one hand holding up her head. She'd dropped the blanket she'd had around her shoulders onto the floor. This close to the fire, she didn't need it.

Long, dark hair fell to the chaise and pooled there. He wanted to wrap the length around his hand as he kissed her. Then he wanted to wind it around his cock.

She looked relaxed, in charge. And so damn sexy, he had the overwhelming urge to go over there and fall on her like a beast.

He managed to restrain himself. But only barely.

"So tell me, Erik. Do you and Keegan usually do one woman together? Is that the only way you can get it up?"

Keegan coughed from the bar area. *Bastard.* His so-called best friend was enjoying the hell out of watching her tie him in knots.

The corners of her mouth twitched, as if she knew Keegan was laughing.

He considered ignoring her but found he wanted to talk. Wanted her to talk, as well. "No, it's not the only way. But we've learned women can be very...*grateful* for the pleasure we can give her together."

"And how did you discover this?"

"In college." Keegan answered as he returned with a glass in each hand. He handed one to Julianne and the other to Erik then made a return trip for his own. "And we found we were good at it."

She took a sip of her drink. "Do you two have a thing for each other?"

It was a common question women usually asked because they thought he and Keegan were bisexual. "Nothing sexual, no."

"And Erik's the only one I would ever trust in this situation." Keegan sprawled back into the chair he'd occupied earlier. "We work well together."

And lately, it was the only way he got laid.

"Do you like to watch each other?"

Again, Erik got no sense that she was asking because she found it distasteful. She was simply curious. She wanted to know how they worked. He liked that about her.

Hell, he liked pretty much everything about her.

"It's not that simple." He thought about it for a second then looked to Keegan for help.

Keegan just sipped his drink and let him swing.

After a heavy sigh, Erik continued. "It's not like watching porn. It's more like sharing an orgasm with someone who appreciates it as much as you do."

Not that that made it any clearer. Still, Julianne nodded as if she understood.

"So if I get up," which she did, "and walk over to you," she stopped in front of Erik, staring down at him, "and tell you to take your clothes off so I can fuck you on this couch, Keegan will enjoy it?"

"Fuck yeah."

Erik heard Keegan's muttered response loud and clear. And apparently, so did Julianne.

Her lips curved in a sensuous smile that made it hard for him to breathe.

"Then take off your clothes, Erik. You look a little warm."

Erik had turned the heat up not long after she'd dropped her coat. He hadn't wanted her to be cold. Now the room felt like a sauna. But Erik was pretty sure that had more to do with his internal temperature than the actual room temperature.

With her hands on her hips, she watched as he leaned to the side to put his glass on the table next to him then reached over his head to pull his shirt off. If she was going to fuck him right here and now, he wanted to feel her skin against his.

Her gaze skimmed over the scars on his arm and body but, again, she didn't seem to be affected by them. When he reached for the button on his jeans, she followed his hand. As he lowered the zipper, he heard her take a deep breath as he bared his cock to her.

The explosion had hit his right side, his arm and face taking most of the damage. His legs had mostly been spared, although there were a few spots on his right thigh. His cock had been completely unaffected and now jutted up from his groin, ten inches long and three around.

Women had been known to lick their lips when they saw him. Before.

Julianne looked into his eyes and smiled.

"Is that all for me?"

God, yes. "Absolutely. Why don't you climb on and I'll give you a good ride?"

"I think I will."

With a few quick movements of her hands, her panties and her corset dropped to the floor and she stood naked in front of him.

He sucked in a sharp breath, feeling like he'd been kicked in the gut.

Jesus, she was gorgeous. Her breasts were firm and high, at least a C-cup with just enough jiggle to prove they weren't fake. They were tipped with tight, light pink nipples. Her generous hips were curved and he couldn't wait until she turned around so he could see her ass. This woman wasn't anywhere near model skinny and was all the more beautiful for it.

He didn't have a lot of time to admire her, though. She took two steps forward, grabbed his shoulders and planted her knees on either side of his hips. Her pussy hovered inches above his cock and he felt the heat of it sink into his body.

God damn, she made him ache. He tried not to show how affected he was but it was becoming harder to breathe with each passing second. His hands clenched into fists at his sides but he couldn't contain the urge to touch her. He grabbed her hips, her skin hot and smooth as silk.

Tugging her closer, he nearly had her exactly where he wanted her. But she stiffened her arms and held him away. She stared into his eyes, forcing him to hold her gaze. Lifted one hand from his shoulder, she cupped his cheek. The ruined one.

The urge to jerk away flooded through his body, almost overwhelming. But he knew if he did, she'd just reach for him again. Or she'd move away.

He didn't want her to move unless it was onto his dick.

Forcing himself to stay still, his gaze never straying from hers. That connection sank deep inside him and put hooks in places he hadn't allowed anyone to touch in years.

"I'm going to fuck you now."

Her voice rasped against his libido, making it hard for him to breathe. His lips parted but he had no idea what to say. All he could do was swallow hard and keep his hands on her hips so she couldn't get away.

Something fluttered onto the cushion next to them, drawing her attention away.

A condom. She left it there for the moment, taking her own sweet time.

Reaching between them, she grabbed his cock and began to stroke him. A slow, steady pump that had him gasping for air in under a minute.

Christ, if she kept that up, he'd blow way too soon.

As if she knew, she tightened on him, her pace becoming faster, her grip tighter. Maddening.

His hips wanted to pump but the angle was wrong. If she'd just fucking sit on his cock, take him high and deep inside her, he could relieve some of this building pressure. And when he started to groan every time her palm rubbed over the head of his cock, he'd had enough.

Before she realized what he was doing, he released one hand from her hip and grabbed the condom. She released her grip on him so he could roll it down his shaft. Then holding it at the perfect angle, he grabbed her hips and brought her down.

They both gasped as he plunged inside, her pussy tight and wet around him. So hot. It made him want to fuck her hard and fast until he came, pumping her full of his cum.

He barely managed to hold onto his restraint. He didn't want to hurt her but she looked a little stunned, her lips parted and her eyes dazed.

"Julianne. Tell me you're okay."

Her eyes closed and, as he watched, her tongue slicked out to lick her lips. His cock throbbed in response as he heard her suck in a rasping breath. His gaze dropped to watch her breasts as she drew in another and another.

God damn, she had gorgeous tits. He wanted to taste them.

"Oh, my God."

His gaze flew back to her face as she whispered those words. With his hands back on her hips, he gave her a shake, just enough to make her eyes fly open and his cock pulse inside her at the sensation.

"Julianne. You gotta answer me. Are you okay?"

Her lips curved in a slight smile. "I'm fine. More than fine. Just fuck me. Now. Right now."

His entire body tightened as lust made him feel even more feral than normal. Then he took her at her word.

Using his hands to guide her, he lifted her up then let her

fall back down. Every movement made her already clenching pussy even tighter.

He felt like she still had him gripped in her hand, milking his every movement. Because of the position, he couldn't thrust as deeply as he wanted but gravity helped. She slid a little farther down his shaft each time until she engulfed him to the base of his cock, her gaze never leaving his.

He hadn't looked a woman in the eyes while he fucked her since the accident. Hell, he hadn't been alone in a bed with one either. Keegan had always been there, too. Keegan and his unmarked face had kept the woman occupied while Erik fucked her from behind.

He hadn't realized how much he'd missed that connection, watching her eyes darken and her lids fall until her gaze was a bare slit. Seeing her lips quiver as she sucked in a shuddering breath each time he let her sink back onto his cock.

Her hands gripped his shoulders, each finger a separate brand as she held him tight. Her sheath rippled around him as he stroked her body closer to orgasm. He saw her fighting it off, holding back, and he wanted to snarl as he pumped into her, each movement becoming harder, tighter.

He wanted her to go over first, wanted to watch her come as he fucked her, knowing he alone had made her break.

Winding one hand into her hair, he tugged, causing her head to tilt back, arching her back until her breasts were within reach of his mouth. Bending forward, he put his lips around one tight nipple and drew it into this mouth. He sucked hard then used his teeth to scrape the hardened pebble.

Her groan rippled through his body, causing his hips to thrust a little harder, a little fiercer.

The sounds she made low in her throat made him feel like a beast conquering his mate as he worked her on his dick.

He tasted the salty sweetness of her skin as he licked a path across her chest to her neglected nipple. When he bit down, her hips rotated in a way that made stars flash behind his eyelids.

Jesus, that felt amazing. His cock responded with a jerk, but he grabbed her hips and held her still.

He didn't want to come. Not yet. He wanted to savor this moment, draw every drop of pleasure he could from it.

Pulling away from her breast, he released her nipple at the very last second, making her squirm and murmur something that sounded like a complaint.

"Stop." His voice sounded like ten miles of bad road and her eyes flew open and locked onto his. "Don't move."

She didn't speak and he thought maybe he'd lost her with the caveman routine. But she didn't move, just continued to stare into his eyes.

"I'm not ready to come yet. You feel too fucking good. So fucking tight. When I do come, it's gonna be after a good, long ride. And you're gonna go first. At least once."

Her lips curled into a smile that made his abs clench and his cock dance inside her. "You better hope you can live up to those words. You don't look like you have much control left right now."

Her pussy clamped around him, milking him, tearing at that control. He groaned, biting down on his tongue until he tasted blood, trying to bring his body back under control.

Then he smacked her ass, just hard enough to sting, and watched her expression go slack with pleasure, her lips parting on a gasp.

"I watched you that night at the party." He spoke through gritted teeth. "You never saw me. I watched you try to look inconspicuous but that's not you, is it? That's not the real you." He punctuated his words with another, slightly harder smack. This time she tried to roll her hips. He held her still, forcing his cock higher inside her. "You want someone to see you, really see you. The sexy woman you really are."

Holding her hips again, he started an excruciatingly slow thrust-and-retreat that made her eyes close tight. Every movement made his balls draw up tighter until they felt like solid stone. Not giving in to the urge to come was taking a toll on his body he'd gladly pay forever.

He'd never felt so powerful as he watched each expression cross her face. *He* made her feel this way. *He* controlled her response and brought that look of sheer carnal lust to her face.

It healed a piece of himself he thought broken forever.

With a groan, he wrapped his arms around her waist and gave himself over to the rhythm beating through his veins. Her head fell to his shoulder, her hair trailing over his chest, heightening each sensation.

Turning her head, she sucked his earlobe between her lips then bit it. The pain lasted only a second but it lit a fuse that'd been primed for weeks. Since the first moment he'd seen her.

Catching the ends of her hair, he tugged until she lifted her head. Blindly, he sought her mouth, sealed her lips with his, and shoved his tongue into her mouth to tangle with hers.

Her pussy felt wetter each time he pushed inside, her moisture soaking his cock and balls. Their skin, damp with sweat, fused together.

She moaned into his mouth as she came, her pussy quivering around his cock, her arms tight around his shoulders. He fought against the urge to release, but it was too much for him to take.

Seating her solidly in his lap, he thrust one last time, pouring himself into her until he had nothing more to give.

FIVE

Julianne didn't know how long she lay against Erik, gasping for air.

She'd come so hard, she swore her teeth were loose.

She should feel drained, exhausted. At the very least, sleepy. And she did. To a point.

More importantly, she felt energized.

Inside her, she felt Erik's cock still twitching. Her lips curved into a smile against the smooth skin of his neck on the undamaged side of his face.

Realizing her fingers were nearly embedded in his shoulders, she forced herself to flex them so she didn't draw blood with her nails.

He made a low sound of protest, which she soothed by caressing his nape. When he angled his head to the side slightly, exposing more of his neck, she followed his silent request and rubbed her fingers along the tight muscle.

They sat there, breathing, until she felt his cock slacken and moisture begin to drip between them.

"We're going to ruin this couch."

Her voice sounded husky, sexy, and he responded by turning his face and nuzzling his nose into her neck.

"I don't give a fuck about the damn couch. Don't fucking move."

Since she didn't really want to anyway, she figured it couldn't hurt to give into this demand—until she heard movement behind her.

Keegan.

She'd forgotten he was still there.

Which made her feel guilty for neglecting him. Which then made her feel ridiculous, considering the circumstances.

"I put a towel on the arm of the couch." Keegan pitched his voice low. "I'm just going to—"

"Don't go."

Her head popped off Erik's shoulder and she turned toward Keegan, still standing at the side of the couch. Their gazes connected and it felt right to stare into his eyes while trying to hold Erik's softening cock inside her.

Beneath her, Erik stilled, waiting. She didn't know for what. Did he think she didn't want to be alone with him? That she considered him damaged or scary or some other foolish thing?

There were enough undercurrents in this room to make her feel like she was drowning. The scent of sex surrounded her, the gazes of these two men weighed down on her.

She'd had the best sex of her life tonight and she didn't want that to end yet. She wanted Keegan to stay. She wanted both of them to take her but she didn't know the right words for this exact moment.

Steady fingers gripped her chin and forced her to look at Erik.

"Say it. Whatever you're thinking, just say it."

Erik's voice made her nipples peak and pussy ripple with a fresh surge of desire, so strong it took away her ability to speak.

She shook her head, unable to clear her head enough to say what was on her mind.

Erik continued on. "God, you are *so* fucking beautiful and sexy and brilliant, you make me want to be worthy of your attention. The first time I saw you, I knew we needed you. I swore I had blue balls for a week after that damn reception."

"It's true." Keegan shifted on his feet. "He couldn't stop talking about you. I've never seen him like that before."

Keegan's quiet voice held regret and she grabbed for him, instinctively knowing he was about to back away. She caught his wrist just before he moved out of reach and held on tight.

"No. You're not going anywhere." Taking a deep breath, she forced a little more spine into her backbone. As gracefully as she could, she slid off Erik's lap and stood, grateful her knees held her.

"I'm feeling pretty damn naked all by myself. I want you both to strip. Now."

She held Keegan's gaze as she stroked her hand up his arm, brushing her fingertips through his hair. She'd expected the curls to be wiry. Their softness surprised her. She sank her fingers into those waves and exerted just enough pressure to hold his attention.

Stepping into him until her nipples brushed against his shirt, she tilted her head back and rose onto her toes until their lips were only centimeters apart. When she closed her eyes, she felt his hot breath against her cheek seconds before his lips took hers in a searing kiss.

Keegan kissed her with an underlying sweetness that made her ache low in her gut. Wrapping her arms around his shoulders, she sank into the kiss, giving over to the erotic pull of the sexual tension running between the three of them.

Grabbing her hips, he pulled her tight against his fully erect cock then rubbed her mound against that hard ridge until she wanted to climb him like her own personal Mount Everest.

As if he'd read her mind, he lifted her off her feet, aligning their mouths and bringing her clit into line with the tip of his cock. She wrapped her legs around his waist and lost herself in the carnality of his kiss, tilting her hips until she got just the right friction on her clit.

She could come again with just a few more—

"No way, Jules." Another set of hands grabbed her hips and Erik's naked chest plastered itself to her back. "You don't come again until I'm deep in your ass and Keegan's fucking your pussy."

She broke off the kiss, gasping for air as his words shocked her. Lust blazed through her, stealing her breath, stealing her sanity. She couldn't believe how close to orgasm she could get from only the sound of Erik's voice. She shivered, tucking her head into Keegan's neck.

"Will you let me have your pussy, Jules?" Keegan's voice threw gasoline on the fire. With her legs spread, her sex felt so damn empty, she knew she'd agree to anything these men wanted.

"God, yes. Please. I need it. Now."

"Oh, no. Not yet." Erik ran a hand down her back, stroking her, petting her. "It's our turn to make you beg."

Yes, that's what she wanted—for these two men to give her what she needed.

She wanted to say yes but all that emerged was a moan because Erik had slipped his hand between her legs. He played his fingers over her labia and up to her clit, barely brushing against that little bundle of nerves but managing to make her shudder.

Shifting against Keegan, she opened her mouth on his neck, sinking her teeth into his skin as Erik began a wicked pattern, flicking her clit then moving back to work one finger between her sex lips, going a little deeper each time.

Just a little more...

She tried to wriggle down onto his finger but Keegan's arms tightened and she couldn't move. She was totally at their mercy.

And Erik had none.

He played her ruthlessly, teasing her clit until she was right on the edge of orgasm then pulling back to knead her ass, leaving her high and dry. Erik used his other hand to wrap around her hair and pull her head back so Keegan could take her mouth again.

As he slid his tongue into her mouth, winding around hers, Erik pressed open-mouthed kisses to her shoulder.

God, she felt shaky, desperate. When Erik's hand returned to her sex, tears formed as he worked two fingers into her sex.

Yes. That's what she needed. To be filled, stuffed to capacity.

Two cocks. One man at her back, another in front of her.

Yes, yes, yes.

"Let me have her a moment."

Erik's voice barely registered but she felt her weight shift as he wrapped one arm around her waist and held her against his chest. Keegan grabbed her ankles and unwound her legs from his waist, his motions jerky as he stripped off his clothes. She saw buttons fly off his shirt, making tiny *pings* as they landed on the wood floor. He didn't bother to untie his shoes, just toed them off and shoved his pants down his legs.

Arching her back, she reached above and behind her, her hands curving around Erik's neck, encouraging him to lean forward. He understood what she wanted and let her slide down his front until her feet hit the floor. His hands reached around to cup her breasts, kneading them, pinching the tight nipples with his thumbs and forefingers.

His cock pressed against the small of her back, a hot brand that made her sex weep with wanting. He bit and licked his way across her shoulders as she watched Keegan toss his pants to the side, after pulling a condom from the pocket, and step forward. His cock stood stiff and ready, and she reached for him, wrapping one hand around his shaft while the other cupped his balls.

She rolled them in her hand, watched his eyes narrow to slits. His handsome face tightened into sharp angles and she knew he'd moved past slow and easy and into hard and fast. His gaze flicked to Erik and he made a motion with his head that Erik must have understood.

Swinging her into his arms, Erik took her back to the chaise. Keegan beat them there, throwing himself onto his back, rolling on the condom then reaching for her.

The chaise was wide enough that she could straddle his hips, in no danger of falling off.

She had the brief thought that they'd bought this piece of furniture precisely for this reason but the idea fled the second she positioned her pussy over Keegan's cock and began to sink down.

She got halfway, already feeling that wonderful sense of fulfillment combined with aching need that hit her just before an orgasm.

Opening her eyes, she smiled down at Keegan but his attention was focused on the point where their bodies joined, his expression tight with his desire to fuck her. So easy to read. So wonderful to see.

She couldn't remember the last time she'd seen that look on a man's face. Way too long. Her life lately had been consumed by work, by the grinding need to keep up with her mom's bills.

So much debt. Too—

"Jules." Keegan's hands grabbed her hips, holding her steady. "Look at me."

She hadn't realized she wasn't. Blinking back into focus, she fell into Keegan's gaze, entranced and trembling.

Shifting her weight, she wanted to take him all the way in. Wanted to fill the emptiness inside her with his cock and the warmth of his body and the way he looked at her that made her feel like a beautiful, desirable, *special* woman.

His hands tightened. "Stop, Jules."

She shook her head. "I don't want to stop."

"If you start to ride me, I'm gonna blow and then you won't have the pleasure of me and Erik taking you at the same time. Trust me, you want that."

Strangely, she did trust him. Both of them.

She turned her head, finding Erik beside her with his hand on his cock, stroking himself as he stared down at her.

Smiling, she crooked her finger at him. When he'd stepped close enough, she leaned slightly and took him in her mouth.

The head of his cock felt silky smooth against her tongue and his deep groan made her pussy clamp around Keegan's cock. Keegan's grunt of satisfaction made her smile.

Yes, that's right. I'm still in control.

Concentrating just on the head, she used her tongue to play at the slit and lick all around the spongy tip. Then she sucked hard, her cheeks hollowing. Erik's breath hissed sharply, his free hand going to her head. She thought he'd exert pressure, get her to do what he wanted, but he only let it rest there.

His cock felt like heated iron against her tongue, filling her mouth with his taste and her head with decadent thoughts.

She tried to move her hips again, needing more friction, but Keegan held her steady.

She moaned around Erik's cock, her hands tightening on his balls.

"Fuck." Erik's voice was razor sharp, making her pussy

ripple in response, which made Keegan groan, his hips jerking, pushing his dick farther inside her.

With a gasp, she pulled away from Erik. "Now."

Her voice was little more than a growl, causing Erik's expression to pull into sharp lines. He looked almost cruel but surprisingly, his scars softened his appearance.

She couldn't quite smile, she was in too much need for that, but Erik knew what she wanted.

Keegan's arms wrapped around her, forcing her to lay against his chest as Erik practically threw himself behind her. Keegan's legs spread to accommodate him, spreading her even further, making her pussy fairly burn.

She felt Eric moving behind her then felt a slick coolness dribble between her ass cheeks.

The anticipation was too much. She lifted her head and molded her lips to Keegan's. His groan intensified as she slid her tongue between his lips to taste him. Keegan's hips shifted and his hands pulled her down, keeping his cock buried deep as Erik's fingers spread the lube.

"You've been fucked in the ass before, haven't you, babe?"

One finger penetrated her ass, making her almost desperate for something bigger. *More. Now.* Clamping down, she felt Keegan's cock twitch in her pussy and he pulled away to gasp in air. Good thing, or she might've passed out too.

"Oh, yeah, you know what to expect, don't you?" Erik's voice sounded almost cruel, taunting, but the way he touched her... He wouldn't hurt her. "I'm going to give it to you, babe. Right now."

Pulling out his finger made all those sensitive areas tingle and quake.

"*Fuck.* Erik, hurry the fuck up."

She barely heard Keegan's voice over the beating of her heart but she certainly felt the head of Erik's cock as it pressed against that tiny opening. Forging ahead with steady pressure, he kept one hand splayed on her back, the other gripped her hip.

The pressure of those two cocks lodged inside her built to an excruciating level. Erik's slow, steady progress only added to it. She needed that pressure relieved, needed them to move.

Keegan felt like unyielding stone and Erik... God, Erik spread fire.

She was stretched beyond pain, beyond pleasure. She needed—

"Fuck her now, Keegan."

Keegan groaned as he began to move, too slowly to suit her. He controlled his motions so carefully, dragging against the walls of her pussy so slowly, she almost didn't feel like he was moving. Erik stayed locked in place, his cock a red-hot pole that spread her ass past the burning point.

"God damn it, *move*, Keegan."

She wanted to scream the words but they emerged as a whisper. Even so, they must have affected him because he shoved back in with a hard grunt just as Erik began to pull out.

They moved with a wicked coordination that took her breath away. Jesus, she didn't know if she could take it.

She began to pant as they alternated their strokes. One in, one out. Slow as molasses. Hot as sin. She wanted to move but they had her wedged so tightly between them, she could only manage to shimmy.

And when she did, Erik held her even tighter and spoke into her ear.

"You stay right where you. No moving. We're in charge now."

"I need you to *move*."

"Oh, we will. But right now, I want to enjoy the feel of you so tight around my dick."

"Christ, you're so fucking hot." Keegan spoke into her other ear. "I want to fuck you so hard, you scream."

Yes. Exactly.

But still they wouldn't give her what she needed.

They drew out their thrusts and withdrawals until she floated in a state of heightened arousal. She tried to concentrate, to feel each distinct cock inside her but she couldn't. They worked together so well.

Nerve endings snapped with sensation, her abdomen tight with expectation.

She gripped Keegan's shoulders but now she reached behind her with one hand, coming into contact with Erik's hip. Smooth, sleek skin. She grabbed him, dug her nails in and was rewarded with a hard thrust forward.

Erik's hand slid from the middle of her back to her hair, which he wrapped around his hand then pulled. It didn't hurt but was enough to get his point across.

And she totally ignored the warning.

She moved into Keegan's next thrust, making Erik scramble to stay with her. Her lips curved into a smile when she did the same to Erik and forced Keegan to move to stay lodged inside.

Control was hers once again.

She needed to make only tiny motions and the guys would do what she wanted—fuck her harder.

"Do me. Come on."

Her voice barely sounded like hers and that was okay. She didn't feel like herself. She felt like a goddess being worshipped.

Her men started to move faster. Sweat began to form, coating them all with a light sheen until their skin clung.

She lapped at Keegan's shoulder, the taste of him intoxicating. His chin lifted and she instinctively knew he wanted her mouth there. She obliged, licking at the hollow of this throat then biting the tendon.

"Fuck yes."

Keegan's hips began to move faster than Erik's, his cock swelling, making her even tighter. Behind her, Erik groaned and fucked her harder. Soon they broke ranks, making their own rhythm.

She could barely stand the sensation, could barely breathe.

Another orgasm built but wouldn't break.

God, if she didn't come soon, she might shatter. She might—

With a groan, Keegan came, flooding her with warmth. His body shook beneath her as he pumped into her, triggering her orgasm.

Yes. Finally.

As she shook with the force of it, Keegan ground against her as Erik lunged forward one final time, burying his cock deep as he pulsed in her ass.

The sensitive tissues absorbed those pulses, prolonging her orgasm, stealing her breath and leaving her boneless between their bodies.

SIX

Erik sat on the chair across from the fireplace, staring into the flames. But his gaze kept sliding to the door.

Keegan had taken Jules to the shower in the bath attached to Erik's bedroom upstairs.

He should join them. He wanted to join them.

Then what's stopping you?

Good question.

He could say the bathroom was too well lit but that would be a lie.

The bathroom *would* be pretty damn bright but the truth was he *wanted* to join them. Wanted to be with Jules. And that scared the shit out of him.

Which just pissed him off.

He felt like a fucking coward and it sucked.

After everything he'd been through, could a well-lit bathroom really have the power to bring him to his knees?

No. Because he knew damn well it wasn't the bathroom.

It was the woman. And that might be even more terrifying.

He didn't want a woman in his life. Not full-time.

The business was his wife and mistress at the moment. He

and Keegan were building something. They had plans for the next five years, big plans. And that wouldn't happen if they split their focus.

Jules had the potential to be one huge focus-splitter. And not just for Erik.

He saw the way Keegan looked at her. His best friend wanted her just as much as Erik did, but Keegan, with his stick-up-the-ass, do-the-right-thing hero complex would step back the minute Erik expressed the slightest bit of interest in Jules that wasn't related solely to the bedroom.

So what the fuck are you going to do?

Damn good question.

If he followed them to the bathroom, Keegan would know exactly how he felt about Jules. He wouldn't be able to hide it because Keegan knew him better than he knew himself lately.

But if he didn't follow them, Jules would think he was an uncaring prick. And that wouldn't be right. At least the uncaring part.

He was a prick. He was driven and stubborn and he didn't typically give up on something until he'd caught it.

He'd thought after he'd had her, the gnawing ache in his groin would be gone. It'd only intensified.

He was on his feet before he realized he'd moved.

Fuck this indecision. He wanted to be with her. He'd blocked out this night—this *one* night—for her and he'd be damned if he spent part of it whining like a snot-nosed kid.

When he reached the bedroom, he heard water running but didn't hear voices. The door was open so he only had to walk over.

He stopped in the doorway, jaw clenching at the scene in front of him.

Keegan had her pinned to the wall, fucking her in slow, steady strokes. They were out of the flow of water but they were wet, skin glistening. He wanted to lick the droplets off her beautiful skin.

Keegan had his face turned away from the door and Jules' eyes were closed so neither of them noticed him.

Unlike before, when Keegan had been uptight because he'd felt they were deceiving her by keeping Erik's presence a secret, now he had no reservations. His hips worked with a slow, deliberate pace, drawing out the pleasure Jules was feeling, if the look on her face was anything to go by.

Her expression slack with desire, her hands clenched at his back. Keegan's skin had long red lines left by her fingernails. She'd wrapped her legs around his waist, her ankles crossed at the small of his back. Her hips arched forward on each of his thrusts, moving with him.

Erik couldn't believe he could get aroused so quickly just by watching. But his cock stood at full attention, almost painfully so. Still, he was content in the moment to just watch.

If he was watching porn, he'd be watching Keegan's cock fucking into her body, slow and easy. Instead, he watched her face, the subtle changes that signaled her feelings. How her breath hitched each time Keegan slid back inside. How she bit her lip when his hips began to swing harder and faster.

Keegan shifted her weight in his arms, lifting her higher, getting a better angle. The muscles in Keegan's arms stood out in stark relief as he took all her weight, bouncing her on his cock like he was a carnival ride.

She appeared to love it, moaning as she arched her back, trying to get a different angle, a better angle.

God damn, they looked amazing together.

His cock ached for friction but he didn't jerk himself off. He wanted to take her one last time.

He didn't know if he groaned or made a noise but her eyes

opened and she stared straight at him. Her mouth parted slightly but she didn't say anything, just stared.

She didn't have to say anything.

Stopping to grab a condom from the pile on the counter, he walked to the free-standing shower stall and drew open the door.

Keegan paused when he realized what was happening, his gaze swinging toward him.

Then Keegan smiled, a flat-out grin Erik hadn't seen in months. Years, actually. Not since the fire. It reminded him of the old Keegan. The one who'd come up with wicked schemes to pleasure women. Who'd taken a hell of a lot of pride in making a woman scream when she came.

"I think he wants to join us. Should we let him?"

Keegan spoke as if there was some doubt then rotated his hips, making Jules' eyes flutter shut for several long moments.

Her thighs tightened around Keegan's waist but he'd already started to pull her away.

Setting her on her feet, Keegan turned her so her back was against his chest.

"She's so fucking gorgeous, isn't she?" Keegan's hands wrapped around her waist then slid up until he cupped her breasts in his palms. They overflowed and Erik couldn't wait any longer.

He stepped forward and bent, sucking one pink nipple into his mouth on a hard draw. Her hands sank into his hair, holding him tight, her gasp of pleasure turning to a moan as he bit her, hard. He didn't temper his actions. He was sick of not giving into his desires.

Jules had taken him, scars and all. Now he wanted to take her the way he knew would give her pleasure.

Dropping to his knees, he felt the water hit his back as he spread her thighs with his hands then put his mouth over her pussy. He licked at her clit, playing with the tight little nub while she cried out. He bit her, hard enough to make her gasp then licked between her lips to find her slit soaking wet and not just from the water.

He lapped up her juices then fucked her with his tongue, getting as deep as he could. Her hands yanked at his hair as he worked a finger into her ass, wriggling it in and out until she gasped his name.

She tasted fucking amazing and he would have eaten her to another orgasm if he hadn't had other plans. He pushed her to the brink then pulled back, looking up at her dazed face.

As he stood, rolling on a condom, she maintained eye contact. Keegan also watched him and Erik nodded at his friend, who still wore a grin.

Taking her from Keegan's arms, he lifted her against him, one arm under her ass. When she had her arms wrapped around his shoulders, he used one hand to aim his cock. Then he let her sink.

His cock breached her, her wet heat encompassing him inch by inch. She was so damn tight, her pussy clenching around him, that he had to strangle the urge to come. Once he had his cock entrenched, he nodded to Keegan, not sure he could speak, he was gritting his teeth so hard.

Keegan didn't need to be told what to do. He closed the distance between them, spread her cheeks and worked his cock inside her ass. Keegan didn't go slow. He took what he wanted, making Jules scream with pleasure.

This time, they fucked her hard and fast. No finesse, no stopping them.

He wanted to get her off fast and intense and then he wanted to blow his load. She barely registered as a weight in his arms, only as a pressure around his cock.

His balls tightened and he knew he was close.

Behind her, Keegan kept his own pace and the dueling sensations were enough to light her up.

This time when she came, she flooded him with her juices, pulling her along with him until his cum joined hers. Just as he pulsed one last time, Keegan pulled out, shooting his cum over her ass then rubbing his cock between her cheeks until the last drop had been spilled.

Hanging limply between them, Jules let out a deep breath then laid her head on his shoulder, her lips brushing against his ruined cheek.

He considered it progress that he didn't flinch away.

And he wondered if he'd be able to let her walk away.

KEEGAN SUCKED in a couple of deep breaths, made sure he had his legs under him then reached out to take Jules' limp body from Erik.

Erik held on to her, sliding an arm around her legs and holding her against his chest. Keegan's brows raised and, over her head, Erik scowled at him. The guy looked almost embarrassed as he carried her to the other side of the room.

Setting her on her feet, he wrapped her in a towel then gave her another to dry her hair. Jules gave Erik a sated, sexy smile as she sat on the vanity stool. Erik moved to the side but not too far away and Keegan wanted to pump a fist in the air.

Maybe now Erik would make his way back to the world of the living. He'd been hiding long enough. Too long.

As Keegan grabbed a towel to dry off, he saw Erik do the same just before he excused himself and headed into the other room.

"When was he injured?"

Keegan barely heard Jules' question, pitched low enough that Erik couldn't hear her from the other room.

He leaned against the counter. She deserved the answers Erik would never give her.

"Two years ago. An explosion in the lab. He wasn't supposed to be there that night. The explosion knocked him out. The fire spread fast and he was trapped. But he made it out."

Her eyes glowed with compassion, not pity. "Has he been afraid to go out since then?"

"He's only recently started working in the lab again. The scars were worse at first, and sometimes I think he doesn't realize how much they've faded over the past year. Sometimes—"

"You talk too fucking much."

Erik stood in the doorway to the bathroom, a furious look on his face.

Damn it. He'd probably heard everything and would be pissed as hell that Keegan had opened his mouth.

"Erik—"

"Do you always speak to your best friend like that?" Jules cut in, standing between the two of them. "Is that how you've isolated yourself, here, in this house? You use words to cut off everyone else, don't you? Push them away. Make them think you're a prick."

Erik's eyes narrowed. "How do you know I'm not? I did pay you to fuck me and my so-called friend, after all."

They were back to this shit again. God damn Erik. This time Keegan was going to break the bastard's jaw for disrespecting her this way.

Erik was expecting him to do exactly that. He didn't put up a hand to stop him. And neither did Jules.

Keegan's fist connected with Erik's jaw. He hadn't pulled his punch and Erik's head whipped to the side, nearly taking his entire body with it.

Sonofabitch. That fucking hurt. The bastard's jaw was still hard as a rock. Just like his head.

As Keegan cradled his hand to his chest, Jules stepped up next to him, her arms crossed.

"Feel better now?" she asked.

Erik shook his head, as if settling his brain back in the right spot, then rubbed a hand over the bruise Keegan could see developing.

"Yeah, actually, I do." Erik raised a brow at Keegan. "Do you? I know you've wanted to do that for months now."

Keegan grimaced. Yes, what he'd said was true but... "I won't allow you to be a bastard to her."

Erik immediately turned to Jules and bowed, looking slightly ridiculous with only a towel wrapped around his waist. "My most sincere apologies, Julianne. And my most sincere thanks. I would've never gotten him to take that swing if it hadn't been in defense of you."

Keegan's mouth dropped open before he slammed it shut. The bastard. "Why the hell didn't you just ask me to take a swing at you?"

"Because you wouldn't have done it."

He was right. No way would Keegan have ever hurt him, not after what he'd been through.

Keegan was still shaking his head when Jules rose from the stool and placed herself between them. "I think it's time I went home."

"No."

He and Erik spoke in unison and her mouth curved into a beautiful smile. The woman truly could make a dead man come, as the Stones had said so perfectly.

"Yes, it is. My mom and I have plans for tomorrow... Well, I guess I should say for today. It *is* Christmas Eve."

Neither he nor Erik had a comeback for that one. They

hadn't really planned for the holiday. Erik's housekeeper had set up the tree in the living room. Keegan hadn't even bothered with one at his place.

He'd figured he'd spend Christmas Eve at the office then have dinner with Erik. Their families were in Boston but neither of them had gone home for the past two years. Erik actively avoided his mother and Keegan didn't want to leave Erik alone.

They exchanged a glance, but neither of them had a good reason for her to stay.

Except that they wanted her to.

Keegan had it on the tip of his tongue to offer her a meal before she left, but Erik stepped forward.

"Thank you for coming tonight, Julianne. I'll get your clothes."

FROM THE WINDOW, they watched her drive away in her aging Toyota. Rust was eating away at the body, the right tail light was out and the engine sounded like a herd of braying donkeys being massacred.

"That damn car is a death trap." Erik's jaw felt so tight, he was afraid it would break. "Make damn sure she cashes that fucking check. If she doesn't, I'm going to deposit the money in her bank account personally."

"She'll cash it. She can't afford not to." Keegan sighed. "I'm starting to think this was a bad idea."

No, Keegan had *known* this was a bad idea from the moment Erik had proposed it. Erik just hadn't wanted to listen. He'd been so damn sure this was the only way he could get what he wanted and get her to take the money.

So why did he feel like a Grade-A ass now?

"We'll never see her again."

Another brilliant observation. "When did you turn into Eeyore?"

"When did you lose your humanity?"

"Fuck you." Shit, even he could hear the words had no bite. "You've been watching too many soap operas. Melodrama isn't your strong suit."

Keegan turned to him with a narrowed gaze. "And bitchiness isn't yours."

Erik's mouth screwed into a grimace. "She's gone. Time to move on."

"Neither of us wants to and you know it."

Erik admitted, if only to himself, that Keegan had a point. And that he might have fucked up what could have been a very good thing. He wanted to go after her, bring her back to the bedroom.

"So what do you suggest?"

Keegan just stared out the window.

"Let me think about it."

HER HAIR STILL DAMP, Julianne drove away.

Five-hundred-thousand dollars richer and fighting the urge to turn around every other second.

It was stupid, really. Thinking the three of them had made a connection in any way other than just sex. Neither man had tried to stop her when she left. That in itself should tell her all she needed to know.

And yet...

She didn't think she'd seen the last of Erik and Keegan.

She started to smile.

SEVEN

"...such a shame about Erik. He was such a gorgeous man. Now he's...well. I mean, who's going to want to tie herself to...well."

Julianne Carter's hands shook as she circled the group of five bitches holding court in the center of the Mifflin Ballroom of the Three Oaks Estate. The exclusive event center catered to the Berks County elite--or at least what passed for elite in this southeastern Pennsylvania county where the third largest city in the state was practically bankrupt and the so-called rich didn't have near as much money as they thought they did. Hell, even the so-called regular folk were a bunch of stuck-up, narrow-minded assholes.

"...not for all the money...too bad he's such a geek..."

The women broke out in restrained laughter, making the men in the vicinity look at them with lust. Jules wanted to break her tray over their heads.

Well, shit. Someone obviously forgot to take her happy, smiley pills before she came to work tonight.

Skirting the group of women for the third time, Julianne continued her circuit around the crowded ballroom. The guests had donated a shitload of money to stand around eating beautifully made finger food, drinking way too much middle-shelf liquor and talking shit about men they didn't know the first thing about.

Then again, it wasn't like Jules really knew Erik any better. Just because she'd spent the night with him and his business partner, Keegan, didn't mean she should want to defend them.

After all, they'd only paid her a half-million dollars to sleep with her. And she hadn't heard one damn word from them since.

With a hard-won pleasant expression plastered to her face, Jules stopped at a group of elderly women who looked right through her, never once taking a breath as they scooped up the hors d'oeuvres Jules had helped make that were pretty damn tasty, if she did say so herself.

But the women just gobbled them down as they discussed the absolute indignity of the latest shooting in downtown Reading. How dare those dreaded immigrants bring their trashy problems with them from those third-world foreign countries?

With her tray empty, Julianne headed back to the kitchen, where the noise level was only slightly lower than the ballroom.

"You look pissed, babe. That asshole in the gray suit try to feel you up again?"

Jules gave a small but genuine smile to fellow server and resident smartass, Jon Petrius, who was handsome enough to give the ladies at these functions dreams that would never be fulfilled. "Not him. Just a long day."

"Well, you tell me if I need to spike his next drink, hon."

"And you know we'd all appreciate it," added Lori Raihl. The blonde beauty had been the object of more than her fair share of gropes. "That guy's such a douche."

Jules bumped fists with Lori in complete agreement. "Thanks, Jon, but he's not the problem."

"Any time, ladies."

Picking up another fully loaded tray, Jules made her way out the door and back into the fray.

"...just as rich. Too bad he's not half as hot as Erik used to be. He might've been worth the effort."

Jules nearly tripped over her feet as she passed by that bitch Allison Terre again, and her face must have flashed bright red because Jon raised his brows at her as he passed by.

That cow was talking about Keegan. *Her* Keegan.

Julianne wanted to dump the contents of the tray down the heifer's back.

Sure, Carol would have to fire her but it wasn't like she really needed the money now. She was only here as a favor to Carol. Another favor but so different from the one she'd done two weeks ago.

The one that made her want to drown pretty Alli Terre in sticky kebabs. And shove the pointy little sticks up her narrow little ass.

Bitch.

No, she refused to cause a scene. Wouldn't embarrass Carol like that.

"Oh, Juli. It is you, isn't it? Wow, that looks delicious."

Then again...

Taming her grimace, Jules turned and approached the small circle of women. Most of them were Jules' age, which made them between twenty-one and twenty-three. Jules and Alli had graduated from the same high school, although Alli had moved in much different crowds than Jules. Their school district had encompassed one of the richest boroughs in the county along with the much more pedestrian middle-class neighborhood where Jules and her mom had lived.

Most of the really rich kids had gone to a private school in a neighboring county. Alli hadn't. According to the rumors, she'd been kicked out for "ethics violations" and her parents had "punished" her by forcing her to go to the neighborhood school.

Which, Jules silently admitted to herself, was her being just as bitchy as Alli. The girl was stuck-up and could be a royal witch but she wasn't the second coming of Lindsay Lohan.

"How have you been, Juli?" Alli reached for one of the kebabs on the plate. "I don't think I've seen you since graduation."

"I've been fine, Allison. And you?"

"Oh, Daddy has me working in his office." Alli rolled her eyes as if she'd been forced into slave labor. "I'd much rather be in New York using my degree in some big firm but Daddy insisted I give him a year before I say adios to Berks County."

The other girls laughed and their conversation turned back to a discussion of their "awful" jobs. Alli's daddy owned the largest law firm in the county. The girl next to her was finishing her marketing degree at the University of Pennsylvania in Philadelphia. Another one was working under—can you imagine?—the CEO of her father's fuel-importing business.

Jules faked another smile and moved on.

But not before she heard Alli say, "Oh, we went to high school together. I think she graduated with my class. Not really sure..."

Blinking away the sting in her eyes that was absolutely *not* tears, Jules started back on her circuit.

KEEGAN STOOD at the door to the ballroom, scanning the occupants for any sign of the woman he ached to see.

Carol had told him Jules was working tonight but he wanted to make sure before he walked into this pit of vipers.

Don't be such a pussy. Get your ass moving.

The voice in his head was Erik's. Too bad the guy wouldn't take his own advice because it was damn good.

So go the hell inside already.

He would, just as soon as he—

There she was.

Across the wide ballroom. Dressed in the white shirt and black skirt the catering company required of their servers. The uniform was supposed to make them fade into the background. On Jules, the shirt hinted at her gorgeous breasts, the skirt hugged a perfect ass and the short-heeled pumps she wore made her legs look amazing.

Jules would never fade. Not even amid the fancy dresses worn by the other women.

Just in the few seconds since he'd caught sight of her, he'd watched two guys check out her ass as she walked by.

He wanted to smash their faces with his fist.

But he couldn't blame them.

Even with her long, dark hair drawn back in a sleek braid and barely any makeup, she was still the most beautiful woman in the room.

Keegan would punch any man who said she wasn't.

Of course, Jules would probably like to take a swing at *him*.

Hell, he'd actually like it if she wanted to take a swing. The alternative—that she wouldn't want anything to do with him or Erik again—was much worse.

She'd walked out the door of Erik's house two weeks ago and Keegan had wanted to drag her back to bed before she could make it to her car.

Erik had said wait.

He'd wanted to say fuck waiting. She'd captivated him. It hadn't just been about the sex. He wanted to get to know her, discover everything about her. That night had been about more than money for him. He'd thought Erik had felt the same.

The next day Keegan had wanted to call her but it'd been Christmas Eve. He'd planned to spend it with Erik but Erik had shocked the hell out of him when he told Keegan he was going home. So Keegan had bowed to the guilt trip laid by his church-every-Sunday mom's guilt trip and gone home. He'd spent four days eating his mother's cooking and thinking about Jules.

But when Keegan had returned and said he wanted to call Jules, Erik had said wait, just a little longer, and locked himself in the lab with their new project.

Keegan waited, not wanting to set off Erik, hoping maybe she'd call. Which hadn't happened.

What did you expect, dickhead? That the woman you paid a half-million dollars to have sex with you and Erik would want to have anything to do with you again?

Fuck.

Exactly.

Damn it, he shouldn't have come. He'd only embarrass her if he walked in and tried to start a conversation.

True, no one here knew about their deal, about that one sex-filled night they'd spent together. But she might be embarrassed and that was the last thing he wanted.

Then again, he didn't think Jules embarrassed easy.

Fearless was a good word to describe her. Confident. Sexy as all hell.

He wanted to add "his" to that list. Hell, he wanted to add "theirs."

Erik wanted the same, even if his best friend refused to admit it. Erik's scars, physical and emotional, gave some explanation for his behavior.

So what's your excuse for standing out here like a fucking pussy?

All he had to do was push open the door and walk in, get her alone and tell her—

What?

That the night they'd spent together had been the best fucking night of his life and he wanted to repeat it for the rest of the foreseeable future?

Probably a good place to start.

And the problem is...

All the other people in the room. Those fine, upstanding pillars of society who thought they had a right to comment on others people's lives.

Erik had been fed up with those kinds of people growing up in Boston, the ones with the kind of wealth that made some people assholes.

Erik hadn't been an asshole when they'd met at Princeton. He and Keegan had hit it off almost immediately as lab partners in first-year electrical engineering. It'd been a partnership that'd only strengthened when they'd created Tin Man Biometrics.

And now that TinMan was making an obscene amount of money, he and Erik were getting invites to parties like this. Parties Keegan avoided at all costs because they were mostly meat markets and all the small talk and the innuendo and all the bullshit made him want to tear his hair out.

But he'd brave this one for a chance to talk to Jules.

Still, he wished Erik was here with him. A united front always worked better than a divided attack.

It's how they managed their business, particularly after the lab explosion that had left Erik disfigured. And a hermit.

Keegan had thought, maybe, after that night with Jules, *maybe* Erik would return to the land of the living. But even though Jules had drawn Erik out into the light that one night, Erik had managed to entrench himself even further in the shadows by the time Keegan had returned from the holiday.

So that left Keegan to stalk Jules.

And maybe he wouldn't use the word "stalk," at least not out loud.

Fuck it. He was going in.

He'd dressed for the occasion in a suit and tie, hoping he wouldn't stick out and could move around without attracting attention.

Which would be almost impossible, he realized. He knew a lot of people in the room because when TinMan had hit the Fortune 500 list, the doors into the inner sanctum of Pennsylvania's elite had opened to them.

Invitations to events like this, which weren't much more than an excuse for people with a certain amount of money to get shit-faced, talk about politics and bitch about how the government was raping them over taxes.

Before the explosion, Erik had handled this crap. Keegan had been more than happy to be miles away in the lab.

After the fire, Erik had guilted Keegan into stepping in. Even though he totally sucked at small talk, did not want to bitch about taxes, and was in no way looking to hook up with a junior exec whose daddy had the last name of someone who'd signed the Constitution.

Jesus H. Christ. He *had* become a fucking pussy.

With a disgusted breath, he started working his way around the room again.

Jules hadn't seen him yet and she appeared to be heading back to the kitchen. Good, that would give him enough time to grab a drink at the bar and scope out a place for them to have a few minutes alone to talk.

"Whiskey. Neat."

In seconds, the bartender slid his drink across the polished mahogany bar. Keegan took a long swallow, hoping like hell the alcohol took the jagged edge off his nerves. He felt ready to bust out of his skin.

"Hello, Keegan. I was hoping I'd see you tonight."

Fuck.

Showtime. Plastering on what he hoped was a pleasant smile, Keegan turned. "Allison, Katherine. Nice to see you."

The women exchanged a look then turned brilliant smiles on him that made him want to run the other way.

They were pretty enough, both blond and blue-eyed. Everything about them screamed privileged, from their perfect hair to their expensive dresses and shoes. They looked exactly like the women Erik's parents had tried to set them up with when the business had started to take off.

"We're so glad you were able to make it. We've been wanting to invite you..."

And that was about all Keegan heard because Jules walked out of the kitchen with a loaded tray and began her circuit around the room.

As the women continued to talk, Keegan made sure he kept his eyes focused on whichever woman was talking at the moment, smiling when it seemed appropriate, nodding occasionally, but always aware of where Jules was in the room.

Her tray emptied before she got close enough to notice him and he was forced to endure more torture from two of the most eligible women in the state. They wanted him to join some board they were involved in. Something about theater or the arts. Something he'd probably think was deadly boring if he was really listening.

Not that he had anything against the arts in general but right now he had other things on his mind.

Namely, the beautiful woman who'd rocked his world to its foundation.

And even if Erik wouldn't admit it, she'd done the same for him.

Keegan would get her back, no matter what he had to do or promise her.

With one eye on the door to the kitchen, he bided his time.

JULES' heart threatened to pound out of her chest.

Keegan was here. Holding up the bar with Alli and one of her cronies on either side of him.

Luckily for Alli, he looked bored out of his skull. If he'd shown any kind of interest, she might've found herself yanking Alli out of the room by her hair then indulging in a good old-fashioned cat fight.

Which was stupid.

They hadn't called.

And she was so totally pissed about that.

Seeing Keegan just made it worse.

He must have just arrived. She knew she hadn't seen him before.

But now that she had, she didn't know if she could go out there and pretend not to know him. Couldn't act like he was a stranger when she'd shared one of the most amazing experiences of her life with him. And with Erik.

Was Erik here too?

No. He wouldn't come out of hiding for something like this. Too many people staring at him.

She would've scratched out anyone's eyes who dared look at him sideways.

And...she was being crazy. Absolutely nuts.

Obviously they hadn't wanted anything more to do with her or they would've contacted her.

It'd been sex. Damn good sex, but still...just sex.

"Hey, Juli, everything okay?"

Two other servers stood behind her, trays loaded, frowning at her.

"Oh, yeah, sorry. Just..." She shook her head then pushed through the door.

She told herself she wasn't going to pay him any attention.

It was total bullshit.

At least she could try not to cross his path. With this many people, no one would ever realize she was avoiding one man.

Drawing in a deep breath, she deliberately didn't look in the direction of the bar and headed for the opposite side of the room. *After* making sure he was nowhere in sight.

She focused on not tipping her tray and not tripping over her feet but nothing seemed to be working right.

The tray felt unbalanced, her feet felt unattached. Her heart wouldn't stop racing and her throat felt like she'd swallowed sawdust.

And her brain wouldn't stop either.

Had he come here to see her? Had he known she'd be here?

No, that was stupid. Why would he come here to talk to her? Why not call?

Stop. Just stop.

With only a half hour to go until the mixer ended, people were drinking more and eating less. She couldn't hide in the kitchen like she wanted to.

And she couldn't stop looking toward the bar. She tried not to but it was impossible.

She caught sight of him out of the corner of her eye several times.

Then he wasn't there.

Blinking, she took another, closer look.

Still not there.

A prickle of awareness made the hairs on her neck stand on end.

He was watching her. She could *feel* his gaze.

She refused to give him the satisfaction of showing she was rattled. Bothered.

Dying to talk to him. Touch him. Tear his clothes off.

She was pissed at herself for wanting more, for thinking there should be more.

They hadn't called.

So why was he here?

Probably had nothing to do with her.

Put him out of your mind. Do your job. Go home and figure out why you haven't decided what you're going to do with the rest of the money.

Her smile had faded so she plastered it on again as she finished her circuit. Her tray was still half full by the time she got to the hallway that led back to the bathroom. Her hands trembled and she set the tray on the nearest table.

There was an alcove at the end of the hall just before the bathrooms that offered some privacy.

She needed a few minutes. To pull herself together. Get her game face back. No way did she want Keegan to know how he affected her.

They hadn't called.

She blinked hard and fast at the burn in her eyes, glanced quickly over her shoulder to make sure no one was paying any attention to her then slipped down the dimly lit hall and into the alcove.

The alcove was darker than the hall and much quieter than the main room. She took a deep breath, trying to get her heart back to a normal rhythm. Force her brain away from thinking about that night.

Damn Keegan for showing up and ruining the tiny bit of calm she'd managed to hold on to.

She'd left that night without a single regret. Still didn't have any.

Except that they hadn't called.

She sighed. "Well, what did you expect? Total devotion in exchange for good sex?"

"I thought it was pretty damn good sex but I might be biased."

Jules gasped and spun around to find a silhouette in the doorway.

She knew who it was right away. Even though she couldn't see that his hair was dark brown with red highlights and just a little too long or that his eyes were a clear, almost navy blue. But she *knew* it was Keegan.

That voice held a slight Irish accent from his childhood. His family had moved to the States when he was twelve.

She'd looked up him and Erik online. Sue her.

They'd earned their first million by age twenty-six. Their company, TinMan Biometrics, made high-end security equipment for billion-dollar companies that wanted to keep their secrets secret.

They'd come up with some revolutionary development that had been way too technical for her to understand. But she understood how smart they were, how brilliant they had to be.

That night she hadn't known much more than their first names and the fact that her friend Carol had told her she could trust them. And since she trusted Carol...

Her chin tilted up. "What are you doing here?"

Damn it. She wanted a do-over immediately. Her voice had sounded timid, shy. Almost hurt. And that's not how she wanted him to see her.

Stiffening her back, she stared straight at him, although it was so dark in the little room, she couldn't make out his eyes. Or his beautiful mouth. Or the cheeks that were covered with freckles.

Damn it, the man was gorgeous. And not as old as she'd thought. He and Erik were only nine years old than her, which made them both thirty.

"I was invited," Keegan said, reminding her that she'd asked him a question. "And I knew you'd be here."

Her racing heart kicked into another gear, and she swore her stomach flipped. That had almost sounded like he came to see her specifically.

She wanted to ask if he had but maybe she didn't want to know. If he hadn't then she'd make a fool of herself. But if he had...

What then?

He took another step into the room, letting the drape covering the entrance fall behind him, making it even darker than before. Suddenly the room felt about as big as a broom closet. With a lot less air than it'd had a second ago.

And that was so totally *not* how she wanted him to see her, panting because he was in the room.

Crossing her arms over her chest, she tilted back her chin, trying to see him through the shadows.

"Which doesn't explain what you're doing here. Right now."

He took another step and another, until he was only inches away from her. This close, she had to tilt her head back to continue to hold his gaze, which she could barely see in this light.

Which didn't stop her from trying to see his mouth.

She *so* wanted to kiss him. Wanted him to kiss her. Wanted to torment and tease the hell out of him before she let him kiss her because she was still pissed at him for not calling.

For making her *want* him to call her.

"I wanted to see you again."

She bit back the words that immediately leaped to her tongue, knowing they'd come out wrong. She couldn't ask him if the only reason he wanted to see her again was because he wanted to have sex. Because he'd turn the question around and ask her the same.

And in the mood she was in, she was afraid she'd say something really stupid, like ask how much he was going to pay her this time.

And what would you do if he quoted you a figure?

"I thought that was obvious. I came to see you."

God *damn* him. He'd said the absolute right thing.

She fought back the smile that wanted to curve her lips. "It's been two weeks. I didn't think I'd hear from you again."

She wanted to ask about Erik, wanted to know if he knew Keegan was here. Wanted to know if they had talked about her. But she didn't want to be disappointed if that answer was no.

"We weren't sure you'd want to see us again."

Had they thought she was only in it for the money?

You had sex with two men you didn't know for a half-million dollars. What were they supposed to think?

God, everything was so fucked up. Money did that. It screwed up everything, whether you had a lot or not enough.

"And I guess you couldn't be bothered to ask?"

As her eyes grew accustomed to the low light, she realized she could see him better.

And maybe that wasn't a good thing.

Because now, she wanted to throw herself at him.

Forget the fact that she was supposed to be working. That she was pissed off at him and shouldn't want him. That they had nothing in common.

None of that mattered as he came even closer.

She couldn't stop remembering his gentleness that night, the way he'd made her feel like she was valued. And, oh God, the man made her seriously hot.

"We've been...busy." She caught his grimace. "Things going on at work."

Something in his tone made her think those "things" at work weren't all good.

"Is everything okay?"

His head cocked to the side. "I'm not sure. But I want it to be."

He wasn't talking about work. And she was suddenly very aware that they were totally alone.

She sucked in a short, sharp breath. "And what exactly do you want?"

God, she knew what she wanted. Keegan naked, fucking her in this tiny little room, half-dressed, hard and fast.

And wouldn't that just show everyone how much of a slut you really are?

No. Just no. Fuck that kind of thinking. What was with her?

He continued to stare at her. "I want you to come with me. Now. We'll have dinner."

So not just sex? "Will Erik be there?"

He paused. Did he think she didn't want him if Erik wasn't there? Or that she didn't want to see Erik?

"He will be."

Something in his voice made her ask, "Does he know you're here?"

Again, Keegan paused and she wondered if she should've kept her mouth shut. Maybe she'd gotten the wrong impression. Maybe Erik didn't want to see her again. Maybe only Keegan wanted to see her. Maybe—

"Yeah, he knows."

Okay, now what? She absolutely hated the fact that she didn't have the answer. Hated that these two men made her doubt herself. When her dad had left, she'd made a promise that no man would have the power to make her second guess herself ever again.

"Doesn't he want to see me again?"

"He does."

Then why haven't you called?

She wanted to scream in frustration. And, damn it, she wanted to see his face. Keegan had been so easy to read that night and there was something going on here that she was missing.

Maybe it'd be better if she never saw either of them again. Just stopped this before—

Keegan wrapped one hand around her neck and pulled her forward, crushing his mouth against hers, making her head spin —and stopping the steady stream of doubts.

EIGHT

Oh God, she'd missed this.

She'd only had Keegan for one night but, apparently, that had been enough to make him an addiction.

Her body pressed up against his and every nerve ending got an immediate jolt of adrenaline that zipped through her like lightning. Moaning into his mouth, her arms wrapped around his shoulders, she clung to him.

As her nipples tightened into hard, sensitive points, she wanted to tell him to put his hands there. Wanted him to unbutton her plain cotton shirt so he could get to her skin.

But she didn't want to break the kiss.

Instead, she shoved one hand into his shaggy waves and wrapped the strands around her fingers, curling around them so he couldn't get away.

Not that he seemed to be thinking about getting away.

He kissed her like he wanted to devour her. Like he couldn't get enough of her. It made her lungs tighten and her head swim.

The hand on her nape was a solid weight, his fingers a hot brand on her skin. His other hand grabbed her ass and pulled her against his hips. The hard ridge of his erection pressed against her stomach and she rocked into him.

God, yes. Please.

She wanted to lift her leg and wrap it around his hip but her skirt was too damn tight so she had to content herself with rubbing her mound against him.

His mouth moved over hers like liquid fire as her free hand stroked from his neck to his shoulder, where her fingers dug into his tight, flexing muscles. She heard him groan deep in his chest, felt his mouth shift position as he forced his tongue between her lips to invade her mouth.

Heat and lust and only faint traces of whiskey. He wasn't drunk.

She was the one who felt drunk, even though she hadn't had a sip of alcohol. Who felt as if all of her constraints had fallen away.

She needed more, but their bodies weren't aligned correctly.

Lifting onto her toes, she tried to get his cock at just the right position to rub against her clit. The several-inches difference in their height frustrated her, had her wanting to climb him like her own personal, lean-muscled tower.

She wanted to be closer. *Needed* to be closer.

As if he'd read her mind, Keegan shoved both hands under her arms and lifted her off her feet.

Yes. His cock fit into the vee of her legs and she damned the fabric preventing her from getting that cock inside so she could ride him until she came.

She hadn't wanted to admit it but she'd been in a constant state of arousal since she'd left that night two weeks ago. Whenever she thought about it, her body responded with a rush of heat, her pussy grew wet and she could barely breathe.

She'd wanted—

With a jerk, Keegan pulled back and she gasped at the

sudden withdrawal. But before she could protest, he grabbed the hem of her skirt in one hand and wrenched it to her hips. Cooler air caressed her bare thighs as her sex drenched with her juices.

Then he cupped her between her legs and took her breath away.

"Fucking hell, Jules." His voice held a deep, raspy command that made her shiver. "Tell me to stop. Tell me now or I swear I'm going to fuck you against the wall."

She didn't want him to stop. She wanted him to shove his fingers inside her and ease a little bit of this ache. She wanted to drop to her knees and take him in her mouth, right here, right now, where anyone could walk in on them.

She wanted him to want her so much he shoved his pants down until he could release his cock and impale her with it.

And then she wanted him to fuck her hard and fast.

Later, when she could think straight, she'd want him to take his time.

But not now.

Now—

He set her on her feet and dropped to his knees, so quickly she didn't realize what was happening until he shoved both hands beneath her skirt and grabbed her panties. He took enough care not to rip them as he yanked them down her legs but he didn't waste any time.

Panting like she'd just run a marathon, her hands fell onto his shoulders to steady herself. The low light seeping into the little room from the hall wasn't enough to allow her to see him clearly—but she didn't need to see. Only to feel.

His lips pressed against her hip and she felt the scrape of teeth before his mouth opened on her clit. The suddenness of the act, the quick flick of his tongue and the two fingers he shoved into her pussy threw her body into shuddering pleasure.

A moan escaped her, so loud in the small room, as she squirmed in his hold. She wasn't trying to get away. God, no. She wanted more.

She pressed her hips forward, wordlessly telling him she needed more pressure. Wanted more of him.

Keegan gave her more than she'd been expecting but still not enough. He fucked her with his fingers, pushing her to the edge of orgasm then letting her hang there as he pulled out and played with her labia, backing off just enough so she didn't come.

She had the barest presence of mind not to scream at him to stop playing with her and fuck her.

Her fingers threaded through his hair, tugging at the silky thick strands. Her head had fallen back and she thrilled to the sound of Keegan sucking and licking at her pussy.

She could barely breathe even though her lungs worked overtime.

"Keegan, please..."

He paused and she nearly screeched with frustration.

"Please what?" She felt his breath against her skin, and her stomach contracted with lust.

"Please make me come." She punctuated her breathless statement with a tug on his hair, trying to pull his lips back to her.

He resisted, his mouth not *even* close to where she wanted it.

"Is it only my mouth you want?"

It took her a few seconds to understand what he was asking, he'd scrambled her brains that badly. She looked down, seeing only the outline of his head at her waist.

"No, that's not all I want."

He nuzzled his nose against her mound. "Say it. I want to hear you."

Her fingers tightened in his hair. "I want you to fuck me. I want you to shove your cock inside me. I want you to do it right here. Right now."

She wanted to make sure he had no doubt about what she wanted but she'd never spoken to a man like that in her life. She had no sexual hang-ups. Hell, she'd already had sex with this man for money. A half-million dollars that had saved her and her mom from a lifetime of debt.

And left her with a craving for two men she was afraid would become an addiction.

With her breath stuck in her throat, she watched Keegan rise to his feet. It was still too dark to see every nuance of his expression, but when he plastered his mouth over hers again, she knew he was just as hot for her. The increased heat of his body felt like a furnace blast against her skin.

The lyrics from Nelly's "Hot in Herre" ran through her head and she wanted to laugh but she didn't have the breath. He stole it from her body, heightening all her senses. Her clothes felt way too constricting, the air on her bared thighs a tease.

His hands roamed her body until one came to rest on her ass. He squeezed and fondled. Then, suddenly, her feet left the floor as he lifted her. Her legs parted, her skirt hiked up far enough that she could wrap her legs around his waist.

Groaning, Keegan put his free hand between her legs, dipping his fingers back into her.

"Keegan."

"Fuck me, Jules. You're soaking wet."

"That's exactly what I want to do. Right now."

The hand between her legs left but didn't go far. She felt him tear at his pants, felt him shudder when she bit his neck.

Her pulse pounded through her body, her pussy tight and aching, her clit throbbing. She wanted to taste his skin, suck on him until she took his essence inside her.

She heard the sound of his zipper releasing and her body reacted with a surge of lust.

"Put your legs down, sweetheart." Keegan's voice rasped in her ear. "Just for a second. I need a condom."

A condom. Yes, that was good.

Her feet hit the floor and her hands reached for his cock. His groan echoed through the small space as she wrapped her fingers around him and stroked with a hard, twisting motion.

She remembered what he liked, what he'd liked that night.

"Fuck. Yes. Harder."

His tone was barely above a growl and she stepped closer, giving it to him harder with one hand as she slipped the other between his legs to fondle his balls.

His mouth lowered to her neck and she tilted back her head to give him better access while she stroked his hard cock. Silky, hot skin over a rock-hard shaft.

Her pussy wept and the frenzy in her blood made her feel drugged.

What did this man do to her?

"Christ, Jules. Your hands are fucking amazing."

She gave him a squeeze. "Don't you dare come until you get inside me."

"Then I've gotta put this on. Now."

His hands reached for his cock and she released him reluctantly, only long enough for him to roll on the condom. She had her hands on him a split second later.

His mouth descended again and then they were moving. Her back met the wall to the left of the entrance, not hard enough to hurt, just enough to let her know she'd hit something. In the next second, Keegan was lifting her again.

Wrapping her legs around his waist and her arms around his shoulders, she arched back, tilting her pelvis forward and moaning when her pussy pressed against his cock.

"Ah, fuck."

Keegan's voice had dropped another octave and she shivered in reaction as he lifted her even higher, until finally, he had her positioned just where she wanted to be.

About to be impaled on his erection.

She sought his mouth again as she shimmied her hips until she had the tip of his cock lodged at her entrance.

As if he'd read her mind, he thrust as she released a little bit of her hold on his shoulders and felt him spread her wide.

"Oh God."

Her arms tightened around his shoulders as he started to thrust, hard and fast. Exactly how she needed it. She was past the point of slow and easy. She needed him to pound her. To take her, to make her let go. Make her *his*.

Every thrust made her gasp, her hips tilting to get him deeper. Every retreat made her want him to come back. Harder.

Suddenly, Keegan stopped. She started to give him hell but he covered her mouth with his hand.

Then she heard it. Voices in the hall. Female voices.

She froze. At least, as much as she could. Her pussy contracted around him, causing his cock to throb. He shuddered against her, pressing his mouth to her neck as if he was afraid he'd give them away.

"...going to make her...doesn't know what...how could he..."

She recognized Alli's voice and, though she couldn't make out exactly what she was saying, she could tell Alli was pissed.

What would the woman say if she discovered Jules and Keegan bare-assed and doing the deed only a few feet away?

Another woman spoke, her voice lower and undistinguishable. Then their voices were silenced completely as they entered the bathroom.

She was on the verge of coming. Her body ached for it. If she didn't orgasm soon, she was going to scream.

Turning her head, she dislodged his hand and pulled his head down so she could put her lips directly on his ear. "Move. Now."

His cock pulsed and she felt the level of control he was exerting over his body as he held himself still.

"Are you sure?"

She bit his earlobe and it wasn't a nip. It was hard enough to make him wince. "If you don't, I'm going to lose it and everyone's going to know where we are and what we're doing."

"I don't give a fuck about anyone else, Jules." He punctuated his words with a slow withdrawal then a fast, hard thrust. "I only care about you."

Then he began to move again, slower this time, as if that would keep her quiet.

It only made her want to scream at him to move faster, fuck her harder. Turning her face into his neck, she opened her mouth on his skin to stifle any noise she made.

Already she felt her pussy tightening around him, clutching at him. Her heels dug into his ass, urging him on. Her hands found their way into his hair again and she wound the soft strands around her fingers and tugged.

Keegan's labored breathing sounded in her ear, and she thrilled at the desperate sound. His hips began to move faster until he hit the pace he'd been at before.

And hit the spot inside her body that lit her up like an electrical current.

She clutched at him, her body tightening until she thought she couldn't stand it anymore.

And then she came, so hard her entire body shuddered.

She couldn't quite stop the moan that emerged from her mouth and Keegan twisted his head to slam his lips over hers and shut her up.

Even so, she couldn't stop the guttural sound as her body

convulsed around him, sucking him deep and dragging him along with her.

In seconds, she felt his cock swell then pulse inside her.

As aftershocks wracked their bodies, they remained there for several minutes until her legs began to shake.

Keegan's arms loosened and he lowered her to her feet, pulling down her skirt before turning her to the side and easing her onto the small bench along the side wall.

Still surrounded by so much darkness, she felt disoriented and off-center, sated but still so damn horny.

"Jules, are you okay?"

Was she? Hell if she knew.

"I need to get back to work."

It was the first thing that came to mind. And it was true. People would be wondering where she was. Someone would eventually come looking for her.

"Fuck."

She barely heard Keegan's muttered curse but she did hear him zip his pants before he sat down beside her.

"Jules—"

"No." She popped off the bench, trying to stem the tide of emotion that wanted to swamp her. What the hell had she done? "I have to go."

"We need to talk."

She shook her head. "No, I need to get out of here before someone comes looking for me."

She couldn't be seen with Keegan. Everyone would know what she'd been doing. And when they saw Keegan, they'd know *who* she'd been doing.

And why do you care?

"Damn it, Jules—"

Running her hands down her skirt to make sure it covered everything it needed to, she turned and practically ran out of the alcove. She'd almost made it up the hall before she heard Keegan come up behind her.

"Wait, Jules. Just listen—"

"No." She sliced her hand in front of her, not quite meeting his eyes. "I can't. Not now."

"Then come—"

"Sorry to interrupt. Hello again, Keegan. I didn't realize you knew Julianne."

Alli stood behind them, her expression leaving no doubt that she knew what was going on between Jules and Keegan. And she wasn't happy about it.

Damn it. She'd forgotten about the women in the bathroom.

Had Alli heard her and Keegan in the alcove? Or had she come out of the bathroom now?

Jules didn't give one shit what this woman thought about her. She never had, not in high school, not now.

But she had enough brain cells left to realize Alli could make things awkward for Keegan and Erik, who traveled in the same, small circles.

She didn't want to get caught up in all this bullshit. Didn't want to be at the center of someone else's drama again.

But you'd love to be in the middle of Keegan and Erik again, wouldn't you?

Keegan barely glanced at Alli as he stepped closer to Jules, allowing Alli more room to pass them. Completely blowing off the other woman.

"Jules, we need to talk."

God, she wanted to. But it wasn't going to happen.

Turning away from him was the hardest thing she'd ever done.

Walking away without a backward glance nearly killed her.

. . .

KEEGAN WATCHED JULES WALK AWAY, her back ramrod straight.

Damn it, he'd cocked that up for damn sure.

He wanted to go after her, wanted to throw her over his shoulder, shove her into his car and take her the hell away from here. Back to Erik's. Back to where this obsession had started.

"Sorry. Did I interrupt something?"

He turned toward Alli, whose tone suggested she knew exactly what she'd interrupted. And that she didn't like it.

And he didn't give one flying fuck about that.

He wanted to tell her, yes, she had interrupted and to get lost, but he couldn't do that to Jules. Apparently Allison knew Jules. He wouldn't put it past Allison to make Jules pay for any slight from Keegan.

If these people ever found out that he and Erik had paid Jules a half-million dollars to have sex with them, Jules would never stay in the area. She'd pack up and leave.

And he wanted her to stay.

He forced a smile. "No. Are you ready to go back to the party? I'm afraid I have to leave in a few minutes. Late conference call."

He started to walk up the hall, not waiting to see if Allison followed.

"Sounds like business is good."

Business was booming. TinMan Biometrics had more than they could handle and they were scrambling to screen and hire technicians, which was harder than it should be. They'd already weeded out one applicant who'd been hired by a rival firm to spy. Corporate espionage was an unavoidable fact of business.

"It is," he answered, not really wanting to get into a conversation with Allison but unable to simply walk away. He knew she wouldn't take the slight well and he didn't want her to go after Jules for any reason.

"Which is great for local business." Allison stayed by his side as they made their way across the room. He tried not to make it obvious as he searched for Jules. But she was nowhere to be found.

"We try to keep as much as we can local. Good for everyone."

And that was the God's honest truth and something Keegan totally believed in. At any other time, he'd be happy to tell anyone who asked how important it was to build a strong base of operations.

But right now, all he wanted to do was find Jules, apologize for practically forcing her to do him in that closet then convince her to come with him. He couldn't leave it like this.

He had to tell her he hadn't meant for that scene in the closet to happen. Jesus, the more this situation progressed, the worse it got.

Allison continued to try to draw him into conversation as they walked across the floor to the bar where her friends continued to hold court. But as soon as she was safely back in that circle of hell, Keegan made his excuses and got the fuck out of Dodge.

He wanted to head straight for the kitchen but Allison and her friends were watching. He'd never get there unnoticed.

God damn, he was an idiot. Erik had said as much. Then again, Erik was being a prick so he guessed they were even.

Frustration made him want to climb the walls so he decided to get some air. Grabbing his coat from the coat check, he stalked out to the parking lot. The frigid January air hit him like a blow to the face and he buttoned his coat and shoved his hands into his pocket for the walk to his car.

Throwing open the door to his new Challenger, he threw himself in the front seat and considered his options.

Shit.

He pulled out his phone.

"I told you not to go. You struck out, didn't you?"

Erik didn't bother to say hello.

"Fuck you."

Erik grunted. "Did you honestly think it'd be that easy? That she'd just say, 'Oh, Keegan, thank God you're here. I've missed you so much. Take me away from all this.'"

Anger warred with frustration. "At least I fucking tried. You're too much of a pussy to leave the fucking house."

"I'm at the lab, dickwad, so I have left the house."

"You can hide just as easily there."

"I'm not hiding. I'm working."

Keegan bit his tongue on the words crowding his throat. Yes, he was pissed and yes, he was taking it out on the one guy who didn't deserve it. But it was the one guy who could take it.

"Fuck." Keegan blew out a breath. "I screwed up."

"I take it you saw her."

"Yeah."

Erik paused. "How bad did you screw this up? Hell, how could you fuck this up even more?"

Shit. Did he tell Erik he'd fucked her up against a goddamn wall? Had he broken their unwritten code? No fucking the object of the other guy's obsession. But what happened when the woman was the object of both of their fantasies?

When he didn't answer for more than a minute, Keegan heard Erik take a deep breath. "Jesus, Keegan. What the fuck did you do?"

He slammed his hand against the steering wheel, not as hard as he wanted because he didn't want to damage the car but hard enough to send pain radiating up his arm.

"Shit."

"Oh hell. You sonovabitch. What did you do?"

Through the open line, Erik's rough, angry breathing came

through loud and clear. Keegan tried to think of a way to tell Erik exactly what had happened without coming off like a douche.

"What the *fuck*, Keegan. I told you not to go. How bad is it? Did you make her cry? I'm gonna bust your head open, you stupid—"

"I fucked her. Alright? I fucked her in a goddamn closet. I couldn't keep my damn hands off her."

The other end of the phone went deadly silent.

Erik was beyond pissed. Which proved, without Erik ever saying a word, that he wanted Jules just as much as Keegan did.

"I'll fix it. I don't know how but I'll—"

"Did you hurt her?"

"*What?* You know I'd never fucking hurt her."

Not physically. Not ever. But he'd probably done a number on her emotionally.

"Shit." Erik's voice held a definite sneer. "I know that, asswipe. I know you'd never hit her. But you did hurt her, didn't you?"

"She was already hurt. We didn't call her. We should've fucking called her."

Another pause. "I know. Okay, I know. God *damn* it."

Something clattered in the background on Erik's end and Keegan figured something metallic had just gone flying in the lab. Hopefully it wasn't anything important.

They both went silent then.

"Call her," Keegan said. "Call her and ask her to come to the house. I'll follow her over. You talk to her then I'll throw myself on her mercy."

"Yeah, like she's gonna want to talk to me."

"Erik, we've got to do something. This situation is getting fucked beyond imagination. We gotta fix it."

Another silence but this time, Keegan knew Erik was thinking.

"Fine. I'll call you back."

Keegan hung up and settled back in the seat to wait.

"HEY, did something happen out there? You look flushed. Are you feeling okay?"

Jules pulled a smile for Lori, who frowned at her as she began cleaning up the kitchen.

"My stomach's a little unsettled. I'm not needed on the floor anymore so I figured I'd help us get out of here faster."

And keep away from Keegan.

"Alright." Lori didn't look convinced but she headed back out the door. "Just make sure you go home and get some sleep. You're starting to look pretty sick."

She did feel sick but not because she was coming down with something. Unless stupidity was in the same league as the flu.

She must have lost her mind. That was her only excuse for what she'd just done with Keegan.

The slight ache in her bare pussy, because Keegan still had her panties. The shaky muscles in her thighs...

Stupid.

But, oh my God.

She nearly dropped the trays she was stacking just thinking about Keegan and that little alcove.

Anyone could've walked in. Anyone could've seen them. And the gossip would start again.

That bastard she'd met at an event three years ago, who'd seemed so decent, had turned out to be a complete asshole. A married asshole.

But she'd been the one to take all the shit for his failed

marriage. How the hell anyone had ever found out she'd been the foolish nineteen-year-old who'd believed his bullshit about having just gotten out of a horrid marriage and how he thought they'd clicked, she'd never really found out.

But someone had and his wife had gotten hold of her phone number and raged at her for days. Vile texts and horrible voice messages. She'd to get her phone number changed.

That incident had almost, *almost*, made her swear off guys for good. But she knew she couldn't let one dickhead ruin her for the rest of her life. She enjoyed guys. She enjoyed sex. She didn't have a lot of hang-ups about it. If she liked a guy...if he treated her well and she wanted him...why the hell shouldn't she enjoy herself?

She'd more than enjoyed herself with Keegan and Erik.

And that was the problem, wasn't it?

She'd thought there'd been some connection between them, something that went deeper than just the money and the lust.

Damn it, she'd *wanted* them to call.

"Hey, you really don't look good. Why don't you take off for the night? We can manage without you."

Jules looked up to find Carol, standing by her side. She and Carol had struck up a friendship from the moment Jules had interviewed for this job with the catering company when she was seventeen. Carol was several years older but they'd recognized a kindred spirit in each other.

Which meant Carol knew her better than a lot of people, her mother included.

When she didn't answer right away, Carol frowned at her then pulled her out of the kitchen and into the room just behind it, where they kept the dishwashing machines. "What the hell happened? Spill it."

Leaning back against the stainless steel counter along the wall, she took a deep breath. "Keegan was here."

Carol nodded, not looking surprised. "And..."

Jules took another breath. "And things got a little out of hand."

"What?" Carol's blue eyes widened. "Did he—"

"No. Wait." Jules held up one hand. "Nothing like that. God, this is coming out all wrong."

Carol crossed her arms over her ample chest. "Then just tell me exactly what happened."

Sighing, Jules shook her head, trying to put things in order. "I needed some space. I headed for that little alcove down the hall before the bathroom. He followed me. We had sex. He left."

Carol's mouth opened but nothing emerged for a good ten seconds. "That... That... *Keegan*? Really?"

Grimacing, Jules sighed then let her head fall back as her eyes closed. "Shit. That's exactly what happened and not at all what happened. I'm being such a bitch."

"No. No, you're not. This whole situation—"

"Is becoming a clusterfuck of the highest proportions. I know that. And they're not totally to blame. I agreed, Carol. I took the money and I screwed them and I had a damn good time doing it. I just need to realize that that's all it was to them. A good time and a charitable donation. Christ, they can probably write it off on their tax return next year."

"Jesus." Carol lifted a hand to rub her forehead then pushed her hands through her shoulder-length blond hair. "They managed to fuck this up royally, didn't they?"

"No, I'm the one who fucked it up. I...let myself think there could be more to whatever it was we did."

"Oh, now wait just a minute. They never told you why they asked you to come to the house that night, did they?"

"They said they saw me at their company's reception. They

wanted me. They found my weak spot and exploited it. My mom's debt."

Carol grimaced. "Damn them. Yes, I know that's exactly what it seems like, but they're not that cold. You've seen Erik but I'm not sure you know how really screwed up he was after the fire."

"You mean how screwed up he still is."

"Yeah, I guess that's exactly what I mean. The guy was gorgeous before the accident. I mean, we're talking male-model perfection. He was used to getting whoever he wanted, when-ever he wanted. And Keegan isn't too hard on the eyes either. Together, they were irresistible."

Carol paused and Jules found herself holding her breath, wanting more, needing to hear more.

"And then the explosion changed everything." Carol shook her head, sighed. "Erik withdrew from the world and it drove Keegan crazy. Keegan loves the guy like a brother. I know some people think he's got a thing for Erik, a sexual thing but I'm not one of them."

"How do you know them so well?"

"I was one of the first people they met when they moved here for the business. My sister...she's a real estate agent. She helped them find the property. She fixed me up with Erik."

Jealousy pricked at Jules. She wanted to tear at beautiful Carol's perfect hair like a raving bitch.

Which Carol must have been able to see because she held out one hand, her expression turning rueful. "Trust me, I was willing, but Erik wasn't interested. And Keegan was never my type. But the guys are dedicated to working with local busi-nesses and they hired me to handle their events. Our friendship just happened. They really are great guys. But then the accident turned Erik into this lifeless, bitter shell. It was like...watching cut flowers die. Does that make any sense?"

Jules nodded, completely understanding. "But why me?"

"Chemistry? Fate? Hormones?" Carol shrugged. "Who knows? But for the first time in two years, Erik wanted someone more than he wanted to hide."

"But he wasn't *going* to come out of the shadows. If I hadn't figured out he was there, he would've hung back and watched me and Keegan. And that's all."

"Do you really think you ever would've known Erik was there if he didn't want you to?"

Okay, Carol had a point. If Erik had only wanted to watch, he never would've stepped out of the shadows. She didn't know him well. Hell, she barely knew him at all. But she'd learned enough about him that night to know Carol was right.

"Then what the hell happened with Keegan tonight?"

Carol shook her head. "No idea. I only know that it's totally out of character for him. Keegan's a sweet guy and I don't mean that in a bad way. He and Erik run the business together but Erik had been the public face until the accident. After that, Keegan was forced into the role. It's not one he likes. I think he got used to Erik handling all the messy stuff. Keegan's good at smoothing, at tying up the loose ends. They're both brilliant engineers and, when they work together in the lab, it's like they read each other's mind. But they're two very different men otherwise."

It wasn't only engineering where they seemed to read each other's mind. When they'd fucked her together, it'd been like nothing she'd ever experienced. The way they worked together...

"Didn't Keegan say anything at all tonight?" Carol prompted.

"He wanted to talk but I couldn't keep my hands off him. And afterward, I was too freaked out. God, what an absolute mess."

"So call him. Let him talk."

Jules couldn't stop shaking her head. "Maybe I should just cut my losses and run."

She looked up at Carol for any hint that she agreed but her friend just stared at her.

"If that's what you think you should do." Carol raised her eyebrows. "But you know that's not what you want."

No, it wasn't. Jules was starting to work up a good mad. At herself. At Keegan for waylaying her. At Erik for not calling.

"Hey, Jules." Lori stuck her head into the room and held out Jules' cell. "This has been ringing for the past few minutes. You left it on the table. Thought it might be important."

Jules took the phone and gave Lori a weak smile. "Thanks. I better check to make sure it's not my mom."

"No problem. Hey, Carol, that bitchy blonde is looking for you to settle up. Jon's been deflecting her but he's getting to the end of his rope with her. Sorry."

"Go on." Jules waved her friend to the door. "I'm fine. Sorry I laid all this shit on your doorstep."

"Well, technically I brought it to your doorstep first so I feel kind of responsible. Just think about what I said, okay?" Then Carol rolled her eyes and straightened her shoulders. "Off to be the boss. Not as much fun as you might think."

Carol left but Jules knew her friend loved owning her own business, even with all the headaches. It's what Jules had always wanted and the money Keegan and Erik had given her might actually make that dream come true one day.

She wanted to bang her head against the wall. Her thoughts just kept going in circles.

Checking her call record, she realized she didn't recognize the number but whoever it was had called four times. Someone wanted to reach her badly.

She hit redial. The phone rang once before being picked up.

"Jules."

Erik. She'd recognize that voice anywhere. It had that distinctive rasp, the one that sent a shudder through her body. It held the same power as Keegan's accent.

"Yes." She wracked her brain for something else to say and came up blank. First Keegan, now Erik.

"How are you? Are you okay?"

No, she really wasn't but she wasn't going to admit that. "I'm fine. Why are you calling?"

Okay, that had sounded steady. So far, so good.

"Can you come to the house? I'd like to talk."

"Why?"

"Because we should've done this the day after."

"Are you talking about the day after you and Keegan paid me or the day after we actually had sex?"

Okay, maybe not so steady.

"Yes."

She waited for him to say more, to say anything. He left that hang there.

The silence grew uncomfortable after several seconds and finally she couldn't stand it anymore. "Fine. Will it just be you or will Keegan be there too?"

"Do you want Keegan here?"

"He told you what happened tonight, didn't he?"

Erik paused. "We can talk when you get here."

Damn him, he wouldn't rise to her bait, to the slight sneer in her tone. Fine. "I can be there in half an hour."

"I'll be waiting."

NINE

"She's on her way."

"Good. Apologize for me. Tell her I was a total dick."

"You can tell her yourself. Get your ass over here."

Through the phone, Erik heard Keegan blow out a breath. "No. She won't want to see me. And I already started on the tequila."

Fuck. When Keegan drank tequila, it was bad.

"Keegan—"

"No. You can handle this one. I'm fucking sick of handling shit. I've done enough damage for the day."

"Shut the fuck up and get over yourself. If you really did fuck up so badly, then you need to be the one to beg her forgiveness. Don't be even more of a dick."

Keegan fell silent and Erik wondered if he'd pushed his friend too far. When Keegan was depressed, the guy could stay silent for days. Like, not talk at all. It made Erik want to yell in his face just to snap him out of it.

Finally he heard Keegan sigh. "Too late."

The call went dead.

Sonuvabitch.

Erik wanted to throw the phone against the wall but managed to rein himself in. Barely. He had half a mind to drive over to Keegan's house and drag him back before Jules arrived.

Since Keegan only lived about a mile away, that wouldn't be a problem. It'd take Jules at least half an hour to get here. If she even showed up.

Damn it. What the hell was he supposed to say to her?

Keegan usually handled this stuff, the messy stuff with women. Erik had been the one to make first contact but Keegan had been the one to smooth everything over when Erik was a dick and blew them off after a couple of days.

Christ, he really had been an ass. He'd learned his lesson when the one girl he'd really liked had blown him off. Desiree. Beautiful girl. He'd actually thought about asking her to marry him senior year at Princeton. But she'd turned around and dumped his ass.

He'd drowned his sorrows for an entire weekend. Keegan had been the one to pull him out.

He didn't want to fuck this up. He wanted to get to know Jules. She drew him in, like no one ever had before.

Pacing the hallway, he was glad he'd told Jane and Bill Carlson to leave early today. He'd employed Jane to take care of the housekeeping and cooking and her father, Bill, was damn handy with a wrench and a hammer. And this old house needed a lot of work.

He'd planned to do the renovations himself, had chosen the house because he loved a challenge. And this house was definitely that. He'd seen the potential right away. Keegan had laughingly called it a money pit and bought property down the road where he'd built a brand-new, modern home. Green all the way, from the cork floors to the solar panels on the roof.

How the hell he and Keegan worked so well together was still a mystery to some people. Erik knew their differences filled in the gaps in each other. Which is why Keegan needed to be here to help him fix this.

Too late.

He heard her car pull up out front. He knew it was hers because he recognized the engine noise. That deathtrap she drove should be condemned. Hell, they'd given her more than enough money to get a new car in addition to paying off her and her mother's bills.

Probably shouldn't bring that up.

Yeah, the money was going to fuck up everything, wasn't it?

Didn't it always?

He didn't hear the bell ring as he walked to the door but he hadn't heard the car drive away either. Which meant she was probably still in it. Talking herself out of seeing him.

He couldn't let her do that.

His pace quickened and, by the time he got to the front of the house, he was running. Throwing open the door, he stepped onto the porch and nearly knocked her off her feet.

"Whoa. Sorry."

He reached for her, grabbing her shoulders so she didn't go tumbling back off the porch. She reached for him at the same time, her hands landing on his abdomen.

They ended up closer than he'd expected to get to her tonight.

And just where he wanted her. Plastered up against him.

She stared up at him, her dark eyes wide, rimmed with red.

Had she been crying?

Shit.

"Are you okay?"

He forced the words from his dry throat as he slid his hands from her shoulders to her hips, pulling her even closer.

"Yes. I'm fine." She tried to take a step back but he wasn't about to release her. Not yet. Maybe not at all tonight. At least, not until she heard him out. "You can let go now."

He ignored her, holding her gaze. "What if I don't want to?"

She blinked up at him, and he could have sworn he saw tears forming right before she sniffed and dropped her gaze.

"Well, I want you to. I agreed to talk. Not...anything else."

He opened his mouth to tell her exactly what he was thinking—that now that she was here, she was his—and shut his mouth. Obviously, the caveman routine hadn't gone over well with Keegan. Guess he'd have to try a different approach.

He took a step back, releasing her shoulders, and gritted his teeth when she released him as well.

"Okay then, come on in and we can talk."

He waved her into the house. Habit had him turning away from her so she couldn't see the full extent of his scars, letting his hair fall over his cheeks. She passed by him without a glance, waiting for him to close the door behind him before he headed down the hall.

He'd intended to take her into the library where they'd spent those hours together two weeks ago, then thought better of it.

Settle her down. Get her used to him again.

Maybe she hasn't called because she doesn't want to look at your hideous face again.

Turning abruptly, he headed to the kitchen. Neutral territory, he figured.

And the farthest room from the front door. If she wanted to leave, he'd at least have some time to convince her to stay before she actually got out the door.

"Have a seat." He waved at the round oak table in the curved alcove with windows overlooking the backyard. "Do you want something to drink?"

"I'll take some water."

Well, she didn't sound pissed, so that was good.

He grabbed a bottle for her and a soda for himself, then steeled himself before he turned back to her.

She'd kept her coat on. As if she didn't intend to stay. Not the puffy pink thing she'd worn last time, that'd hidden a ball-busting corset that made him want to beg her to let him take it off. This jacket was leather and short, stopping at the top of her tight black skirt. It hung open to expose the plain white, button-down shirt.

Her hair hung in a braid over her shoulder, the end brushing against her breast.

Yeah, looking at her breasts was probably *not* going to help him keep his hands off of her.

Keeping the table between them, he sat and pushed her water across the expanse. When he'd withdrawn his hand, she took it.

Now what? What the hell did he say? She wasn't exactly giving him any openings here. Might as well just rip off the bandage.

"Keegan told me what happened. Do you want to talk about it?"

Her head popped up and those dark eyes locked onto his. "Why should I want to talk about it with you? Why exactly would I want to talk about *any* of this with you?" She shook her head. "You know what? This is a mistake. I never should've come here. Not now. Not before."

So that's where they stood. This quicksand was deeper than he'd thought. But now that he was standing in it, he might as well fight all the way down.

"Bullshit."

Her mouth dropped open and her eyes widened. And the tears receded as anger built.

Good. Anger he could deal with.

"If you hadn't wanted to talk about it, you wouldn't be here."

It took a few seconds but he saw her realize that he'd read her correctly. But she wasn't happy about it and he braced for battle.

Which showed just how much he really didn't know about her.

As he watched, the anger drained out of her. She didn't deflate though, didn't break down. She took a deep breath and straightened her spine.

"You're right. I do want to talk."

His turn to take a deep breath. "Okay. Lay it out for me. Whatever it is, just spit it out."

Her gaze bored into his. "You didn't call. Neither of you. And I was stupid enough to think you would." Each word she spoke came out precisely. And cut like a scalpel. "I can't help feeling used. Which is totally stupid. You paid me to have sex with you. And Keegan. You *paid* me and it was more than enough to clear out any debt my mom and I had. You knew about that. I don't know how but I know you knew we needed the money."

Erik was afraid to move, afraid to breathe. Every word out of her mouth was underlined with pain and each one dug into his chest like an ice pick. His brain whirred like a pinwheel in a tornado. What the hell did he say? What *could* he say?

Nothing, because she continued. "I was so stupid because when I left that night, I thought I'd hear from you again. I thought one of you would call. We'd do dinner. We'd— Hell, I don't know, go to a movie. Do something normal. But this isn't a normal situation, is it?"

She paused and he knew she was waiting for him to speak up.

"No, it's not." He sighed, a hard exhalation of breath that

reeked of his frustration. "But you're not stupid. Not by a long shot. I wouldn't want you so damn badly if you were."

Her eyes narrowed, wary and focused totally on him. And she kept silent, waiting.

"Don't make any mistake there. I *do* want you. So does Keegan. He wanted to call. He wanted to call and ask you out the next day but it was Christmas Eve and you said you were spending it with your mom. Then it was Christmas and we had family commitments. And when we got back to the lab last week, we had other shit going down."

He wasn't about to lay that on her. That was business. This wasn't. Never had been despite the money.

"Yeah," he continued, "we knew about your mom's situation. We knew you needed help. We knew we wanted to give you the money. And we both knew we wanted you in bed between us."

"And you didn't think I'd want you if it weren't for the money."

There it was again. That elephant in the room.

Her gaze slipped to the side of his face, looking at his scars. Instead of dipping his head and letting his hair cover them like he normally did, he resisted the urge. She'd done it on purpose but he didn't think she'd done it to hurt him.

And when she finally looked into his eyes again, he knew it. No pity. Only empathy. He knew the difference because of her.

And that's why there was no way he was letting her leave.

Christ, his cock practically pounded against the zipper in his jeans, he was so hard.

"No, I didn't think you'd want me. But I'm not as stupid as I was then."

They fell silent, staring into each other's eyes. He wanted to reach across the table and pull her over it. Hell, he wanted to strip her naked and fuck her hard and fast on top of it.

Then he'd text Keegan and tell him to get his ass over here so they could take her on his bed.

He'd dreamed about her every friggin' night. Woke up hard and unsatisfied every morning. He wanted to ease the ache in his gut right now.

"Keegan didn't go to that reception tonight to nail you to the wall. He only went to talk."

Her lips twisted in a sneer. "Then he obviously has a different meaning for the word 'talk.'"

"It's not entirely his fault, Jules." He raised a hand before she could say the indignant words gathering on her tongue. "It's mine. I told him to wait."

"Why?"

Because I think I've finally found a lead on who might've sabotaged the lab and caused the fire that disfigured me. Because I need to prove to Keegan that I'm not crazy.

And Jules would've made it impossible for him to think clearly.

"Because I was an ass."

"So because you admit it, that means everything's forgiven?"

"No. But give me the chance to make it up to you."

Her expression showed just how futile she thought that was. "How?"

"Honestly, I was hoping you'd have a suggestion."

She blinked. "Isn't that kind of a cop-out?"

He couldn't be sure but he thought she might have almost smiled. Maybe he hadn't totally lost his touch with women.

Then again, he had no idea what to say to that except... "Yeah. I guess it is."

Damn, he was totally blowing this.

"Hey, would you like something to eat? I haven't had dinner yet and I'm starving."

"Is this your subtle way of getting me to cook for you?"

He gave her a mock-angry frown. "Hey, are you dissing my abilities to perform in the kitchen? I'll have you know I'm perfectly capable of fending for myself."

The fact that he had a housekeeper who fixed most of his meals notwithstanding.

He didn't wait for her answer, just headed for the fridge where he pulled out the fixings for an omelet.

"No, I'm not dissing your cooking abilities. I just... I thought..."

He set all the stuff on the island counter then reached underneath for a bowl. "Thought what?"

"Well, you seem to know everything else about me, I figured you knew that I plan to open my own restaurant one day."

He actually *had* known that. Carol had told him. "What do you like to cook?"

Rising, she walked over to the island. "American comfort food but high-end. Lobster mac and cheese. Sirloin cheesesteak sandwiches. Different but recognizable."

After cracking eggs into a bowl, he started to whisk. "Sounds good. Where do you want to set up shop?"

"Philadelphia maybe. King of Prussia. Not around here."

"So you want to run away to the big city, huh?"

He and Keegan had run as far from the big cities as they could. And now Erik wouldn't move back for all the business in the world. All those people staring at him. Jesus, it'd be hell every day.

"I want to get away from here, that's for damn sure." Her tone held a hard note. "Growing up in a small town might sound like a great idea, but when you don't want to conform or fit into the little box everyone thinks you should fit in..."

Things hadn't been great for her growing up. She'd had a reputation apparently, for something that wasn't her fault. Carol had told him about the affair she'd had. About the man who'd lied to her and made her out to be some kind of home wrecker.

Erik would gladly bash the guy's face in.

"So don't. But don't let small-minded people keep you down."

He realized what he'd said the second the words left his mouth and looked up to find her staring at him with raised eyebrows.

"Not the same thing and you know it," he said.

She reached across the island and ran her finger down his cheek. The disfigured one. He flinched away. He couldn't help it.

But she followed him, putting her hand flat on his cheek. He barely felt it. The scar tissue was thick and didn't allow for much sensation. Which just pissed him off. He wanted to feel her hand on his skin.

As if she'd read his mind, she lifted her other hand to his opposite cheek. And now he felt the full effect of her touch. It nailed his feet to the floor. He wouldn't have been able to move if he'd tried.

Her fingertips stroked along his skin, sending shivers of sensation through his blood, straight to his cock.

If he wasn't careful, he'd make the same mistake Keegan had. He'd let his dick do the thinking. Couldn't say he didn't understand completely, but *one* of them had to be the better man tonight.

"Jules."

"Yes."

Aw hell. That was definitely not going to make him behave. Not that word, said with that husky tone in her voice.

"Do you like onions?"

It took a few seconds but her lips curved in a smile. "Maybe you should leave them out."

"Okay. Sure."

She withdrew and he cursed silently when she was no longer touching him.

"So, are you planning to go back to college?"

She shrugged. "Maybe for some business courses. College was never on my radar. I couldn't stand high school. Why willingly sign up for more torture? I went to the vo-tech for the culinary program. That was really the only reason I graduated."

"College isn't for everyone."

"Some people think you're stupid if you don't."

"And some people are idiots. Some of the stupidest people I know have a college degree. I figure it all evens out."

Her smile was small but genuine. "I guess it does. So tell me, Erik. Don't you want to have sex with me again?"

His hand froze in the act of beating the eggs. "More than I want to breathe. Is that why you're here?"

Her gaze dropped. "I don't know why I'm here."

"Bullshit." He said it with no edge, no snark, no sneer.

After a few seconds, she nodded and her gaze lifted to his again. "Okay, fine. Why am I here?"

She looked at him with such vulnerability and he was struck by how young she looked.

Rationally, he knew she was only twenty-one but she'd never seemed that young. She had a maturity beyond her years.

Until this minute.

And now he felt every one of those nine years separating them.

Christ, what a mess. And it was all his fault.

"Because you know what we shared wasn't just sex."

The words were hard for him to get out because he was admitting something aloud he'd barely admitted to himself.

And he should've known she wouldn't let it go at that.

"So what was it to you?"

He paused and, after several seconds, Jules huffed. "Are you really not going to talk to me? Am I the only one who has to spill their guts?"

After a few more moments of silence, she shook her head. "Damn it—"

"When you left, I had every intention of calling you, of setting up a date. A real one. With the three of us. Then...I got some information about the explosion that I had to investigate."

"What information?"

"Nothing I want to discuss now." When she looked like she wanted to argue, he held up his hand. "No, I want to talk about you. About us. We can talk about anything else you want later. Right now, I want to talk about us."

"Is there an us?"

"What would you say if I told you I want there to be?"

Her turn to pause. "I'd have to say I'm so screwed up in the head about all of this that I'm not sure what I want anymore. All I really do know is that I want you."

His cock tightened painfully and his hands curled into fists as she began to walk around the counter. "Jules, I'm trying to be—"

She put her hands on his face again and pulled him down for a kiss. And he let her.

TEN

Erik locked down every impulse to grab Jules and toss her onto the nearest flat surface.

As her lips moved over his with a desperation he could taste, his lust built until it reached an almost feral force.

He resisted for all of two seconds then gave in to the raging desire to take whatever she wanted to give him.

When her mouth opened and her tongue licked at his lips, he opened to her.

God damn, she tasted fucking amazing. He wanted to kiss her for-fucking-ever.

His arms wrapped around her body, caging her. She wouldn't be able to move unless he allowed it. And he wasn't going to. Not for a damn long time.

She'd come to him. She'd given him her permission. He was going to take her at her word. Or actions, as the case happened to be.

With his tongue in her mouth, he swore he was drugged by her taste. It made him reckless. Made him forget that only seconds ago he'd been ready to be noble and not fuck her brains out.

Now he didn't think he could take another breath without having her.

Their lips still locked, he picked her up in his arms. Hers wrapped around his shoulders immediately and she clung to him as he headed for the stairs at the back of the kitchen.

The stairwell was narrow and he bumped his elbows so many times he was sure they'd be black and blue tomorrow. He didn't care.

He almost stumbled as they reached the second floor and he had to release her mouth to get his bearings, flinging one hand out to steady himself against the wall. Her mouth immediately landed on his neck, where she sucked on the tendon beneath the skin, biting and licking and driving him crazy.

That side of his neck was mostly scar-free so the skin was more sensitive there. Almost too sensitive. Every swipe of her tongue made electricity zing through his body. His cock felt like it was going to burst out of his jeans.

Stopping to make sure he had his feet under him, he let his head fall back as she worked her mouth from his neck to his lips.

Her hands shoved through his hair and she tugged until he stared directly into her eyes. "You better be taking me to a bed."

"Damn right. And when we get there, I'm going to strip you naked and tie you to it."

He saw her eyelids flutter and her gaze darken. "I might let you."

"You already gave your consent. You're here. And now you're mine."

He felt her shake, heard her breath hitch but she held his gaze. And didn't let go.

She'd accepted him before, scars and all. Now he'd see if she accepted even more of him.

He started to walk again, his bedroom on the other side of the house from this set of stairs.

She never said no. She never said stop.

By the time they reached his bed, he hoped like hell he had enough control to take her the way he wanted and not just fall on her like an animal. But, Jesus, he craved her.

Only his obsession with finding out what had happened that night in the lab kept him from hunting her down.

Now, he tossed her on the bed. She bounced once before stabilizing herself with her hands on the mattress, still staring up at him.

"Strip."

Swallowing hard, she hesitated, eyes widening as if in fear.

Damn it. Maybe she was just too damn young to handle all of him. Maybe—

Her lips curved in a slight grin. With an easy grace, she rose to her knees, her hands lifting to the front of her shirt. Her gaze held his and he couldn't tell if she needed reassurance that he hadn't turned into some kind of raving lunatic or if she was as turned on as he was.

Her fingers worked their way down her shirt buttons. She didn't go slowly, didn't do it as a tease. When she got to the bottom, she yanked the tails out of the skirt and shrugged it off her shoulders, letting it fall to the side, leaving her in a flesh-colored bra that managed to be sexy without being overt.

Then again, maybe it was because *she* was wearing it.

Now, her hands went to the fastening on the back of her skirt and he heard the zipper release. In the next second, she slid to the edge of the mattress and stood. The skirt fell down her legs, revealing matching bikini panties and a garter.

God damn, the girl slayed him.

His jaw hurt from clenching it, to keep from demanding she go faster. That she get on her knees and suck him off. Jules brought out the caveman in him. And he wasn't sure that was a good thing.

Because in the back of his mind, he wondered if he was just a curiosity for her. Just the man who'd saved her and her mother from a life of poverty and worry. Maybe she felt she owed him.

At this moment, he didn't care. She was here and he was going to take whatever she gave him.

Bastard.

So be it.

She leaned to the left, her breasts jiggling as she toed off her shoes. Now she was at least two inches shorter.

He felt like he towered over her. It made him want to toss her onto the bed and consume her.

"Take off the panties. Leave the rest. Then take off my clothes."

Her head tipped to the side, her braid falling over her shoulder. "That's an awful lot of demands."

"All you have to say is no."

She thought about it. He saw her weighing the pros and cons and he hoped like hell that the pro column came out ahead. If it didn't, he'd have a world-class case of blue balls.

After what seemed like an eternity, she moved her hands, her thumbs catching in the strings of her bikini panties, which then disappeared down her legs.

His chest contracted until he thought he wouldn't be able to breathe. When she reached for the hem of his t-shirt, it released in a rush.

He raised his arms to allow her to pull the shirt over his head, trying not to wince as that dark gaze made a thorough catalogue of his scars.

Yes, she'd seen them before but he didn't think he'd ever get used to anyone looking at what had once been flawless skin.

She reached for his jeans as soon as the shirt dropped from her hands and finally his cock got some relief from the tight denim. Which hadn't seemed that tight when he'd put them on this morning.

His lungs began to work overtime as she went to her knees, dragging his jeans and underwear with her. With her mouth only inches from his cock, his fingers curled into fists at his sides so he didn't reach for her and pull her mouth to his erection.

Her breath brushed against his abdomen, hot and moist, before she rose again.

As if she'd realized the balance of power was shifting, she looked up at him through her lashes. Overtly sexual. Devastatingly hot.

"I believe you said something about tying me to the bed."

Fuck. His cock jerked, his balls tightening until he could barely stand it.

"Pull the comforter off then lie face down on the sheets."

Her eyes widened and she opened her mouth but he shook his head. "Do it."

With a raised eyebrow, she went.

JULES GRABBED the comforter and pulled it to the foot of the bed then crawled onto the mattress and lay on her stomach.

Was she really going to do this? Was she really going to let him tie her down and do whatever he wanted to her?

Had she finally lost her mind?

Or was this some sort of weird reaction to having sex with Keegan earlier? She'd fucked him so she had to fuck Erik too?

Or was she just that horny?

She thought maybe it was a combination of all of the above. And right now, she didn't care.

She burned. All over. Her breasts ached. Her pussy ached. Sex with Keegan hadn't been enough.

How screwed up was that?

The sheets felt cool against her skin and her nipples puckered almost painfully.

"Reach for the top of the mattress and spread your legs."

Swallowing heavily, she did what he wanted. The cool air on her pussy almost made her close her legs again.

She heard Erik moving around, felt the mattress shimmy beneath her then something soft wrapped around one ankle. Sucking in a sharp breath, she tensed when he tightened the strap, tugging her leg closer to the edge of the mattress. Seconds later, he'd strapped her other ankle and tightened that one, leaving her legs spread wide.

"I'm going to do your hands together. Let me know if it's uncomfortable and I can split them."

She nodded, not trusting her voice. She couldn't catch her breath and she didn't want Erik to think she was frightened. She wasn't.

Turning her head, she watched him reach between the mattress and the headboard and draw out a wide black strap with double cuffs.

When he had her hands restrained, he stepped back to look at her. His cock stood almost straight up and made her breathe even harder.

If he didn't touch her soon, she might cry.

And that would be utterly humiliating.

But she was beginning to believe she was totally out of her league here. She'd considered herself experienced. Able to handle any situation.

What she was feeling for these two men wasn't anything she was prepared to handle.

Not that she was about to pull out now.

She shuddered as Erik touched her, just the tips of his fingers down her spine.

"You have the most gorgeous skin I've ever seen." He

stroked the hollow of her back just above her ass then palmed one cheek before squeezing the other.

Her eyes closed as she absorbed the warmth and roughness of his skin. Her breath caught when she thought he might reach between her legs to play with her pussy but he continued down her thigh.

When he removed his hand, her eyes opened but she couldn't see him, couldn't see what he was doing. Disoriented, she writhed, pressing her mound into the mattress, trying to gain a little relief.

She felt over-wound and over-stimulated, even though he'd touched her so sparingly.

Need more. Need it now.

When the bed shook, she sucked in a breath, realizing she'd been holding it.

She felt him pick up her braid and seconds later, her hair spilled around her shoulders, teasing her skin.

Then he put one hand high on the inside of each thigh, kneading her flesh. Moisture seeped from her needy sex.

He didn't say a word as he began to stroke her, his hands smoothing over every inch of skin he could reach. His knees were between her legs. She felt the hair on his legs graze her inner thighs and she knew he could see her pussy clearly.

Was he looking? Could he see how wet she was for him?

His palms felt rough against her skin, calloused. They had some scarring but it didn't turn her off. Nothing about this man turned her off.

She had a moment to wonder if the reason he wanted her face down was because she couldn't see his scars but then he tapped her ass and said, "Lift."

It took her a second to compute what he wanted then she lifted her hips off the bed. Something cool and firm slid under her. A pillow held her body away from the bed.

And exposed her sex even more.

"So fucking pretty."

He didn't touch her again for several seconds and she began to wonder if he was ever going to.

Then he ran one finger along the seam of her sex and sent a shudder of desire sweeping through her. She tried to close her legs, even though she knew she couldn't.

"Every night, I dreamed about this." His voice made her skin break out in goose bumps. "About you naked on my bed. I wanted you here."

"Then *do* something."

"I plan to. I just don't plan to rush it."

She felt the bed move but she couldn't see what he was doing. Then she felt the heat of his body as he put his hands on either side of her torso and leaned forward. His mouth landed on her nape, planting a kiss there, then moving to the side and laying a string of them along her right shoulder. Her left.

Every now and then, she felt the scrape of his teeth and she shuddered, muscles tightening, before he began to make his way down her back.

He bit and sucked and kissed, arousing her to a fever pitch with only his mouth. He was halfway down her back when he stopped. Her lungs stuttered and she found it nearly impossible to breathe as she waited for him.

Finally, she felt something brush against her lower back. But it wasn't his mouth.

He scraped his beard-roughened cheek against the hollow of her back, just above her ass, and her body reacted as if he'd shocked her.

Barely able to breathe, sensation pulsing through her, uncontrollable and raw, Jules sank deeper into a state of heightened awareness, where each rasp of his whiskers, each brush of his fingers against her skin, made her pant for more.

His hands moved now, grabbing her ass before smoothing down her thighs. When he bit her on one ass cheek, she flinched, though not from pain.

"Erik. Please."

His answer was to bite her other cheek.

Could he smell her arousal? He had to be able to. She wanted him to—

"You are so fucking wet, I can see it from here. I want to draw this out all night but, Christ, I can't do it. I've got to..."

He put his mouth between her legs and swiped his tongue at her sex. Every nerve ending in her body lit up and sharp hunger sliced through her. She moaned, every muscle in her body clenching.

He licked at her like she was his favorite flavor of ice cream. The tip of his tongue flicked out to play with her clit, stimulating it until it ached painfully. He refused to give her exactly what she wanted. Instead, he drove her so close to the edge that she felt, finally, she'd fall. But then he'd pull back and she'd nearly pass out from the unrealized culmination.

He licked at her labia, playing with the sensitive lips and sucking on them. Then he drove his stiffened tongue into her body and fucked her with it.

Not enough. Not nearly enough.

Her legs strained against the straps holding her down and he smoothed his hands from her thighs to her calves, easing the aching muscles.

When he pulled away, she wanted to scream but heard the crinkle of foil and her body stilled with anticipation.

"Hurry."

He pressed a kiss to the bottom curve of one ass cheek before she felt his knees wedge her legs even farther apart.

As he leaned over her, his cock nestled into the valley of her ass, making her whimper as he rubbed himself against her.

"Do you want me?"

He whispered the words in her ear and they reverberated like a heavy bass line in her stomach.

"God, yes."

"Good." His words were practically a growl. "Because I can't wait any longer."

He slid his cock between her cheeks twice before he groaned and pulled away.

But not for long.

She took a deep breath as his cock prodded the entrance to her body. Rubbing the tip against her, he groaned as he smeared her wetness all over his shaft. The stimulation made her suck in a breath and hold it, waiting for the moment he breached her.

He made her wait until she couldn't take it any longer.

Then he took her in one, hard thrust. His cock filled her, stretched her, made her moan in ecstasy. He filled her completely, gave her a sense of satisfaction that competed with the raw lust eating away at her.

When he'd gotten as far inside as he could and she felt his hips press against her ass, he stopped and held still. One hand grabbed her shoulder while he held his upper body away with the other.

On his knees between her legs, he thrust again, gaining even more ground. Stretching her. Pushing her limits.

Then he started to move and she knew she hadn't begun to test those limits.

The pace he set had her on the verge of flying apart but the hand he had on her shoulder tethered them together. He held her tight, calmed her down to the point she could sink into each sensation without being overwhelmed by them.

His cock scraped against her inner walls, already highly sensitized, and she felt it clear to her toes. Her sheath tightened around him as he groaned out her name. His hips continued to rock against her, his thighs smacking against her ass.

She was right on the edge of exploding, her body tight. She kept trying to close her legs, to close around him, but she couldn't because of the restraints.

Behind her, Erik slowed, lowering his head until his forehead pressed against her back and she felt his breath against her skin.

"Christ, Jules. You're making me crazy."

"How do you think I feel? Move, Erik. Now."

"I don't want this to end."

"Then don't be an idiot and not call me later. But right now, you have to move."

He moved and she felt him lay his cheek against her back. The one that was scarred so badly. She wanted to reach around and touch him, let him know that his scars really didn't bother her but then he began to move again and she could do nothing except let him take her along with him.

His pace wasn't as frantic now. He was more focused, more determined.

Going boneless beneath him, she wallowed in every sensation until she couldn't hold back any longer.

She came, her body jerking against the restraints as she contracted around him.

Through the blood pounding in her ears, she heard him groan out her name. Felt his cock swell and jerk inside her.

He rode her through it, pushing her higher until she literally couldn't process the feelings coursing through her.

When he finally stopped, he collapsed over her, surrounding her with his scent, his warmth.

Leaving her sated.

But knowing something...someone...was missing.

"I'M NOT GOING."

Keegan barely recognized his own voice as he stared into the heights of the cathedral ceiling in his living room.

The room wasn't spinning. At least, not yet, though he'd polished off almost an entire bottle of tequila since he'd gotten home.

Yes, he was drunk. No, he didn't feel any better.

After he'd left the mixer—after he'd banged Jules up against a wall—he'd driven home with the single-minded purpose of getting falling-down drunk.

And forgetting what a prick he'd been.

Christ, he needed to apologize. He should've done it right away, should've made her listen. Instead, he'd let her go.

Had she gone to Erik's? Was she there right now?

You could be there too if you weren't such a dick.

But he didn't think she'd want to see him again.

Why the hell would she? He'd upset her. He'd used her.

And now she probably thought he was a prick.

You are a prick.

He took another swallow, trying to drown out that voice in his head.

You should go over and see if she's there. Apologize.

He snorted. "Yeah. Go spy. That's real mature."

But was it spying if Erik had told him to show up?

Even though he was mostly drunk—as opposed to being completely drunk and a sloppy mess sitting here unable to think at all—he knew why Erik wanted him there.

They worked well together. They always had. Together, they could handle Jules.

But do you want to handle her together?

That was the half-million-dollar question, now, wasn't it?

They both wanted her. They'd both had her.

Now what?

He and Erik worked together. They owned a business together.

Throw a woman into the mix—No, throw *Jules* into the mix and things would get messy.

Not just messy. They'd get downright fucked up.

Things are already fucked up.

Alright, he seriously needed to drink more to drown out that asshole voice in his head.

But he didn't want any more to drink.

He wanted to see Jules. He wanted to watch her while Erik fucked her then he wanted to join them and make her scream.

Shit.

He got up, catching the arm of couch before he fell back onto the cushions. Hell, maybe he should sleep this off. He wasn't a mean drunk but he was a sappy one. If he went over there, he didn't know what'd come out of his mouth.

Spying his phone on the sofa table, he grabbed it to text Erik. Ask what was going on.

And what if he doesn't get back to you?

He needed to grow some fucking balls and go to Erik's. The gravel lane that connected his house to Erik's was mostly level and it wasn't like he'd be stumbling along. The one-mile walk in thirty-degree weather would clear his head.

Grabbing his coat, he headed to the front door. He'd been smart enough to change out of his dress shoes and slacks when he'd gotten home, pulling on a pair of jeans instead. At the door, he pushed his feet into a pair of battered black Chucks then headed out.

The moon was no more than a sliver of silver in the sky, when he could actually get a glimpse of it through the clouds. There were no streetlights along the stretch but he wasn't worried about wild animals or traffic. Occasionally, the nearby farmer's cows got out of their grazing land and wandered onto Keegan's property. But he didn't think the small wooded area that straddled his and Erik's land held anything more than deer, raccoons and skunks. And a shit-ton of squirrels and rabbits.

After growing up in large cities—first Dublin then Boston—he'd had culture shock moving here. It was too freaking quiet at night. No traffic noise, no sirens. And holy hell, it got dark.

He liked having his own space but being close enough to Erik that they could see each other in minutes. Watch a game together, eat dinner together, talk business. Some people thought they were too close. Those people were assholes who had no friends of their own and needed to get a life.

Fuck. He'd thought this walk would help but it was just giving him more time to screw himself up in the head.

And it was fucking cold.

He put his head down and trudged on.

Since this lane led to the back of Erik's property, he couldn't tell if Jules' car was parked out front. He debated going out front to check then talked himself out of it.

If it was there, he might not go in.

Punching in the code to open the back door, he stepped into the mudroom off the kitchen. The only light he could see was the one over the sink. Erik left that one lit all the time. He didn't like coming into a dark house.

Keegan paused, listening. Heard nothing.

He considered calling out but didn't want to bother him—them—if they were...busy.

Walking to the front of the house, he didn't see anyone.

But there, in the front window, he saw Jules' car.

He sucked in a breath then forced himself to release it slowly.

If they weren't down here then he knew where they were.

His body still felt the effects of the alcohol but his head had cleared.

Now what?

He had to know. Had to see with his own eyes.

He turned to the stairs to the second floor.

JULES DIDN'T KNOW what prompted her to look at the open door.

Maybe she'd heard some small sound. More likely it was just a coincidence that her gaze happened to go there.

Erik had released her from the restraints but they hadn't moved from the bed. He'd curled against her back, tucked her into his body and wrapped his arms around her.

Neither of them had caught their breath yet and she needed a shower.

She wanted to drift off to sleep and give her brain a rest but it just kept working. Thinking.

And then there was Keegan.

Standing in the shadows of the hall outside the bedroom room.

Staring at her.

She saw Keegan's face perfectly in the glow from the hall light. And his expression made her breath catch in her throat.

Behind her, she felt Erik freeze and knew he saw Keegan, as well.

Their gazes met and held.

Just before Keegan turned and walked away.

ELEVEN

"Keegan! Stop!"

Keegan had known going to Erik's house this late had been a mistake of immense stupidity.

He'd known Julianne was here. He'd seen her car parked out front.

And when he'd walked into the house and realized she and Erik weren't anywhere to be found on the first floor, he should've left right fucking then.

But had he?

No, of course he hadn't.

Shaking his head, Keegan bounced off the wall as he stumbled down the second-floor hall, away from Erik's bedroom. His head throbbed with an ever-increasing headache and he lifted a hand to rub at his temples. Which only made it worse.

He needed his feet to move faster. He needed to be...somewhere else. Anywhere else.

"Christ, I knew this was a mistake. Shoulda stayed the fuck home."

"God damn it. Keegan, don't fucking make me run after you."

Ignoring Erik's voice, Keegan kept walking. He had to get to the front door, get out of the house. If he just kept walking, eventually he'd get away. He needed to get away.

"Keegan. Stop."

His footsteps faltered. That wasn't Erik.

His chest muscles contracted as if he'd taken a solid blow to the solar plexus. He sucked in a sharp breath then released it in a rush.

Damn it. Don't stop now.

He took a few more steps, to the top of the stairs, then paused. Behind him, the floorboards creaked as someone walked up behind him. Tensing, he waited, waited...

The hand that fell on his shoulder was not Erik's. It was small, delicate...and had the power to destroy him.

Get a grip, asshole.

Christ, he was one stupid bastard.

"Don't go," Jules said. "Not like this."

He considered ignoring her, forcing his feet to continue down the stairs until he reached the door. From there, all he had to do was turn left. He didn't have to worry about his car. He'd walked because he'd been too drunk to drive. Now he definitely wasn't drunk enough.

The buzz that had allowed him to think coming here was a good idea in the first place had worn off the moment he'd seen Erik and Jules together in bed.

And you're an utter fucking asshole because you were the one who fucked her up against a wall earlier tonight like an unfeeling asshole.

"I shouldn't be here."

The words falling out of his mouth sounded slurred, like he was still drunk. Which couldn't be right because he felt stone-cold sober inside his own head.

"Then why are you?"

There was an edge to her voice that cut into him like a dull knife. And he deserved it. He totally deserved whatever she threw at him.

Christ, if she told him to get the hell out, it'd be only what he deserved.

Forcing himself to turn, he expected her to be pissed, almost expected a slap.

Instead, her dark gaze held worry. For him? He sucked in a breath. Why would she be worried about him?

She *should* want to hit him.

"I don't know why I'm here."

"Bullshit." Her tone held only the slightest bit of anger and, again, he wanted to shake his head. Why the hell wasn't she raging? Hell, he was pissed off at *himself* on her behalf.

So when he crossed his arms over his chest and glared down at her, the edge in his voice came through. "Fine. Then tell me why I'm here, Jules. When I'm the last person you should want to see right now."

Out of the corner of his eye, he saw Erik put his back against the wall and let his head tilt back. From this angle, Keegan saw barely any of the scarring on Erik's face. He looked like he had before the explosion. Before the damage to his face had made him a recluse.

Until the night they'd seen Jules for the first time. That night, she'd been dressed in the same, plain black-and-white catering uniform she'd been wearing earlier when he'd—

Damn it.

Now she wore Erik's t-shirt and probably nothing else.

His gaze dropped to her bare legs, her feet planted wide. She'd crossed her arms under her breasts and through the thin cotton, he could see her nipples poking into the fabric.

Christ, just put a knife through his fucking heart already.

He wanted to drop to his knees, put his arms around her waist and pull her against him.

Then he'd pull that shirt up around her waist and put his mouth—

No. There he went, thinking with his dick again. And that's exactly what had gotten him into trouble already tonight.

His gaze lifted back to hers, narrowed and glittering. "Yes, I'm pissed at you, Keegan. But not for the reason you think."

Confusion made his head swim but he refused to show it. The sooner he let her tell him off, the sooner he'd get out of here. Which was what he wanted.

Bullshit.

His chin lifted. "So tell me what I'm thinking and how I'm wrong. Am I thinking I should've called two weeks ago? Am I thinking I should've kept my damn dick in my pants tonight and talked to you instead of taking advantage of you?"

"Oh, please." Her face screwed up in a frown, which he found hot as fucking hell. "If I hadn't wanted you tonight, you would've had my knee in your balls."

Out of the corner of his eye, he saw Erik wince and run a hand through his hair. He hadn't bothered to get it cut for a couple of months and he used the length as a screen to hide behind.

But Keegan had noticed he'd been doing less of it lately... since that first night with Jules. The night this had all started.

"Then why didn't you? Why didn't you knee me in the balls? I fucking deserved it."

Her eye roll was worthy of an Oscar. "Jesus! How can you be so freaking dense and so insanely smart?" She actually stamped one bare foot, her hands curling into fists at her sides. "You know what? Maybe you're right. Maybe there *is* nothing to talk about. Maybe this is all just—"

"Stop. Just...stop." Erik's voice cut through the lust and the anger and the guilt raging in the air between Keegan and Jules. "You two need to figure this out on your own—"

"Oh no." Jules turned and took a step back so she could see both of them, pinning Erik in place with a pointed index finger. "You don't get to bug out on this. You're right. We need to talk. All three of us. Right now."

No one moved.

Keegan flashed Erik a look but Erik was staring at Jules. The lust on Erik's face made Keegan's guilt flare white-hot and he knew exactly what he had to do.

"Fine." Keegan nodded at Jules. "You wanna do this? Let's get it over with now."

JULES SUCKED in a deep breath as Keegan turned and headed downstairs, calling over his shoulder, "I'll be in the study."

For a second, she stood there, listening to his footsteps on the stairs. She found herself holding her breath, waiting for him to open the front door and leave.

She only released that breath when she heard him come to a stop somewhere in the front of the house. The floors in this old place announced every move you made. Which made it a miracle that Keegan had snuck up on them.

Then again, she hadn't really been paying much attention to anything other than Erik.

God, she wanted to close her eyes and crawl into a hole but she'd gotten herself into this mess. Now she needed to dig herself out.

Even though she had no idea what the hell she was going to do when she did.

Well, what do you want *to do?*

Good question. And no easy answer.

She wanted this entire mess to just go away. She wanted to return to the first night she'd met Erik and Keegan and enjoy that time again. That night had been...amazing. Special.

She'd thought it'd been a one-night-only event.

And then everything had gotten so screwed up.

"I assume you'd like to get dressed before you go downstairs."

Erik's quiet statement roused her from her muddled thoughts and she raised her head to look at him. His expression showed nothing but the stillness of his body said so much.

Her head began to throb and she just barely managed to keep herself from rubbing at her burning eyes.

"Yeah, I think that's probably best."

Although she didn't kid herself that Erik or Keegan would have any uncontrollable urges to take her hard and fast again, even if she paraded around naked.

Then again, with these two... Who knew.

Hell, she was so screwed up right now, she didn't think she'd say no.

And why would you?

Two hot guys wanted her. And she'd had them both at the same time.

It was the basis for thousands of romcoms—minus the sex, of course.

Yeah, but look how it's turned out? Those stories usually have happy endings.

Okay, she really needed to stop talking to herself and talk to them.

Erik watched as she turned toward his bedroom. He'd pulled on his jeans only, his body bare from the waist up. Every time she saw those scars on his body, she wanted to run her fingers over them, stroke them so he didn't think she was repulsed by them. She truly wasn't.

And the scars on his face made her want to press kisses to them. She couldn't make them all better, couldn't heal him physically. But she could show him he was still desirable.

Yeah, you're a real humanitarian.

With a shake of her head, she headed back to the bedroom. But just before she crossed the threshold, she stopped and turned. Erik hadn't taken his eyes off of her. His very hungry eyes.

Grabbing the hem of his shirt, she pulled it over her head and tossed it to him. For several seconds, she stood there naked, totally gratified to see the hunger turn to absolute lust. And to see the physical evidence in the growing bulge behind his zipper.

Then she turned and walked into the bedroom.

Tease.

She thought about that as she pulled on her panties and bra. But her brain skipped a beat when she thought about putting on her catering clothes.

Gross. But she refused to walk out there half-naked.

Which was ridiculous.

"Fuck."

She dropped onto the edge of the bed, took a deep breath and let her head fall forward.

Now what?

What did they do? What should she say? What *could* she say?

Something dropped onto the bed beside her and her head snapped up.

Erik stood at the foot of the bed, where he'd set a pair of sweat pants and a t-shirt.

"I didn't figure you wanted to put on your clothes."

Her gaze met and held his, even as her eyes burned. "Thank you."

He grimaced and huffed, the sound holding so much self-disgust she almost smiled. "Yeah, I'm a real gentleman. Come down whenever you're ready. We'll be there."

He walked out without a backward glance.

And all she could think was, *God, the man has a great ass.*

"Ugh."

What the hell was wrong with her?

Pulling on Erik's clothes, she tried not to think. Which was easy to do for a few seconds because his scent drenched her, a mouth-watering mix of sandalwood and sharp citrus.

It made her hungry again. Horny.

For both of them.

Which made no damn sense, at all.

She wanted to fall on the bed and flail around, just for a few seconds, like a toddler having a temper tantrum. Instead, she took a deep breath, closed her eyes and tried to clear her mind, at least for a few minutes.

But all too soon, she was trying to make sense of all the different thoughts running through her head.

This isn't right. You need to let one of them go.

Damn it, she didn't want to. Call her selfish. She didn't care. It was their own damn fault for spoiling her that first night. She wanted both.

Yeah and how's that going to work?

People in this town already thought she was a slut. What would they call her if she started hanging out with two guys? Two older, wealthy guys? Who'd already given her money to sleep with them?

"*Argh.*"

No more stalling. Straightening her back, she stood.

She knew what she *should* do. Now, she just had to do it. Taking a deep breath, she headed downstairs.

As her foot hit the last step, she almost faltered, her knees wanting to lock so she couldn't go any farther.

She pushed ahead.

And when she stepped into the only room on the first floor with light shining through the doorway, she caught back a sigh.

They'd taken up positions on opposite sides of the room. Keegan sprawled in a leather wingback chair, staring at the wall beside him. Erik stood in front of the bay window, hands shoved in his pockets, bare shoulders hunched.

Both seemed to be in deep thought and she had a few seconds to observe them before Keegan turned and snagged her gaze. She didn't make a sound but Erik must've heard Keegan. Or maybe they were just that attuned to each other that Erik sensed a disturbance in Keegan's force.

She would've laughed at her own joke if it'd been even the least bit funny.

Neither of them spoke so she crossed her arms over her chest.

"So, how do you want to do this?"

She sent the question out there, not really knowing how they'd respond. Not sure how she wanted them to respond.

Keegan spoke first. "I don't think that's the question you want to ask, Jules."

She thought about what he'd said for a few seconds before she realized that's exactly what she'd meant to say. "Actually, it is."

Keegan's brow furrowed as he thought that over, like he was trying to find the bombshell hidden in her words.

It took him at least half a minute but he finally shook his head. "I'm not sure there is any way to work this."

She'd expected him to say something to that effect but it still hurt. "So you don't even want to try?"

He rose from the chair with an explosion of movement then

began to pace. "Try what? A relationship between the three of us? Are you serious? How the hell would that even work?"

Her heart pounded, her lungs tightening with anxiety. And anger. "I don't have a clue. I've never done it before. I guess the question is would you even want to see if it could work? I know you and Erik have taken other women to bed together before. You're too good at it."

Erik snorted but didn't turn from the window. And he didn't say anything. Keegan sliced a vicious look at his friend but Erik continued to ignore him.

"So...," she infused as much sarcasm as she could in her tone. "Let me guess. You didn't do relationships. You only did sex."

She knew she was right when Keegan stopped to glare at her before continuing to pace. When she slid a glance at Erik, she saw he'd bowed his head.

Her hands went to her hips as her temper continued to build. "So that's your response? Ignore me? Not going to work. Why the hell did you come to that reception tonight, Keegan? If you didn't want anything to do with me, why didn't you just leave me the hell alone?"

His lips twisted. "I just wanted to make sure you were okay—"

"Bullshit." She slashed a hand out in front of her, and he halted in his tracks. "Jesus, could you please not lie. If that's all you wanted, how did we end up fucking in a *closet*?"

Keegan flinched and the blush leached out of his cheeks. "I'm sorry. You're right. That's unforgivable. So slap me. Tell me to fuck off."

He took a step closer and she had a brief flash of fear. She'd been hit by a man before, by the one man who never should've laid a hand on her. Her father had slapped her when she'd confronted him. After he'd left them. After he'd cleaned out the bank accounts and moved in with his new girlfriend.

But as Keegan drew closer, she saw his anger wasn't fueled by rage. It was directed inward.

"Why don't you just tell me why you're afraid to even try?"

When his gaze flashed at Erik, she knew what she was thinking was right. This wasn't only about her. This was about Erik, as well.

Maybe Keegan really did have sexual feelings for Erik that he wasn't willing to admit. Maybe she was simply a scapegoat. Or a stand-in.

Her anger started to get the better of her.

"You want him, don't you? I was just a way to be able to have him. Christ, I've been such a fool."

Keegan had been shaking his head almost since she started to speak. "That's not it. God damn it, Jules."

"Then explain why you look at Erik like you have something to say to him but don't know how. What could you possibly not be able to tell him?"

A tense silence fell and she heard two sets of heavy male breathing. With another shake of his head, Keegan turned away from her, yanking his hand through his curls. Which was exactly what she wished she could do. Sink her hands in his hair and pull his head down so she could kiss him. Then she wanted Erik to plaster himself against her back and kiss his way down her neck to her shoulders.

But apparently, it was all just a stupid dream on her part.

They'd used her for their own purposes and she'd been paid. She should've stayed away.

"God damn it, Keegan." Erik's voice startled her out of her thoughts and she looked up to find him closer than he'd been. Actually, he was closer to Keegan. "Say it. Go ahead, just fucking say it."

Keegan's hands curled into fists at his side for several seconds before he made a conscious effort to release them. "Whatever you're thinking, you're not right."

Erik shook his head, his expression sarcastic. "How the hell would you know what I'm thinking? We don't fucking talk anymore."

"That's not all on me." Keegan finally turned to face Erik and Jules knew she'd just been sidelined. But she didn't move.

"I know that." Erik shook his head but this time didn't look away. "I know I've been a bastard. But that's not her fault. Don't make her pay for things I'm guilty of."

"You're not guilty of anything."

"And neither are you!"

Erik was shouting by the end but she didn't flinch this time. She couldn't take her eyes off Keegan. He looked so tortured, she almost felt sorry for him. Sorry she'd started this.

"I don't know—"

"Don't fucking *lie*," Erik shot back. "Did you really think I wouldn't get it? Why you've been so damn apologetic? You walk around like a kicked puppy. What happened to me was *not* your fault."

"But *I* should've been there that night!"

Jules' eyes popped wide.

Oh wow. That explained so much.

Erik scraped a hand through his hair and pulled it back, apparently forgetting, for once, to keep the scarred side of his face covered. "Jesus, Keegan. When the hell are you going to let that go? What happened to me was *not* your fucking fault. The fault's with whoever set up that explosion."

As Keegan shook his head, Jules frowned at Erik. "You think someone deliberately tried to hurt you?"

Erik turned to face her. "I think so, yeah."

She turned to Keegan. "And you don't?"

Keegan closed his eyes and shook his head. "I never said that."

"You don't have to say it." Erik's voice sounded flat. "I can read it in your face. You think I'm delusional—"

"Oh, that's utter fucking bullshit." Keegan's hands clenched into fists at his sides. "You're not delusional."

"I know that. I know there's a goddamn reason why that burner blew other than a simple malfunction."

"You think someone sabotaged your lab?" she asked.

Both men turned toward her but she kept her eyes on Erik, watching him come closer.

"Yeah, I think someone deliberately set it to blow."

"Do you know who?"

Erik shook his head. "I have some suspicions but nothing concrete. Not yet."

"And you're driving yourself crazy trying to figure it out." Keegan slammed his fist again the wall. "You need help, damn it."

Erik threw his hands in the air. "And there you go. You think—"

"Fuck it, you know that's not what I meant. If you really think someone rigged that explosion then you need to hire someone."

Apparently this was an ongoing battle between the two of them but she couldn't help but ask, "Why won't you get someone to help you with the investigation?"

"Because what if he's wrong?" Keegan's voice held a bitter tone. "What if whoever we bring in proves him wrong? You're never wrong, are you, Erik?"

Erik shook his head, his expression bitter. "Oh, please. You know that's bullshit."

"Then why won't you let me hire someone?"

"What if this was an inside job? What if we bring someone

in and tip off whoever did it? No. I can do this. I just need a little more time."

"And in the meantime, you leave me to keep everything else going. This is supposed to be a partnership, Erik."

They seemed to have forgotten she was there again, squared off against each other.

She should leave. She couldn't help them with this and she felt useless. And slightly guilty for pushing them into this discussion, although apparently, they needed it.

Erik sighed loudly. "I know I've been preoccupied but I've been putting in as much time as I can on that new pad and—"

"Jesus, I'm not questioning your schedule." Keegan shook his head. "I'm fucking worried about you. After that last operation, you walked around like a fucking zombie. These past few months you started to come back to the land of the living but you're still not here completely. When you saw Jules, I thought..."

Thought what?

She looked at Erik, watched another flush creep into his cheeks. He didn't look at her and she wasn't sure if that was deliberate or not. She'd begun to feel like she was at a tennis match.

"Don't." Erik's voice had a sharp edge to it. "Don't put that on her."

"I'm not putting anything on her." Keegan shook his head. "But admit it. The first time you saw her, you finally started acting human again."

They stared at each other for several seconds before Erik's gaze slipped toward her.

"Is that true?" She wanted to know. She knew she'd been his first after the accident. He'd told her so. And Carol had practically said the same thing earlier tonight.

After several seconds, Erik nodded with a sharp jerk.

She frowned. "Why wouldn't you want me to know that?"

Erik just stared at her as Keegan released a frustrated sigh.

"Because he doesn't want you to feel obligated. God damn it, Erik. Just tell her how you fucking feel."

Erik's gaze slid to Keegan. "Because that's exactly what you're doing, right?"

Keegan's jaw locked and she had that sensation of being on the outside again. Locked out. Maybe there really was nothing romantic between the men. But they had one hell of a complicated relationship.

And she was making everything worse.

"I'm leaving."

She couldn't take it anymore, this constant push and pull. Was she crazy thinking they could build something between the three of them?

Definitely crazy. It would never work.

"No."

Two male voices spoke in unison. Two pairs of intense eyes locked onto her. Determination shone from each of them. But she wasn't backing down.

"You two need to work this out. I can't help you."

Erik reached for her, wrapping his fingers around her wrist. "Don't go."

"I have to."

"No, you don't." Keegan had stepped up behind her, enclosing her between them. "Neither of us want you to go."

"And what if I don't want to stay? Would you keep me here against my will?"

It was a pretty shitty thing to say and she wanted to take the words back immediately, especially when she felt Keegan go rigid behind her and watched Erik's expression harden into a mask.

When he released her, she wanted to grab for him but

managed to curl her fingers into her palms. She couldn't play this seesaw game. It wasn't fair. To her or them.

"Do you think we'd do that, Jules?"

Keegan's voice held a hint of ice she'd never heard before.

Frustrated, she threw her hands up and took two angry steps away from them, giving them both her back.

"No, I don't think that. You two are screwing with my head and I hate this."

Behind her, dead silence.

Which just fucked with her head even more.

Forcing herself to take a deep breath, she reached for calm. But knowing they were there, just as screwed up as she was about this, didn't help.

But they're both here.

The thought lodged in her brain and wouldn't leave.

They're here and they want you.

No, she shouldn't be thinking about sex.

And yet, she couldn't *stop* thinking about it. For the past two weeks, all she'd done was obsess over that night.

And you could have that again. Right now.

All she had to do was turn around and tell them. Tell them she wanted them. They wouldn't deny her.

And is that fair? To any of you?

Right at the moment, she didn't care about fair or unfair. All she cared about was easing the ache deep in her gut. The ache these men created simply by being in the same room.

Finally, behind her she heard movement.

She held still, waiting, unwilling to move. Biting into her bottom lip, she sucked in a deep breath.

Had Keegan left? She didn't want him to leave.

Or had Erik retreated?

A hand grasped her shoulder and her eyes closed.

Only to fly open again when another body moved in front of her.

She found herself staring into Keegan's dark blue eyes.

Which meant that was Erik's hand on her shoulder, the hand now smoothing down her arm, sending erotic shivers through her body.

Keegan's eyes were rimmed in red but they were clear. Sober.

His mouth, when he sealed it over hers, was hot and demanding. The same as Erik's when he pressed it to her shoulder.

Feet anchored to the floor, her hands curled into fists. She was almost afraid to reach for either of them for fear they'd pull away. She knew that was ridiculous but it didn't make her move.

Her lips stayed still beneath Keegan's mouth, waiting. For what, she wasn't sure. Her skin heated at Erik's touch as he stroked his hands down her arms to the hem of the shirt.

When his hands slipped beneath it and splayed across her lower back, she shuddered and Keegan released her mouth, though he didn't step away.

"This is your last chance to run, Jules. If you really don't want to be here, you need to go now. If you stay..." Keegan's breath as he spoke fanned against her cheek, making her lashes flutter to stay open. "This is where you're going to be all night. Between us."

She drew in a sharp gasp as Erik tugged the shirt up and over her head in one swift motion. Bared from the waist up, she didn't feel exposed. She felt desired.

Erik's arms wrapped around her from behind, pulling her against his chest. His erection pressed against her lower back and she couldn't help but wiggle against it. His groan echoed in her ear.

Her gaze snapped up to Keegan's face, but his eyes were

focused on her body. Watching Erik's hands stroke her belly before moving up to cup her breasts.

When Erik began to play with her nipples, tugging on the tips through her bra, her eyes fluttered shut but Keegan grabbed her chin in his hands and tilted her head back until it hit Erik's shoulder. Her eyes flew open and locked onto Keegan's.

"He's going to play with you until you come." Keegan's voice was nothing more than a dark rasp. "Then we're both going to make love to you. On the couch, on the floor, against the wall. In the middle of the damn room. I don't give a fuck where. We're going to give you what you want. And we're going to make sure you enjoy it."

Oh, God. She had no doubt she would. Her skin broke out in goose bumps, sensation shivering through her.

This was what she'd wanted. So why was she afraid to move?

Maybe because she was afraid she'd break the tenuous truce. Between them. Between her and them.

Erik's teeth sank into the tender spot joining her neck and shoulders as Keegan's arms crossed over his chest. The slight pain sent a shock through her that jolted her against the cage of Erik's arms. They tightened around her even more and, for a second, she felt helpless.

God, it made her wet.

Her eyes closed again and this time Keegan didn't tell her to keep them open. The darkness heightened her sense of touch, and every inch of skin pressed against Erik's felt like it was on fire.

Erik's fingers plucked at her nipples, teasing them into hard, aching points. The cooler air of the room brushed against them, pebbling them. Her skin soaked up the heat from Erik's hands until it sank into her veins and made her blood boil.

Leaning back against him, she finally let her hands reach

behind her. She slipped her fingers into the waistband of Erik's jeans, scratching at his skin. Her fingers fumbled at the button but from this angle, she couldn't undo it. So she contented herself with cupping his erection through the material.

Erik's chest rose and fell against her back in a furious rush even as one of his hands began a slow slide down her stomach.

He took his own sweet time but finally his fingertips pushed beneath the hem of the baggy sweatpants she wore. His sweatpants, actually. She wished he would get rid of them. Shove them down her legs and get her naked.

She lost all sense of shame when she was with these men because they made her feel as if nothing she did was wrong. Or bad.

She wanted to strip them, as well. Keegan's physical perfection made her want to lick him from head to toe. Even Erik's scars held their own dark attraction. Or maybe it was just the fact that he'd survived.

She sucked in a sharp breath as Erik's hand slid over her mound then arrowed straight between her legs.

"Fuck, you're wet."

His fingers slid over her clit and through her slick pussy lips, teasing, rubbing. Making her wetter.

She was already so close...

Moaning, she arched her back and rubbed her ass against his cock.

"Make me come, Erik. While he watches."

She opened her eyes now, looking right at Keegan. His jaw so tight, it looked ready to crack. But his gaze stayed on hers.

"Shove the pants down, babe." Erik spoke directly into her ear, the words felt more than heard. "Let him look."

She obeyed without hesitation, hooking her thumbs in the waistband and pushing down. The material fell without much help and, in seconds, she stood there naked.

Now Keegan's gaze dropped and didn't rise. The burning ache between her legs intensified because she knew he was watching Erik play between her legs.

Erik's fingers stroked along her labia as his thumb pressed against her clit. Without entering her, he worked her body closer to orgasm. She felt it coiling inside, tighter with each stroke. Her hips began to move in rhythm with his hand, seeking more.

She hadn't realized her eyes had closed until she felt Keegan step close enough that she felt his heat searing her.

When she opened her eyes, her first view was of Keegan's chest. Broad, strong. She leaned forward and put her mouth on him, right over his heart. She swore she felt it pounding against her lips. Sucking in a breath, she filled her lungs with his scent until it mingled with Erik's and her own arousal.

Erik chose that second to release her and she let out an unhappy moan as she reached behind her.

Keegan chose that moment to replace Erik's hand with his own. He took a second to wet his fingers in her juices before he parted her sensitive lower lips and began to fuck her with his fingers. Long, slow strokes, in and out. Stretching her, filling her. Giving her friction. Just not enough.

Erik's arms wrapped around her again, his hands molding to her breasts. Her back arched, her pelvis tilting toward Keegan, inviting him deeper.

He didn't take her invitation. He withdrew and she gasped, wanting him to return. But Erik was there, twisting her head so he could take her lips. Overloading her senses.

Vaguely, she heard the sound of a zipper releasing but Erik's kiss engaged her mind and body, hot and drugging.

Yes. This. Exactly.

She jolted when Keegan's hands gripped the backs of her thighs but she wasn't surprised when her feet left the floor.

As Keegan stepped into the vee of her thighs, she wrapped her legs around his waist, her back braced by Erik's chest, Keegan's hands on her hips. Suspended between them, she had no fear they would drop her. She trusted them implicitly with her body.

With other, more delicate things...

She moaned when the tip of Keegan's sheathed cock pressed against her swollen labia, demanding entrance to her body. She gave it to him willingly. Her body parted for him then enclosed the head. It lodged there, stretching her, making her want more.

Her moan echoed through the room as she wrapped her arms around Keegan's shoulders.

The sense of fullness in her pussy increased as gravity took hold and she slid farther down his cock. Keegan held her poised there for several seconds, his breath a harsh rasp in her ear. His arms were tight bands around her, his body throwing off heat like a furnace.

Then he moved, his erection shifting inside her, hitting points that made pleasure shimmer.

Keegan turned and she caught a glimpse of Erik, eyes narrowed, bare-chested. And staring at her with so much heat, she clenched around Keegan in reaction.

Groaning, Keegan lowered them onto the couch and she lost eye contact with Erik as Keegan sank even deeper.

Taking her face between his hands, he stared into her eyes. "Move, Jules. I took you earlier. You take me now."

God, yes.

Heart pounding, she rose up on her knees, careful not to let him slip out of her, then started to fuck him. Slow and steady, feeling every inch of him as he filled her.

Now there was no frantic urgency that had consumed them earlier tonight. She savored every second, each drag of his flesh against hers. His cock felt thicker, hotter. His gaze burned as he stared at her. He released her face to grab her hips, keeping a tight grip on her but not dictating her motions.

She had total control as she rode him, loved watching him hold himself in check when she knew he wanted to move. Keeping her motion steady, she worked them both into a deepening state of eroticism.

She wanted to drown in it, to stay here as long as possible because the rewards would be much sweeter later.

Keegan held still beneath her, his breathing a harsh rasp. He watched her with the intensity of a predatory animal. She was surprised by that focus because he'd been so visibly drunk earlier.

Now he looked totally sober. And oh so very sexy.

Gripping his shoulders tight, she found a rhythm that kept them both hanging. Her thigh muscles trembled but it wasn't from exertion. She wanted to go faster, harder.

Right here, right now, she was in control and she planned to keep it. She was determined to hold on as long as she could.

She kept up the pace for several seconds before sinking deep and holding. Watching Keegan, she saw his eyes narrow and his jaw tighten, felt his fingers dig deeper into her hips.

She felt his restraint, knew he wanted to thrust, but he wouldn't take the reins away from her. She planned to repay him for his trust very soon.

But first...

"Erik."

She looked over her shoulder to see Erik standing where they'd left him. Arms crossed over his chest, his eyes held an avid gleam.

Releasing one hand from Keegan's shoulder, she crooked her index finger at Erik and watched the corners of his mouth tilt up. Erik rarely smiled. She could count on one hand the number of times she'd seen him do it.

She liked knowing she could make him. She also liked knowing he would indulge her.

Walking toward them, he never lost the smile. It made the scars on the right side of his face pull and twist. Instead of focusing on the reminders of the ordeal he went through, she looked into his eyes. She wasn't turned off by his scars and they weren't all that he was.

Despite what those bitchy women had said earlier tonight, he was not ruined.

As she held Keegan tight inside her, heard his heavy breathing in her ears, she waited for Erik to cross the room. He took his own sweet time and she felt Keegan's control begin to fray. His fingers flexed on her hips and his cock throbbed in her pussy. She tightened around him, making him swear under his breath.

She petted Keegan's chest but didn't take her gaze away from Erik. When he finally stood beside her, she pointed to the cushion next to Keegan.

"I don't want you to feel left out."

He didn't move right away, just stared down at her for a few seconds.

"I don't ever feel left out when you're around, Jules."

Her heart twisted at the restrained emotion in his voice. "I'm going to reward you for that." She grabbed his waistband and pulled him closer when he didn't move fast enough. Every slight motion made her aware of the thickness of Keegan's cock in her pussy and the control he was exerting not to move.

And she knew he wouldn't, not as long as she wanted him to keep still. No matter what it cost him.

"Kneel here. Close enough that I can reach you. Then I'm going to suck you."

Keegan groaned, low and deep in his chest, and she felt the sound rumble through her from his cock into her pussy. Erik's gaze narrowed until his dark eyes were mere slits.

He didn't move on her command but, after a few seconds, he closed the steps between him and the couch.

When he knelt on the cushion she'd indicated, she reached for the button of his jeans with both hands, shifting on Keegan's cock and making him thrust just enough to keep himself seated deep.

She had to stop for a second because the sensation was so damn good.

Her hands began to shake as she forced the button through the hole.

"No more buttons," she muttered as the button proved stubborn. "Snaps. Jeans should only have snaps."

"I promise I'll remember that the next time I go shopping," Erik muttered, though he didn't attempt to help her. Instead, one hand went to the back of her head to sink his fingers into her hair. He didn't pull her closer or tug her head back. He just rubbed the strands between his fingers.

Tilting her face up to him, she flashed him a quick smile and watched his lips part to draw in a deep breath. Her heart thudded almost painfully in her chest at the thought that she could whip these men into as much of a frenzy as they did her.

Every time they touched her, she felt it. In the pulse of Keegan's cock in her pussy and the weight of his hands on her hips. And in the pounding pulse at the base of Erik's neck and the rigid length of his body next to her.

The control her men exerted as they allowed her to take control, once again, was more than just a game to them. It was a commitment. At least, that's what it felt like.

But was it a long-term one? Or was she seeing something that wasn't there?

Questions for another time because, right now, she wanted to shut off her brain and lose herself in these men.

After working each of the four buttons through their holes, she pushed Erik's pants down, releasing his cock.

It sprang forward, thick and hard, and she bent forward to rub her lips against the tip.

Erik's fingers tightened in her hair for several seconds but he didn't yank or pull. Keegan shifted slightly, and she slid a glance sideways to find him watching her. Which made her want to put on a show for him as she pleasured Erik.

She tilted her head to make sure Erik could see as she opened her mouth and took his cock between her lips.

She wanted to watch Keegan but she couldn't keep her eyes open as the decadent sensation of firm, hot flesh glided between her lips. Combined with the throbbing cock in her pussy, her body began to sink into orgasm almost immediately. Her sheath contracted around Keegan's shaft, wringing another heartfelt "Fuck me" from him. But he didn't move.

Erik couldn't hold still. His hips jerked forward when she took him all the way to her throat and held for long seconds before retreating, her tongue flat against the underside of his cock until only the tip remained between her lips.

Above her, Erik's tortured breathing rang in her ears as she continued her slow torture. She wanted to draw this out, make it last as long as possible. Show them how good they were together.

And hold off the decisions that would have to be made.

"Fuck, I love your mouth." Erik's voice was a low growl. "So hot."

His response sent a shiver through her and she sucked hard enough to make Erik groan.

"Come on, Jules. Get him off so I can make you come." Keegan had leaned forward so he could speak directly into her ear. "You're gonna come so fucking hard. I promise you're not gonna want to move for days."

She was already exactly where she wanted to be. Why would she ever want to move?

But she did want to come. The ache in her pussy needed to be soothed.

She quickened her pace, cupping one hand between Erik's legs to stroke his balls, making his cock pulse in her mouth. Then he started to move, a slow, jerky rhythm.

Her free hand reached out and Keegan pressed his palm against hers, weaving their fingers together, holding her tight. Then he began to move, as well.

At first, the dual motion threw her off her rhythm and she let her men take over. Erik gripped her head to hold her steady, not forcing himself too deep. Keegan's hips thrust slowly at first but picked up speed quickly, as if he couldn't help himself.

Keegan's hand on her hip and the one gripping her hand tightened, anchoring her to him, while Erik began to match Keegan's pace. Deliberate or not, the men's synched movements made her burn hotter.

She began to move with them. Let her tongue glide down Erik's cock as he sank it deep in her mouth then swirled it around the tip when he withdrew. On his last retreat, she let him slip completely from her mouth then smoothed her lips down the shaft to place a suckling kiss at the base before working her way back up.

With her lips positioned at the tip once again, she blew a stream of air over the head and felt his cock leap, bumping against her mouth.

"Go ahead, babe. Tease me all you want."

Tilting her head until she could see Erik's eyes, she smiled up at him. "I plan—"

She moaned when Keegan thrust and held, hitting a particularly sensitive area inside her.

Her eyes snapped closed as desire rocked through her, making her breath catch in her throat.

"Don't stop now, Jules." Keegan's gravel-tinged tone battered at her senses. "We're just getting started."

"Absolutely," Erik chimed in. "I wanted to come now and again later. You're not leaving tonight."

She moaned in delirious pleasure. Again sounded good. Later sounded like a promise.

"Between us all night." Keegan's thrusts increased in speed until she felt like limp jelly. "Where you should've been."

Yes. It's what she'd wanted since Christmas Eve morning when she'd woken in her bed alone. She'd wanted to be back here with them.

She ramped up her own technique now, using her vaginal muscles to clamp around Keegan's cock and sucking hard on Erik's.

It became a delicate game, but she wasn't sure what the prize was because they were all going to be satisfied when they finally collapsed.

And that moment was coming faster than any of them had anticipated.

She heard the hitch in Keegan's breathing and felt his increasingly unsteady rhythm as he thrust into her. Erik wasn't far behind, though he was more careful not to be rough. Which meant he still had a slim grasp on his control.

And that was unacceptable.

She started in on him with abandon, chasing his orgasm as hard as she did her own. Her body cranked closer with Keegan's every thrust and she let her mouth work Erik harder, drawing harder on his cock, sucking him deeper.

Erik's fingers tightened in her hair and he thrust hard, his cock stretching her mouth until it tingled and burned.

Humming around his length, she slid back to the tip and sucked in a deep breath as Keegan released her hand so he could put both of his on her hips. Then he took control and started to pound into her. The change in rhythm made the base of his cock hit her clit at a different angle and she started to come.

She sucked in a breath and exhaled on a moan, which made Erik groan in concert with Keegan.

As Keegan's cock began to pump his cum into her pussy, Erik's twitched then he began to spill into her mouth.

Both men groaned, holding deep, clutching at her as if she might try to get away.

She could barely think, much less consider getting away. Sensation washed over her, finally taking her under, and she let her men hold her up.

TWELVE

Erik's thigh muscles quivered as Jules tilted back her head, letting his cock slide from her mouth.

Sinking into the corner of the sofa before his legs betrayed him and dumped his ass on the floor, he watched as she sank against Keegan, his friend's arms curving around her back to hold her against his chest.

Holy shit. They were gonna kill themselves if they kept this up. But what a way to go.

He met Keegan's gaze, still glazed with lust. And no lingering trace of guilt.

Good.

Yeah... Now what?

Julianne sighed, drawing his attention down to where she rested her head against Keegan's shoulder, eyes closed and hair mussed from his fingers.

Beautiful.

"Time for bed. Everybody upstairs."

He looked at Keegan, ready to shoot down any argument he planned. But Keegan shocked the hell out of him when he nodded.

His bed was big enough for the three of them. They'd already proven that. But tomorrow—well, later today, actually—he was going out and buying an even bigger bed. He'd get rid of a few pieces of furniture if he needed to. Hell, he'd take down a damn wall.

"Need to text my mom, tell her I won't be home."

Jules' voice sounded sleepy but peaceful and her mouth held a slight smile.

"I'll find your purse. Keegan, take her upstairs."

Without a word, Keegan rose from the sofa, settling Jules more securely in his arms. Her arms encircled Keegan's shoulders and her cheek rested against his chest but her eyes were on him.

"Bossy."

That one word held a hint of amusement that was reflected in her eyes. But it didn't manage to totally wipe away the worry he could still see there.

Tomorrow morning, they'd have time to talk.

"That's why they pay me the big bucks."

Keegan huffed. "Well, you're not my damn boss and we get paid the same."

"True. So just go the fuck upstairs, okay?"

Jules' mouth curved even more as Keegan curled his fingers around Jules' arm until only the middle one remained straight.

Then Keegan headed toward the door to the hall. "Bring me a bottle of water."

"Sure."

"And a bottle of Tylenol."

"I live to serve."

"Fuck you," Keegan threw over his shoulder as he disappeared into the hall.

Erik didn't let himself stop to think. He headed toward the hall where he knew Jules had dropped her purse.

Grabbing it, he steered back toward the kitchen, where he grabbed three water bottles then he practically ran up the steps, taking them two at a time.

He forced himself not to run down the hall to his bedroom.

But when he walked through the doorway, he had to catch back a groan.

Jules lay in the center of the bed, eyes closed, dark hair spread all over a pillow. Keegan lay next to her, his eyes closed, as well.

Good, they could all use some rest. Apparently none of them had been sleeping much since the first night they'd spent together. Setting the bottles on the bedside table as quietly as he could, he headed for the bathroom.

He didn't realize he was grinning until he caught a glimpse of himself in the mirrored medicine cabinet. Without thought, he ripped open the door because he really hated to look at himself, grabbed the bottle of painkillers, then closed the door, his eyes automatically veering away from the glass.

Coward.

Yeah, he was. And he didn't want to be anymore.

He forced himself to lift his gaze and look at his reflection.

He didn't bother with the mostly unscarred side of his face. Sometimes that made him just as crazy as looking at his scars.

Now, he focused on the right side. On the worst of the damage. Forced himself to really look.

And it was bad. No way around it. You could see where the grafts had been done, where the skin was different. Ruined. That side of his mouth also had damage that made it look misshapen. Deformed. Although...it wasn't as bad as it'd been before. Or as bad as he thought it'd been before.

The color was off in places, and the texture was rough, but...

No. No sugar-coating. It was still pretty damn awful. After all the operations, he'd finally come to grips with the scars on his body. Mostly because he could cover those and not think about them.

But his face... That made people gape and stare, their eyes filled with pity. He could deal with stares. But the pity...

How did Jules even manage to look at him much less let him have sex with her?

Because maybe it's not as bad as you think?

For the first year after the fire, the image staring back at him in a mirror had been a monster, frightening to him and everyone around him. His mom had actually cried. His dad had even shed a few tears. His girlfriend at the time, the woman he'd considered marrying... Probably better not to even think about her.

It'd taken him months to look in a mirror and then several more to chance it again.

Only to be disappointed after the subsequent operations when his image had changed. But not enough. After that fifth surgery, when he'd said no more, he'd had a lingering sense of grief that he'd battled with anger.

And by throwing himself into work and hunting for the person who'd caused the explosion.

"Jesus, Erik, what the fuck are you doing? I thought you were bringing me the damn Tylenol?"

Erik's gaze shifted from his face in the mirror to Keegan, standing in the doorway behind him.

Turning, Erik tossed the pill bottle at Keegan, who caught it with one hand, grimacing like it hurt.

"Headache start already?"

Keegan nodded, spilling out three pills, then dry-swallowing them before walking over to the sink to get some water.

Erik moved out of his way, heading for the door, but stopped before leaving the room. "Don't get any smart ideas about going anywhere." Erik tossed over his shoulder before leaving. "She'll be pissed and so will I."

A huge sigh from Keegan, who looked at him in the mirror. "I'm not leaving. But your shitty bed's lumpy. And short."

"Don't worry, I'm getting a new one—a bigger one—tomorrow. Today. Whatever."

Keegan wanted to say something. Erik saw it in the muscle throbbing in his jaw. He waited, ready to smack down anything Keegan said that would fuck with the decent mood he was in right now.

Only to feel let down when Keegan just shook his head.

"Shut the door on your way out."

Erik did.

Jules was still asleep when he walked back to the bed. He didn't let himself overthink his actions as he slid beneath the covers and lay on his back next to her. Curled on her side, he felt each breath against his shoulder. His right shoulder. If he didn't move and she didn't move, the first thing she saw in the morning would be his ruined face.

Turning on his side to face her, he let himself stare. The dark smudges under her eyes showed she wasn't sleeping well.

Join the club, babe.

Which was total bullshit. He didn't want her to suffer because of him. Them. But she had been. He and Keegan had put those dark circles there.

Or maybe he was being totally self-centered and her fatigue had nothing to do with them.

She sighed, shifting beneath the covers, and he reached for her, his hand curving around her hip.

Her eyes cracked open and she stared at him.

"Closer."

He smiled at the slightly grumpy tone of her voice. "Are you cold?"

"A little."

"Then come here."

She twisted over onto her other side then wiggled her way back into him, ass against his thighs, her back to his chest. With a soft grunt, she pushed her hair back and settled her head on the pillow again. He wondered what she'd do if he twisted that hair around his fist, spread her legs and sank into her. Again.

Christ, he didn't think he'd ever get tired of her.

Restraining the urge, he wrapped an arm around her waist and pulled her even closer.

The bathroom door opened, spilling light into the room. When the light shut off, he heard Keegan pause before he started walking again.

He waited for Keegan to head toward the door...and nearly pumped his fist in the air when Keegan moved to the other side of the bed and slipped beneath the covers.

It was dark enough that Erik couldn't see him but he heard his friend sigh.

"Lay still," Jules demanded in a sleepy voice. "Stop thinking. Go to sleep."

Good advice.

Erik closed his eyes.

KEEGAN'S EYES opened to a room still dark.

Made sense. He typically woke by 6:30 a.m., no matter if he'd gone to bed only an hour before or had been drinking or whatever.

His internal clock was a ruthless son-of-a-bitch he wished he could shoot on mornings like this.

His head ached, despite the painkillers, but the slim arm wrapped around his waist burned. And not in a bad way.

No, it made him want to grab the hand splayed across his stomach and push it down to wrap around his morning erection.

Which throbbed almost as badly as his head.

And if he knew Erik at all, he knew the guy would wake up and want to fuck Jules hard and fast. Together.

At least, he knew that about the old Erik. He'd started to see glimmers of that man again.

He fucking loved that Julianne had brought Erik out of the dark hole he'd fallen into. Erik might not have crawled out completely, but he was a hell of a lot closer to the rim than he'd been a month ago.

And almost all of that had to do with the woman whose soft skin made him want to lick her from head to toe.

Behind him, he heard two separate sets of breathing, deep and even. Probably both still asleep.

Could he get up without waking either of them?

Why the hell do you want to get up?

For the first time in years, probably since before Erik's accident, he had the urge to indulge himself. To take without feeling like he didn't deserve...whatever it was he wanted.

And this morning he wanted Jules until his stomach ached and his muscles seized. He wanted to roll over and get inside that tight pussy and let Erik take her ass.

He wanted to do her fast and hard, no holding back. No restraint.

He knew Erik wouldn't object to being woken. Would Jules?

Find out.

Not giving himself time to talk himself out of it, he shifted around so he lay facing her.

Her eyes remained closed, her breathing deep. Her lips were parted only the slightest bit and he had to bite back a groan as he thought of those lips wrapped around his cock, like she'd taken Erik.

Christ, the things he wanted to do to this woman...

Not now. At least, not all of them.

Could he work his way inside her before she opened her eyes?

Did she sleep deeply enough that he could wake her with an orgasm?

A slight movement behind Jules drew his attention. Keegan eased himself up on one elbow, careful not to jostle her. He looked over her shoulder to find Erik blinking sleep out of his eyes.

It took only seconds and then Erik's eyes began to gleam, letting Keegan know his friend had read his mind. Or at least correctly interpreted the lust on his face.

His lungs had to work harder as he looked back at Jules. Her long hair partially obscured her face but when he inched closer, the tip of his cock brushing against her mound, her lips parted on a sigh and her hips thrust the tiniest bit forward.

The slight patch of hair on her mound brushed against the underside of his shaft, making him suck in a sharp breath.

"Fuck."

He hadn't said it loud but it must've been just enough to rouse her.

"Okay."

He barely heard her but he definitely understood what she was telling him when her hands reached for his hips, stroking down until she petted his thighs.

"Both. Together."

He had no trouble understanding her this time. Her voice, still rough with sleep, made his cock harden even more.

Grabbing her leg and lifting it onto his thigh, he positioned his cock with one hand and pulled her onto him with the other.

He nearly swallowed his tongue. "God damn, you're already wet."

She moaned, eyes still closed. "Good dreams. So hot."

He forced himself to work into her slowly, to let her feel every inch of his cock in her pussy as he went deep then held, rubbing the base of his cock against her clit when he did.

She moaned again as her head tipped back and Erik's head bent to rest on her shoulder.

Keegan felt Erik moving behind her, felt her quiver as Erik petted her ass before he rolled over on his other side to grab something from the bedside table.

Shit. Condoms.

Erik tossed one at him, which he caught out of the air. He didn't want to pull out of her wet heat but he wasn't going to betray her trust either. He'd gotten a clean bill of health the last time he'd been at the doctor but, until he exchanged that information with Jules, he wasn't going to let her think he didn't care about her.

The next time, if she okayed it...no fucking condoms.

He pulled out, her hands clutching at his shoulders as she moaned. He made short work of it but Erik had been faster.

"Oh my god."

Jules bowed forward, though she couldn't move much, sandwiched between them as tightly as she was.

Behind her, Erik's eyes closed as he worked his way into her tight ass, his expression contorting with pleasure just before he leaned forward and pressed his face into the back of her head, nose buried in her hair.

As she gasped, her fingers clenched on Keegan's hips. Pulling at him. Her lips pressed an open-mouthed kiss against his chest, her tongue flicking out to taste his skin.

If that wasn't an invitation he didn't know what was.

As if he'd read Keegan's mind, Erik stilled, waiting. Keegan didn't need to be told twice. He pressed inside her again and, this time, the fit was almost too tight.

But Jules didn't complain.

"More." Her mouth moved over his skin, brushing against the base of his throat. He tilted his head back, wanting her to do it again as he thrust. When she did, he rewarded her by seating himself deep enough to press against her clit.

Reaching for him with one hand and reaching behind her with the other for Erik, Jules moved just enough to set the pace.

Slow. Steady. Maddeningly steady.

Lust built at the lazy slide of skin against skin. The stiffened points of her nipples dug into his chest, a sharp contrast to the softness of her stomach against his. Her mouth continued to press increasingly fevered kisses to his chest until he cupped her chin and lifted her mouth to his.

He kissed her hard, hearing her moan low in her chest as their lips melded. His tongue slid into her mouth and played with hers, coaxing her into gliding against his with the same rhythm .

Behind her, he heard Erik's breathing hitch, felt his hips pick up speed and knew he was close.

Erik thrust deeper as Keegan pulled out until only the tip of his cock remained enclosed in her sheath. Jules moaned and wriggled as much as she was able. The motion appeared to inflame Erik.

"Fuck me, baby. Yes."

Erik's raspy growl made Keegan want to pound into her as well, but he held still. He let Erik find his rhythm until he began to groan and pump his release into Jules.

Erik's orgasm must have triggered hers because he felt the strong convulsions of her pussy sucking him deeper.

His cock twitched, the tug in his balls letting him know he

wasn't going to last long. He held out long enough for Erik to pull free and flop onto his back.

Then Keegan released the reins. He let his hips swing hard and fast, pulling her down onto his cock to increase the contact, to fill her even more.

She cried out, her arms winding around his neck to hold on as he pounded into her. He didn't hold anything back, his arms crushing her against him, his mouth covering her lips and devouring her.

It took him longer than Erik but that was deliberate. He wanted it to last, to draw it out until he couldn't see straight and she wouldn't think to leave the bed.

His arms tightened even more and his mouth demanded her complete acquiescence. This time, damn it, she wasn't leaving.

His orgasm built until he couldn't hold it back. It practically kicked him in the ass as his cock jerked hard as he pumped into her.

At least a minute later, he loosened his hand from her hair and eased back enough that she could take a deep breath.

Her contented sigh made him want to pump his fist in the air and, behind her, he heard Erik release a short, amused laugh.

"And good morning to you, too."

Her lips tilted into a smile as she spoke, and finally she cracked her eyes open.

Keegan let himself stare into that dark gaze, his own mouth curved in amusement.

"Sleep okay?" he asked.

Her smile broadened. "For as long as I was allowed to sleep, yeah."

"Blame Keegan." Erik rolled onto his side again, his arms wrapping around Jules to fit her into his body. "He's the ass who can't sleep beyond the crack of dawn. Hell, even in college he was up before the fucking chickens."

"Roosters." Jules yawned, her eyes squeezing shut as one hand entwined with Erik's. Her other curved over Keegan's shoulder.

He fucking loved the way she didn't make either of them feel left out. And that it seemed instinctual on her part.

He just realized he had no idea if she'd ever been in a three-way relationship before. Not that it mattered, but she seemed to be handling it...them...well.

Then again, so far, they'd only had sex. There was no relationship.

"Fuck. Keegan's starting to think. I swear I can hear his gears creaking." Erik leaned up on one elbow behind Jules. "And that's not a good thing this early."

Keegan gave Erik the finger instinctively but Jules grabbed his hand and brought that finger to her mouth, sucking on the tip and forcing a groan out of him.

When she released him, his brain was blank and she wore a pout.

"I'm hungry. One of you two had better be able to make something more than cereal. I need food."

Erik's eyes were already closed. "That's his job. Pancakes, dude. The lady's hungry. And so am I."

Keegan was used to Erik's demands. And it was his own damn fault that Erik thought he could get away with it because Keegan actually liked to cook. It was like working in the lab except he was using pots and pans instead of robots and computers.

So, though he wanted to stay in bed, he knew Erik wasn't going to feed her. And if they wanted to keep her in bed all day, the least they could do was feed her.

Leaning forward, he kissed her, gratified that her lips clung when he pulled back after a few seconds. "I'll be back. Don't go anywhere."

"Don't plan to." She yawned again. "Don't be gone long."

"Yes, your highness."

Her eyes closed but he saw her nose wrinkle before she smiled. "Damn right."

He rolled out of bed and headed for the bathroom then raided Erik's walk-in closet for sweats.

The bedroom was warm but he knew the rest of the house would be ball-shriveling cold. Erik's idea of a comfortable temperature was miles apart from his.

Before he left the room, he turned to find them asleep again. Erik had Jules' head tucked beneath his chin, the rest of them covered by the bedding.

He closed the door behind him as he stepped into the hall.

JULES HAD FALLEN BACK to sleep but Erik didn't let himself.

He'd gotten good at forcing his body to shut down no matter what was going on. It'd become a safety mechanism, taught to him by a former SEAL who'd been a therapist at the rehab hospital where he'd spent the better part of two years.

Jimmy Cochran had lost an eye and a foot in Afghanistan and was one tough bastard who hadn't let him slide. Along with Keegan, who'd kept Erik involved with the business in every way possible during those early, blurry months of recovery, operations and rehab, Jimmy was the second person Erik felt he owed his life.

Neither Jimmy nor Keegan had let him wallow in his misery too long. They'd poked, they'd prodded, they'd pissed him off until he'd finally done as much as he thought he could do. And then they pushed him farther.

When had he hit the wall that'd stopped his forward momentum?

Probably when he'd left the rehab hospital that last time six months ago. After he'd said no more operations.

Which was right about the time Keegan had started looking like the weight of the world rested on his shoulders.

And yeah, that was partially his fault. Okay, mostly his fault. He'd returned to work full time but his concentration had been divided.

Before the accident, he'd had two things on his mind: building the business and getting laid. He'd never had a problem with either. He'd been twenty-seven, their firm had gone from decent to holy-shit-we're-rich and they'd had more money than they knew what to do with.

And the women... God damn. Whoever, whenever, wherever. He'd never had a problem getting laid but with the money they were making, women literally slipped their numbers into his pockets anywhere from business events to bars.

And then he'd met Anne Corcoran a few months before the explosion and he'd thought maybe, just maybe, she'd been the one.

Smart, sexy and career-minded. A woman who knew what she wanted and went after it. Which had been him. Keegan had never entered into the equation because Anne had expressed no interested in him and Keegan hadn't been remotely interested in her.

And then... Boom.

He'd gone from immense possibilities to nothing but pain.

Anne had stuck around a month or so but he hadn't blamed her when she finally told him she couldn't take it anymore. Which had been a blessing because he couldn't look at her anymore.

She'd reminded him of everything he'd lost.

The very few times he'd ventured into society after the explosion had shown him, in no uncertain terms, how different his life was going to be from there on out.

Which was why he'd thrown himself into finding out who'd rigged the explosion.

He had no doubt someone had sabotaged the lab. There were just too many coincidences, too many pieces that didn't fit. He didn't want to believe it was someone who worked for them but all signs pointed to it being an inside job. And that would devastate Keegan.

Keegan didn't want to believe the accident had been rigged, didn't want to think someone hated them enough to want to hurt them.

Erik didn't think it had anything to do with hate. No, he was pretty damn sure it had everything to do with money. Contracts they were getting that older, more established companies were not.

Erik didn't think the plan had been to hurt him or Keegan. He was pretty sure the explosion was supposed to go off at night when no one was around. It'd only been dumb luck that he'd still been in the lab finishing something Keegan had started.

Which was why Keegan still carried that enormous mountain of guilt on his back. And why he'd agreed to Erik's scheme to get this woman in their bed.

Well, that had worked out pretty damn well because here she was.

Yeah, so now what?

Probably should've given that some more thought.

Three-way sex didn't need much planning.

A three-way relationship? That needed a fucking twenty-page manual. And neither he nor Keegan wrote their own instruction manuals. They had people to do that for them.

Jules had been right. They'd never had a relationship with

any of the women they'd double-teamed. Probably because they hadn't known how to work it.

They were going to have to figure it out and fast because neither one of them was giving her up.

She accepted him, scars and all, and he had a serious jones for her, to the point where he couldn't stop thinking about her, day and night.

And though he probably wouldn't admit it, Keegan had fallen pretty damn hard. Hell, he'd practically fucked her in public. And for Keegan, that was like declaring his eternal love.

The guy didn't do casual. And he didn't do PDA lightly. Though he'd never admitted it, Erik thought there was something in Keegan's past that made showing affection equal to crying like a girl if someone hurt his feelings.

They'd never talked about it. Hell, lately they didn't talk about anything that didn't relate to the business...or wasn't about Jules.

Below in his kitchen, he heard Keegan banging around, opening drawers and cabinets, probably cursing him because he didn't have the high-end toys Keegan did in his. Erik's kitchen was nothing like Keegan's, all shiny and stainless and spotless.

His was utilitarian, more country farmhouse than high-tech. Considering he had a housekeeper who made most of his meals, he didn't really need more than a microwave, a fridge and a stove.

Erik angled up on one elbow to stare down at Jules. Utter relaxation made her look years younger than twenty-two. Too young to have taken on so much of her mother's debt. Then again, her father, according to Carol, had been a rare bastard who'd left them high and dry.

If he ever met Jules' dad, the guy wouldn't leave in one piece.

Erik wanted the opportunity to get to know her. He didn't want her to have to worry about work or money.

Yeah, and how are you going to manage that when Keegan wants the same thing?

They'd figure something out. He and Keegan always did. Hell, they'd managed to create a multi-million dollar company from nothing and not argue about the little shit. They saved those arguments for the big stuff, the projects they worked on. And those arguments always got worked out.

They'd work this out too.

WHY THE FUCK weren't all the dry ingredients in the same damn cabinet?

Yeah, it was a stupid ass thing to be pissed off about but, Christ almighty, why the fuck was the flour in with the canned goods and the sugar in the cabinet with the dishes?

And did Erik *not* own a non-stick frying pan?

Fuck.

Well, he had seen a cookie sheet somewhere so scones it was. Grabbing the ingredients from their various and unorganized spots, he dug into his memory for his grandmother's recipe.

The simple routine of measuring and mixing and kneading helped him regain his stability. He'd been shaken when he'd left the bedroom.

He still hadn't figured out why exactly.

While the scones baked, he started the coffee machine, willing it to go faster. He needed at least a gallon this morning if he was going to be at all sociable.

He didn't want to fuck this up for Erik. Didn't want to give Jules any excuse to leave.

Grimacing, he grabbed a cup out of the cupboard, wanting to be ready the second the pot filled.

Alright, so maybe he didn't want to fuck this up for himself, either.

But how the hell were they going to work this? Wouldn't either he or Erik eventually be a third wheel? Did they take turns being a third wheel?

Maybe it'd be best if he did what he'd planned all along and stepped out of the picture.

Erik needed her—

No, that wasn't giving Erik enough credit. The guy had come through a major ordeal without losing his sanity or his strength. Yeah, he'd basically become a recluse but everyone had issues, right?

But just because he'd gone through hell and back, did that mean Erik should automatically get dibs on everything?

"Christ, you sound like a two-year-old," he muttered as he finally poured himself a cup of steaming caffeine. "She's not a toy."

She had her own mind and, if she wanted to date both of them, or even just have sex with both of them, that was her choice.

Right?

So did they make up a schedule and put their initials on the dates they wanted to take her out or did they just skip the whole dating thing—

Wait, they'd already done that.

He shoved a hand through his hair, pushing it out of his face. Christ, they'd fucked this up but good.

So how the hell did they get it back on track?

The timer dinged and he glared at it. He needed more time to think, damn it.

But his avoidance delay was over.

Time to be a grownup.

———————

THE FIRST THING Jules noticed was the smell of warm pastry. Then fresh coffee.

Her stomach grumbled loudly just as she realized she wasn't in her own bed. There was a warm, naked body behind her and one gorgeous guy setting a tray on the table beside the bed.

"You missed your calling, man. You should've been a chef."

Erik's voice was pitched low enough that it wouldn't have woken her, if she'd still been asleep.

"That smells amazing."

Opening her eyes, she shifted onto her back so she could look up at Keegan, who was reaching for one of the three mugs on the tray.

Surprisingly, he met her gaze head-on. "My grandmother's scones recipe. She was an amazing cook."

"Maybe you could teach me that one. I'm always looking for good recipes."

"Sure." Keegan nodded as he reached for Erik's t-shirt that she'd been wearing last night and handed it to her. "If you'd like."

Pulling the shirt over her head, she released her hair from the neckline and threw it over her shoulder. Usually she braided it before bed but last night...she hadn't thought about it. Ugh. She didn't want to think about how it looked now.

"Here, lean forward."

Erik piled pillows behind her so she could sit upright before he slid from the bed. Her gaze automatically went to his naked backside. While scars marred his skin, it couldn't hide the fact that the man was all lean muscle beneath. After he'd pulled on his boxers, he sat back on the bed next to her and reached for the mug Keegan held out.

The next few minutes were quiet as they drank coffee and ate amazingly good scones.

And totally avoided any and all conversation.

She tried not to let the silence get to her, tried to pretend like sharing breakfast in the morning after sharing a bed all night with two guys was normal.

But it wasn't. At least not for her.

After two scones and a cup of coffee, she'd had enough. And it didn't seem like either of the men were going to start the conversation.

"So now what?"

Neither of them looked surprised by her question and neither pretended not to understand what she meant.

Then again, neither of them had anything to say either. Erik took another swallow of coffee, his gaze shifting from Keegan then back to her. Keegan kept his gaze on her.

"I guess that depends," Keegan finally said. "What do you want to happen now?"

That was the half-million dollar question, now, wasn't it?

"When I took the money that night...I didn't think I'd ever see either of you again. I mean, why would I? We had sex, you gave me money and I left. A simple transaction—"

"There was nothing simple about that night." Keegan's tone held an edge of frustration she totally understood. "I—We never intended—"

"Yes, we did," Erik cut in. "Admit it, Keegan. You knew from the moment you saw her you wanted more than a one-night stand. So did I. And the minute you realized that, you went into martyr mode. You sacrificed your feelings for mine."

Now Keegan looked directly at Erik, a frown settling on his features. "What the fuck are you talking about? I didn't sacrifice anything. Christ, tonight I practically hunted her down like a stalker."

"I know. And then you dragged your sorry ass home and almost drank yourself into a coma because you want her so badly and you think you shouldn't because I want her. And poor Erik, he needs all the help he can get, right? I'm so fucking scarred and pathetic that no woman would want to be seen with me. But wait, here's this beautiful woman who doesn't seem to mind that he's damaged. So what if I can't think when I'm around her, I'll let him have her."

Jules had to make a conscious effort to close her mouth. It'd been hanging open in shock.

Erik wasn't pulling any punches and Keegan looked like he was about to keel over if he took too many more.

They'd argued about some of this last night, before they'd been derailed by sex. Again.

And Keegan just seemed to take it. She wanted to stand up for him, wanted him to stand up for himself. To challenge Erik like he had last night. She understood why Erik was pissed about the way Keegan treated him. Erik didn't want to be broken anymore but Keegan kept the illusion alive.

It was a vicious cycle.

Did she really want to be caught in the middle of this drama? Was it worth it?

"Do you really want to fight over her like a pair of dogs with a bone?" Keegan finally answered Erik's accusation, his voice a barely audible snarl. "Because that's what this is beginning to look like."

"Stop it. Right now. No more."

Once again, they turned toward her, mouths closed.

Erik had a haughty look on his face, one that suited him, and Keegan's determination showed in the rigid line of his lips.

"Is it always like this between you?"

They exchanged a look that didn't include her at all. Neither of them answered. They just turned back to her, still silent.

Not letting her in.

She shook her head. "If you can't even answer that simple question , how can we move forward?"

Erik's gaze narrowed. "So you're saying you're willing to try?"

It was her turn to pause, to think carefully about what she wanted to say.

Did she really want to do this considering the conservative area they lived in and that people already had judged her to be a slut? Then again, what was one more black mark on an already soiled record?

Do you really want to give them up? Or are you ready to pull on your big girl panties and go after what you want?

"Yes, I'm willing to try. Are you?"

Both men glanced at each other and she wondered if they'd thought she'd never agree and that would be the way out.

Then Keegan said, "Dinner tonight. Seven o'clock. We'll pick you up."

She hesitated for a millisecond before her chin lifted.

"I'll be ready."

THIRTEEN

"And you're going out with *two* men? Not just one man who's bringing another along as a friend?"

"Yes. Two men. They're friends, they own a business together and they both want to take me out."

Jules' mom gave her "the look," the one Jules recognized from her childhood.

She'd seen it thousands of times as a teenager as she'd smashed through boundaries, convinced she knew what she was doing, and gave a (sometimes) implicit middle finger to whoever told her she couldn't do something.

Amazingly, her mom still spoke to her, still loved her.

"And you're going where?"

"I'm not sure."

"And what do they do for a living?"

Tricky, tricky. Her mom was no fool. She knew this had something to do with their debt being paid off and Jules wondered, for about the millionth time, if she should just come clean.

Slipping simple gold hoops through her ears, Jules glanced at her mom in the mirror.

With her dark brows raised and her arms crossed over her chest, she looked pretty much the same as she had when Jules was a teenager, not buying her excuses for why she was late getting home.

Her mom knew there was a hell of a lot more going on than just a date.

"They run an electronics company."

She didn't plan to add that they ran a multi-million dollar electronics company.

Slipping her feet into red pumps, she turned to check her reflection in the long mirror in her bedroom, the walls still sporting the black and purple paint she'd christened them with in her senior year of high school. Actually, she still loved the color combination. "I'll have my cell. Don't worry."

Her mom gave her the "other look," which basically meant "Yeah, right." Another expression Jules was familiar with.

Her mom worried about everything and had since Jules had been born, apparently. Not that she didn't have good cause to worry. Her husband *had* been cheating on her. That lump in her breast *had* been malignant. And Jules *had* slept with two men to get the money to pay off their debt.

Turning to face her mom, Jules leaned in for a hug, so happy to feel the strength in her mom's arms as she returned the hug. For a couple of years, Sara Carter had barely been able to lift her arms.

"Julianne, you'd tell me if something was wrong, wouldn't you? You know you can tell me anything, right?"

"Yes, mom." She infused her tone with just enough teenage boredom that her mom actually laughed. "I'll be fine."

Her mom gave her another tight squeeze before taking a step back. "I'll always worry. Mothers never stop."

"I know. It's just...complicated."

Complicated didn't begin to describe what she felt for

Keegan and Erik. Or what she'd done to get the money. Or the first night they'd spent together. Or last night and this morning. Or even this dinner.

With a sigh, her mom walked to the doorway then turned and gave her a resigned smile. "Everything's complicated, honey. Some things just take a little more work. You have to decide if it's worth it, I guess. And don't think for a minute that we're finished with this conversation. I want to hear all about this date tomorrow."

Which was her mom's not-so-subtle way of asking if she'd be home tonight.

Jules just said, "Don't wait up for me. I'm not sure when I'll be home."

Or if she'd be home at all tonight. Would they ask her to stay with them again tonight?

"Alright, sweetheart. Just...be safe."

With a little wave, her mom disappeared and Jules sank onto the edge of her bed.

Damn it, she needed to tell her mom the truth. The secret weighed on her like a boulder around her neck.

After she'd paid off their last credit card and the final bill from the hospital, she'd briefly considered telling her mom she'd won the lottery but that would've been too easy to check.

She'd come up with a version of the truth. A very wealthy man had offered her the money in exchange for a service, which she'd assured her mom had not been illegal, dangerous or life-threatening.

Her mom had been stunned speechless and had tried to get Jules to tell her everything but Jules had held her ground.

Would her mom be horrified at what she'd done to clear their debt? Would she understand that Jules had had every intention of turning the money down if she hadn't been attracted to the man who'd offered her a half-million dollars to sleep with him?

Would her mom think less of her when she found out she'd actually slept with *two* men for the money? And that it'd been the best sexual experience of her life?

Would her mom understand why she was attempting to pursue a relationship with those same two men, not because they'd saved Jules and her mom from poverty and despair but because she actually liked them?

Glancing at the clock, she realized it was one minute until seven and the guys would probably be on time.

Standing, she made sure her dress wasn't wrinkled. She'd gone with basic black, tailored and elegant enough for dinner with two millionaires. She'd bought it at an outlet but the style was classic enough that it'd aged well. She knew she looked good in it and the red, spike-heeled pumps set it off perfectly.

She'd fit in wherever they planned to take her, unless it was one of the chain restaurants near the mall or a dive bar in downtown Reading. She didn't think either of those possibilities was going to happen. Not with Erik along.

As she headed toward the front of their one-story ranch, the doorbell rang.

Crap, she'd wanted to be there to open the door before her mom could badger Keegan with a thousand questions. She didn't figure Erik would get out of the car.

So she was shocked when she realized both men stood in the living room, shaking hands with her mom.

Standing in shadows of the hall that led to the bedrooms, she let herself stare.

Oh my, her guys cleaned up fine.

Keegan wore a dark suit with a white shirt. Erik had paired gray pants with a black shirt. Neither of them wore a tie, and the couple of undone buttons at the tops of their shirts made her want to undo the rest.

They looked sleekly casual and elegantly handsome and oh, so very rich.

Her mom was making a valiant effort not to stare at Erik's scars, focusing on his eyes instead. Her smile was strained, though, and she could tell her mom wanted to reach out and hug him. That's just the kind of person she was and Jules wouldn't wish her any other way.

They'd barely gotten beyond basic greetings when Keegan noticed her. His gaze locked onto her in the shadows, as if he had x-ray vision, drawing her out to them.

"It was nice to meet you both," her mom said when Jules joined them. "I'll talk to you tomorrow, dear. Have a good time."

The way she said that last bit, Jules could've sworn there was a question mark on the end of it. But her mom headed toward the kitchen with a smile and a nod.

"We made reservations for Judy's On Cherry," Keegan said. "Okay?"

From working in the catering business, she knew the food was amazing, though she'd never eaten there before. Too pricey for her budget.

"Of course. I'm fine with wherever you'd like to go."

"Then we should get going. Our reservations are in fifteen minutes."

The car sitting out front shouldn't have been a surprise. The BMS was new and black, sleek and smooth. Just like it's owner.

Erik handed her into the front seat while Keegan got in the back. Erik slid into the driver's seat then pressed pedal to the floor and they took off.

Or that's what it seemed like. She'd never ridden in a car that practically glided along the road. And it was so well insulated, she heard no outside noise. Even the engine purred,.

The radio pumped out something that sounded like Sinatra and the leather seat conformed to her body like a lover.

She watched Erik's hands on the steering wheel, strong and long. In the rearview, she saw Keegan watching her. When their gazes met, she smiled and saw his mouth curve upward in response.

"Your mother looks well." Keegan's voice broke the silence. "How long has it been since her last treatment?"

"Almost eighteen months and there's been no recurrence of the cancer."

"That must be good to know."

"It is. It's just...I keep waiting for the other shoe to drop. Know what I mean?"

"Yeah, I know a little something about that." Erik's voice held an edge, but not hard enough to cut. As if he was consciously dialing it down.

She wasn't sure how she felt about that. She liked his edge. She didn't want him to be a different person for her.

"So what are her plans now that she's cancer free?"

They passed the rest of the drive with careful small talk, so different from the angst of the previous twenty-four hours. Almost like everyone was on their best behavior, as if this was a first date... Well, actually, it was.

She couldn't consider their first encounter an actual date considering the money they'd given her. And last night... She didn't know what to call last night except one hell of a roller coaster ride.

By the time they parked in the lot across from the restaurant, she'd dropped out of the conversation completely, content to listen to them talk.

She loved the sound of their voices, Keegan's with that tiny hint of an accent and Erik's with the damaged rasp. It was kind of ridiculous really, that she got wet listening to them talk about a professor they knew from college who'd become an internet sensation for a video on robotics.

When Erik turned off the car, he turned to look at her, eyes narrowed. "Are you okay?"

She smiled, making sure she glanced over her shoulder to include Keegan. "I'm fine. You two don't need anyone else to carry on a conversation. You do just fine on your own."

And she could stick her foot in her mouth just as easily as they could hold a conversation.

She held up one hand as both men opened their mouths.

"Wait, wait. That didn't come out right."

And both mouths shut. Amazing.

"I didn't mean that in a bad way so please don't take it like that. You two have a real friendship. That's great. I never had that with anyone. I mean, yeah, I had friends in school and I have friends at work and Carol is almost like a sister to me. But you two not only finish each other's sentences, you actually know what the other is thinking before he says it."

"Are you saying it turns you off?" Keegan glanced at Erik, as he got out of the backseat then opened the door to help her out.

"No, not at all."

The cold night air made her shiver as they crossed the street to the entrance and Erik put his arm around her shoulders, drawing her into his side.

"It's just that I've never met anyone like either of you."

Keegan huffed out a laugh. "That's probably a good thing."

She considered her response as they walked into the restaurant. She'd stepped away from Erik, who helped her remove her coat while Keegan walked up to the hostess stand.

It wasn't until she'd turned back to join Keegan that she noticed how rigidly Erik held himself.

Frowning, she searched for the cause...and found it in the woman behind the stand. She stared at him, open shock on her face. Jules recognized that shock. She'd felt it too when she'd first seen Erik.

Then the look was gone, the woman smoothing out her expression and waving them up the stairs to the dining room.

Keegan flashed Erik a look then caught and held her gaze before nodding at her to follow the hostess.

Taking Erik's arm, she walked with him up the stairs. By the time they reached the second floor, she realized she was holding her breath.

God, this must be hell for Erik.

All these people looking at him, staring. A few noticed him right away, did a double take, eyes widening before quickly looking away again.

They had to walk past several tables and the pattern repeated at every single one. Someone would look up as they passed, notice Erik and either look away immediately then whisper something to their dinner companion or they'd openly stare for several seconds before blinking, like they were coming out of a trance, and looking away.

Two people did manage to smile at them, two women who nodded and smiled sadly at Jules. As if she were some saint who'd taken pity on a ruined man.

That was almost worse than the stares and unconscious gasps.

By the time they reached their table in a dark, secluded corner, she was ready tell the lot of these well-dressed assholes to mind their own fucking business or she'd knock a few of their teeth out.

"Jules. Hey, are you okay?"

Keegan had asked the question but she turned to see Erik staring at her with raised eyebrows. Sitting with his back to most of the room, he slowly started to smile.

Then he laughed and Jules smiled in return. How could she not?

"I'm sorry. I didn't think it would be this—"

"Don't apologize." Erik shook his head and covered her hand, curled into a fist on the table, with his. "I'm a big boy. I can take it."

"Don't you want to go around making faces at people and growling? Some people are just so...so...."

"Pathetic? Clueless?" Keegan offered.

"Rude? Obnoxious?" Erik added.

Keegan leaned back in his chair, almost smiling. "Insufferable? Moronic?"

"Dude, your Irish is showing." Erik picked up the menu. "You bust out words like that with that accent and normal American guys don't stand a chance."

"True." Keegan flashed Jules a grin before picking up his menu. "You never could compete."

The waitress interrupted whatever Erik had been going to say. She was probably Jules' age, maybe a little younger, and had a face that probably won her a mint at the poker table. She nodded at each of them, made eye contact with Erik without blinking, took their drink orders and disappeared.

"Hell, it was never even a close competition before." Erik continued to study the menu, a quirky smile on his lips. "I had to go and fuck up my face for you to actually pull ahead of me."

She was so surprised at Erik's joke at his own expense that her lips parted on a silent gasp.

"Yeah, well apparently you screwed that up too because Jules seems to find something about you interesting. And I'm guessing it's not your amazing personality. So what do you say, Jules? Was it his personality or his wit or his looks that drew you in? Because it certainly wasn't his charm."

She started to laugh, trying to keep it from being an all-out bray with unladylike snorting, but she couldn't help herself.

Erik looked at her with a gleam in his eye then glanced at Keegan for a bare second before returning his attention to the menu. "And you know shit about charm. Let me tell you about the time he fell for the TA in our second-year e-lab."

The anger she'd felt at the way people looked at Erik slowly retreated as her dates put on The Keegan and Erik Show. They were a little rusty at it but she saw how effective it must've been in college.

Keegan's sincerity shone through in everything he said. When he told her she looked beautiful, she knew he meant it one-hundred percent. And when he smiled, she felt like the clouds had just revealed the warm summer sun.

Erik had smooth charm to spare. He knew what to say and when and how to make a woman feel like she was only person in the room. But it was his underlying intensity that made a woman want to leap over the table and throw herself at him.

Combined...they were deadly to a woman's ability to say no. And they made dinner pass way too quickly.

She barely remembered what she ate and soon forgot that there were other people around them. Three hours flew by. Two bottles of wine, dinner and dessert consumed.

Most of the restaurant had cleared out by the time Erik said, "I guess we should get out of here. Looks like they're ready to close down for the night."

She bit her lip as they settled the bill, Keegan grabbing it before Erik could get his hands on it. Would they ask her back to one of their houses? She'd never been to Keegan's and she was curious. Or would they deliver her home like this was a regular date, where they each gave her a peck on the cheek and said good night?

She didn't want the night to end. It'd been fun, flirty, sexy and exhilarating.

She hadn't had a night like this in...well, she couldn't remember.

So much worry and stress the past several years had made her feel old. Like she'd skipped all the good parts of being twenty-something and headed straight into the pressures of being an adult with too much responsibility.

While she never would've said anything to her mom, she'd felt like she was drowning.

Now that the debt had been cleared and she'd met two amazing men, she wanted to let loose, have some of the fun she'd missed.

"Are you ready to go?" Keegan asked.

"Only if you're not taking me back to my house."

Erik had already stood but now he leaned over her shoulder and put his mouth close to her ear. "And where would you like to go?"

Keegan still sat across from her, watching them. When she met his gaze, his head tilted back. "Would you like to come back to my house tonight?"

"He's actually got an even bigger bed than I do." Erik low rasp made her shiver.

"Yes, I would. Can we leave now?"

"Hell, yes," Keegan said, his words a little louder than he'd probably intended.

She didn't care who heard him. Didn't care who saw when she pressed a kiss to Erik's mouth then Keegan's before they headed for the stairs and the exit.

She glanced at the wait staff still on the floor as they were leaving, thoroughly enjoying the shock on some of their faces.

Hell, if they were going to do this, she wasn't going to hide it. If Erik was willing to come out of the shadows for her, she was going to kick down the rest of the walls.

But she didn't think Erik was going to be the problem.

Keegan had let her kiss him but withdrew immediately, letting Erik put his hand on the small of her back as they walked down the stairs.

The drive back to Keegan's home was mostly silent but this time, that silence held a charged sensuality.

When Erik finally pulled to a stop in front of a contemporary building that would look more at home in California than the rural outreaches of Pennsylvania, her panties were soaked.

She really needed to get a handle on her libido.

Then again, why? Why try to tame this feeling? They were hurting no one—

"Shit."

Keegan's low curse drew her attention as he pulled into the three-bay garage. There was another car already parked in the space at the far end and Keegan looked at it like it was a snake.

"I take it you weren't expecting company?"

There was a tone in Erik's voice that made her realized they knew whose car was sitting in Keegan's garage.

And they weren't happy about it.

"What the hell is she doing here?" Erik glanced over his shoulder at Keegan, his mouth set in a firm line.

"And why the fuck didn't she call first?" Keegan added.

"Christ." Erik shook his head. "Can we leave before she realizes we're here?"

"Too late. You know her. She was probably watching through the front window."

"How the hell did she get in your house?"

Keegan grimaced. "I gave her a key."

"Well, you're a fucking idiot."

Jules was tired of being left out of the conversation. "Are

you two going to tell me who's here or are you just going to let me hang?"

At that moment, both men's attention turned toward that open door.

Where a beautiful blonde now stood. Pale gold hair hung in a sleek fall to her shoulders. Wide blue eyes watched them, one eyebrow lifted. Her features had the perfection of selective breeding and her clothes screamed wealth and status.

"Who is she?"

Erik sighed. "My sister, Katrina."

Keegan gave a matching sigh and turned to her with a grimace. "And my ex-fiancé."

FOURTEEN

"Fiancée. You were engaged. To Erik's sister."

Jules stared at the door the woman had disappeared through, a ten-ton weight now settled on her chest.

Which was stupid. It wasn't like she didn't know they'd had lives before she'd met them.

Why this made any difference at all...

With a muttered curse, Erik shoved himself out of the car then opened the door to help Keegan out.

She took his hand and let him, operating on autopilot.

Her heart hammered against her ribs as she tried to tell herself it shouldn't matter.

But the fact remained that she didn't know as much about these two men as she should.

As you want to.

Once again, she'd taken a leap without looking. Or even wondering what was on the other side.

She should know by now that she usually ended up in quicksand.

Through the pounding of her pulse in her ears, she heard

Erik slam the driver's door then he stopped next to Keegan in front of her.

A united front.

"Jules, look at me."

She looked up at Keegan, saw the burning anger in his eyes. Then she looked at Erik and saw the flush on his cheeks that made his scars stand out in sharp contrast.

She wanted to reach up and stroke Erik's cheek. Wanted to wrap her arms around Keegan's shoulders and hug him.

Both men looked a little shell-shocked.

She didn't want to leave them. But if she stayed...

Did she really want to meet Erik's sister? Who also happened to be the woman Keegan had wanted to marry?

"It was years ago." Keegan's voice sounded like he was being strangled. "We both realized it was a huge mistake and called it off."

"Give the guy credit for coming to his senses before he actually walked down the aisle." Erik's voice held an edge sharp enough to cut.

Neither of them sounded thrilled to see Katrina.

"So why is she here?" she asked.

Neither man answered, exchanging a glance that made her want to smack the backs of their heads and force them to spill their guts.

Finally, Erik sighed. "Keegan, you should take Jules home. I'll deal with Kat until you get back. I'm sorry, Jules. I had other plans for tonight but—"

"I could wait until you're finished talking to her."

The words were out of her mouth before she could stop them, and they sounded so pathetic, she had to fight a wince.

But she'd had her own plans for tonight that involved a lot of naked skin and her in bed with her men. All hers. All night.

Keegan and Erik exchanged another quick look, their lips flattening into straight lines.

Keegan shook his head. "Trust me, it's better if I take you home."

Okay, maybe they didn't want her here. Didn't want her to meet Katrina.

She nodded, a chill running up her spine. "Of course. I'm ready whenever you are."

Erik muttered a barely audible "Fuck" as Keegan grabbed her hand.

"No, damn it, it's not fine." Keegan shook his head. "We weren't expecting her, Jules. We didn't invite her. Hell, I'm not sure why the hell she's here."

Erik sighed and she and Keegan switched their attention to him.

"I'm kind of afraid I do," Erik said.

Keegan's gaze narrowed. "What the hell. Have you talked to her lately?"

Erik grimaced though he cleared it quickly. "She was at Christmas dinner."

Total shock made Keegan's mouth go slack. "Shit. Seriously? In the same room as your mom?"

Erik rubbed a hand along the side of his neck. "My dad insisted. Told her she had to show up. Doesn't matter. Let me deal with this while you take Jules home."

They both focused on her again and she forced herself to hold each man's gaze in turn.

"I had a great time tonight. Thank you for dinner."

In unison, both men said, "Fuck."

Erik took a step forward and put his hands on her shoulders, bending down to look straight into her eyes. "Damn it, Jules. I'm not trying to get rid of you. I don't want you to go. I want to spend the night making you come and watching Keegan fuck you until you pass out. Then we'd start all over again."

She shivered, her pussy clenching at the images Erik had conjured with his words. God, yes. She wanted the same thing.

But you don't always get what you want, do you?

Keegan huffed out a sigh. "Fuck it. Jules, you're coming in. I'll set you up in the den, Erik and I can find out what the hell she wants, then we'll get rid of her. She's not staying here, that's for damn sure."

"I'll take her back to my place." Erik stepped away from Jules and ran a hand through his hair. "Damn it, I wish she would've called first."

Keegan turned to Erik. "Then tell her we have plans and to come into the office tomorrow. We can deal with her there."

Erik shook his head, though she wasn't sure he was saying no.

When a short silence fell, she felt compelled to fill it.

"I take it you and your sister don't get along?"

"Actually," Erik rubbed at his eyes, "we used to get along just fine. She's just...not a happy person lately."

Keegan snorted. "That's putting it mildly."

Sighing, Erik turned toward the door. "Look, just let me deal with this. I'll take her back to my place and come back. Then we can put her out of our minds until tomorrow morning." Turning, he smiled at Jules. "And concentrate on other, better things."

Jules loved when Erik smiled like that. It made her tingle from the inside out. But when she turned to Keegan, he was staring at the door Erik's sister had disappeared through. A scowl marred his expression and she felt her heart stutter.

Did he still have feelings for Katrina? Would he tell her what had happened between them? Did she even want to know?

"Keegan." She put her hand on his forearm. "I'll go home if that's what you want. I don't want to cause you and Erik any trouble with your families."

Maybe their families didn't know about their unusual love lives. Maybe the men wanted to keep it that way.

And maybe that's how this relationship would always be. Maybe their date tonight had been the exception. Maybe they'd never be able to acknowledge their relationship publicly.

After all, Keegan and Erik ran a company worth millions. They held a certain position in society.

She...didn't.

Keegan cupped her face in his hands, startling her. Then he lowered his head and kissed her, so long and deep, she started to feel her body give in almost immediately.

When he pulled away, she sucked in a deep breath.

"She's not my family."

Keegan's gaze bored into hers, the promise of what was to come later making her burn. Her cheeks were flushed and she probably looked like she'd just been thoroughly kissed.

She didn't care.

Keegan turned toward the house, lacing his fingers with hers as Erik put his hand on the small of her back. "Let's go see what the princess wants."

ERIK WAS PRETTY sure he knew why Kat was here.

He hadn't invited her. Would never have thought she'd actually show up. Especially not at Keegan's. Her history with his best friend was contentious. And that was putting it mildly.

He'd expected her to call after she'd dug into the information Erik had given her at Christmas. It'd been the only way he could think of to handle this problem.

Kat had access to resources Erik didn't, resources Erik needed for his investigation into the explosion. An investigation Keegan was reluctant to pursue.

Biting back a sigh, he followed Jules into the house. He really wasn't looking forward to Keegan's reaction when he found out Erik had involved his sister in their business. Keegan would be pissed. And with good reason. If Keegan had gone behind Erik's back and involved his sister, he would've been ranting and raving by now.

Instead, Keegan paused in the kitchen to squeeze Jules' hand and give her a slight smile before taking a deep breath and heading toward the front of the house.

Following behind Keegan, Jules looked around with an interested gaze as they passed through the formal dining room and into the great room in the front.

Unlike Erik's comfortable mess of a home, Keegan's was all straight lines, lots of white accented with dark browns and blues. Starkly modern. No clutter, no mess. It fit Keegan to a T. It'd drive Erik crazy to live in this minimalist wonderland.

Except for Keegan's great room. The cathedral ceiling, the stained-glass window high on the front wall, the massive book-shelves on the back wall that went from the floor to the second-floor ceiling held books and art. A huge stone fireplace took up most of one of the side walls, and comfortable furniture spread through the room.

Everything had a place here. The only thing out of place was Kat.

Erik loved his sister but he'd never understand why Keegan had thought they'd make a good match. They were just so different.

Keegan had a heart, and Kat... Well, Kat had lost hers awhile ago.

His sister turned as they entered the room, and Erik

watched her expression harden until her lips looked like they might actually crack.

This is a very, very bad idea.

But it was too late now. Might as well put their shoulders back and bulldoze through it.

Stepping away from Jules, whom Kat studiously avoided, Erik walked up to his sister and wrapped his arms around her.

"Hey, sis. Good to see you. What brings you all the way down here?"

With a heavy sigh, his younger sister allowed herself to soften in his arms for just a few seconds, reminding him of how, at one time, they'd been bound by a common enemy.

Then he'd gone away to college and had never returned, and Kat had been left to fend for herself against their mother. It'd made her brittle. Not in the sense that she was easily breakable but that she was fractured inside. Yes, she'd shored up the outer façade, but you could see the cracks every now and then.

Old anger rose inside. Their mother had one hell of a lot of misery to answer for, which would never happen because their mother thought she was right.

When Kat pulled away, she gave him a small smile. "I tried your house first but the housekeeper told me you'd gone out with Keegan. So I decided to try here. Sorry if I'm," her gaze skittered over his shoulder and her expression flooded with bitterness, "interrupting anything."

Giving her a warning look, he crossed his arms over his chest. "Obviously you have something you thought I'd want to hear."

When her gaze reconnected with his, her expression became serious. "I do. I thought I should deliver it in person, and I thought Keegan might be interested as well."

The tone of her voice suggested otherwise, and Erik locked

down the urge to sigh even as he battled the anger trying to get out.

"And maybe," she continued, "we want to make this conversation a little more private."

Keegan muttered, "God damn it," before Erik cut him off.

"Keegan. Why don't you take Julianne into the media room and get her settled."

"That sounds like a good idea," Jules agreed immediately. "I could stand to take my shoes off."

With a curt nod, Keegan led Jules out of the room. Keegan had installed a state-of-the-art theater, where they mostly played videogames. Damn things looked awesome on that seventy-inch screen.

But the only games Erik wanted to play tonight were with Jules, and that meant hearing what Kat had to say, then taking her back to his place for the night. Where he'd leave her to return here.

Kat was going to love that.

Tough shit.

His sister continued to stare at the doorway through which Jules and Keegan had disappeared.

"All right, Kat. What'd you find?"

Her gaze sliced back to his, her mouth pulled into a sneer. "Still playing your dirty games? Does she know what you expect from her? Or haven't you told her about yours and Keegan's fucked-up games?"

And there she went, straight for the jugular and back into the hell that had nearly torn apart TinMan Biotronics after she'd called off her engagement with Keegan.

Erik steeled himself against the rising tide of anger, staring at her with a steady gaze. "Do you really want to rehash this? I thought you'd put it all behind you."

Kat rolled her eyes and started to pace. "I thought I had, too. Then I saw Keegan and... I want to tear his eyes out."

"I thought you were seeing someone."

"I am." Her mouth twisted. "He's actually a nice guy. And he's not interested in sharing me with anyone."

"Keegan wouldn't have shared you, Kat. You know that. He told you that."

"Because you're the only one he shares with. He told me that, too. That he's never shared a woman with anyone else. Why do you think that is, Erik?"

He knew exactly why, but this was an old argument, one he would never win with her.

After a disastrous affair during her last year of college, and an even more horrendous stay at a psych hospital mandated by their mother, Kat had met Keegan and thought he was the one. The one to fix her.

Stupid Erik had thought maybe she'd been right. Hell, even Keegan had thought so. And Keegan *had* loved her. It just hadn't been enough for Kat and her demons.

Because Keegan had brought his own demons to the relationship. Keegan had thought, by marrying Kat, he'd be cured of wanting to share women. He'd be normal. Like his parents.

But as their relationship had progressed, Erik knew Keegan was never going to get through to his sister's cold heart. Finally, Keegan had seen the light, but by then, Kat had heard the rumors and confronted Keegan. She'd nearly had another breakdown, though this time, she'd managed to avoid being committed.

Erik sighed. "Are you going to tell me what you found out, or are we going to end up pissed off and screaming at each other again?"

He'd had enough of those bouts to last him the rest of his life.

Nodding, Kat became all business. She was so good at submerging her feelings. But her eyes... He caught the lingering hurt before she could hide it.

One more thing you can't make better.

"You're right," she said, meeting his gaze straight on. "I'm sorry. I talked to Stilinski, gave him the information you gave me. You're right. It was Eggert Labs."

"I'M REALLY sorry about this, Jules, I had no idea she—"

"I realize that, Keegan." Jules smiled at him but it was a struggle when she had all these wild thoughts banging around in her head. "And there's nothing to be sorry about. I know you and Erik had lives before I met you."

She just hadn't known Keegan was engaged to Erik's sister. He and Erik would've been family. Talk about fucked up.

Keegan grimaced. "Yeah, but I know how my engagement to Kat must look to someone who knows about...our preferences."

"You really don't have anything to explain to me."

"Yeah, I do."

She waited but he still seemed to be debating what to say. So she decided to give him a little help.

"When did you meet her?"

He smiled, just a quick twist of his lips. "Our senior year in college. Erik didn't talk about his family much. They're kind of...dysfunctional."

She raised her eyebrows and he laughed, sounding a little more like himself. "Yeah, I know how that sounds. But Erik's family might have a lock on crazy."

Kicking off her shoes, she sat on the nearest black leather couch and pulled her legs under her while Keegan remained standing, leaning against the wall in front of her.

"What about your family?"

He didn't stop to think. "Traditional Irish Catholic. I'm the oldest of six. When I was eight, my teacher realized I understood high-level math and knew I needed advanced training. When I was ten, my parents sent me to live with my aunt and uncle in Boston so I could eventually attend MIT. By the time I was in college, the rest of my family had moved, as well."

"Must have been tough, being away from your family that young."

His smile was a little more natural now. "As much as I fought with my brothers and sisters, I missed the hell out of them when they weren't around. My aunt and uncle are great, but they didn't have kids. They were kind of at a loss as to what to do with me so they overcompensated. I'll admit I was fairly well spoiled."

"Sounds like you had a good childhood."

"I did." He glanced at the door and his expression tightened again.

She wanted to make this better for them but had no idea what to do.

"You should go out there and back up Erik."

"Yeah, I should."

Instead, he walked over to the couch, put both hands on the cushion behind her head, and bent to kiss her.

Hard and demanding. She wanted to melt into the couch and let him follow her down. Her stomach clenched, her heart stuttered, and she reached for his shoulders to hold him to her, kissing him back with as much passion as he put into it.

Groaning low in his throat, he made her shiver in response as she opened her mouth to his tongue. He flicked it against hers, teased and taunted, making her shift restlessly on the cushion, an ache building low in her gut and radiating to her pussy.

When he pulled away, his cheeks flushed and his eyes

intent, she smiled up at him, stroking one hand against his cheek.

"I'll get Erik to take her back to his place, but he'll be back. We have plans for you."

She smiled, a little of that weight leaving her chest. "I'm not going anywhere."

"Good. I don't want the night to end yet."

After another brief, hard kiss, he turned and stalked out.

Leaving her alone with her jumbled thoughts.

BY THE TIME Keegan got back to Erik and Kat, they were huddled over a file, side by side on the couch.

Stopping in the shadows of the hall before they noticed him, he watched as they discussed...whatever they were discussing so intensely. Kat had a law degree that she used to defend her father's consulting firm from whatever sludge might be tossed its way. And since Arthur Riley consulted with some of the richest men in the country, she made a healthy amount of money and wielded a fair amount of power. What business exactly Arthur consulted on, Keegan had never understood completely.

And because of the nature of her work, Kat had never wanted to talk about what she did. At least, not with him. And since she didn't understand what he and Erik did, they hadn't talked about that either.

What the hell *had* they talked about when they'd been together?

Damn if he could remember.

He only remembered that when they'd decided to call off their engagement, months before the explosion, there'd still been a lot of hard feelings between them. Keegan had hang-ups he freely admitted to. Kat had hang-ups she couldn't bear to think about much less talk about.

Even so, he'd loved her. He'd thought their hang-ups would eventually work themselves out if they loved each other enough.

Turns out neither of them had.

A lot of blame to go around. And it'd put Erik in an awkward position that Keegan had always regretted—

Erik's head snapped up and his gaze latched on to him, eyes gleaming in triumph.

Shit. He knew that look.

Keegan wanted to turn around and go back to Jules.

But it was Katrina who spoke first. "I apologize for showing up unannounced, Keegan. I didn't mean to screw up your plans."

Her expression held no hint of the disgust he remembered seeing on her face only minutes ago. Obviously Erik had said something to her about her earlier comments.

Or maybe not, if the surprised look on Erik's face was any indication.

"If you don't mind lending Erik your car," she continued, "he can take me back to my hotel."

"What hotel?" Erik frowned. "You don't have to stay at a hotel. You can stay with me."

Katrina shook her head. "I don't want to interrupt your...life."

Grimacing, Erik sighed. "Kat—"

"Take the car and take her where she wants to go."

Keegan just wanted her gone. Yeah, he sounded like a prick, but at the moment he didn't care.

Katrina's mouth tightened into a scowl at his callous tone, and Erik rolled his eyes in exasperation, but Keegan didn't want to deal with her. Not tonight. Old wounds and regrets would make him bitter, and that's nothing he wanted to bring to bed with Jules.

And he *wanted* her in his bed. So far, they'd only been in Erik's.

Why the hell that mattered didn't make sense, but then Keegan didn't want to examine his feelings right now.

He'd already pulled the keys out of his pocket and dangled from his finger. The anger he thought he'd worked out of his system years ago burned like a dull ache in his gut.

This time, though, it wasn't directed at Katrina... Well, maybe that wasn't exactly true. He was pissed off that she'd just appeared, like a bad memory he wished he could erase.

But there were other issues...

With a ragged sigh, Erik stalked toward him and grabbed the keys.

Then he leaned in and spoke low enough that Katrina wouldn't hear them. "I'll be back as soon as possible. Try to keep it together until then."

"I'm not in danger of falling apart."

Erik just stared at him. "I'll be back as soon as I can."

Katrina didn't look back as Erik waved her toward the kitchen. Keegan stood there, listening as the door closed, as the engine started and the garage doors opened.

He couldn't help but look out the front window to make sure Katrina was in the car with Erik.

Irrational?

Yeah. Maybe Erik did have reason to be worried about him.

Which just made him all the more irrational.

Fuck. He should take Jules home because she wouldn't want to be around him when he got like this.

She'd gotten a glimpse of him in one of these moods two nights ago at the reception. When he'd fucked her in that closet. He'd attributed his behavior to alcohol, but maybe he just needed to be honest and admit that that person was a part of himself he tried so damn hard to keep under wraps.

"Keegan?"

Jules stood in the hall, watching him, her expression curious.

Closing the distance between them silently, he watched her watch him with a steady gaze. She didn't look worried or frightened or even concerned. She looked like she knew exactly what he wanted. And was fine giving it to him.

If she hadn't, would he have stopped?

Luckily, he didn't have to think about it because the second he wrapped his hand around her neck and drew her against him, she tilted her head back and let him consume her.

Her hands settled on his chest, fingers spread across his pecs, her warmth seeping through his shirt. She didn't push him away, which probably would've made him grab her closer. No, she stroked him through his shirt, making his nipples peak under the cotton.

Wrapping his free arm around her waist, he plastered her lower body against his, pressing his already throbbing erection against her lower stomach.

He thought about shoving her dress up to her hips and pushing down her panties, but he didn't want this to be a repeat of the reception. If he got her skirt up, he'd have his fingers inside her in seconds and would be hell-bent on making her come. And it'd be too damn fast.

So he focused on kissing her. On her soft lips beneath his and the firm mounds of her breasts pressed against his chest. He heard her breath hitch as his tongue pressed against her lips, demanding entrance. Wanting to taste her. Needing her to give up everything to him.

He felt his need to dominate rising like a tidal wave. He

should pound it down, keep it contained. Part of him knew that's exactly what he should do.

Another part of him wanted to say, "Fuck it," and release the reins.

At the thought, they slipped a little farther from his reach.

He fucked her mouth with his tongue, her neck bent back and her lips parted, giving him access. The hand on her neck tightened for a second before he made a conscious effort to loosen his grip. Still, he couldn't let her go completely.

He wanted more.

As he pulled away, her lips clung to his for a moment before she retreated and blinked up at him.

"Take the dress off." His voice sounded like a growl, deep and demanding. "I don't want to rip it."

She hesitated, as if she'd heard something in his tone or seen something in his expression she didn't like. That millisecond pause made his pulse throb through his body, made his blood boil.

His hands threatened to tighten into fists at his sides so he shoved them in his pockets, out of sight. He'd never hit her, never hurt her. He'd rather throw himself in front of a bus. But he might've reached for the dress himself. And yeah, he would've ripped it off.

In the next second, she pulled her hair over her shoulder and turned to present him with her side.

"I need help with the zipper."

Looking over her shoulder at him, she didn't smile. But he definitely saw heat in her eyes.

He took a deep breath before he reached for the tiny tab mostly hidden in the side seam of the dress. Tugging it down, he watched the dress gape, revealing a hint of black lace before she turned back to him and began to shimmy the dress down her body.

The black lace was her bra, which cupped her breasts with half moons of fabric that left almost nothing to the imagination and made his mouth water.

He would've reached for her then but she bent slightly and his gaze slid down the graceful line of her back before he heard the slither of fabric as the dress fell to the floor. She snagged it before it lay in a complete heap then held it out to him with her index finger.

"Got somewhere I can hang this?"

Swallowing hard, he tried not to let his tongue hang out of his mouth.

She stood before him in that black lace bra, a pair of matching panties that were more string than bikini, and thigh-high stockings that magically clung to her legs without the aid of a garter belt.

And then there were the black patent leather, spike-heeled pumps.

The bra made her breasts look like they were about to fall out, the panties made him want to fall to his knees and lick them, and the shoes... Hell, the shoes made him want to lay her on her back so he could grab her ankles in one hand, hold her legs up to his shoulders, and pound his aching cock into her.

"In the bedroom."

She raised an eyebrow at him. "And that would be where?"

"Up the stairs. Door to the left."

He saw her gaze dart around the room until she found the floating circular staircase that could've been mistaken for a work of art. The ebony risers seemed to magically hang in midair around the center marble column.

When her gaze returned to him, she shook the dress at him until he reached for it.

Then she turned and headed for the stairs.

His mouth dropped open at the sight of her walking away

from him. Her panties didn't cover her ass completely, and the creamy skin between the thigh-high stockings and those panties practically called out for his hand to either smack her or stroke her. Maybe both.

He watched her cross the room and begin to climb the stairs. At the first bend, she caught his gaze and crooked her finger. His lips curved in a smile that had a hard edge to it.

Oh yes. He definitely wanted to smack that ass.

He didn't want to rein himself in. Didn't want to hold anything back. He'd been doing way too much of that lately.

With her dress clenched in his hand, he stalked to the stairs. She'd started up again as soon as he'd moved but he caught up to her midway. His eyes followed her ass the entire way.

By the time she reached the top of the stairs, his jaw was clenched so tight, he thought it might crack if he tried to speak. His hands had tightened into fists, crushing her dress. He'd get it dry-cleaned for her. Good as new.

He just hoped he didn't destroy it before they got to the bedroom. Hoped he didn't destroy whatever feelings she had for him when he got her on his bed. Because he was in a mood to dominate. Wanted to throw her over his lap and spank her ass then he wanted to fuck that ass.

He recognized the desire for what it was, knew his life had spun a little out of his control tonight, and he didn't like that feeling.

Rein it in.

Fuck that. It's all he felt like he'd been doing for the past few years. Reining it in. His emotions, his fears, his insecurities.

And now was definitely not the time to let them fuck with his head.

Jules didn't need his shit. Not on top of everything else. Hell, Erik couldn't deal with his shit either.

That meant he *had* to rein it in.

"Whatever you're thinking, I'm not sure I like it."

They'd reached his room and he hadn't even realized it. As she pushed through the half-open door and into his space, she looked around like she'd never seen anything so interesting.

Walking to the bed, she stood by the side of the king mattress that had never been shared with anyone other than a few one-night stands.

Which was just so fucking pathetic. Erik had never joined him with a woman here. Their threesomes had always taken place at Erik's.

He forced those thoughts out of his head. "I'm not thinking of anything other than getting you in my bed."

She glanced over her shoulder with a wry smile. "That's bullshit, Keegan. But I'm going to let it slide for right now." Turning, she faced him completely. "Come here."

His hand clenched on the dress. "I don't think you want to give me orders right now."

Her gaze narrowed, and he knew she was trying to figure out what he was thinking, trying to decide how to handle him.

Before she could come to a decision, he laid her dress on the nearest piece of furniture then closed the short distance between them and wrapped his hand around her neck.

He felt her still beneath his hand, almost like a deer in the headlights. But he didn't see any fear in her eyes.

If he had, he would've torn himself away and locked himself in another room until this burning lust passed and he could make love to her without wanting to spank her ass until it was bright red.

"What do *you* want?" Her question was almost a whisper, her gaze interested.

He paused, fighting the need to tell her exactly what he wanted.

"Keegan." She lifted one hand to stroke his jaw. "Just say it."

"I want you." He barely got the words through his gritted teeth.

Her mouth twisted in disappointment as she pointedly glanced at his crotch. "I can see that. Tell me what I can't see."

He felt the muscles in his jaw jump, saw her try to figure out what he was thinking. "I want something you might not want to give."

"Try me."

FIFTEEN

Fascinated, Jules looked into Keegan's eyes and saw something she hadn't seen there before. Something that made her heart pound.

Keegan had always seemed like the stable one, the one who planted his feet and didn't sway even in hurricane winds.

Last night at the reception, he'd shown a crack in that façade.

Tonight...that crack had widened.

And her excitement grew.

She'd already soaked through her panties and now she felt a fresh rush of moisture slick her sex. She wanted to clench her thighs against the ache between them. Wanted Keegan to throw her on the bed and ravage her.

And yes, she meant ravage. The way he looked right now... she loved it. It made her feel wicked and wild and a little dirty.

Considering all she'd already done with Keegan and Erik, a session of one-on-one should be almost routine.

But nothing with either of these men could be considered routine.

Keegan shook his head, as if trying to shake out his thoughts. "Maybe we should wait until Erik gets back."

"No." She took another step toward him, closing the distance so that her breasts just brushed against his chest. "No, I don't want to wait. I want you, Keegan."

His jaw continued to clench, a muscle jumping under the skin. She wanted to lick it, bite it. He looked like he wanted to bite her, too.

"Jules—"

He cut off when she put her hand over his erection straining against his pants.

"Come on, Keegan. You know you want—"

Grabbing her by the shoulder, he spun her around until she was facing the bed. Then he plastered his body against her back, wrapping his arms around her waist.

"I know exactly what I want," he whispered in her ear, his breath making her shiver with desire. "I want you bent over this bed with your legs spread so I can stand and fuck you, hard and fast. I want you to come so hard it's almost painful. Then I want to fuck you again, with you on your back this time, staring up at me with your ankles at my shoulders. And then I want your ass. I want you to beg me to take your ass."

Her lungs had tightened with excitement to the point that she could barely breathe. Her mouth hung open and her throat was so dry, she could barely swallow.

She was almost glad he couldn't see her face because she was worried he might mistake her intense, almost painful desire for shock.

Yes, she was shocked but not in a bad way.

She was shocked because he'd finally let go.

And she couldn't wait for him to start.

"Then what are you waiting for?" Her voice could barely be heard over his labored breathing. "Fuck me, Keegan."

She heard him growl, felt the rumble of it against her back. And then she felt him move.

One hand moved to her shoulder, pressing her down until her chest hit the mattress. Her head turned to the side as he kicked her feet apart just enough that he could stand between her legs.

She wanted to wriggle back against the cloth-covered erection she felt brushing her ass, but the second she started, he smacked her ass with his palm.

She sucked in a sharp gasp as sensation rushed through her body from the point of contact. Her nipples tightened, her clit swelled and her pussy clenched.

Good god, she felt...amazing. The sting hurt but... It hurt so damn good.

She sucked in a breath, moaning through her clenched teeth.

"You have the most beautiful ass." His voice had gotten deeper. Harder. "I love the way my handprint looks on your skin."

Sweet hell. That shouldn't make her want him to do it again. It did.

She deliberately arched her back so her ass would brush against him again.

And he smacked her again.

Groaning louder this time, she nearly melted into the mattress. As it was, her upper body felt as if every muscle had gone liquid while her legs hardened into stone to keep her standing.

"Keegan."

The hand on her shoulder tightened as she heard his zipper release. Then he flipped the tails of his shirt onto her back and rubbed his cock between her cheeks.

He felt hot, sleek, and hard, and she wanted him to stuff

every inch inside her, but she couldn't manage to get the words out. Instead she began to move with him as he stroked his cock against her.

"I'm not going to take your ass yet. That'll have to wait because if I take you there now, I'll be too rough. But I'm going to pound your pussy."

"God, yes. Please."

The hand on her shoulder released her abruptly and she cried out before she heard the crackle of foil.

Damn it, she was really beginning to hate condoms for the intrusion they were.

Then she didn't have the brain power to think because he put one hand back on her shoulder to hold her steady, used his other to line up his cock with her pussy then shoved himself deep with one stroke.

The sudden sensation of being empty to being stretched so tightly made her shudder and lock around him. She didn't know whether she was trying to keep him out or get him deeper.

The silk comforter felt cool against her front, her ass still tingled from his smacks, and now her pussy burned as he began to hammer his cock inside her.

With one hand on her shoulder and the other on her hip, he held her immobile.

Under his command.

She was so close to coming already, she felt her pussy ripple in anticipation.

Keegan must've felt it as well, because he groaned and shoved so deep, his balls slapped against her clit.

"Oh my god. Keegan—"

He fucked her even faster, his hips slamming against her ass even as she felt his cock begin to pulse inside her.

Her pussy responded with a short, sharp orgasm that only made her want more.

But Keegan was already retreating.

With a groan, she reached for him, trying to hold him to her. She couldn't.

He pulled out so fast she gasped, but in the next second, he grabbed her around the waist, flipped her over onto her back, then dropped to his knees beside the bed.

She barely had time to breathe before he put his mouth over her pussy and began to push her toward another orgasm.

She sank one hand into his hair to hold him close while the other curled into the comforter, anchoring her to the bed. She seriously felt like she might fragment into a thousand little pieces when she came again.

And she would come. Keegan would give her no other option.

His lips and tongue worked together to work her into a state where she rested right on the edge of flying apart. His tongue licked inside her with long, leisurely strokes, but when he pulled out, he nipped at her clit with his teeth, the sharp sensation making her back bow off the bed.

He knew exactly what to do to make her body respond to his tiniest movement.

Holding her thighs apart with his hands, his fingers gripped her tight. Her thighs wanted to close around him, hold him tight, but he used his superior strength to keep her open. She liked that. A lot.

She liked when he licked her. He did it with an intensity that made her shudder. Her body released itself from her control and gave itself over to him.

Grazing her clit with his teeth, he made stars flash beneath her eyelids. Then he tugged on it, making her moan at the sting and writhe when he licked away the slight pain.

Her pussy clenched hard, needing to be filled, but she could barely breathe much less string two words together to ask for what she wanted.

Apparently Keegan could read her mind because he slid two fingers inside her and started to fuck her with them. It wasn't enough. It wouldn't be enough until he fucked her with his cock but it helped...to wind her up even more.

Her heart pounded against her ribs so hard she thought it'd be bruised.

His fingers stretched her, the roughness of his rhythm making her arch into each thrust, push herself against his mouth, seeking more.

He fed on her for long minutes, making her sink a little deeper into a state of intense pleasure with each second. Her body, however, was still climbing to another peak, which he pushed her toward relentlessly.

When she finally reached it, every muscle in her body seized in ecstasy. Crying out his name, she tightened her fingers in his hair, making sure he kept his mouth on her through the entire orgasm.

When her pussy finally stopped spasming and she lay there gasping for air, she wanted him to lie on the bed beside her. Wrap his arms around her and hold her against him.

She felt him move and opened her eyes to see him on his feet, staring down at her.

Their orgasms hadn't abated the heat she still saw in his eyes. Surprisingly, she felt an answering heat lingering in her sex. When he lifted his arm to wipe his mouth on the back of his hand, she bit back a moan. The act looked so decadent because she knew what that wetness was. Her.

"Roll over, Jules. Get onto your knees. I want to fuck your ass."

Her eyes widened and her gaze immediately shot to his groin.

And yes, he was hard again. So hard, his cock very nearly stood straight up against his stomach. Thick and long and...

Jesus, she couldn't breathe.

It got worse when he began to unbutton his shirt, revealing that beautiful chest and sculpted abs. He'd only taken the time to shove his pants low enough on his hips that he could take out his cock, but as soon as he threw the shirt to the side, he stripped off his pants and underwear, taking his socks along.

Now he was totally naked and she wanted to stroke her hands along every square inch of his body. But she was already moving to do what he'd commanded. And there was no doubt it was a command.

Rearranging herself took some effort because her limbs felt like wet noodles. But her anticipation made her go as fast as she could.

The glide of a drawer opening caught her attention. By the time she had herself positioned, he kneeled onto the mattress behind her.

Closing her eyes, she settled her forehead on the comforter, expecting to feel his cock pushing at her back entrance. Instead, she felt his hand stroke along her ass.

"So fucking smooth. And pale."

The smack of his palm against her ass sounded like a gunshot and made her buck forward. Again, it didn't hurt. But it lit up every nerve ending in her body.

Her moan sounded like a sob. And when he did it again, she bit her bottom lip so she didn't cry out.

"You like that, don't you?"

"Yes."

"Why? Answer me, Jules."

"Because it hurts but it doesn't."

His palm rubbed the heated spot on her skin before he pulled back and smacked her twice on the opposite cheek.

"And when I fuck your ass, how does that feel?"

"So good."

"So do you. So damn tight and hot."

Cool, slick liquid dribbled between her ass cheeks and she shuddered. His fingers followed, spreading the lube.

"I'm going to fuck you now, babe. Hard. But I don't want to hurt you. You tell me if it's too much, okay?"

"Just do it, Keegan. You won't—"

His cock butted against her, increasing the pressure until she opened to him. The intensity of the sensation made her mouth drop open as she sucked in air. Fingers grabbing onto the comforter, she tried to anchor her body but Keegan kept pushing, taking more of her and filling her until she swore she couldn't take any more.

Then he'd pull out but not all the way. And his cock seemed to expand until her nerve endings sizzled around him. Her pulse pounded in her ears as her muscles tightened around him. Another orgasm built as he began to thrust. The sensation was almost more than she could bear. This position made her feel vulnerable, exposed, and that intensified her need.

"God, Jules."

Keegan's voice made her body tighten like a fist around him, made him groan as he began to pound into her like he'd promised.

Relaxing as much as she could, she let him have her, let her orgasm wind her up as the hand on her shoulder tightened and so did the one on her hip. The force he used to hold her and the increasing power behind his thrusts made her feel out of control. And adored. And so hot, she felt sweat bead along her hairline.

She only needed—

The hand on her hip slid around her front to tweak her clit. Shards of extreme pleasure radiated from the contact and she came, shudders wracking her body so hard, Keegan had to hold her up with his arm around her waist as he pumped his release into her.

He held her there until his cock stopped pulsing then pulled out slowly. Her sensitive nerve endings spasmed as he did, making her moan. And shake.

With a loud exhale, Keegan collapsed onto the mattress, taking her with him. Wrapping an arm around her waist, he tugged her into the curve of his overheated body.

They lay there as minutes ticked by, their breathing the only sound in the room, sweat cooling on their bodies.

She knew she needed to go to the bathroom and clean up but she didn't want to move.

Especially not when Keegan held her close against his still-heaving chest and pressed his lips against the back of her head.

"Lie still. I'll be right back."

His voice was a low rumble that touched off a miniquake of reaction in her pussy. If he wanted, she'd be ready to go again right now.

She might not have the strength to participate but she'd certainly enjoy the ride.

After another kiss pressed to her cheek, she felt the mattress shimmy then cooler air coated her back.

She made a slight sound of protest and heard him huff out a laugh. "I'm going to fill the tub. I'll be back for you in a second."

Since a bath sounded heavenly, she decided she wouldn't protest. Much.

"Hurry."

"Back to you, yes."

She heard something in his voice that made her open her eyes to look at him. He stared down at her with a burning intensity that made her shiver. And want to burn in his arms again.

Then he turned and disappeared into the attached bath. She heard water run, heard the toilet flush, then he was back.

And she realized she'd watched the doorway with a gaze that had never wavered.

God, Keegan had a beautiful body. Long, lean, muscled but not beastly. She wanted to bite his pec and kiss her way down his torso to follow the line of dark hair straight to his cock. Which looked like it could be coaxed into readiness sooner rather than later.

"Keep looking at me like that and you'll never get in the tub."

She smiled up at him, loving the fact that she could make him hard with just a look. "Maybe I wouldn't care."

He stopped by the side of the bed, his cock at the perfect height for her to wrap her hand around and—

"Hey!"

He scooped her off the bed and strode back to the bathroom. "If you're good, maybe we can christen the tub."

She liked the sound of that. "Are you trying to tell me you haven't had another woman here?"

He didn't answer as he walked into the bathroom, and she stared up at him, watching his expression. His grimace told her that's exactly what he wasn't saying.

"Let me know if it's too warm."

Biting her lips to hide a smile, she took a second to check out the room. Dark marble in shades of blue and tan. Lots of straight lines. Except for the tub. That was white, oval, and inset into the floor. And big enough to host a party of five.

"Oh my god, I think I love your tub. I could swim laps in here."

He stepped into bubble-filled water, the level coming up to mid-thigh before he set her on her feet. She stood on her own for a moment as he settled onto the bottom then quickly sank into the water to sit beside him.

In the next second, he resettled her between his legs, wrapping his arms around her and tucking her head under his chin.

The water temperature immediately loosened all her muscles and she melted back into him with a sigh, breathing in the slight coconut scent of whatever he'd put in the water.

"Okay?"

She sighed. "Oh yeah. I want to take this tub home with me."

"You're welcome any time."

She liked the sound of that. She liked the way he held her against him. Liked the way he brushed her hair back from her ear so he could bite at the lobe and make her shiver in reaction.

"So," she teased, "I never would've figured you for a bubble-bath kind of guy."

He paused before answering. "I bought it for you. Because I was hoping you'd be here tonight."

Oh wow. The quiet sincerity in his voice made her breath hitch. Despite the fact that she felt too relaxed to move, she turned to kiss him. Cupping his face in her hands, she settled her lips on his for a deep, lazy, sensual kiss.

She kissed him with all the heat stoking low in her body, stroking her lips over his, sliding her tongue between his lips. His arms tightened around her but he let her lead, let her dance her tongue along his and taste him.

He tasted like heat and dark desire and her pulse began to pick up speed.

A sharp *clack* caught her attention and she pulled away with a gasp, turning toward the sound.

Erik stood just inside the door, hands pulling his shirt over his head. The noise she'd heard had been his belt hitting the marble floor. He hadn't taken the time to change at home and the look on his face made her lungs tighten.

"Room for one more?"

He didn't make it sound much like a question, but she nodded just so he didn't get any stupid ideas. "Of course."

His gaze shot to Keegan's in a flash, and she felt Keegan's chin brush her temple as he nodded.

In seconds, Erik had his pants and underwear off and was sliding into the other end of the tub.

"Fuck, I love this tub," Erik said as he sank into the water up to his shoulders, hiding the scars on his body. "I've been thinking about redoing my bathroom just so I could put one in."

"I told you to when you were having the renovations done." Keegan released her to put his arms on the rim.

For a brief second, she wondered if he was trying not to hurt Erik's feelings then she realized Keegan was silently telling her to go to him.

Keegan must have seen something in Erik's expression she hadn't because Erik looked fine. Calm, even.

Until she took Keegan's hint and shifted to Erik, wrapping her arms around his shoulders and kissing him with the same passion she'd given Keegan when Erik had walked in.

But where Keegan had let her lead, Erik wove his fingers through her hair and took over immediately.

He kissed her like he was afraid she might try to get away, like he was desperate for her. She couldn't say she didn't like it and she let him have what he wanted.

Letting her body relax against him seemed to give him the signal he was looking for. She'd already felt his erection press against her hip so she knew he wanted her. She just hadn't realized how ready he was.

Pushing her away, he repositioned her until she was on her knees. Urging her to spread her legs, he drew her forward again until she straddled his hips. Then he held her steady when she would have dipped her hips to rub her clit against his cock.

"If you don't want this right now, all you have to say is no."

She lifted one hand to his face, brushing her fingertips along his scarred jaw to his lips, then leaned forward to follow the same line with her lips. "I know exactly what I want. Why do you think I'm on the verge of coming again when I've already done it twice already?"

Erik's mouth twisted into a smile and his gaze flashed over her shoulder toward Keegan for a second. "Twice, huh? Well, damn. I guess I have my work cut out for me."

She heard the strain in his voice now, but she didn't think it had anything to do with her or Keegan and how many times she'd orgasmed. And she hated to think that she could add to his stress level.

"Why don't you lean back and let me do the work for a change?"

His smile eased a little bit more toward normal. "Why would I even think about turning down an offer like that?"

She smiled, letting all the desire she felt for him show through. "I was hoping you wouldn't."

Closing the few remaining inches between them, she reached for the condom he'd set on the edge of the tub before getting in and handed it to him. She leaned back just far enough for him to be able to roll it on then moved back where she'd been, with her pussy brushing against the length of his cock.

With each movement of her hips, she watched his chest rise and fall more quickly, heard his breathing roughen. His hands tightened on her hips but didn't dictate her movements. He let her take the lead.

After Keegan's earlier dominance, she realized she had a little of that in her, as well.

And here was a willing subject, offering himself up to her.

So she teased the hell out of him.

She rubbed herself against him. Her pussy, her nipples, her lips. Wherever they touched, she stroked.

Leaning in to lick his earlobe, she pressed her breasts against his chest, her hands petting along his shoulders then down his arms. She felt the rough skin of his scars, felt the familiar pang of empathy that quickly turned into the fierce desire to make him experience more ecstasy than he'd ever had in his life.

Groaning, he leaned his head back to rest on the rim of the tub. She followed him down, kissing her way from his ear to his neck as her hands stroked back to his shoulders.

All the while, her hips continued to rock her pussy against his cock.

When she finally couldn't take it anymore, she let one hand drift down his chest to pull his cock away from his stomach and line it up with her channel.

His groan made her smile. And when she settled herself over the head and began to sink down on him, that smile spread as he released her to grip the rim of the tub so he wouldn't pull her down.

"Such a gentleman," she whispered in his ear as she raised herself up, almost releasing him. "You'll let me fuck you however I want, won't you?"

"Anything you want, babe. You know you can have it."

"Keegan took me earlier. Fucked me hard and fast and I liked it. But it made me want to do the same to you."

His eyes opened and he stared straight into hers, lust gleaming in the dark depths. "I have absolutely no objection to that."

Without warning, she sank onto him, taking him all the way in.

"Aw fuck, Jules. Yes."

He stretched her tight, her labia swollen and tender from Keegan, her ass still overly sensitive. It made her want to ride him hard, feel that burn radiate through her entire body.

Wanted Erik to burn with her, this time in a way that made him hers.

Behind her, she heard Keegan's harsh breathing, wondered if he was stroking himself in time with her and Erik. She wanted to look but found herself transfixed by Erik's expression. Harsh desire and frantic yearning proved to be a potent combination.

Her orgasm started low in her body. Her pussy tightened around his cock until he groaned, his eyes closing and his head falling back as she rode him harder and faster.

She saw the exact moment he gave in and let her have him. His cock swelled then begin to pulse deep inside her, prolonging her orgasm until she could no longer hold herself up and slumped forward onto his chest.

Erik anchored her to his heaving chest with an arm curled around her shoulders. And even though his breathing nearly drowned out all other sound in the room, she still heard Keegan's low groan behind them.

She decided she wasn't moving for the next week.

———————

ERIK WOKE when the bed shifted.

Lying on his stomach, he opened his eyes, blinking in the dark as he realized he wasn't at home.

He was at Keegan's. The previous night came back in a flash and he turned to catch a glimpse of Keegan's back as he closed the bathroom door behind him. Beside him, Jules continued to sleep on her side, facing away from him.

Without a second thought, he rolled until he was spooned around her. Wrapping an arm around her waist, he pulled her even closer. She snuggled into him with a sigh, her body warm, her skin so fucking soft.

Damn, he could get used to waking up like this. He *wanted* to get used to waking up like this.

The three of them. Together. Making love all night. Having her waiting for them when they got home. Having her with them all the time.

It sounded like a dream come true.

And would probably never happen.

After they'd showered last night, they'd fallen into bed, Jules between them. There'd been no discussion. Erik had simply picked her up and laid her in the middle of the bed. Keegan had taken one side, Erik had taken the other.

It'd felt right. Exactly the way it was supposed to be.

This morning...

He sighed. This morning they needed to talk.

Because after his conversation with his sister on their way back to his house, Erik had come to a few realizations.

The door to the bathroom reopened and Keegan walked out, wearing a pair of boxers. He slid into bed again but lay on his back, one arm under his head, the other across his stomach. Just enough light seeped into the room that Erik could see him staring at the ceiling.

"What time is it?"

Keegan turned, his gaze sweeping down to Jules before looking at Erik. "Around six. Why are you awake already?"

"Because I'm not asleep."

Keegan gave him the finger. Then turned back to his examination of the ceiling. "Go back to sleep."

"What are you going to do?"

"Probably get up. I've got work to get done."

No, he didn't. Their work wasn't the kind you could bring home unless he was talking about paperwork. And Keegan hated paperwork. Both of them did, which was why they had assistants.

"She'll be pissed if you're not here when she wakes up."

The "she" in question shifted against him, sighed, and said, "Yes, she will."

Keegan turned again. "Sorry. We didn't mean to wake you. It's still early. Why don't you try to get some more sleep?"

"I'd rather be awake with you two." One of her hands rubbed along Erik's forearm. With the other, she reached for Keegan, settling her palm on his chest. "You're an early riser, aren't you?" She yawned loudly. "We're gonna need to work on that."

That sounded like she planned to spend more time in bed with both of them. Erik definitely liked the sound of that.

Keegan laughed, a bare whisper of sound. "Yeah, that's not gonna happen."

"He's been like this as long as I've known him," Erik said. "He's the only person I know who can get two hours of sleep and still wake up with a smile."

"Yeah, well, I wasn't raised with a nanny who brought me hot chocolate in a platinum mug every morning."

Erik grinned at the old dig, though it was mostly true. He'd had a nanny and she'd made him hot chocolate every morning until he'd moved away to college. His mother certainly never did, though.

"Yeah, yeah, you were deprived. Your hot chocolate only came in a silver mug."

"Sounds like neither of you had to worry about money growing up."

Erik grimaced. "Shit. Sorry, I don't mean to—"

"No, no. I didn't mean that the way it sounded." She squeezed his arm. "I'm just curious. Keegan talks about his family. You don't."

He tried not to tense but couldn't help it. Her hand began to rub along his arm again. Soothing.

"That's because mine's pretty messed up."

"My dad cheated on my mom while she was fighting breast cancer, cleaned out their bank accounts, spent the money on strippers, and then left us to clean up his mess. I know a little something about fucked-up families."

Yeah, she did. If he ever found her father...

Erik's arms tightened but he forced himself to think about what to say. Since she couldn't see his face and the room was still mostly dark, he almost felt insulated from the past pain.

And he didn't want to shut her down on this. He knew he had to be willing to share part of himself if they wanted to keep her here. He would share this.

"My mom is a stone-cold bitch," he started, dragging out each word like he was pulling teeth. "She's one of those women who looks like a mannequin, dresses like a model, never goes out of the house without makeup, and has the emotional capability of a gnat. My dad married her because she looked great on his arm and her pedigree matched his. They had two kids because that's what was expected. After my sister was born, they moved to separate bedrooms and Kat and I tried to be ghosts."

A weight had settled on his chest, a weight he'd become used to over these past three years. Only when he was with Jules did he not notice it as much. Instead of focusing on it, he focused instead on the heat radiating from her body, easing his muscles.

"Sounds cold."

He hugged Jules closer, but he couldn't continue to hold Keegan's gaze. Keegan knew all of this. Didn't mean it made it any easier to talk about. "We coped. My mom was harder on Kat. Her teen years sucked, and by that I mean they were hell. We both went to private schools but we lived at home. Kat wasn't allowed to play sports so she didn't have that outlet. I was expected to play soccer. My dad played and so did his father, so it's kind of a family tradition. Luckily, I was good at it. Played almost all year round. Kept me out of the house."

"Do you still play?"

"I did until the—" He refused to say accident because now he knew it wasn't. But he didn't want to get into that fight now. Not with Jules here. "Until the explosion."

"Do you miss it?"

"Yeah. I do."

"Then why don't you go back?"

He hadn't even considered it. "Too busy."

Keegan's eyebrows curved upward. Erik's jaw tightened at the challenge, but there was no way he'd respond now.

"What does your sister do?

"She's a lawyer, much to my mother's regret."

"Seriously? Your mom's upset that your sister's a lawyer?"

"Mom wanted her to go to college to find a good husband. Not a career."

"That's...kind of medieval."

"My mother had emotion bred out of her. My grandparents were pretty much the same. I didn't see them much growing up. I saw my mom cry once. After the explosion. And I'm pretty sure that was only because she knew I'd never look the same and she couldn't handle that."

Jules fell silent then, though she continued to stroke her fingers along his arm, which began to give him other, more exciting ideas.

But there were still some things they needed to discuss.

"So have I scared you away with my dysfunctional family talk? You've met Kat and you're still here so I guess that bodes well for the future."

She stopped stroking his arm, her hand coming to rest on his forearm. "And what kind of future are you looking for?"

He knew what he wanted to say. He was more than ready to

tell her exactly what he wanted. Full-time and exclusive. The three of them.

Keegan's gaze remained steady on his. "You sure you want to do this now?"

"Now's as good a time as any, I guess," Erik replied.

"Then how about we do it over coffee?" Jules suggested. "I need some caffeine."

Keegan nodded and sat up, but not before squeezing her hand.

"How about some blueberry pancakes to go with the coffee?" Erik sat up, trying not to grin. "I'm kind of hungry."

Keegan gave him a look Erik knew well. The finger that followed made Erik lose the fight with his grin.

Jules' stomach growled at the same time and Keegan's smile became more natural. "Pancakes it is."

Sitting up, Jules didn't try to hide her nudity with the sheet, looking totally confident and so fucking hot, Erik almost reached for her. He managed not to but just barely.

She turned to him with raised eyebrows. "So if Keegan cooks all the time, what do you contribute?"

Damn, she made it almost impossible for him to be good. Hands curled into fists so he didn't grab her, he turned and slid off the bed, grabbing his underwear from the chair along the wall where his clothes had ended up last night.

"I make a mean martini."

From across the room where he was pulling on a pair of sweats and a long-sleeved t-shirt, Keegan snorted. "In his dreams." He walked to a dresser, rummaged around. "Here, Jules. This shouldn't be too big and I think I've got a pair of—yeah, here." He handed her a t-shirt and a pair of flannel pants. "They'll be big but they've got a drawstring. Erik, you know where the sweats are."

"Next time, pack a bag."

Erik had spoken the words casually but there was nothing casual about his meaning.

Jules turned to him, eyebrows raised. "That assumes there'll be a next time, doesn't it?"

"Then I guess Keegan better make breakfast fast so we can talk this through."

Erik used his most calm, reasonable voice, the one he only pulled out when he saw Keegan starting to lose it.

Keegan wasn't in any danger of losing his shit, but his brain wasn't where Erik needed him to be. Which was aligned with his. They needed to present a united front if they were going to tie her more tightly to them.

It's what he wanted so that's what they'd do.

And even though Keegan hadn't said anything, Erik knew it's what he wanted as well.

Keegan caught and held his gaze and Erik nodded, which just made Keegan sigh.

"Breakfast in fifteen. Don't be late."

Which Erik took to mean, "Don't get distracted and try to get in Jules' pants."

And he would have if he was a total douche. Which he was not.

Instead, he nodded, waved Jules into the bathroom in front of him, then waited for her to emerge with her face washed and her hair in a ponytail on the top of her head.

She looked like a teenager, dressed in oversized flannel pants and baggy t-shirt, with no makeup and her hair swaying back and forth.

Giving him a sidelong glance, she stopped by the door to the hall. "Don't give me that look. You heard what Keegan said. You won't get any breakfast if we're not down there."

He smiled back at her, the action coming much more naturally with her than it did with anyone else. "Yeah, but you know if we don't show up, he'll come looking for us."

She tried to curb a smile and wasn't quite successful. "But I need to eat, especially if you want to...play more later."

Heat hit him low in the gut, making his already half-hard cock rise to full hard-on. "Then by all means, please, go downstairs. I'll be there in a few minutes."

With a full smile this time, she slipped out of the room.

True to his word, it only took him five minutes to join Keegan and Jules, who were already at the table.

Keegan didn't look up when he entered but Jules did. Her smile was warm but her eyes... She'd been thinking a little too much.

Walking over to the stainless behemoth that was Keegan's stove, he served himself a stack of pancakes, flipped the ones on the griddle that needed to be flipped then took a seat at the square black table in front of a bay window overlooking the backyard.

Erik took a bite of Keegan's excellent pancakes and swallowed. "Here's what I think. Keegan and I have made it clear we want you. We...Well," he shot a look at Keegan, who simply stared back, "I have no problem sharing you with Keegan for as long as you'll have us. You don't seem to have a problem with that so let's just get this part out of the way."

"What part?" Jules looked genuinely curious, a slight curve to her lips as her eyes narrowed.

"The part where this gets messy with other people's opinions and ideas about morality and the way things should be."

"And how do we manage that?"

Keegan's quiet voice and intense stare let Erik know he had his partner's undivided attention. And that Keegan wasn't quite as onboard as Erik would like.

"By letting everyone think she's seeing only you, Keegan."

Keegan's gaze narrowed even farther but it was Jules who said, "You mean hide the fact that I'm sleeping with both of you."

Erik nodded. "I don't want you to take any shit because of us. I know how cruel people can be when they think you're doing something they think is wrong." He glanced at Keegan. "We both do. So when we go out, you're Keegan's date. You hold his hand. You kiss only him. I'm just along for the ride. No one will think twice."

Her gaze narrowed on his. "Is this because of your scars? Do you think that because of the way you look, no one will have any doubt that I'd only want to see Keegan?"

He nodded again. "Yes. Exactly. What we do in private is no one's business. Society and their morals can all go to hell."

"Then why can't we just tell everyone to fuck off and *do* what we want?" Jules asked.

"Because you live here." Erik leaned forward. She had to see that he was doing this for her. "You work here. Your mom lives here and she's already dealt with enough crap. I don't want to give you up. I believe this is the only workable solution for all of us."

She paused and he had no idea what she was thinking, her expression calm. Even her next statement didn't give him a clue.

"So you want me to lie to everyone and tell them I'm only dating Keegan."

Was she pissed? Was that the hard tone he heard in her voice?

"It's not a lie. You are dating Keegan. No one else needs to know our personal business."

Keegan and Jules exchanged a glance before transferring all of their attention back to him. He felt the weight of their stares like a physical force.

Jules wanted to say something, something he wouldn't like.

Why? He couldn't understand why she wasn't immediately agreeing to his plan. It really was the only viable solution, especially for Jules.

And Keegan should be backing him up on this. But when he looked at his friend, Keegan looked pissed.

"What's wrong?" he asked Keegan.

"Nothing." Keegan shook his head, meeting his gaze head-on. "Not one damn thing. If that's how you want to play this, I'm fine with it if Jules is."

"You don't sound fine."

Keegan didn't respond to him. Instead, he turned to Jules. "It's not up to me. Are you okay with this?"

She hesitated long enough that Erik thought she was going to say no. Then she nodded slowly. "If that's what you want, Erik, then I'm fine with it, too."

Yes, it's what he wanted. It's what was best for all of them.

So why did it seem like neither Jules nor Keegan were as thrilled as he was?

SIXTEEN

"Did you have a good time last night?"

Jules hadn't exactly sneaked into the house but she had been hoping not to have to face her mom. At least, not right away.

After Keegan had dropped her off, giving her a lingering kiss in the car before walking her to the front door, she'd been hoping to have a few hours to herself to think. Sunday mornings her mom usually went to breakfast with her best friend, Cookie, before they headed to an early movie.

Apparently not this morning.

"Hey, Mom. What are you doing home?"

Her mom stood in the doorway to the kitchen, wearing an expression all too familiar to Jules from her wild-ass teen years.

"I thought maybe you'd want to talk."

More like Mom wanted to talk. And since she loved her mom, she nodded. "Can I change first?"

"Sure, honey. Come back to the kitchen then. I made cookies last night."

Ooh, definitely a serious talk when Mom busted out the homemade cookies.

"Sounds good. Give me a few minutes."

She ran through the shower, threw on sweats and an old, soft t-shirt proclaiming her mom's love of Abba, and headed back to the kitchen.

Her mom already sat at the table, staring out the small window into the tiny backyard of the tiny single home Jules had grown up in. Somehow, her mom had managed to keep the house out of the bank's hands. And after Jules had paid off all of their other debts, she still had more than enough money to pay off the house. Which she planned to do...as soon as she came clean about how she'd gotten the money.

Heading for the fridge, Jules poured herself a glass of milk then sat across from her mom and snagged a cookie.

"So, your dates from last night." Her mom didn't waste any time. "They gave you the money, didn't they?"

She sighed and took a bite of cookie loaded with chocolate chips. "Yes."

"And what did you have to do for it?"

She held her mom's steady gaze, needing to choose her words carefully. She didn't want her to hate Keegan and Erik. "Can I give you a little background first? It might help."

Her mom's eyebrows lifted. "Background. Sure. Background is okay."

She started with Erik and how he'd gotten his scars, knowing it would soften her mom's defenses. Explained how Erik and Keegan had built TinMan into the company it was today, a very successful company that continued to grow. Told her how they'd been friends in college, how they'd stuck together, even when it looked like they could lose everything they'd worked for because of the explosion.

"They sound like amazing men." Her mom took advantage of Jules' pause to get more tea. "That still doesn't tell me why they gave you enough money to pay off our debt and then some."

No, it didn't. "A few weeks before Christmas, I waitressed their Christmas party for Carol. Erik saw me, wanted to ask me out but..."

"His scars," her mom said.

"Yeah, his scars. He sat in a room by himself watching the party on monitors, connected to Keegan through an earbud."

Her mom's expression melted with compassion and Jules knew it was time to drop the rest.

"Erik didn't think I'd ever consider going out with him so he and Keegan offered me half a million dollars," she sighed as her mom's eyes widened with shock, "for one night. For me to have sex with Keegan so Erik could watch. I wasn't supposed to know Erik was there but I figured it out. And before you have a meltdown, please realize that I never would've gone to bed with either of them if I hadn't wanted them. Not for all the money in the world."

Her mom's eyes widened. "Oh, honey—"

"Don't freak." Jules held her hands up in front of her. "Okay? Just...try not to freak. I like them, Mom. Both of them. A lot. But they're a package deal and I'm okay with that. They treat me great." And holy hell, the sex was awesome. But she wasn't going there with her mom. Not yet. Maybe not ever. "They treat me more than great, actually. They both have issues but name me one person who doesn't. And what we do in private shouldn't matter a damn to anyone."

Her mom took a deep breath, nibbling on her bottom lip as she formulated an answer. "Is this...relationship serious?"

"Do you mean are we talking rings and place settings? Not yet. We're having fun. We're getting to know each other. But, yeah, it could be serious."

Her mom shook her head. "Wow."

"That's it? That's all you have to say?"

Her mom laughed but the sound held no amusement. "I'm not sure what you want me to say. You just told me two men paid you to sleep with them and you did it to pay off our debt."

Jules winced at the disappointment in her mom's tone but she had to get her to see that wasn't the entire story. "That's not why I slept with them. Yes, the money got me to Keegan's house that first night but that's not why I stayed."

"And why did you stay?"

"Because I connected with them. Because we fit together. Because when I'm with them, I feel part of a whole."

"Oh, honey, don't you think you're rushing into this whole arrangement pretty fast?"

"I know it seems fast but I'm not talking about marrying them. I'm just talking about spending time with them."

Grimacing, her mom walked to the fridge, reached in, and pulled out the carton of chocolate milk before sitting opposite Jules again.

"I'm not going to pretend I like this." Her mom shook her head. "Or understand it. But the money..."

"I know what it looks like. But I'm not sorry I took it. And I refuse to give a damn about what other people say. Those men saved our asses. And even if you take the money out of the situation completely, I'd still want them both."

Her mom took a sip of chocolate milk then a bite of cookie. "People are going to talk."

"I know. And I'm willing to put up with it. But Erik..."

After a short pause, her mom prompted, "Erik...what?"

"He wants me and Keegan to pretend we're dating and that Erik's just a third wheel."

"Well, it's not pretend if you actually *are* dating." Her mom started to look a little less stressed. "And it seems like the perfect solution. It'll keep the gossips at bay."

"Mom, the only people whose opinions matter are the ones in this with me. Keegan and Erik. And you. " She paused. "When Dad—"

"No." Her mom shook her head. "Your dad's gone. He did what he did and we survived. What other people said hurt, but nothing hurt worse than what that man did to our marriage and our family. I'd cut off his balls if I thought I could get away with it. But he gave me you and it's really hard to hate a man who gave you the most wonderful thing in your life."

Jules didn't know what to say about that so she grabbed her mom's hand across the table and squeezed.

"Sweetie, I still don't see a problem with the way Erik wants to handle things. It seems like a good idea. We live in a small town, not Philly or New York. People are going to talk. And it's going to get bad. Erik's suggestion seems reasonable."

"And I don't want to lie about our relationship. I'm pretty sure part of the reason Erik wants it this way is because he wants to remain in his little hole, away from the world."

"I don't see how letting people believe you're only dating one of these men would be lying. Although I see your point about Erik. But he's a grown man, honey. You have to take him as he is because you're not going to change him." Her mom's wry smile popped out. "I learned the hard way that men aren't going to change their ways and there's nothing you can do about it."

Jules shook her head. "No. I can't believe that. If I do, then there's no hope for Erik to get on with his life."

"He was here, wasn't he? He took you out to dinner. What else do you want from the man?"

The question made her stop and think and the only thing she could come up with was, "Maybe everything."

"ERIK," Keegan called out as he opened the front door to Erik's house. "You home?"

"No, he's not. He went to the lab. What do you want, Keegan?"

Keegan stifled a sigh as he pulled the door closed behind him.

Katrina stood in the doorway to Erik's living room. Dressed in jeans that looked starched, a cream cable-knit sweater, her blond hair combed back and held with a clip at her neck, she looked wealthy, imperious, and cold. If she had superpowers, she'd be able to freeze a man into a block of ice at a hundred paces.

Maybe other people saw her differently but he didn't think so. She'd always been like this, at least for as long as Keegan had known her.

She'd been a challenge and, yeah, he realized that'd been part of her appeal. He'd wanted to be the man who cracked through that outer shell. He hadn't realized it wasn't a shell. That hardness went all the way through.

Reaching for calm, because all he wanted to do was shake some of that attitude out of her, Keegan stood his ground, "Hello, Katrina. How are you?"

Staring at him through narrowed eyes, she didn't answer right away. Probably looking for hidden meaning in his words.

After a few seconds, she sighed. "I'm fine. Thank you for asking."

Oh, so very polite. He could do polite. And get the hell out before he said anything to jeopardize what seemed like a truce.

"I'm glad to hear that. Sorry to have disturbed you."

He turned to leave but before he could, Katrina said, "Keegan, wait. Can I have a few minutes of your time?"

He smoothed out his expression, made sure none of his impatience showed. It'd only make things worse.

Facing her again, he nodded.

Her hand rose to play with her necklace, a heavy gold chain with what had to be a five-carat sapphire hanging from it. "Erik came to me for information. I just wanted you to know that I never would have poked my nose into your business otherwise."

Keegan's stomach tightened into a lead ball. "What information did he want from you?"

Katrina's chin went up and she managed to look down her nose at him even though she was several inches shorter. "I found the company that ordered the sabotage."

That lead ball became a red-hot bubble of lava. "And how exactly did you do that?"

Her mouth thinned even more. "By looking. For three years, you and Erik trusted the police to do their job. They didn't. They wrote off the explosion as an accident because it was easy and it was made to look like one. They didn't dig deep enough. And you kept telling Erik to let it go, to forget—"

"I wanted him to move on. Jesus, can't you see he needs to let this go?"

Finally, he saw emotion shimmer in her eyes. "How can he when every time he tries to talk to you about the explosion, you deflect him onto something else or blow him off? Damn it, Keegan, why were you so sure no one rigged that explosion?"

Katrina's voice had risen to a level he hadn't heard since the night she gave back his ring. Actually, she'd thrown it in his face but he couldn't think about that now. Not on top of the bombshell she'd just dropped.

"I'm not. Is that what you want to hear? I'm not sure the explosion wasn't sabotage. I also know if it was, someone inside our company might've helped. But letting Erik wallow in the past and what happened isn't going to help him deal with his scars. He needs to come out of this on his own."

"And finding out who was responsible will allow him to do that."

Keegan's anger started to boil. "You haven't been here. But I have. Every single day. I see how he struggles. And now, when he's finally started to come out of his shell, you show up and—"

"*I* show up?" Katrina was livid now. Her pale skin flushed bright red. "I show up and...what? Do you think I'm here just to interrupt your depraved games? Are you serious?"

"We don't play games." He bit off each word. "Just because you don't appreciate the lifestyle—"

"Lifestyle? Now your sex games are a *lifestyle*? I guess your new *friend*," she made the word sound like the filthiest curse, "lives the same lifestyle? How lucky for the three of you."

"I know you don't understand." He kept a vicious hold on his temper, which had almost reached the critical boil-over point. "I know you don't approve. But just because you think it's wrong doesn't mean you get to stick your nose in where it doesn't belong."

Katrina's eyes widened as that barb hit home and he felt like a complete and utter ass. Erik and Katrina had been close when they were younger. He knew Erik held some deep-seated guilt where she was concerned. He also knew there was something in Kat's past that had made her the way she was. But neither he nor Erik had been able to discover what that was.

"Damn it." Keegan rubbed the knot at the back of his neck. "I didn't mean that the way it sounded."

"No, you meant it exactly the way you said it. And trust me, I don't want to come between you two. Not again. But when my brother asks for my help, I give it to him. And now that I have, I'm going."

She turned on her heel and would've made a dignified exit except Keegan caught her arm. "Katrina, stop."

She did but she wouldn't turn to look at him and the arm he held went rigid as stone. "I don't want you to touch me."

He released her immediately. She sounded almost like she was going to cry. Which had to be his faulty hearing because the only time he'd ever seen Kat cry had been after Erik's accident. Which apparently hadn't been an accident.

"I'm sorry." He took a breath, put his thoughts in order. "I'm sorry for the way things ended between us. We both said things we shouldn't have, and I wish I could go back and do it again, but it doesn't change the fact that we were never going to be compatible."

She sliced a glance over her shoulder at him. "You're absolutely right. And we should remember that the next time we meet. Let's just retreat to our own corners now and go back to ignoring each other. I need to get my bag. My taxi will be here in a few minutes. Goodbye, Keegan."

She disappeared up the stairs before he could say anything more.

He stared after her for several long seconds before heading back to his car.

He needed to get to the lab.

SEVENTEEN

Erik had meant to do some testing on the new retinal scan they'd been perfecting for the past two years but he hadn't been able to concentrate.

Kat's discovery about Eggert Labs' sabotage wasn't unexpected. He'd known the explosion had been deliberate. And until TinMan had come along, Eggert had had a lock on the biometric security market.

So a little friendly sabotage made to look like an accident should've been expected. In the corporate world his dad worked in, it was part of doing business.

He didn't think whoever had ordered the sabotage had meant to harm anyone. Erik had simply been in the wrong place at the wrong time.

But now that he had evidence, it was damn hard not to want to go after them and bring down the behemoth. He and Keegan had both interviewed with Eggert before deciding to start their own business. They hadn't wanted to be wrapped up in corporate red tape while they worked.

So what are you going to do with the information?

He should hand it over to the police, let them do more digging. But a part of him wanted to exact his own revenge.

Sitting in his personal lab station, he spun his stool in a slow circle, his eyes open but not focused on anything.

What he really wanted to do was punch old man Eggert, owner of Eggert Labs. He had a tight leash on his company and he would've known what was happening. The bastard had even sent a card and flower arrangement after the accident.

What he wouldn't give to stuff that arrangement right up—

Shit.

He threw the tiny screwdriver he'd been holding at the table, swearing when it missed and fell to the floor.

Between his anger over the explosion and his thrill of victory after getting Jules to agree to his plan, there was no way he was going to get any work done. Even though it was Sunday and no one else was here to bug him, his brain was too fractured to work with any efficiency.

He kept flashing back to earlier today. Yes, Jules had agreed to this plan but neither she nor Keegan had seemed happy about it. He couldn't quite figure out why.

Didn't matter. They'd realize soon enough that this was the right way to handle the situation. None of them needed the hassle their relationship could bring if it went public.

Yes, last night's date had gone well but people would talk. They always did. Rumors would start. He didn't care if they talked about him, but he didn't want Jules to have to go through that again. Carol had relayed some of those rumors about Jules, though she assured them they held no truth.

Yes, she'd had an affair with a married man, who she'd had no idea was married. Erik figured he and Keegan were damn lucky she'd agreed to spend more time with them after they'd bribed her to have sex with them. It'd been an arrogant, selfish move and it'd been all his idea.

Still, it would work out for the best. It had to.

"Why the fuck did you go behind my back and get Katrina involved in our personal business?"

Erik's head snapped back at Keegan's harsh question.

His partner stood in the doorway to his lab, leaning against the frame as if he'd been there awhile. Maybe he had.

Taking a few seconds to formulate a reply, Erik gauged Keegan's emotions. Pissed but not furious. And not holding back his anger.

Good. He was glad to see the old Keegan reappearing. He'd seen more of that guy in the past few weeks than he had in the last two years.

"Because I needed to know what happened that night and she was willing to help me find out. I knew it wasn't an accident. Kat was the first person to actually listen to what I was saying and run with it."

"God damn it, Erik. It's not that I don't believe you. It's—"

"Bullshit." Erik felt his own anger immediately begin to churn. "I wish you'd just fucking admit that you thought I was chasing my tail on this one. Well, I'm not, so now we have to figure out what we're going to do."

Keegan didn't hesitate. "We give the information to the police and that's that. We let them handle it."

"They didn't handle it the first time, did they? They ruled it an accident, basically said it was my fault. Like I had a plan to blow the damn lab up with me in it. They were fucking incompetent. No, we find the dirt and go after them publicly. Hit them where it hurts. Strike at their reputation. Then we turn the information over to the cops and let them clean up the aftermath."

A muscle in Keegan's jaw started to flex, but he kept his mouth closed tight.

Erik shook his head in disgust. "You have nothing to say?"

"Yeah, I do. You're becoming obsessed again."

That stopped Erik dead. "What do you mean 'again'?"

"You know what I mean. You got like this a year ago. You barely ate or slept. All you did was try to figure out who rigged the explosion."

"So now you believe that someone deliberately sabotaged our lab? Well, damn, it only took you two years."

"Fuck you, Erik. That's not fair. Of course I want to know what really happened. I want whoever blew up our lab to rot in jail. And then I want you to let it go and actually live your damn life. Not spend every waking minute thinking about what happened to you and plotting revenge. I want you to move forward."

"What the fuck more do you want from me, Keegan? Jesus, I'm working. I'm even dating, for Christ's sake."

"And that's a great start. But it's not enough. And you know it."

"What exactly do you want me to do? You're not my psychiatrist, damn it."

"No, I'm not." Keegan crossed his arms over his chest. "And you don't have one of those anymore because you decided you were done."

"Because I was. I don't want to talk about my parents to anyone. I don't want to think about how I felt when they took off the bandages. I just want it all to disappear."

"And you know that's not going to happen. Erik—"

"No. I'm done. You're not the one living in my skin. You don't get to tell me how to feel or how to live my life. I don't give a fuck what other people think of me."

"What about Jules?"

"What about her? She's fine with our arrangement."

"How the hell would you know that? You pretty much told her what was going to happen. There was no discussion."

"This is the best solution to the problem and you know it."

Keegan looked like he wanted to keep arguing but managed to swallow whatever he was going to say. Instead, he said, "You're so fucking stubborn and you have an answer for everything, don't you?"

"For this, yeah, I do. Because it's the only solution."

Keegan took a deep breath and let it out on a sigh and Erik knew he'd gotten Keegan to give in.

"So when are we going to see her again?" He was done hashing this out. Time to push forward. Isn't that exactly what Keegan wanted?

"Don't you mean when will I call her to ask her out so we can see her again?"

Erik just stared at Keegan, holding on to his own temper.

Keegan shook his head. "I told her I'd call Tuesday. I assume you don't have anything planned."

He felt that jab like a blow to solar plexus. "You know I don't."

"Then I guess I'll see if she's available for dinner."

"And afterward, you can come to my house."

And get Jules in bed between them.

Sounded like the perfect plan.

And in the meantime, he'd figure out what he was going to do with the information he'd received from his sister.

"SO YOU REALLY DIDN'T KNOW?"

"Had no idea he was a guy. That'll make you think twice about saying yes to a date with a former lover's friend."

Jules laughed at Keegan's story as they walked through the door into Erik's home. They'd had a great dinner, talked about everything and anything, shared a few drinks, and managed not to bring up the one sore spot between them.

Jules found it amazing that after four dates with Keegan over the past ten days, they still found new subjects to discuss.

Guess that's what happens when you date men instead of boys.

Keegan might be soft-spoken when they were out in public but he had a dry wit she adored. They could talk for hours and never repeat themselves or fall into an awkward silence.

The only time that happened was when Erik's name came up. Then she'd felt they were missing a vital piece of the puzzle of their relationship.

"Sounds like you two had a good time tonight."

Erik smiled as he walked into the front room to meet them and her heart did a little happy dance as she turned toward his voice.

He's here. Now we're complete.

She crossed the room to wrap her arms around his waist and lift her face to his for a kiss.

When his lips settled on hers, he practically took her breath away. Pure domination laced with burning lust. She felt seared through, her lungs singed and every nerve ending energized.

When he finally let her up for air, she could only blink up at him for several seconds as he stepped away.

Did his smile look a little forced?

"We did," Keegan answered Erik's questions, walking over to stand by Jules' side and casually pulling her back against his chest, holding her there with one arm around her chest. "What'd you do all night?"

Erik didn't answer right away, his gaze tracking Keegan's movements before he looked up at his face. "Kept busy. Caught up on paperwork. Where'd you go tonight?"

"Viva. Good food. Nice and intimate."

A tiny muscle in Erik's jaw started to twitch and now she knew his smile was forced. "Good. So, either of you want a drink?"

"Not for me, thanks," Jules said. "I probably had enough at dinner."

"Keegan?"

Keegan shook his head. "I'm good."

Well, okay, then. They were all good. Now what?

Erik nodded, his expression pulling into a stiff mask that made his scars seem more prominent. His unscarred cheek had a slight red tinge and she wondered if he'd been drinking before they'd arrived. She hadn't tasted alcohol when he kissed her but...

And what would it matter if he had? He was a grown man. He didn't have to answer to anyone.

Including her.

"Then I guess I'll be drinking alone."

Was she imagining the hard edge she now heard in his voice? Why had this suddenly turned difficult?

The first night she and Keegan had gone out alone had been a little awkward but they'd managed to get through it before they'd hurried back to Erik's and spent several hours in bed. They'd repeated that the second date last Friday and again on Monday.

By Monday's date, however, she and Keegan hadn't mentioned Erik once. Which had made her feel disloyal.

Except he'd said this arrangement was what he wanted. He'd pushed the two of them to go out without him, to show the world they were a happy little couple, not some freak show with three heads.

But here, in the privacy of Erik's house, they could get their freak on all they wanted.

And they did. So much so, Jules would bet they'd broken the record for most orgasms in one night.

It'd be totally amazing...if she didn't feel like Erik was slipping farther into the shadows. Backsliding.

And they were allowing him to do it.

Erik poured himself a glass of whiskey from the bar across the room and took a healthy swallow before turning back to them.

With a little nudge from Keegan, Jules headed for the couch. Keegan kept going and sat on the chair opposite her.

There was definitely something up with him tonight and it made her stomach curl in on itself.

If this night was like the rest, they'd have a drink—or Erik would have a drink—then they'd head up to Erik's bedroom and make love for hours.

Since it was Friday and she had the day off tomorrow, she'd taken Erik's advice and packed a bag. Just a small one but her mom had known what she had in it. She hadn't said anything but Jules had seen that hint of worry in her eyes.

At least she wasn't making herself sick over how she was going to pay the bills and keep them in their home.

Keegan had grinned when he saw the bag but he hadn't said anything about it. He'd taken it from her and put it in the backseat. Where it remained, she realized. Keegan hadn't brought it in with them.

Oversight? Or had he done it deliberately? She wasn't sure what was going on in Keegan's head but it was increasingly obvious that something was.

Erik could sense it as well, and his confusion was quickly turning to frustration. Walking over to the couch, he leaned down to press a kiss to her lips before sitting on the couch next to her.

Then he stared straight at Keegan.

"Want to tell me what's going on?"

With Erik sitting so close to her, she felt how tightly he was holding himself. As if he was waiting for a blow.

A swirl of confusion settled low in her belly and she turned to Keegan. His expression made her want to reach out and stroke away the lines of tension around his eyes. She hadn't seen them during dinner, when it'd just been the two of them. Now...

Her lungs felt tight, almost as if they weren't working correctly.

Suddenly Keegan stood. "I'm not staying. I'm sorry, Jules. I just..." He stopped and ran a hand through his hair. "I just don't think I'd be very good company tonight. Dinner was amazing. Thank you for going with me. But...I think it's better if I leave."

She wanted to protest, wanted to reach for his hand and tell him not to go. Not because she didn't want to be alone with Erik but because she wanted them both. Together.

She felt something intangible starting to tear apart at the seams.

Erik's eyes narrowed and he rose to his feet as well. "Why?"

"I just told you." Keegan spoke slowly, a hint of an edge in every word. "I don't think I'll be good company tonight."

"Did something happen? Something between you and—"

"This has nothing to do with Jules."

Erik's frown held a world of confusion. "Then what the hell's going on with you? You've been miserable at work this past week. You don't talk much, and when you do, it's like pulling teeth."

"I've had a lot on my mind."

"Yeah, so have I, but I'm not acting like a dick."

"No, you're retreating again." Keegan's tone started to rise and the hair on Jules's neck stood on end. "Well, I'm sick of playing this game, Erik. I'm sick of watching you curl back into your hole, where you can hide and everyone comes to you instead of you coming out to meet them."

"What the fuck are you talking about?"

"I'm talking about the fact that after one date, you decided, for the three of us, that it would be better if *I* dated Jules. And you know, I'm not complaining. Not one fucking bit because there is no one else I would rather see."

Erik shook his head, true confusion starting to replace the anger. "Then what the hell's going on?"

"I have bent over backward to make this work." Keegan turned toward the door and started to walk away before turning on his heel and getting in Erik's face. "But it's not. Because you're still broken."

Jules cringed as Erik's eyes widened. He looked like Keegan had slapped him. "What the fuck—"

"Don't. Don't fucking deny it. I thought you were starting to come out of that hole you'd dug for yourself two years ago. The one that I allowed you to build, so yeah, I'll take some of the blame for this. Hell, a month ago I would've taken all the blame. But I'm not going to. Not anymore."

"I'm not living in a goddamn hole. I'm living my life the best way I know how to right now. I saw the way people looked at me that night we took Jules to dinner. I saw how they looked away. But did you notice how they looked at Jules? Did you even fucking care? No, you didn't. And you know why? Because your guilt is always right there. You wear it like a fucking badge of shame. You've got quite the fucking martyr complex, don't you?"

Both men were breathing like freight trains, staring each other down. Jules realized she was holding her own breath and sucked in air.

"Don't try to turn this back on me." Keegan sliced his hand

through air. "If you really wanted to live your life, you'd grow a pair and come *out* with us."

"That's what this is about?" Erik looked dumbfounded. "Seriously, you're pissed because I didn't come out with you and Jules on your dates?"

"No, you know that's not it. You're deliberately misunderstanding me."

"Then explain it so the feeble-minded among us can understand."

Keegan pulled back as if Erik had punched him. "Is that what you believe I think about you? That you're somehow mentally diminished because of the explosion?"

Erik's hands curled into fists at his sides, and Jules wanted to reach for him, wrap her hands around his, and make him uncurl his fingers. She wanted to step between them and make them stop but she was afraid they might not even see her.

"Isn't that exactly what you think? You've been treating me like a fucking invalid for years—"

"Because that's how you *acted*. God damn it, Erik—"

"No." Erik held up one hand. "Just...enough. It's bad enough you finally got the nerve to say exactly what you're thinking, but that you did it in front of Jules makes it so much worse."

Erik turned to her and she saw a torrent of pain and anger in his eyes.

"I'm sorry, Jules. I think it's probably best if Keegan takes you home tonight. I don't think I'll be in the right frame of mind to entertain."

"Erik—"

She and Keegan spoke at the same time but Erik cut them both off.

"That's it. I'm done. You've said what you wanted to say.

Apparently you've bottled that up for a few years. Do you feel better now, Keegan? I fucking hope so."

Erik turned to face Jules then and he wiped away the furious look on his face for her. But he couldn't rid himself of the deeper flush on his cheeks. That flush highlighted his scars and made her chest ache.

He'd never be without them. She knew that.

And maybe, just maybe, he was too damaged emotionally to ever have a normal relationship again.

"I'm sorry for trying to spare you drama we'd cause whenever we went out together, all three of us. It'd be a circus. You know that, Jules. We were both too fucking selfish to give you up. I honestly thought this was the best solution for all of us. Obviously, I was wrong."

"Erik, stop." She heard the pleading in her voice but couldn't stop. "Why don't we all take a deep breath and sit down and talk about this."

Erik just shook his head. "I think we're beyond that, babe. And I'm truly sorry."

Then he bent over the couch, over her, and sealed their lips together. "Let Keegan take you home. I'll talk to you soon."

With one last, burning look at Jules, Erik turned and walked out of the room.

EIGHTEEN

"You need to go back. You need to talk to him."

Keegan's hands tightened on the steering wheel as he drove Jules home. He heard her voice through the pounding of his pulse in his ears, heard the concern. Still, he shook his head.

"No. He made himself clear enough. He doesn't want to talk to me and he can be damn stubborn when he's angry."

Silence descended, so thick he swore he felt it press against his skin.

He glanced at Jules to find her staring at him with wide eyes.

"Angry? Are you serious?" She sounded shocked. "You practically tore his heart out. How can you not see how hurt he was?"

Because Erik wasn't hurt. Erik didn't get hurt anymore. The scar tissue from the burns had toughened him, inside and out.

Keegan's chest tightened but he forced himself to say, "He's not hurt. He's pissed because I told him the truth. Everyone's let him wallow for too damn long. Revenge is going to eat at him and warp him until there's nothing left of the old Erik and I can't watch him do that."

"Then you have to help him."

Frustration tasted like acid in his throat. "Do you think I haven't tried? Do you think I don't want the bastard who did this to him to rot in jail? Of course I do. But if I tell Erik to send the information Katrina dug up to police, he'll say no."

"You don't know that."

"Yeah, I do. He wants to go after Eggert himself. You haven't known Erik as long as I have, Jules. You don't know him like I do."

She fell silent again and he felt her tension ratchet up another notch.

Sonuvabitch. You're an idiot. Are you fucking trying to alienate her?

Between this tension with Erik and the uncertainty with Jules, his head was spinning. What the fuck was wrong with him? His stomach rolled and his fingers began to ache with the force of his hold on the steering wheel.

"Shit, Jules, I'm sorry. I didn't mean—"

"No." She held up one hand and he bit off the rest of his words. "No, you're right. I don't know either of you as well as you know each other. But have you considered that maybe you're too close to the situation to see it clearly?"

He wanted to growl, he was so fucking frustrated. Yes, he was too damn close to the situation. He and Erik had known each other too long and cared for each other too damn much not to be.

He loved the guy like a brother, their lives entangled in so many ways. He couldn't imagine going to the lab and not working beside him or spend a weekend without catching a meal or hanging out. Just the thought created a knot in his stomach.

Since the accident, their relationship had become even more complicated as they spent more time together. Other friends had drifted away. Some because of Erik's accident, some because they just hadn't done enough to keep them close.

And then they'd added Jules to the mix...

Jesus.

He took a deep breath. "What I think is that Erik just needs a few days to cool off. Katrina laid a huge amount of shit on him all at once. He needs to process."

"And then what?" Jules's disbelief came through loud and clear. "You think he'll just decide that you're right and that's the end of it?" She paused. "Would you?"

No, of course he wouldn't.

Still... "He just needs some time. Kat waylaid him—"

"No." She turned more fully in her seat toward him. "You know this isn't his sister's fault, right? She's just the messenger."

One who hated him enough to try to screw up his relationship with Erik. "Who'd be more than thrilled if Erik and I never worked together again."

"Do you really believe that?"

"I know it. She told me as much after Erik decided he wasn't going through with any more operations."

"Well, obviously he didn't listen to her because you two are still in business together."

Yeah, they were.

But for how long?

Christ, had just a few words completely screwed up their working and personal relationships?

Damn Katrina—

No. No, he knew that wasn't fair. As much as he'd like to blame Erik's sister for this, he knew it wasn't her fault. Not all of it.

She loved Erik. At least as much as she could love anyone, she loved her brother. And Erik had always been protective of her. Erik had bit his tongue when he and Katrina had started to date. And when they'd gotten engaged, the only thing Erik had said was, "You better be really sure you know what you're doing because if you hurt her..."

He'd left the rest unsaid, but Keegan had known what Erik meant.

And when he and Katrina had called it off, Keegan had expected Erik to call off their fledgling partnership.

He hadn't, though, but that was only because Kat had told him not to. At least she'd been able to get past the bitterness that had consumed her to see that what he and Erik were building was better than anything they could have made apart, and they'd gone on to build TinMan into the company it was today.

Keegan had to believe they'd survive this as well.

"Keegan?"

He sliced Jules a quick glance, saw the worry in her eyes... and realized he wasn't the only one with something to lose here.

"Yes?"

"Promise me you'll go back and check on him. As soon as you drop me off."

"I plan to." The words dropped out of his mouth immediately and he knew he hadn't said them just because she wanted him to.

Her mouth twitched into a sad smile that quickly faded. "Good."

He grabbed her hand lying on her thigh. "Don't worry. We'll figure this out."

Her smile reappeared for an even shorter amount of time. "I hope so."

Hating the worry he heard in her voice, he squeezed her hand. "He's stubborn, not stupid. We'll get through this. Just... don't abandon us."

Her fingers slipped between his and clung. "Of course not."

But she looked less than reassured when he forced a smile for her.

And the pit in his stomach opened a little wider.

They reached her house minutes later, the silence widening the chasm growing between them. A chasm he didn't know how to fix. He had way too much stuff running through his head right now.

Most of the house was dark; the only light he could see shone through the window next to the front door. Jules's mom was probably already in bed. It was close to midnight and most of the houses on the street were dark.

The growing need to turn around and drive back to Erik's made every muscle in his body tighten. They should hash this out now. The three of them. Together.

But he knew if they did, he and Erik would go right back to yelling at each other. And he didn't want Jules to see that.

We'll figure this out. Then we'll worry about Jules.

Jules got out of the car without saying a word. She didn't wait for him to open the door for her. She even got to her bag in the backseat before he could help her.

Walking beside her to the front door, he wanted to wrap his hand in the long, silky hair that hung down the back of her coat. Wanted to pull her against him and seal his mouth over hers and kiss her until she melted against him.

He wanted that so badly, he had to fist his hand in his pocket to keep from reaching for her.

When she stopped at the door and turned to face him, her sad excuse for a smile made him want to punch the brick wall.

"Thanks for dinner. I really..." She sighed. "You know I enjoy spending time with you, don't you, Keegan?"

His heart began to race but instead of pumping his fist in the air, he settled for a nod, lifting his hand to cup her cheek. "Yeah, I do. And I hope you realize the feeling's mutual."

She nodded, rubbing her cheek against his palm. "Talk to Erik. And call me. Soon."

"I will. Jules..."

Her lips curved into a sweet smile. Rising on her toes, she pressed a heated kiss against his lips. "Good night, Keegan."

ERIK STALKED THROUGH HIS HOUSE, wanting to throw something, but the person he wanted to throw something at wasn't here for target practice.

Instead, he headed to the basement.

When he'd remodeled the house, he'd had the basement completely redone into a gym. He'd made sure the area was open and bright. And had no mirrors. That's the main thing he'd hated about going to physical therapy...all those damn mirrors.

Now dressed in sneakers, gym shorts, and a tank top, he started with the bench press but shoving heavy metal around wasn't doing it for him tonight.

So...treadmill.

Setting the speed at a steady eight-minute mile, he pounded away. It was always slow going at first. He used to run outside but after the accident... Well, he didn't do much of that anymore.

Mostly he used the gym at the lab. They'd had it installed as an incentive for their employees but he and Keegan—

His foot nearly slipped and he had to jump onto the stationary sides to get his balance.

Damn him.

What right did Keegan have to talk to him like that?

The right of a best friend, maybe?

His jaw tightened until he swore it'd pop out of joint.

But Keegan had him all wrong. How could his best friend

not know how important the information was that his sister had brought?

How could Keegan expect him to ignore the fact that their major competitor had tried to cripple their business and nearly killed him in the process?

All right, no. Keegan didn't want him to ignore it. Keegan wanted him to pass it off to the cops. Who'd already bungled the investigation the first time, according to his sister.

Anger began to burn in his gut again and he kept pushing the speed higher.

It'd been three fucking years since the explosion. Three years of pain and heartache and operations and coming to terms with the fact that he would never be the same person he'd been before.

But you are the person Jules takes to bed with her.

He nearly lost his footing again but managed to keep steady. Punching in a lower speed, he adjusted his pace and sucked in air until he could breathe regularly. He hadn't realized he'd been gasping.

Would she have liked him before the explosion?

He'd like to think the answer to that question was yes but... he wasn't the same person.

That guy had been interested in two things—making money and getting laid. Okay, three. Partying.

And three years ago, Jules hadn't been old enough to drink and had been supporting her mom through her cancer treatment.

Christ, he was an ass.

But that didn't change the fact that Keegan continued to want to stick his head in the sand about what had happened. Wanted to let it go.

He couldn't let it go.

With a sigh, he brought the treadmill to a walk then finally to a full stop.

Sweat dripped down his body, his clothes soaked through. He should go upstairs and take a shower then head to bed. Hopefully he'd worn himself out enough that he could sleep.

Because he had a hell of a lot to sleep on.

Grabbing a towel from the pile on the weight bench, he turned—

And found Keegan sitting on the stairs, staring at him.

"You almost killed yourself on that thing." Keegan shook his head. "Erik—"

"Why are you here?"

Keegan drew in a deep breath and let it out in a rush. "Jules thought we should talk."

Erik tilted his head back. "Just Jules?"

Keegan's jaw tightened. "No, not just Jules."

Tossing the towel away, Erik took the stairs two at a time, passing Keegan without a glance, knowing he'd follow.

Without a word, he headed for the kitchen to get some water, Keegan close at his heels. The anger he thought he'd worked out of his system was creeping back, curling his hands into fists.

Fuck water. He needed something stronger.

For so long he hadn't been able to drink alcohol. It had fucked with all the pain pills and antibiotics and other shit he'd been taking. In the past year, he'd been able to tolerate a drink or two at a time. But he hadn't gotten crazy, sloppy drunk. Not like he used to do. Before the explosion.

Some people might say he'd matured.

Well, tonight was the night he proved them wrong.

As he stalked to the bar near the fireplace, he was acutely aware of Keegan's measured footsteps behind him. For some reason, the sound made him furious. He felt the rage building, felt it singe his stomach.

By the time he'd poured a glass of whiskey and downed half of it in one swallow, he knew he wasn't going to be able to hold his tongue this time.

Earlier, with Jules between them, he'd barely kept his tone civil. Every word Keegan had said had made him bleed. Erik wanted to return the favor.

Keegan walked up beside him and poured himself a drink when Erik didn't offer.

They stood next to each other in silence for at least a minute.

Finally, Erik turned to face his best friend. But he didn't say anything and Keegan took the cue.

"I don't think you're an invalid." Keegan continued to stare at the wall in front of him. "And I'm not unaware of how people looked at Jules that night."

Erik waited, knowing Keegan wasn't finished. Not trusting himself to say something that would make them start yelling at each other again.

And this time, he wasn't sure they wouldn't say something irrevocable. The fact that Keegan had returned didn't mean much. Erik had known he would. If he hadn't come back tonight, he would have tomorrow. Keegan couldn't bear to let things fester.

Erik could go days without talking if someone pissed him off.

"You want to go after Eggert," Keegan said. "I get it. I do. I just...don't think you'll be satisfied with the result."

Erik frowned. "What do you mean?"

With a sigh, Keegan turned to face him, his expression tired. Sad. "Short of blowing up his lab, what can you do to him that will make what you went through better?"

Erik wanted to rip into Keegan's logic, tear it apart bit by bit. He'd had years to think about what he would do when he discovered who'd torn his life apart. None of those scenarios involved handing over the information to the police so they could fuck up the investigation even more than they had already.

"Nothing will ever make what I went through better."

"Exactly." Keegan's steady gaze held his. "Give the information to the cops and let them handle it."

Erik held on to his temper by a thread. "And what if they don't do anything? What if they can't do anything? No. I'll handle this my way. And I need you to be onboard with that."

"And if I'm not?"

"Then I need you to back away."

"Erik—"

"No. Just listen to me."

Keegan looked like he was biting his tongue but he nodded.

Erik took a deep breath. "You have no idea how I feel. How utterly fucking pissed off I have been for so damn long. It's eating me up from the inside. For three years, it's been a living, breathing cancer in my gut. The rage never goes away. All the therapy in the world isn't going to make it better. No amount of talking about it or ignoring it is going to ease it. Bringing down Eggert for what he did... That will make it better."

"How do you know? Erik, you could end up just like the bastard who did this to you."

"Do you honestly think I'm going to go blow up his labs? Do you really think, after what I went through, that I would purposely put anyone else's life in danger the way mine was?"

Keegan had the grace to look ashamed. "No, I don't think you'd ever do anything like that."

"Then why can't you trust me to handle this?"

Keegan shook his head and looked into his almost-empty

glass. "I told you. I don't want you to crawl in that hole again. The one where all you think about is screwing the person who screwed you. I thought..."

Since Erik didn't know where Keegan was going with that, he said, "You thought what?"

"I thought we were going to take our relationship with Jules to the next level."

Erik's guts twisted and he tried to tamp down the surge of emotion. "Have you really thought about what that relationship might be? Seriously, how does a three-way relationship work in the real world? And she's only twenty-two. We gave her enough money to do whatever the hell she wants. She's talked about culinary school. The good ones are in New York and Philadelphia, and those are only the local ones. The great ones are in Europe. Do we really want to tie her here?"

Keegan's gaze remained on his glass. "I'm not talking about tying her anywhere."

"But *we're* tied to this place. This is our home. This is where we work. Our entire lives are settled *here*."

Keegan's jaw flexed. "Do you think I haven't considered these same things?"

"I'm not really sure you have." Erik shook his head when Keegan finally shifted his gaze to meet his. "No, just listen. I'm trying to be reasonable here. We set this up thinking it was for one night. And it was a damn great night. So fucking great neither of us wanted to let it go."

"And neither did Jules."

"No, she didn't. But, god damn, she's young. And she's got dreams. Just like we did when we were her age. We made our dreams a reality. Why shouldn't she have the same opportunity?"

Keegan poured himself another drink then began to pace. "Maybe I don't want to be fucking reasonable about this."

"And maybe it's not our call."

"Then why don't we let her make that decision herself?"

"Because I see her struggling to work out her position between the two of us and maybe there's just no solution."

Keegan stopped in front of the fireplace, spearing him with a glance. "And what the fuck does that mean?"

Erik took a deep breath. "Maybe that means I step back."

Keegan shook his head. "From what?"

"From between the two of you."

Keegan shook his head, a faint sneer on his lips. "And what would that solve? Do you think she'll want to continue seeing only me?"

"Don't you?"

Keegan's eyes flashed wide. "Christ, Erik. If she wants to continue seeing anyone, it'll be you. Don't you see the way she looks at you? She's halfway to being in love with you and you want to back away and let me take your place? No way."

"Fuck that, Keegan. I see a young woman who's had a rough life and now she's dating two men who gave her a shitload of money and great sex. She hasn't had to deal with the reality of a relationship with two guys and how she'll be treated by the rest of the world. You just don't get it—"

"Oh no, I get it. You're letting your experience overshadow every aspect of our lives—"

"We have separate lives, Keegan. Or have you forgotten that?"

Keegan blinked. "I thought we were partners."

"We are. We're business partners." And the sooner Keegan realized that their business partnership and their friendship should no longer mix with their personal relationships, the better.

"We're friends first." Keegan's voice held a fierce tone. "We agreed that's how we'd run our business."

"Of course we are. But we're not lovers. We don't owe each other every minute of every day. At some point, we're going to have wives and children and actually spend a holiday apart."

Eyes narrowed, Keegan stared at him with an intensity that practically burned. "Is that what this is all about? You want me to back off?"

Just the thought made Erik cringe but he covered it with a shrug. "I'm saying maybe we've become too dependent on each other."

Keegan just stared at him, like he was trying to read his mind. If he could, he'd probably only hear static.

Erik was forcing words out of his mouth, but he wasn't sure they were what he wanted to say. He only knew he had to do something.

In some ways, Keegan was right. Erik could lose himself bringing down Eggert. At this moment, it was a price he was willing to pay. Even if it meant he lost Jules and Keegan.

You don't really mean that.

Yes, damn it, he did.

And now he was fucking arguing with himself.

He needed to stand firm. For all of them. He'd been an anchor around Keegan's neck for too damn long, stopping the guy from having a life of his own. This whole situation just proved it.

"You're actually serious, aren't you?" Keegan shook his head. "You're going to trash this relationship for revenge?"

Erik rolled his eyes, forcing himself to sell a position he didn't completely believe in. "You sound like a damn TV show. That's not what I'm doing. Damn it, Keegan. How can you be so thick? I'm practically giving Jules to you on a plate and you're fighting me!"

"She's not a fucking carnival prize!"

A bright flush suffused Keegan's cheeks and now Erik saw

not only anger but hurt in his friend's eyes. Stiffening his back, he shook his head.

"I know that. I also know she shouldn't be stuck in between us any longer."

Keegan slammed his glass onto the nearest table, so hard Erik expected it to shatter.

Good metaphor, huh?

"Jules insisted I come back here. She wanted me to talk some sense into you. But you're just not going to listen."

"I heard everything you said. I just don't think you're right."

Silence fell and every breath he took felt like he was drawing broken glass into his lungs. But he kept his expression clear, refused to let Keegan see his conflicting feelings.

This had to be done and it had to be done now.

Erik set his own empty glass next to Keegan's. "I'm going to bed. I'll see you Monday morning."

Minutes later, in his room, he heard Keegan's car start then drive away.

He sat on the edge of his bed and stared at the wall for minutes before he threw off his clothes and crawled under the covers.

NINETEEN

"I didn't expect to see you this morning. Is everything okay?"

Sitting at the kitchen table, Jules had her head propped on her hand, staring out the window into their tiny backyard. It looked so desolate out there without the flowers her mom cultivated spring through fall.

Her mom said digging in the dirt helped her work out a lot of her anxieties during her cancer treatment.

Jules did the same with bread dough. Which was why, at 8:30 in the morning, she already had a loaf in the oven and had just put another in a bowl to rise.

"No, I don't think it is."

"Okay." Her mom poured a cup of coffee and joined Jules at the table. "Tell me what's going on."

"I think...I might not be seeing Erik anymore."

Her mom's expression didn't change. "And why do you think that?"

"Because last night he and Keegan had a fight."

"About what?" her mom prompted when she paused.

"Keegan accused Erik of being broken. And I'm not sure he's wrong."

Her mom frowned. "Broken how?"

"Like maybe he'll never be able to live a normal life. Maybe the psychological damage is too severe. Or maybe he just doesn't want to move on with his life."

Her mom nodded, as if she understood completely. Jules certainly wished she did.

"And what if he is? Would that change your feelings for him?"

"No," she answered immediately and truthfully. "But I'm not sure my feelings will change what he wants."

"And what is that?"

"To get back at the people who caused the explosion."

Horror plainly showed on her mom's expression. "Someone actually tried to kill him? Oh my god, that's awful."

"They didn't want to kill him. They only wanted to damage the lab. They didn't know he was working. But...yeah, someone set up the explosion to look like an accident."

"Well, I can certainly understand why he'd want to punish whoever did it. If I could've blamed someone for my cancer and taken out my anger on them, you're damn right I would have."

"But this isn't cancer. It's a crime. Keegan wants Erik to give the information to the police. Erik wants to handle it himself."

"And that's what they're fighting about?"

"I think that's only part of it. They just seemed so angry at each other for something they should've been able to talk out. I don't know how to help."

Her mom shook her head. "Honey, I'm not sure you can. These men have known each other for a lot of years. They own a business together. They have a relationship you might never be able to be part of."

Wincing, Jules realized her mom had put into words exactly what she'd been worried about. "So what do you think I should do?

"I think you need to give them a few days. Let things cool off. If they come to you, that's great. But..."

Her mom sighed.

"But what?"

"But I think you should be prepared."

Her mom's sad, apologetic smile made Jules's heart hurt but she didn't need to ask what to be prepared for.

It would be nothing good.

"CAROL?" Jules stuck her head through the open office doorway Monday morning. "Can I talk to you for a minute?"

Her friend's head popped up from behind her laptop screen, a smile curving her lips. "Sure, Julianne. Come on in. What's up?"

Jules walked into Carol's office behind the kitchens she'd built for her catering business. She loved the open work space, the granite countertops, and the professional-grade ranges. When she was here, she felt like she was in her element. Like she belonged.

"I've been thinking about something and I wanted to run it by you."

Closing the laptop, Carol leaned back in her chair and gave Jules her entire attention. "Absolutely."

Even though she'd rehearsed exactly what she wanted to say, it was still difficult to get the words out. Sliding into the seat opposite Carol gave her an excuse to stall just a little more but finally she couldn't any longer.

"I'm thinking about attending the CIA in the fall."

Carol's eyebrows arched higher as her smile spread. "Oh, wow. That would be great! I mean, I'll be sorry to see you go but it's a great school."

The Culinary Institute of America was one of the leading culinary schools in the country. Jules had never even considered applying because she knew she wouldn't be able to afford it. It'd been nothing more than a pipe dream.

Now...

She had the money. But it meant she'd have to move to New York.

Away from her mom, her friends, her job. Away from Keegan and Erik.

"I'm not sure yet," she hedged. "But my mom's doing really well and now...now I have the money."

More than enough to pay her tuition and room and board. Thanks to Keegan and Erik.

Who were the reasons she hesitated.

"And the problem is...?"

Carol's tone suggested she knew what the problem was.

Sighing, Jules propped her elbow on the arm of the chair and let her head fall into her hand. "I'm not sure I want to leave."

Carol nodded, her expression sympathetic. "And does that have something to do with a couple of mutual friends?"

Jules bit her lip, knowing this was exactly why she'd come to Carol, but afraid to discover that maybe Erik and Keegan had already moved on. It had been three days since Keegan had said goodbye after that night. Both men had promised to be in touch. Neither had.

She'd gone from upset to pissed off to depressed and back to pissed off.

Today, she was just worried.

"Have you seen them lately? Or heard from them?"

Carol shook her head. "Not for a few weeks. I...thought they were busy. With you. Did something happen?"

"Yes. And no. Jeez, everything is just so screwed up."

Carol's face twisted in sympathy. "And so much of this is my fault. I'm sorry, Jules, I never should've—"

"No, Carol. No. It's not your fault. I could have said no."

Carol grimaced. "But I knew you wouldn't. I knew you needed the money. And I knew I couldn't loan you that much. I knew you and your mom had gotten all the credit you were going to get. I knew this was such a screwed-up situation to begin with and I did it anyway. But I honestly thought..."

Carol's eyes closed as she shook her head, taking a deep breath.

"Thought what?" Jules prompted.

Carol stared straight at her. "I honestly thought you'd be good for them. I've known them for years. I've seen how Erik's situation has affected them both. I know you didn't know them before but...Erik was one of those people who had a good time no matter what he was doing. He genuinely loved life and he dragged Keegan out of his shell."

Leaning back in her chair, Jules listened, nodding at Carol to go on.

"Erik's accident changed them both at a fundamental level, and I really thought they'd never recover. That it would tear apart their friendship and their business. But what it did was draw them tighter together and alienated everyone else. I couldn't bear to watch. Then they saw you and I saw a spark of that old life come back into Erik's eyes."

Jules shook her head. "Did you honestly think one night with me would solve all of Erik's problems? Because I think everything's gotten so much worse."

"So tell me what happened."

As Jules told her about the previous night, she saw Carol's expression become more and more distressed until finally she held up her hand. Jules had just gotten to the part about the accident being rigged.

"Oh my god. Poor Erik. He must have been devastated. And Keegan... Jesus. So what are they going to do?"

"I'm not really sure. I haven't seen them since early Sunday morning."

Carol fell silent for several seconds, her gaze boring into Jules's as she sorted through what Jules had told her. And what she hadn't.

"So let me guess. Erik said something stupid, Keegan tried to smooth it over, and they ended up pissed off at each other and not talking. And now you're caught in the middle."

It was close enough that Jules nodded. "Pretty much, yeah. I haven't heard from them since then. And I'm afraid I won't."

"Do you want to? Hear from them again, I mean. Or is that why you've decided to finally move on with your life and go to culinary school?"

Jules's nose wrinkled as she grimaced. "I guess it would be nice if I figured that out, hmm?"

Carol smiled. "Yes, it would probably make your decision much easier. But then, I'm not sure anything will make this decision easier." After a short pause, she said, "Jules...can I ask... do you love them?"

Jules didn't answer right away. She didn't want to blurt out "Yes" and have Carol doubt her. She took her time to think.

"Honestly, I don't know. What I feel for them is so wrapped up in how we first met and the sex and the emotion and, truthfully, the money just complicates everything."

Grimacing, Carol nodded. "Money usually does."

"It's just...I think I do. Love them." And just saying the words out loud made her heart thump in agreement. "But what if..."

She couldn't finish the sentence because she wasn't sure she knew what she wanted to say.

What if they don't love me back? I'll be heartbroken twice.

"Yeah, that's a big 'what if,' isn't it?" Apparently Carol understood. "I honestly don't know what to tell you. I love those guys like brothers but I know how they can be. They're stubborn as hell and they both think they're right about everything. Being in the middle of that is difficult, I'm sure. Just...don't let it scare you away. Not if this relationship is something you really want."

And is it?

Was it worth fighting for? There was just so much involved, from Erik's scars to Keegan's guilt, from the money that would allow her to leave this place behind to her guilt at wanting to leave her mom.

And that didn't even take into account what people in their community would think when they found out she was sleeping with both of them. Some of them already had a less-than-good opinion of her.

"It just seems like there's too many hurdles." The words came out in an almost whispered hush, and shame curled in her gut. "And that sounds like I'm taking the easy way out."

"Honey, no one could ever accuse you of running from a difficult situation. And even if they did, they don't know you and you shouldn't give a shit about what they think."

Jules nodded. "But you know it's just not that simple. Erik and Keegan have a business. A hugely successful business. They have to deal with people from all over the world—"

"Now wait a sec. Are we talking about the same men?" Carol's amusement shone through her wry smile. "Keegan hates that aspect of the job, dealing with the boardroom stuff. Erik used to handle it before the acci—well, before the explosion. But even he didn't really have the patience for it. Yes, he loved the party aspect of it but he hated the actual business aspect of it. Now, you know he won't go near a cocktail party. Keegan does some of the social appearances when it's absolutely necessary but he hates it even more than Erik, I think. They hire people to handle that stuff."

"But their reputation—"

"May be slightly dinged if a few narrow-minded people decide to stick their noses in other people's business. But they are *way* too good at what they do for people to discount simply because they both choose to love the same girl."

"And what if they don't love me? What if I never hear from them again?"

Carol huffed. "Then they're idiots and I'm going to go smack them. I honestly don't see that happening but, Jules, the relationship has to be right for you, too."

Carol paused, as if she could tell she'd hit a nerve. And she had. Jules hadn't really thought about the situation in those terms before. In how it affected her personally.

"The guys already know how to deal with each other," Carol continued as Jules's head continued to spin. "But you have to deal with both of them and that could drive any woman over the edge. Have you really thought about what your life'll be like if you make this relationship permanent? About the reality of living and loving two men day in and day out?"

When Jules just stared at her, Carol's lips quirked.

"Sometimes what we want isn't what we need. Sure, a buffet is great but you know if you gorge, you're going to make yourself sick."

BY THURSDAY AFTERNOON, Keegan was ready to climb the walls.

He and Erik hadn't spoken since Saturday night. Erik had deliberately evaded him at the lab and Keegan had let him. And if he were being the least bit honest, he'd admit he hadn't gone out of his way to run into Erik.

So they were both in avoidance mode. *Great.*

What sucked was that Keegan didn't know what to do about it.

Sitting in his office, which he rarely used unless he wanted to make a phone call away from the noise and general chaos of the lab, he stared at the wall.

He and Erik had hired the best people they could find for the jobs they'd created but they'd also hired people they could get along with. The three developers had come from Princeton, were a few years younger than he and Keegan and just as brilliant. To a degree, they all shared Keegan and Erik's sensibilities and their slightly offbeat approach to science.

They also had an additional five technicians and an office manager who kept them all on a short leash. They'd hired Sandra Keating five minutes into her interview when she'd told them she'd raised five boys with her Navy husband around the world and had never seen a group of people more in need of a drill sergeant than this building of misfits.

When Erik had been in the hospital, she'd been one of the first people to visit. She'd sat by his bed, held his hand, and kept him informed of everything going on at the office. She'd never once cried in Erik's presence, but Keegan had caught her sobbing in her husband's arms when he'd come to pick her up.

Keegan had still been in shock at that point, going from the hospital to the lab with absolutely no purpose or direction. Seeing Sandra, who always looked so calm and collected with her perfectly styled blond hair and polished nails, break down had knocked Keegan out of his free fall.

The office had needed someone to step up and pull them all back together. Keegan had managed it. Barely.

Now Sandra entered his office in her sensible shoes and her

khaki pants and white blouse and stared at him with the same look in her eye she'd given Erik when he'd first come back to work and refused to go to a staff meeting. Erik had been there minutes later.

"All right, I want to know what's going on and what's going to need to happen to fix it."

Keegan blinked before he could stop himself. "I don't know what you're talking about."

Sandra cocked her head at him, eyes wide, and Keegan braced for the snark attack. "Oh really? So you haven't noticed that you and Erik haven't been in the same room together at this entire week? Or that you haven't spoken to him all week? Or that the staff is starting to wonder if they're going to have jobs next month if you two don't figure out your shit and kiss and make up or whatever the hell you need to do to fix whatever happened?"

Her husband might've been the one in the service, but Sandra was the family's commanding officer. And TinMan's, too. He and Erik owned the business, but she kept it running like a well-oiled machine.

Since Sandra appeared to want an answer and didn't look like she was going anywhere until she got it, Keegan nodded. "We'll figure it out. There's nothing to worry about."

Sandra's eyes widened even farther. "Okay, that was the lamest bullshit I've ever heard come out of your mouth, Keegan." Her hands went to her hips and Keegan sat a little straighter in his chair. "What the hell is going on? And don't tell me nothing. I certainly know that's not true."

"It's...complicated."

"Son, life's complicated. Did you two have a lovers' spat?"

Keegan sighed, knowing Sandra didn't mean her question literally. She'd asked point blank when she'd taken the job if he and Erik were a couple. She'd quickly pointed out she wasn't homophobic. She made it clear she believed everyone had a right to love whoever they wanted, so long as it wasn't a kid or livestock. She only wanted to know because working with a couple was a completely different dynamic than working with two friends.

"We've had a...disagreement. I'm sure we'll be able to work it out."

"You know your Irish comes out when you're lying. Surefire tell, kid."

He grimaced before he could hide it. Sandra, of course, saw it. Turning, she shut the door behind her then sat in the chair opposite him.

"Now, you want to tell me what's really on your mind? You know I don't blab and you both looked like you got kicked in the nuts this past week. I'm cracking you first because you're easier but I'll be going after Erik next. Now spill. I don't like to see my guys bleed."

Keegan thought it over for barely a second. Sandra had worked with them for more than five years. She knew them almost as well as she knew her own children, and he trusted her implicitly.

"We've been seeing a woman."

She barely batted an eye. "We? As in, you're both seeing the same woman?"

"Yes."

A pause. "At the same time."

That wasn't a question but he nodded anyway.

"And how's that working out for you?"

Sighing, he shoved a hand through his hair. "It was working fine until about a week ago. Or so I thought."

Now her eyebrows lifted. "Seems to me it wouldn't work at all, but knowing how connected you two are... Maybe you want to walk me through what happened."

So he did, laying it all out for her.

At first, he couldn't hide the blush that flooded his cheeks. He never talked to anyone but Erik about relationship stuff. Hell, even he and Erik didn't talk much. They just barreled ahead and damned the consequences.

But the more he talked, the easier it got. He and Erik often relied on Sandra to see things they didn't, especially things that dealt with interaction between multiple parties.

Of course, for Sandra, that sometimes involved knocking heads together, figuratively and literally.

When he finally finished, she cocked her head and looked at him for several long seconds. "So let me get this straight. You bribed this girl with half a million dollars to sleep with you and Erik. A girl who needed that money to pay for her sick mother's hospital bills. A girl you knew couldn't really say no."

He sucked in a sharp breath as her words slapped him. Every one of them was true. "Yes. We did."

"And when that night was over, what happened? Did you call her?"

"No, I went to see her."

"You? Alone?"

"Yes."

"And...?"

"And we had sex." He had to force the words from between his gritted teeth.

Sandra sighed. "And after that?"

"I left her. I fucking left her to deal." Exploding to his feet, he began to pace. "I let Erik pick up the pieces with her, but when I walked in on them together... I was a total ass."

"And what did she do?"

His turn to pause. And think. "She forgave me."

"And you and Erik have been, uh, dating her since then. And by date you mean actually taking her out and buying her dinner? Unless you're using the word 'date' in a completely different way than I'm used to."

"No, Erik and I actually took her to dinner at Judy's."

Sandra's eyes widened in true surprise. "Erik went along? Actually *went* to the restaurant when other people were there?"

"Yeah. I thought..."

"You thought he was fixed."

Keegan grimaced. "No, not fixed. But maybe, just... Fuck, I don't know." He shoved a hand through his hair and yanked, letting his scalp burn. "Yeah, maybe I thought he was finally fixed."

"So this girl has some magical power to heal all of Erik's wounds *and* fix your terminal case of the guilts?"

"Shit. I know it sounds ridiculous. I'm not stupid. But I thought, maybe..."

"He was starting to believe he could live again." Sandra's compassion bled through every word. "I get it, Keegan. Really, I do. And I'm encouraged to hear he actually went to the restaurant. Hell, I would've thrown a damn party if I'd known."

"Yeah, well, don't throw that party just yet. After that night, he told me he wanted me to take her out by myself. His excuse was that he didn't want people to talk about her. He didn't want her to have to deal with the gossip."

She made a face that indicated she agreed. "Sounds reasonable."

"No, it wasn't. He only suggested it so he could go back in his safe little cave."

"Is that all?"

He considered telling her about the explosion, but they hadn't decided exactly what they were going to do with that information yet. Hell, they hadn't talked period. It was stupid but talking about their three-way affair was easier than talking about the fact that the explosion had been rigged by one of their biggest competitors.

Or maybe his priorities were just totally fucked up.

"Keegan?"

"Jesus, am I being a complete and total ass?"

"No." Sandra's concise answer made him breathe an immediate sigh of relief. "But...for three years, Erik's considered himself the monster in the closet. That's not going to change overnight because he's fallen in love or because you want him to be fixed."

"I know that. I do. I just..."

"Don't want him to be broken anymore. I get it, Keegan. I want the same thing. But Erik has to want it even more than you do. And I'm not sure he's there yet. You pushing him might set him back." She shrugged. "Then again, if you don't push him, he might never move forward. You have to find a healthy balance."

"Yeah. And how the hell do I find that?"

"Sometimes," Sandra's smile turned bittersweet, "sometimes you don't. Sometimes you just have to barrel through and hope like hell that everything comes out for the best in the end."

"And what if it doesn't? What if I fuck this all up by forcing him too far, too fast?"

"Then you'll know you at least tried something. But first, you need to apologize to this girl. It sounds like you really screwed her over."

They had. They'd both treated her like shit. He should've called, should've checked in on her. Instead, he'd avoided her like a coward.

"I know. I have to call her, apologize. Beg for mercy, even. But..."

Sandra's eyebrows quirked. "Erik."

"Yeah."

"Well now, that's the trickier problem, isn't it? You two haven't talked at all?"

She made it sound like they were teenage girls having a snit. And she probably wasn't far off the mark. He did feel somewhat like a teenager, all raging hormones and out-of-control emotions.

"Not since it happened. We've avoided each other this entire week and—"

"Yeah, no shit, Keegan. Haven't you noticed everyone's been giving you two a wide berth? They figured it would pass in a few days. When it didn't, they came to me, figured I'd have the guts to find out what's going on."

Keegan's lips twitched into a quirky grin. "Don't you always know everything?"

She raised an eyebrow at him. "Yes, I do. And don't you forget it. Now. What are you going to do about your Erik problem? Because I think once you fix that, everything else might fall back into place. But I think you need to be prepared for when it doesn't."

ERIK SAW Sandra walk into Keegan's room.

They were talking about him. And Jules. And this whole fucking mess.

He wanted to be pissed. He couldn't help but envy Keegan for having someone to talk to.

He also knew Sandra had approached Keegan first because she knew Keegan would give her the ammunition needed to approach him next.

Sandra might not have been in the Navy herself, but she would've made one hell of a submarine commander. She worked better under tense circumstances.

And it had been tense this past week.

He and Keegan needed to talk. He knew that. He even knew a lot of this problem was his fault.

Even though Keegan couldn't—

No.

He had to stop that. Keegan had only been trying to help, although he'd gone about it totally the wrong way.

Because I basically cut him off at the knees.

And he hadn't called Jules.

Hell, that might be worse than any of the other shit he'd pulled the last time they'd been together.

He should've stayed. They should've hashed this out together. Like adults.

Christ, he'd been an idiot. Worse, he'd hurt two of the people he cared most about in the world.

So now what did he do?

"Hey, Erik, you okay? You've been standing here for a few minutes."

Erik turned to find one of his tech assistants standing behind him. Her expression held a little worry, a little apprehension, and a whole lot of "Damn, I really hope he's not losing it again."

"I'm fine, Lynne. Did you need me for something?"

Relief at his normal-sounding answer made her pretty face soften immediately.

"Yes, actually, we think we may have found a way around that short in the circuitry panel."

He waved a hand in front of him to have her lead and Lynne smiled. Right at him. Looking him in the eyes, her gaze never sliding to his scars.

He saw no sign of pity at all.

When had their team stopped looking at him like he was a freak?

Had he really been so blind?

Following Lynne into the main lab, he found two more assistants and Tommy, another engineer, all grinning like kids on Christmas morning.

It was infectious.

He smiled for the first time that week. And hoped like hell that he and Keegan could repair their friendship as easily.

"JULES. Hi. It's Erik. I know you probably don't want to talk to me but I'd like to see you. If only to apologize."

He paused, tried to think of what else he could say to her answering machine that wouldn't sound like so much whiny bullshit on Friday morning.

He couldn't, so he finished with, "Please call me back. I look forward to hearing from you."

The second he hung up, he wanted to erase that lame-ass message and start over.

Hell, he should've pleaded and begged and messaged her a picture that had him on his knees begging her to talk to him.

Then she'll think you're a nutcase.

Tossing the phone on his desk, he leaned back into his chair, barely registering the low hum of voices from outside his office.

Yesterday had been pretty much a whirlwind after he'd seen Sandra go into Keegan's office. One of their engineers and his assistants had found a way to keep their new board from shorting out. If they hadn't found the flaw, the board would've been useless.

He and Keegan had actually smiled at each other across the room as they talked with their team, congratulating everyone. The day had ended with pizza and beer in the company common area.

Somehow, he and Keegan had managed not to say a word to each other.

Erik hadn't wanted to make a scene, not at the office. He'd planned to talk to Keegan today. He'd figured the offices were neutral territory. He'd corner him in his office after he'd spoken to Jules and—

His phone rang. The name on the screen read Jules and his heart began to pound.

Taking a deep breath, he hit answer. "Hello, Jules. Thanks for calling me back."

"Hi, Erik. How are you?"

Better now that I'm talking to you. "I'm fine. And you?"

"I'm good, thanks. I'm glad you called. I was thinking maybe we could get together tonight. If you don't have plans. I'd like to talk to you."

Just the two of them? Alone? "Sure. That'd be great."

She exhaled, as if she'd been holding her breath waiting for his answer. "I thought maybe I could come to your house. Would that be okay? I'd have you over for dinner but my mom has book club—"

"No, really. My house is fine. How about seven?"

"Great. I thought I would cook for you, if you wouldn't mind?"

Why would he mind? "Sure. Of course. That's fine."

"Okay. I'll see you then. And Erik?"

"Yeah?"

"Just so you know, I plan to see Keegan tomorrow night."

She didn't want to see the two of them together. He took a deep breath. "No problem."

He swore he heard her sigh through the phone. "I just want to be upfront—"

"Jules. It's not a problem. I'd like the chance to talk to you alone as well."

She paused. "Okay. Then I'll see you tonight. Bye."

She hung up before he could say anything else.

Setting the phone back on the desk, his first instinct was to head for Keegan's office. To talk about how they could work on her from opposite sides and get her back into bed between them.

Which meant he and Keegan would actually have to speak to each other.

Then again, maybe he'd wait until they'd talked to her separately, found out what she was thinking.

If the only reason she wanted to see each of them was to tell them it was over... Well, that would be painful.

If she was talking to them separately to tell them she only wanted to date one of them... What would he do?

He knew what he would've done before the explosion. If she'd picked him, he would've taken her up on her offer then he would've used every skill at his disposal to get her back in bed with him and Keegan.

Yeah, right.

Damn conscience. But it was right. He would've told himself she'd made her decision and he was only abiding by what she wanted. He'd have taken what she offered.

Could he do that to Keegan now? Could he stab him in the back over a woman? After everything they'd been through together?

Shit.

He didn't think he could. Hell, he'd like to think he *wouldn't* do it. Ever.

He picked up the phone. Put it back down.

And the damn thing rang.

He snatched it up again. His sister.

Well, hell. A visit and a phone call in the space of a week. What the hell was wrong now?

For a brief second, he considered letting it go to voice mail.

Selfish bastard.

He answered.

"Hello, Katrina."

"Erik. I'm so glad you picked up. I...I'd like to talk to you about something."

He sat up, hearing something in his sister's tone he hadn't heard in years. A fragility that actually made him doubt for a second that it really was Katrina.

"Are you okay, Kat? You sound shaky."

"Actually," she laughed, a sound so fake he really began to worry, "that's why I'm calling. I know this is completely and utterly over and above the limits of what I should expect, even from my brother, but..."

"Just spit it out, Kat. What do you need?"

A huge sigh. "I need a date for a company function, and since I don't know any suitable men and it's kind of a big deal, he must be decently handsome and well-spoken but willing to keep his mouth shut for long periods of time. And he has to act like he adores me."

"Uh..." Kat's request was so unexpected, Erik's brain stuttered to a stop for a second. "Seriously?"

"Yes. I'm dead serious."

He paused again, his brain finally starting to turn. "And why would you want to take a guy to a company function? You never have before. What makes this one different? And—"

"I don't need the third degree, Erik." Her voice bit at him like a lash. Then she drew in an audible breath. "I just...I need you to help me with this. Please."

There it was again. That fragile note in his sister's voice. Kat never let her nerves show. It'd been drilled into them by their mother from birth.

Never show your weakness. Someone will use it against you.

"Just to be clear," he wanted to be absolutely sure what she needed from him, "you want me to set you up with someone to take you to a party and have him be your devoted slave for the night." He almost added, "And you don't have one friend who's willing to set you up," but quickly swallowed that.

His sister didn't really have friends. Not like he had Keegan. She'd always been a loner, prickly and cold to outsiders. Okay, to almost everyone who wasn't Erik. By the time she'd dug herself out from under their mother's thumb, it'd been too late.

"Yes. That's what I want. If you have to pay him...well, I guess that's how it has to be."

"Katrina, what the hell—"

"Can you just do it, Erik? Please. Just...do it."

He didn't think twice. "Of course."

"Thank you." Another sigh, like she'd lost a weight off her chest. "Now, have you done anything with the information I found for you?"

His turn to sigh. "No, not yet."

"What are you waiting for?"

Hell, he didn't know. "What do you think I should do with the information, Kat?"

She paused. "Honestly...I don't have a clue. I think you need to do whatever you think is best. If that means taking it to the police, then do it. But...I think Keegan's right about one thing." He heard the strain in her voice more clearly, knew how hard it was for her to even say his name after all this time. "Don't let it obsess you again, Erik. You've started to come around to something of your old self. The good part of yourself. You've made such huge strides. Don't let this set you back."

"Why does everyone think this is going to send me off the deep end? Jesus, how crazy do you think I am?"

"I don't think you're crazy. I think you're my brother and I don't want to see you hurt any more than you were already. And I think it could be very easy for you to fall back into old habits."

Kat's voice had softened. It stunned him to hear that note of caring in her voice. "And what old habits are those?" he asked.

"The one where you hide yourself in the lab and pretend you're so caught up in work when what you're really doing is hiding from the rest of the world. You are not a monster. You are not hideous to look at. You are so damn lucky to be alive you should want to celebrate that every day."

Kat went silent for several seconds as Erik held his breath, waiting for her to continue. Because she was right. He couldn't come up with a decent argument for anything she'd said.

But this was how he'd lived his life for three years. He'd gotten used to it. Gotten comfortable.

And then Jules had agreed to their proposition and blown his safe world apart at the seams.

Now everyone wanted to gang up on him.

Maybe they'd all left it too late.

No, his state of affairs was no one's fault but his own. He just didn't know if he could fix it. Hell, he didn't honestly know *how* to fix it.

"Erik?"

He heard a vulnerability in Kat's voice that threw him uncomfortably into the past. Before Kat had been able to protect herself from their mother's sharp tongue.

"Yeah."

"Are you—"

"I'm fine, Kat. Honestly. And you're right. I'm just not sure I know how to be the person I was before."

"You don't have to be that person. Frankly, that person wasn't always the nicest. And I know how that sounds, coming from me. I'm a royal bitch." There was no missing the sarcastic bite in her tone. "Anyway, I should get going. Lots of work to do. Seems never-ending lately."

Now she sounded exhausted. "When was the last time you had a vacation?"

"I don't believe I know the meaning of that word." Her tone

was deadpan. "I'm almost surprised you remember what that is as well." She took a deep breath. "Let me know about the other matter, okay? And I would really appreciate it if you wouldn't say anything to anyone."

"No problem. Hey, Kat?"

"Yes?"

"You're a much sweeter person than anyone ever gives you credit for."

She snorted. "No, I'm really not. Talk to you soon."

He hung up. He didn't have a clue why she'd come to him, but he was glad she had. The more he thought about it, the more he realized how far into her shell his sister must have crawled.

Well, it seemed the Riley siblings had more in common than he'd known.

And apparently neither of them knew how to fix themselves.

KEEGAN HUNG up then navigated back to his favorites list to call Erik before he remembered they weren't talking.

Shit.

What the hell did they do now?

When he'd seen Jules's name pop up on his phone, he'd answered before the second ring.

He didn't care if he'd seemed over-anxious. He only knew he was damn glad she'd called.

When she'd asked to see him tomorrow night, he'd nearly pumped his fist in the air before he realized she meant she wanted to see *only* him tomorrow night because she was seeing Erik tonight.

His first thought wasn't jealousy but relief that she'd at least agreed to see one of them.

His second thought was, *Oh shit, she's making a choice.*

He'd been chilled to the bone.

That was the only reason he could think of for her to want to see them separately.

Now he really wanted to talk to Erik.

He was on his feet before he realized it and had taken two steps toward the door before he stopped.

He should wait until Sunday. Until they'd both spoken to her.

If she chose Erik, he'd step away. It'd tear out a piece of his heart but he'd do it.

If she chose him... He'd do whatever it took to get the three of them back together.

And what if that's not what she wants?

His mind went blank.

If she didn't want them as a package deal... If she chose Erik...

Could he live with that?

He'd have to.

And he'd be happy for Erik. Even if it killed him.

TWENTY

Jules took one last look in the mirror on the back of her bedroom door, made sure the cleavage on her plain black long-sleeved t-shirt was seductive but not blatant then ran her hands down the front of her jeans.

She wondered, not for the first time, if she should've worn something more...provocative.

Maybe a dress or at least slacks and a blouse.

She wanted to entice the man into bed but she hadn't wanted to appear like she was trying too hard. Since she was cooking dinner for him at his house, a dress had seemed like overkill. And she didn't really own any nice slacks that weren't for work.

But she looked damn good in these jeans, and her t-shirt clung to her breasts like a second skin. Tonight, she wasn't out to impress Erik with anything other than her cooking. And then she'd show him what he'd be missing if he and Keegan couldn't get their shit together.

"Honey, didn't you say you want to leave by 6:30?" her mom called up the stairs. "It's close to quarter of seven."

"I know. Thanks, Mom. I'm leaving in a minute."

Stepping into her boots, she took a deep breath and headed down the stairs.

At 7:05, she parked her car in front of Erik's home and gave herself a few seconds to breathe before she got out of the car.

He must have been waiting for her because as soon as she stepped out of the car, he opened the door and headed for her.

"I thought you might need a hand getting stuff into the house."

His voice, with that distinctive rasp, made her thighs quiver every time she heard him. It was so damn sexy. She wondered if he knew it or if he could only hear the damage that'd been done.

"Thanks. There are a few bags in the backseat."

By the time she rounded the back end of the car, Erik had already grabbed the bags and waited for her to join him.

The butterflies in her stomach took flight when he smiled at her. She'd grown to crave that smile. He didn't do it nearly enough.

Please, please, please, let this turn out the way I hope.

Her lips curved into a smile and she had to make sure she didn't trip over her own damn feet. That was the hold he had over her.

When she reached his side, he leaned down and kissed her cheek, the smooth, unscarred skin of his face soft against hers.

A nice, sweet, chaste kiss.

"I'm glad to see you."

Jules shivered at the deep, husky growl of his voice and wished he would've gone in for the kill and kissed her like she was dying to kiss him. Lips open, tongues tangling, hands tearing at clothes.

Later, she promised herself.

Now, she just wanted to enjoy his company.

They made careful small talk as he led her into the house then through to the kitchen—the weather, her work, her mom—

and carefully avoided anything that could lead to talk about Keegan or his sister.

Erik helped her as much as she'd let him with dinner. She'd planned for salad, chicken cordon bleu, and risotto. She'd put as much together at home as she could, including making the angel food cake for dessert, but she'd left some things for them to do together.

But Erik proved to be pretty inept in the kitchen, which made her laugh and made him smile.

By the time they were seated at the table to eat, though, they'd begun to loosen up. They somehow got on the subject of superheroes and she was surprised to find out Erik collected them. X-Men comics, to be exact. Since he was a kid. And he loved to read. Neither of which they had in common. She was more into music and movies.

They did find common ground in television. Neither of them watched much of it.

When the dishes were stacked in the dishwasher, Erik asked her if she'd like to take their wine into the study and she realized they'd be alone together in the place where this relationship had started.

She nodded and followed him down the hall.

Instead of sitting on the couch, he went to the loveseat on the opposite side of the room.

Thank God. At least she wouldn't fidget all night as memories of the first night they'd met flooded her brain.

Instead, she forced herself to sip at her wine, not just drain it in one gulp. "So I've been doing a lot of thinking about what I'm going to do with my life."

His gaze snapped to hers. "And what have you thought about?"

She took a deep breath. "Continuing my education. I never went to college. Never had the money."

His head cocked to the side, his gaze never leaving hers. "Sounds like you've made a decision."

"Not entirely, no. I've always wanted to go to cooking school, but ... Well, I've been looking into the CIA."

His eyes narrowed for a moment. "I don't think you're talking about working for the government. Not that you wouldn't look good in a black suit."

She smiled. "No, not that CIA. The Culinary Institute of America. I used to dream about going after high school but we never had the money."

Ah. "And now you do."

Money he and Keegan had given her. He didn't say the words aloud but she knew that's what he was thinking.

He leaned back into the cushion, his gaze steady on hers. "When would you start?"

She sat next to him, trying to read his mind. An impossible task. She had no idea what he was thinking. "In the fall. If I get accepted."

"I can't imagine they'd turn you down. You're too good."

Her smile widened at the sincerity in his tone. "You can't tell that on the basis of one meal."

"True, but what you just made was amazing and Carol talks about you all the time. If she says you can cook, that's high praise."

The smile Jules gave Erik went straight to his cock, making it harden. "Nice to know she has faith in me."

"She's not the only one."

Erik had total faith she'd succeed in anything she attempted.

It also meant she'd be farther away from him and Keegan.

Jules' smile became sweeter. "Thank you."

Fuck. He couldn't help himself. He leaned forward and kissed her.

He hadn't meant to kiss the hell out of her. He'd meant

for them to talk a little, to ease into the intimacy that had come so naturally between the three of them. Yes, they'd been together alone before but that had been different. Unexpected.

Before she'd arrived, all he'd thought about had been seducing her, getting her in bed, making love to her.

And after he'd accomplished that, he'd tackle the other stuff.

But she'd smiled and he'd pounced.

And when she wrapped her arms around his shoulders and kissed him back... Well, hell. He couldn't resist her.

He didn't *want* to resist her.

With a groan, he grabbed her and lifted her over his lap. Her knees parted and settled on either side of his as her fingers sank into his hair.

She gave a tug, setting his nerve endings to tingle. Then she massaged her fingertips against his scalp.

The sensation was incendiary. Lust outstripped his control and the hands he had on her waist yanked her closer, pressing her down against his already hard and aching cock.

He wanted to fuck her. Right here, right now. Just strip her bare and take her.

Christ, he wanted to. But doubts kept creeping in.

They should talk first. Right? Before they took this any further.

Reluctantly, he pulled away, forced himself to stop. To wait until she opened her eyes and looked at him. Really looked at him.

He recognized the glaze of passion in her eyes. He'd seen it before. He was greedy enough to want it all for himself. And that could be a major fuck-up on his part.

"Erik." Jules put her hands on his cheeks and forced him to look into her dark eyes. "Don't think right now. Just kiss me."

Okay, he could do that.

He closed the distance between them and sealed their lips together.

Groaning when the tip of her tongue met his, he wrapped his arms around her back and pulled her tight against him. His cock throbbed at the contact, straining against the zipper of his jeans.

Shoving his hands under her t-shirt, he soaked in the warmth of her skin. It arrowed straight to the cold lump that had settled in his chest since the last time he'd seen her. When everything had gone to shit.

Desperation tried to urge him to go faster. He kissed her with a little more force, a little more aggression than he normally used. He'd always tried to be so careful with her before. Maybe more so than he'd ever been with anyone else.

Because no one else had ever mattered. Not like Jules.

His hands moved with a purpose now, stripping her shirt over her head and dropping it on the floor. Her lacy black bra looked like pure sin, pushing her breasts up and out, Instead of removing it, he left it there as a temptation. His lips landed on the pale mound of one breast.

He licked at the tiny freckles sprinkled across her skin, her fingers tightening in his hair. Following those freckles across her chest, with a short stop to press a kiss over her heart, he let his lips travel to her breast.

When he drew one lace-covered nipple into his mouth, he sucked hard and was rewarded when she sighed and trembled against him.

He was so intent on pleasuring her that he didn't realize she was pushing him away.

Releasing her immediately, he looked up, into her eyes. But she wasn't looking at him. Her gaze was focused down.

"Jules, what—"

"Take your shirt off. I want you naked."

Yes. "Anything you want, sweetheart."

He released his hold on her only long enough to yank his t-shirt over his head before he pulled her back against him..

The heat of her body soaked into his chest, straight through to his heart, beating at an ever-increasing pace. The lace of her bra subtly abraded his skin, raising goose bumps.

God, yes. This was much better.

"I want you to make love to me right here." She smiled into his eyes. "I think this might be the only piece of furniture in this room we haven't had sex on."

"Then we definitely have to fix that."

Grabbing her hips, he lifted her off his lap and set her on her feet before standing in front of her.

She must have read his mind because she had her hands on the waistband of his jeans before he reached hers.

Their hands tangled as they yanked and pulled fabric to uncover skin warm from exertion. And desire.

Jules moved at the same frantic pace, teeth biting into her bottom lip as she worked the button on his jeans. His hands slowed their glide up her arms then stopped as he watched her. Finally, she stopped too and looked up.

"What's wrong?"

Keegan's not here.

"You're beautiful."

She blushed through her smile. "Thank you. And so are you."

If anyone else had said that, he would've told them to fuck off. He would've figured they were yanking his chain.

Not Jules.

Damn it. She'd gotten under his skin and burrowed so deep, he was really afraid that if he lost her, he'd go off the deep end. Finally and irrevocably.

Wrapping his hands around her head, he held her steady for his kiss.

She didn't try to get away. She moved closer until he felt the lace-covered mounds press his bare chest. Warm. Soft. His.

Slipping one hand down her back, he stroked along her skin, fingertips grazing the fine bones of her spine. She arched toward him, as if he'd hit a secret button. And when she let her lips trail from his lips and across his scars, he realized just how much he adored this woman.

And it wasn't just because she could see beyond the scars. It was because she accepted *everything* about him.

Which had included Keegan.

Not now. Can't think about that now.

His hands began to move again, lifting her out of the jeans he'd pushed off her hips already. He didn't get to see if her underwear matched her bra because they went down with the jeans. Didn't care. She was so damn pretty naked.

Finally, he brushed the bra straps off her shoulders and unsnapped it with one hand—it'd been a long time since he'd used that skill—then let it fall to the floor.

He gave himself a few seconds just to stare at her perfection until he couldn't resist. He lifted his hands and cupped her breasts. As he began to knead the soft flesh, her head fell back, eyes closed. Her lips parted as if she were going to say something but the only sound that emerged was a breathy sigh.

He barely registered the fact that she'd finally gotten his jeans down his legs, his entire attention fixed on pleasuring her, getting her to make those soft sounds that drove him crazy.

But when she wrapped her fingers around his cock, his concentration fixed on himself.

"Fuck, Jules. Yes."

His head fell back as she stepped even closer, her teeth fastening onto one sensitive nipple. Heat flamed through his body, racing to his cock and making it swell even more in her hands.

His eyes closed as he sank into sensation, soaking in everything about her. The feel of her fingers squeezing him, the light scent of her skin, the pinch of her teeth on his chest.

This. Yes.

He wanted this all the time. Wanted her to play with him until he couldn't control his response.

With a groan, his head snapped up and he grabbed her hips. She responded with a slight gasp, as if he'd surprised her.

But when he lifted her off her feet, she immediately wrapped her arms around his shoulders and her legs around his waist and held on.

She felt almost weightless in his arms and he began to tease the tip of his cock against the trimmed hair on her mound. Catching her mouth again with his, he kissed her, tongue sinking deep, until she was practically gasping.

Tearing her mouth away from his to suck in a deep breath, she looked straight at him.

"Erik."

He knew what she wanted, heard it in the rough tone of her voice. In the soft pleading in her eyes.

It made him greedy for more, greedy for her longing for him.

"But you feel so damn good. I don't want to stop."

"I promise it will feel better if you come inside. Do it, Erik. I want you."

His cockhead butted against her clit and her entire body shook in his arms. Moaning, she pressed harder against him and rubbed her mound on his cock.

"Damn, that feels amazing."

He wasn't sure he could hold on much longer but he didn't want this to end too soon. If he could, he'd tie her to him and fuck her until they both passed out.

And when they woke, Keegan could—

Shit.

His eyes opened and he saw hers were closed, her face slack with passion.

For him.

Live in the moment.

It was a mantra his former rehab nurse had drilled into his head. He'd never really put much stock in it. Until now.

Lifting her higher, he let the tip of his penis finally brush against the lips of her pussy.

Immediately, she tried to angle herself onto him.

"Hang on, sweetheart. I'm not done playing."

Moving his hips, he coated the head of his cock with the moisture from her pussy. She moaned quietly as he teased her and himself, only stopping when he felt his balls begin to draw up.

Then he started to lower her.

Arching forward, she took him in slowly. He felt her sheath close around the top, the lips of her pussy spreading around the shaft. The farther he pressed, the tighter she got until he wasn't sure he could hold out any longer.

Jesus, his balls tightened and he felt the beginning of his orgasm already. He didn't want to come yet. He wanted to fuck her until they couldn't move and then he wanted to do it again.

If Keegan was here, we—

He shook the thought out of his head and focused every bit of his concentration on Jules.

She looked lost in the moment. Eyes closed, head tilted back so he felt the brush of her hair on his arms, lips parted.

Lifting her slightly, he watched her suck in a deep breath then release it on another moan as he brought her down hard, sinking his cock into her until he couldn't go any farther.

He kept up the pace as long as he could. His heart thundered against his ribs, lungs working overtime to draw in much-needed air.

His cock jerked in anticipation and he moved a hand from her hip to her clit and played the little nub until he felt her pussy grip him like a vise.

As her body went taut, he brought her down one last time, sealed his mouth over hers, and kissed her while he pumped his release into her.

He continued to kiss her long after his orgasm had faded, unwilling to give her up in any way.

When her own climax finally wound down, she melted against him as he practically fell back onto the loveseat. The heat from their bodies kept them warm for several minutes.

They didn't speak. Erik wasn't sure he could get his brain to work coherently anyway.

But he'd have to make the effort soon enough.

He wanted to take her to his bed and keep her under him for the rest of the night. Then again, he didn't want to assume she was staying.

When she finally started to stir against his chest, he made sure not to lock his arms around her. And he stilled when she lifted a hand to caress his scarred cheek.

Though the sensation wasn't as sharp as if she were stroking unscarred skin, he still shuddered in reaction. For so long, no one had touched him. And if anyone had attempted to touch his scars, he would've flinched away, stalked off, or worse.

For years, he'd been a bastard to the people around him. He'd wallowed in self-pity and told himself he had the right.

Poor Erik. He used to be so handsome.

It'd taken this woman to make him see that the person inside was what he should be worried about.

And how did he tell her that without sounding like an ass?

"Erik?"

"Yeah."

"What are you thinking about?"

"I'm thinking about how I can get you into my bed for the night. My furniture has been getting one hell of a workout lately."

She laughed, as she was supposed to, but not for long. "I can't stay tonight. I'm sorry. I work tomorrow and then..."

"You're seeing Keegan tomorrow night."

"Yes. I am."

She stopped and he knew she wanted him to say something. He just didn't have a clue what to say. If she'd said she was going out with any other man, he'd have blown a gasket.

"Does that bother you?" she asked.

"No." It honestly didn't.

"Are you still not talking to each other?"

He stroked a hand along her hair. "You don't have to worry about that. Keegan and I will work things out. We always do."

"But you can't do that if you don't talk."

He knew that. He just didn't know what he could tell her that would ease the worry he heard in her voice. So he ignored it.

Sometimes ignorance really was bliss. And sometimes ignorance was just plain stupidity.

With a sigh, she dropped her hand from his cheek and let it rest on his shoulder. "It's getting late. I should get home."

And that was the last place he wanted her to be. If she were any other woman... if this had happened before the explosion, he'd have been more than happy to send her packing or simply carry her to his bed and make her forget she'd wanted to leave.

Selfish.

"If that's what you want, Jules."

He tried to keep the edge out of his voice because he wasn't upset with her. Not in the least.

He was pissed off at himself.

WHEN HER ALARM went off at 6:30 the next morning, Jules groaned and turned it off with a huff followed by a jaw-cracking yawn.

She hadn't been able to fall asleep until close to two in the morning. All she could think about was Erik. She hadn't wanted to leave him but she knew she couldn't stay.

Not only did she have to work this morning but she couldn't justify spending the night in Erik's bed and, ten hours later, jumping Keegan's bones.

Yes, sex with Erik had been seriously hot but she hadn't planned to have sex with him.

Sex blurred her brain to everything else.

And she needed to be on her toes if she was going to figure out what she was going to do about this relationship. Or even if there was a relationship.

But first, she needed to get through the day.

Carol had a bridal shower booked, and she'd recruited Jules to help her with the cooking and waitressing. Typically, Jules did one or the other, but one of Carol's regular waitresses was laid up with a sprained ankle.

Jules was the only one available on short notice. Most of the women Carol employed were mothers whose children played hockey or soccer or baseball or whatever sport was in season. When they had a day off, they weren't ready to jump in and take someone else's shift.

That almost always fell to Jules and the two other college girls Carol employed.

Usually she didn't mind. Before, she could use the extra money.

Now that she didn't have to worry about money... Well, she couldn't leave Carol in the lurch.

And today's event was going to be sheer torture.

The bride-to-be was a woman Jules had gone to school with. She'd belonged to the popular girls' clique that had included that bitch, Allison Terre. Alli was sure to be at the party.

And if word had gotten around that Jules was seeing Keegan and Erik... Well, Jules could only hope to stay in the kitchen and prep trays.

By midmorning, she'd determined luck had deserted her completely.

One of the other waitresses had a cold, so she had to stay in the kitchen with Carol wearing a mask. Sure, it sucked to wear the mask but Jules wished she had one right about now.

Because no sooner had she started to make the rounds with a tray than Alli had walked into the room.

She hadn't noticed Jules at first. She'd been too busy giving hugs and air kisses to the rest of the guests, all dressed with the express purpose of outdoing one another.

Your inner bitch is showing, Jules. Tone it down.

With a deep breath, she tried but knew it was going to be a losing battle.

Luckily there were more than enough guests for her to avoid Alli, the bride, and their friends.

The older women at the shower didn't bother to look beyond the tray, as they talked about their latest trip to Europe or their Hawaiian cruise with those gorgeous and oh-so-helpful stewards whom they tipped so well for their service.

Eww. Jules had to work hard to erase those images from her head. Most of these women looked like they'd had a few too many trips to the Botox bar and the plastic surgeon. And then to think about them seducing younger men...

Just eww.

But she figured it was better than listening to the women her own age talking about their careers and the men they were dating and how huge the bride's solitaire was.

A little better anyway.

But of course her luck had to run out sometime.

Alli caught her just as she was about to escape back to the kitchen with her partially empty tray.

"Hello, Julianne. We've been seeing each other a lot more lately than I think we did in high school."

Alli laughed as if she found that hilarious but Jules knew it was a dig.

Jules just nodded and smiled and tried to keep walking, but Alli put her hand on her arm. Jules didn't feel threatened. Alli wasn't digging her fingers into her skin but the command was there all the same.

Jules stopped and forced a pleasant smile. "How are you, Alli?"

"Oh, I'm just fine." The other woman's icy blue eyes flashed up and down Jules for a second. "I understand you've got a new man in your life." She paused. "Or is it two?"

Jules bit her tongue to stop her immediate urge to tell the woman to take a flying leap into a volcano.

Instead, she smiled. "Would you like a cucumber sandwich? I'm about to take the tray back to the kitchen for more."

Still holding her gaze, Alli smiled, her expression turning downright mean, and Jules knew the other woman was about to go in for the kill.

"Riley and Malone are big fish for such a small...pond. I'd love to hear all about how you met them. Rumor has it there's an interesting story there."

Out of the corner of her eye, Jules saw two of Alli's friends approaching. Shit. She was about to be surrounded. Like sharks, they must smell blood in the water.

"Sorry, Alli, there's really nothing to tell. And I am working today, so—"

"So is it true, Julianne?" asked Ginger Macintyre, another former classmate of Jules and Alli's. "Are you dating Erik Riley?"

"I'd just like to know how you can stand looking at Erik's face all night and not want to run," the third woman chimed in.

Jules felt every muscle in her body tense and her eyes narrowed down to slits.

Deep breath. No punching the guests. Even if they deserve it.

Jules didn't know the woman but if she hung around with Alli and Ginger, she probably didn't want to.

"I mean, it's such a shame," the bitch continued. "That accident was so totally tragic, I understand why he's not been able to find a woman who'll put up with that."

"At least, not one he hasn't paid for."

Alli threw that zinger in and, while the other women smirked at each other, Alli kept her eyes on Jules.

A flush burned Jules's cheeks as Alli's smile turned hard. But Alli couldn't possibly know that flush was all about anger and not embarrassment.

Jules wanted to pop the bitch in her smug little smile.

And then she wanted to tell Alli and her friends all about the hot, steamy, sweaty sex she had with both men. How they treated her like someone special and not like a toy they'd bought.

"You know, I dated Erik right after he and Keegan moved here," Ginger said. "And I'm not so sure there's not something going on between them. If you know what I mean."

Ginger lifted her eyebrows at Jules, as if they were sharing secrets.

Jules wondered how high the bail would be if she took her serving tray and bashed the women's heads with it.

While Ginger and the other woman started to giggle like teenagers, Alli kept her unnerving gaze on Jules.

"Or maybe their tastes are a little more...unconventional."

Even though Jules had braced herself for someone finding out about her relationship with Erik and Keegan, she hadn't actually thought about what would happen if anyone openly confronted her about it.

Silence seemed the best course of action, but Jules had never been one to back away from a fight. Or know when to hold her tongue, apparently.

Letting her own mouth curve in a knowing smile, Jules leaned closer to Alli, like she was going to share a secret.

Alli's gaze narrowed but the other women moved in with mocking smiles.

"Would you like to hear about how wonderful they are in bed? Because I could go on for hours. And so can they, actually. Or do you want to know about how they wiped out the mountain of debt my mother and I were drowning under because of her breast cancer?"

Ginger's mouth dropped open with each word Jules said. Her friend's eyes were so wide, Jules swore it had to hurt. But Alli... Alli was putting two and two together and coming up with...well, probably the right answer.

"I guess the rumor mill got it right this time." Alli practically spit the words through clenched teeth. "Good for you, Julianne."

"Yes, they *are* good for me, Alli. They're both very, very good."

Without another word, she spun on her heel and headed back to the kitchen.

That bitch. That miserable fucking bitch.

She wanted to go back out there and light into Alli again. Wanted to rip her hair out and have a straight-up cat fight.

But as mad as she was at Alli for putting her in that position, she was just as pissed off at herself for opening her mouth and stooping to Alli's level.

By the time she'd set her tray on the counter where they'd placed the appetizer warming pans, Jules swore she had smoke coming out of her ears.

Jesus, how stupid could she be? The party had barely started. Jules would have to face those women for the next three hours. And knowing Alli, she'd probably told more people and they would tell their friends until everyone out there knew Jules had slept with two men who had then cleared her debt.

She'd thought life had gotten bad when she'd had an affair with a married man. That the nasty glances and the whispering she'd endured at the functions she'd worked were bad.

Add having an affair with two men and taking money from them...

Good thing you're planning to leave, isn't it?

Shit. She should've kept her mouth shut.

"Julianne, what's wrong?"

Carol stepped up beside her, wiping her hands on a towel, her expression full of concern.

Because she didn't want to worry Carol, and because she'd made this mess herself, she shook her head and forced a smile.

"Nothing. Sorry, just a little headache."

More like a migraine beginning to hammer at her skull.

Carol didn't look convinced. "Do you need to sit down for a little? I can—"

"No. Really. I'll be fine."

Carol frowned but sighed. "Okay, but if you need to sit, just let me know."

What she needed was a do-over of the last ten minutes.

What you really need is to figure out what you're going to do with the rest of your life.

And with the two men she wasn't sure she could give up.

———————

KEEGAN STARED at the name on his phone screen, finger poised over the big red no button.

Why the fuck is she calling me?

He should let it go to voice mail. He really had no idea why Allison Terre wanted to talk to him.

Whatever it is, it probably isn't anything you want to get involved in.

He hit "No" and shoved the phone out of reach across his kitchen table.

Fingers drumming out a fast-paced rhythm on the table, he stared at the phone. He should work out, go for a run, anything to get rid of this nervous energy.

Would Erik pick up if he called?

God damn it. He wanted to talk to his best friend about his date with the woman who'd come to mean so much to him in so short a time. But how did he clear up a week's worth of silence with a phone call?

He shouldn't have let it go on this long because now he didn't have a clue what to do.

His phone vibrated, annoying him once again. Allison had left him a message.

With a half-assed growl, he retrieved his phone and called up the message.

"Hello, Keegan. This is Allison Terre." She gave a little laugh that made the hair on the back of his neck stand on end. "I hope you remember me, otherwise I'm going to be totally embarrassed. I called to see if you'd like to accompany me to the next chamber mixer. I know we talked at the last one, but you skipped out before we could have a decent conversation. I'd really love to spend some time getting to know you. If you're not busy, of course. I realize a man in your position doesn't have a lot of time. And I'm sure you don't have a lot of time to meet women in your...circle. Anyway, I just thought I'd throw my idea out there and see if you'd like to go. Give me a call. See you soon."

The message ended and he shook his head.

What the fuck?

Which was about all the time he wanted to give that particular phone call.

He dismissed it with a shake of his head, his brain already working through the problem with Erik. If he could just get his friend to see how self-destructive he was being. How not letting go of his rage against Eggert Labs was going to destroy what they'd built all these years.

But he never picked up the phone.

And when his doorbell rang at a minute past six-thirty later that day, he'd managed to forget the phone call completely and put Erik out of his mind.

So he could completely focus on Jules.

Who looked absolutely stunning in a figure-hugging blue shirt with some kind of design swirled all over it and a pair of jeans that made her legs look five miles long.

She held bags in her hands and had a smile on her lips that he wanted to kiss.

He took the bags instead.

"Come in. It's damn cold out there tonight."

Her smile twisted, as if he'd said something funny, but he had no idea what that would have been.

"Feels like snow," she said, as he closed the door behind her then followed him through the kitchen.

"A little snow would be nice around this time of the year."

She cocked her head at him. "Do you ski?"

"Not in years." He set the bags on the counter. "Erik and I used to—"

"Used to what?" Reaching into the bags, she started to withdraw ingredients, but she turned to give him an encouraging smile. One that didn't quite meet her eyes, he noticed.

"We used to go to Vermont to ski every winter. Before."

Nodding, she continued to unload the bag. "So you haven't gone in at least three years. That's a shame. There are some decent slopes in the area. Maybe you'll want to try those."

He almost said he'd love to but Erik wouldn't go. And it wouldn't be the same without Erik.

"Sure. Do you ski?"

"Nope." Her smile widened. "Never been. Snow is really pretty when you're watching it fall from inside the house. But that means it's really cold outside. And I love to be warm."

She'd be warm if she stayed between him and Erik.

Fuck.

He needed to get his head together, needed to concentrate solely on Jules.

So that's what he focused on while he helped her make dinner and while they ate. She didn't bring up Erik again and they stuck to safe topics that never got boring. At least not for him. Anything Jules had to say was something he wanted to hear.

Especially if she's moaning my name as I fuck her into an orgasm.

He had an erection all through dinner. Luckily, the table hid it because he didn't want her to believe all he thought about was nailing her to the bed. Or the wall. Or on the table.

Of course, he'd take any of those places if it meant he could have her.

Because, holy hell, he wanted her so fucking much.

By the time they were finished eating, he needed a moment

alone so he told her to take the wine into the great room and he'd meet her there after he cleaned up.

She didn't argue, just grabbed the bottle and their glasses and headed off. He watched her walk away until he couldn't see her anymore. The sight of her ass in those tight jeans made him salivate.

He filled the dishwasher without a care for how the dishes were stacked, and he drew it out as long as he could.

But he couldn't stay away from her for long. She was like an addiction.

He found her standing by the window, looking out into the dark. He didn't know if it was coincidence or not that she was staring in the direction of Erik's house.

She turned as he stopped next to her.

"Thank you for dinner."

Her smile made his cock swell. "Thanks for being my sous chef."

"I'm glad you're here tonight. I've missed you."

Her smile became a little more natural as he said exactly what he was thinking. It got him in trouble more often than not but, damn it, he meant it. He didn't want her not to know.

"I've missed you too. That's really the main reason I wanted to see you tonight."

He controlled the urge to pick her up and carry her to his bedroom. "But it's not the only reason you wanted to see me tonight."

She held his gaze. "No, it's not."

Taking a deep breath, he prepared himself for whatever she was about to throw at him. "So what's up?"

Now her gaze slipped and she stared back out the window. "I've been thinking about what I want to do with my life."

The hair rose on the back of his neck and his heart rate increased. "And have you made a decision?"

"I've been thinking about culinary school."

Which would take her away from him and Erik. "Is that what you want to do?"

She sighed. "What I want is to have my own restaurant, and I know if I study at a good school, I'll be a better chef."

Couldn't fault her logic. "Sounds like you've got a plan."

"Oh, I've always had a plan." Her lips twisted in a wistful smile. "I just never thought I'd have the means."

And now she did.

"I understand Carol relies on you quite a bit."

"I love working for Carol. Most of the time." Something passed over her expression, something bitter. "And I love to cook. But..."

"But what?"

She sighed. "I don't know that I would ever be able to make a go of a restaurant here."

"Why not?"

"Because there are people here who would love to see me fail."

He'd take care of anyone who dared screw with her. "Like who?"

A shrug. "A few of the girls I went to high school with, for starters."

"Why would they care?"

"Because they're mean, sarcastic bitches who don't know when to shut up."

The saccharine tone of her voice made him wince. But he heard something else in her tone that made him wonder... "Did something happen? You worked today, didn't you?"

She nodded. "A bridal shower."

His gaze narrowed. "Did you know the bride?"

Another nod. "A few bridesmaids and I went to school together."

"And they said something to disturb you."

She blinked. "I should be used to it by now."

"Used to what?"

"To being their target of choice."

Angry heat gathered low in his gut. "How long has this been going on?"

She shrugged like it didn't matter. "Since high school, really. I wasn't part of their clique. My mom didn't make enough money. I didn't wear the right clothes. Yada, yada, yada. Just not good enough in their eyes. And then I made the mistake of going out with one of their ex-boyfriends and I was a marked woman for the rest of senior year."

"That sounds like hell."

"Isn't high school hell for everyone?" Her laugh didn't hold much amusement. "I know for a fact Allison's father was screwing around on her mother and had at least one illegitimate kid so I'm sure her home life was pretty crappy. She's pretty much still a bitch, though."

"Are you talking about Allison Terre?"

His brain started to replay the message she'd left him, filtering it through what he now knew. That bitch. That reference to not meeting women in his circle took on a whole new meaning.

Jules's eyebrows raised. "Yes. Do you know her?"

"Unfortunately. Her father's firm serves as our lawyer."

And I'm going to make damn sure her father knows it's all his daughter's fault when I fire their ass.

A pause. "Have you dated her?"

"No." He grimaced. "But not for lack of trying on her part. I believe she struck out with Erik as well. We have much better taste in women."

There, that made her smile. "You just made my entire day."

With a sinuous move, she swung her leg over his thighs, wrapped her arms around his shoulders, and kissed him.

Like she was starving for him. Like she'd missed him. Almost as much as he'd missed her.

Christ, he'd missed having her in his arms. Missed the feel of her body pressing against his. Every curve was a temptation that made him want to run his hands all over her. Preferably while she was naked.

For now, he'd be content with this.

He let her kiss him, let her control the action because, as much as he wanted to take over, he didn't want to give her any reason to back away.

For several minutes, all they did was kiss. Her lips moved over his, her tongue tangled with his, as her hands roamed his shoulders and chest.

He kept his hands locked to her hips as she rolled her pelvis until her denim-covered pussy rubbed against his crotch.

Groaning, he tightened his hands as he fought the urge to make her rub against him harder, faster.

He didn't want her to go faster than she was ready, didn't want to do anything to make her pull away.

But after a few minutes, she did, just far enough to touch the tip of her nose to his. "When are you going to learn I'm not fragile? I won't run because you're a little rough during sex. Haven't you figured out yet that I like it?"

He hadn't wanted to hope.

Heat raced through his blood. "Stand up and strip."

His voice held a distinct growl, making her lips quirk up at the corners for a brief second before she maneuvered back to her feet, hands on her hips.

She raised her eyebrows at him. "Make me."

Lust fired at her dare, making him suck in a sharp breath. The look she gave him was pure provocation.

If she wanted to play this game, he wasn't about to say no.

In the back of his head, the niggling doubt that they were stealing this time alone together kept intruding. The more he tried to ignore it, the more he knew it was right.

Just accept it and enjoy her.

Pushing off the couch to his feet, he stared down at her. He liked the way she turned her head to look up at him. Liked how her gaze then made a leisurely inspection of him from head to toe.

Barely holding on to his control, he reached for the hem of her shirt with both hands then pulled it over her head with a jerk. Her hair spilled back around her shoulders, the ends curling over her breasts and brushing against the purple satin cups of her bra.

That would stay for the moment because it looked fucking awesome against her skin.

Next, he reached for her to bring her to her feet then reached for her jeans, flicking open the button, yanking down the zipper then forcing them down her legs.

She'd taken off her shoes when she'd arrived. They sat by the door where he hoped they stayed all night.

"Step out."

She hesitated just a second before she complied.

Her panties matched the bra and made him want to go to his knees so he could rip them away with his teeth. But then he didn't want to damage them because he really wanted to see them on her again.

Actually, he wanted to fuck her while she wore them so every time she put them on, she'd remember this night.

He left the panties where they were.

"Take my clothes off."

She didn't tease him at all this time. Her nimble fingers

discarded his shirt in seconds and went to work on his button fly.

He watched the increasing rise and fall of her breasts, as if she couldn't get enough air.

Join the club, sweetheart.

Every time she tugged a button through its hole, his cock responded by hardening even more. And when she bent to pull his jeans down, he put one hand on her nape and pressed, gently but firmly.

"Suck me, baby. Please."

He could barely get the words out from between his clenched teeth but she must have heard him because she went to her knees, her hands tugging down his boxer briefs.

When his cock sprang free, he breathed a sigh of relief before drawing her head toward him. She gave some resistance but from the look she flashed him, he knew it was token, designed to make him even hotter.

Which she was doing a damn fine job of.

The second her lips touched his cock, he wanted more. More of her mouth, more of her hands, her body. Wanted everything she had to give. And then some.

He let her nuzzle him for a moment, rub the tip of her nose against the shaft, before he clasped her chin in one hand and tilted her head back.

He wanted her mouth. And she knew it.

Her lips parted and he angled his cock down so he could thrust inside.

Slick heat. Tight suction. The slight graze of her teeth.

Christ, he'd be lucky not to blow in seconds.

He started a steady rhythm that had him gasping almost as heavily as Jules. He was careful not to gag her but he couldn't stop. She sucked on him hard as he pushed in then let her teeth graze his skin on the way out.

Fuck. She made him insane. Made him crazy and hot and took him out of himself to a place he'd never been.

Her hands gripped his thighs, kneading the tight muscles. He bent his head to watch her and his cock gave a warning pulse as her lips spread around the tip.

With her eyes closed, she looked as if she were enjoying it almost as much as he was. Jesus, he hoped so because he wanted her to do this for hours.

Just the thought made his balls draw up.

Too soon.

With reluctance, he pulled away from her mouth then bent to pick her up.

With a gut-wrenching sigh, she wrapped her arms around his shoulders and her legs around his waist. His cock bumped against her mound, the satin covering her cool against his heated flesh.

Fuck yeah.

He wanted to impale her on his cock and keep her there until she came around him.

When she started to rub against him, lifting her body up, he realized they were definitely on the same page.

Keeping one arm around her back to hold her against him, he moved to the couch and lowered himself to the cushions. With his arm around her waist, he urged her higher, then used his free hand to guide his cock. He rubbed the tip against her panties, rubbing at her clit.

Her head fell back and her eyes closed. Sucking her bottom lip between her teeth, she bit into it, making him want to do the same. Lowering his mouth to hers, he sealed their lips together for a long, deep kiss.

As she moaned into his mouth, she writhed against him, angling her body so the head of his cock lodged between her lower lips, pushing her panties inside her body.

"Keegan."

He knew what she wanted but he wasn't ready to give it to her yet. He wanted her just as crazy as he felt.

He rubbed and rubbed until her panties were drenched with both their juices and she'd started to moan.

Finally, he reached down to rip her panties to the side. The first touch of his cock made them both shudder, his arms tightening around her.

But somehow she managed to move, working herself against him until she shimmied down his shaft with an indrawn breath.

Jesus Christ, that felt amazing. She was going to kill him.

As he groaned, he released more of her weight and she slid until she couldn't go any farther.

"Jules."

"Oh my god, Keegan." She tilted her head forward and rested it against his shoulder. "You feel so good."

That was all it took to lose the grip on his control.

He lifted her just high enough so that he felt her slide down his shaft. Her grip on him was so damn tight, it felt like a vise. But he slid easily because she was so wet.

Faster.

He increased the rhythm, felt her moving against him. Her breath blew across his neck, hot as a brand. His hips jerked, slamming him higher into her heat.

When she shuddered, he knew she was close. Their movements grew rougher, harder, but they still moved in sync.

If only—

He came, the burst of pleasure so intense he felt it to his toes. How he managed to stay on his feet was a miracle, with Jules convulsing around him and her arms nearly cutting off his air supply.

But he held on to her just as tightly because without Erik to back him up—

Shit.

Lowering his head, he brushed his cheek against her hair and felt her return the caress.

They sat there for several minutes, just breathing, their skin slowly cooling.

He wanted to say something, anything, that would make her stay.

Jules stirred, shifting closer. "I don't want to move but I'm getting chilly."

He ran his hands up and down her back as she snuggled her face into his neck. "That feels great."

"But you're still cold." He looked around the room, realizing he didn't have a blanket on any of the furniture. He'd have to fix that.

"I should get dressed and get home anyway."

Fuck no. "Stay."

"I can't." No hesitation. "I've got to be up early. I'm helping Carol again tomorrow."

It was on the tip of his tongue to ask why she was working when they'd given her more than enough money, but he was smart enough not to say it.

Besides, he knew the reason. Carol was practically family and Jules didn't abandon family.

He wanted to be counted as family. He and Keegan.

His arms tightened and he had to make a conscious effort to relax them. "I really wish you could stay."

Pulling back, she looked him in the eyes. "Me too."

Does she want me to argue with her? Make her stay? Beg her?

Hell, he just might stoop to that. But he didn't want to pressure her.

Instead, he lifted his hand to cup her cheek and held her steady for another kiss. This one didn't devour. It coaxed, played, and lulled them back into that heated place they'd been just a few minutes ago.

But when he pulled back, she wore a rueful smile. "As much as I'd love to do that all night, I really do have to get some sleep."

With that, she grabbed her clothes and slipped into them. He sat and watched, as mesmerized as if she were taking them off.

But she went way too fast. She was finished before he'd zipped his jeans and had to wait for him to walk with her to the door.

Just before she slipped into her car, he grabbed her and planted another kiss on her that left her gasping.

"We'll figure this out, Jules. I'm not giving up."

He hoped like hell she understood what he was saying.

Her smile indicated she did. But that she wasn't sure they could.

"I'll talk to you soon, Keegan."

He stood there until he could no longer see her taillights.

Then he headed back in the house and stared at his phone.

AVENGED SEVENFOLD'S "ALMOST EASY" blared from his phone late Sunday morning and, out of habit, Erik grabbed it immediately.

Keegan's ring.

Shit.

He felt like a dog who'd been conditioned to respond whenever someone rang a bell.

His thumb hovered over the screen. He wanted to answer. Hell, they hadn't talked to each other in a week and it almost felt like he'd lost a limb.

What the fuck should he say?

Sorry I've been such a dick.

Probably a good start.

I gave the information Kat got me to the police.

That would be better but it wouldn't be true.

Fuck.

As he continued to stare at the phone, it finally went silent.

The urge to toss it against the wall of his study had his hand tightening around the case. Just before he knew he'd crush it, he threw it on the chair next to him.

He'd been moody and cranky since waking up. Probably because he had a fucking hangover painful enough to make him consider an ice pick to the temple.

Which wouldn't do anything to alleviate the cold ball of lead in the pit of his stomach.

Had she spent the night with Keegan?

If she had, was that why Keegan was calling? To tell him she'd made a decision between them? Or was Keegan calling because they'd never gone more than three days without talking to each other since the day they met?

Call him back.

Keegan had been the better man and called first. The least Erik could do was return his call. With a harsh sigh, he grabbed the phone. Then sat there staring at it.

Coward.

Fuck it.

He jabbed at the phone and heard Keegan's voice before he got it to his ear.

"I was almost afraid you'd blocked my number."

If he didn't know Keegan so well, he might've missed the dry wit in his tone.

Erik huffed. "Maybe I should have because if you're calling for any other reason than to say you missed me, I'm gonna pout."

Keegan's amused snort came through the phone perfectly. "You're an ass. A stuck-up, conceited ass."

"And you're a whiny bitch."

"Fuck you."

Erik sighed. "Yeah, I missed you too, you prick."

"Good. Now, what the hell are we going to do about Jules?"

Slouching deeper into the couch, he let his head fall back so he was staring at the ceiling. "You do realize all this time we've been focusing on ourselves, we haven't thought about what she wants."

A pause. "Has she said anything to you about going to culinary school?"

"Yeah, she has. In fucking New York." Erik shoved a hand through his hair, wishing his damn headache would give up the ghost. "I don't want her to go."

"Neither do I." Keegan's voice became more somber. "But... there's no way I want to stop her from doing what she wants."

"If she leaves, we lose her."

"We may have lost her already."

They fell silent for several seconds until Keegan took a deep breath. "Have you decided what you're going to do with the information?"

Erik snorted. "Honestly, right now, I could give a flying fuck about it."

"Whatever you want to do with it, I'll back you. I should've said that from the moment Katrina handed it over."

Erik felt a little bit of that cold ball in his gut dissipate. "Then come over and let's talk through it."

"I can do that."

"Of course you can. It's not like your calendar's overflowing."

"Speak for yourself, asshole."

Now grinning, his hangover in retreat mode, Erik decided

maybe things were going to be okay. "Just get your ass over here. We need to make some plans."

JULES STARED at the online application for the Culinary Institute of America.

She'd started filling it out three times already Monday morning before closing the screen and getting up to do something else.

Anything else.

Except the one thing she wanted to do, which was call Erik and Keegan and tell them she wanted to see them.

And what if they're still not talking to each other?

She knew some of that was her fault. She'd come between them.

What if she'd driven that wedge between them even deeper by insisting on seeing them separately?

Damn it. They'd told her they'd never had a three-way relationship. Their three-ways were confined to the bedroom.

Maybe that's how they want to keep it.

She should break it off now. Chalk it up to a learning experience and take the money and run.

And since she'd already taken the money, maybe now was the time to cut and run.

Just the thought brought tears to her eyes.

The past two nights had proved, at least to her, that these two men were worth every bit of trouble they gave her. Worth every headache she'd have to endure. Every dirty look she'd ever get, every whisper behind her back and every thinly veiled innuendo any catty bitch might ever make.

But if I go away to school, if I try to reach that dream, the relationship's over.

It felt like every which way she turned, she hit another roadblock.

Her phone bleated out a convincing moo and an instant smile lit her face.

"Hey, Jon. What's up?"

Jon Petrius's laugh was enough to make her smile widen.

"Hey, pretty girl. Whatcha doin' tonight?"

"Not one blasted thing. What did you have in mind?"

"Gary and I are having friends over to watch hockey. You know you wanna come. Just say yes."

A party. A little liquor. A few friends. "Sounds like that's exactly what I need."

"Good. You haven't seemed like yourself lately so tonight I'm going to get you liquored up then I'm going to pump you for information. And don't even think about holding back."

"I wouldn't dare. What time tonight?"

"You know you're welcome whenever. Everyone else I told to come around six. Flyers and Caps tonight. Puck drops at 7:35. And you know...if you want to bring a friend, you're more than welcome."

She wondered what Jon would say if she told him she wanted to bring two.

"Actually...I may take you up on that. But it would be two friends. Is that okay?"

"Of course, babe. But now I'm curious. Who are you bringing?"

"If they come, I'll introduce you and you can quiz them to your heart's content. If not, I'll tell you the whole story over a bottle of wine. Good wine. You know the cheap stuff gives me a headache."

"Oh please." She could almost see Jon rolling his eyes. "When have you ever known Pete to drink anything cheap?"

Silently, she conceded. Jon's partner had champagne tastes

and could afford it as a partner in one of the largest law firms in Reading.

"I'll give them a call, see if they're free tonight."

"Well, even if they're not, I still want to see you here. Talk to you later, babe."

Ending the call, she stared at her phone for several seconds before punching the button that would connect her to Keegan.

Who answered by the third ring.

"Jules."

Keegan didn't say anything else. He didn't really have to. Just him saying her name with that faint accent made her shiver.

"Hi, Keegan. How are you?"

"Fine. I'm...good. How are you?"

"I'm fine." She took a deep breath. "I was calling to see if you would be interested in coming to a party with me tonight."

He paused. "Just the two of us?"

"No. I'm going to ask Erik to join us. Will that be a problem?"

"Why don't you ask him? He's standing next to me."

Her breath caught in her throat. "You're talking again?"

"We're working on our difference of opinion."

"Is that a fancy way of saying you're beating the crap out of each other?"

Keegan laughed. "No. But I'm not promising it won't come to that before we're finished. Here."

"Keegan—"

"Jules? Hey, are you okay?"

Erik. "Yes. I'm fine. Are you?"

"Better now that I'm talking to you."

Her lips curved in a grin. The man knew how to make her smile.

"Are you doing anything tonight? I wanted to know if you

and Keegan would like to go to a friend's house tonight for drinks and a hockey game."

He paused.

Please say yes. Please say yes...

"If you want us to, of course."

Her heart started to beat again. "Great! That's great. It's probably easier if we meet at my house and go over together."

"That's fine. We'll be there by quarter of five. Does that give us enough time?"

"Absolutely. I'll see you both later."

She ended the call before either of them could back out.

It was only ten in the morning. Seven hours until she saw them again.

They couldn't get here soon enough.

KEEGAN STOOD next to Erik in the elevator, biting his tongue.

He wanted to ask Keegan if this was really what he wanted to do. But he knew if he did, Erik would likely bite his head off. So he kept quiet.

He'd already asked at least five times before they'd left on their field trip this morning. Right after they'd talked to Jules. She'd caught them on their way out the door.

Good timing. It'd taken a little bit of the edge off Erik's nerves. But not for long.

Keegan glanced at the file in Erik's hands, the one Katrina had given him. Erik had almost wrinkled the thing beyond recognition.

Keegan had his hands stuck in the pockets of his dress slacks so he'd stop cracking his knuckles.

They'd barely said a word in the car on the drive to the Philadelphia headquarters of Eggert Labs.

Old man Eggert knew they were coming. They'd had their soon-to-be-ex-lawyer call and request a meeting. They might have let their soon-to-be-ex-lawyer lead Eggert to believe they might want to talk about a possible sale.

They hadn't told him exactly what they were going to do because he probably would've advised against it.

Keegan didn't give a shit what their lawyer thought.

This was what Erik wanted, so this was what they were doing.

Still...

He drew in a breath—

"Don't even open your mouth." Erik sliced him a look. "It's my decision. You agreed. Case closed."

Their lawyer—fiftyish, gray hair, expensive suit—gave them a curious look but didn't speak. He'd met them at the door to the building after they'd parked, they'd exchanged a few cursory words, then they'd proceeded to ignore him. He'd have no bearing on the meeting. He'd added legitimacy to the lie they'd told Eggert to get him to agree to see them.

"I know," Keegan said for what had to be the fiftieth time. "And I'm backing you one hundred percent."

"Then stand beside me and let me handle this."

Keegan caught and held Erik's gaze. "You know I'll be right here."

"Which is why I can do this."

A muted ding announced their arrival on the fifth floor. The doors slid open.

Keegan held Erik's gaze for a second longer then nodded.

They walked out together.

TWENTY-ONE

Erik's palms were sweaty.

Fucking ridiculous.

It was just a party.

Yeah. With Jules's friends.

Which was why his palms were sweaty.

Meeting new people had never been a problem for him. Until he'd lost half his face in the explosion.

Fucking hell. This shouldn't be so damn difficult.

He'd gone to the restaurant, after all, and no one had run screaming.

And after his meeting with Eggert... Well, he should feel like he could handle anything.

But these were Jules's friends. And not only were they going as a threesome, but her friends would see him for the first time. People occasionally said stupid things to him when they first met him. Then he'd get pissed off and respond with something equally idiotic.

He'd learned early on it was better to just not go anywhere.

"Erik. Come out of it. We're here."

His gaze snapped to Keegan's, who was staring at him with narrowed eyes.

"Sorry. Thinking."

He looked out the side window of the now-parked car. Hell, he hadn't even noticed they'd come to a stop. He'd really been zoned out.

"Yeah, well, knock it off," Keegan punctuated his words with a friendly shove, "because if you fuck this up, I'm going to make damn sure you pay for it."

Sucking in a deep breath, Erik pushed out of the car then stopped to look at Keegan over the roof of his Beemer. "Don't you get tired of being my designated prodder?"

Keegan's face pulled into a frown. "What the fuck are you talking about?"

"I'm talking about the fact that you have never given up on me."

"Are you serious?" Keegan's brows rose as he shoved his hands in his pants, probably because of the below-freezing temperature. "You seriously want to have this conversation now?"

Erik rounded the front of the car and stopped a few feet away from Keegan. He looked at his best friend, thinking how much stronger Keegan actually was than him.

"No, you're right. I don't want to have this conversation now. Let's get Jules and do this."

Erik rolled his eyes. "God damn it. Erik. Just once—"

He never finished because Jules had opened the door and was smiling at them. Backlit, she looked like an angel. But he didn't mean the ones that had wings. He meant the ones that wore skimpy lingerie and strutted down catwalks.

Jesus, she was absolutely fucking beautiful, even bundled up in a navy pea coat. His heart beat like a bass drum, he wanted her so damn much.

And if she went away to culinary school...

Fuck. He didn't know if he could cope.

And wasn't that a kick in the ass.

"I'm so glad to see you both."

A deaf man would've been able to hear the relief in her voice as she stepped onto the porch, shutting the door behind her.

Keegan reached her first, bending to kiss her. And not a sweet peck on the cheek either. He put an arm around her shoulders and brought her flush against his body while he slipped his tongue between her lips and made her moan into his mouth.

And Erik's cock responded as if he hadn't just had her two nights ago.

Of course, Keegan had had her last night and he still seemed starved for her.

Erik totally related.

When Keegan finally left her up for air, Erik practically elbowed him out of the way to have his turn.

He kissed the trace of a smile off her lips, hands settling on her hips to pull her forward. She came with no hesitation, her arms wrapping around his shoulders as she arched into him.

Fuck the party. He wanted to go straight back to his place and get her naked and between them.

But he knew this party was a test he had to pass. If he wanted to keep Jules in their lives, well... He had to suck up his fear and step out.

But first, he wanted to enjoy having her back in his arms. She tasted warm, welcoming. Like home.

He let her up for air and so he could look into her eyes and see what she was thinking. Her smile reached her eyes and told him all he needed to know.

Now, he needed to take a deep breath and plow ahead.

• • •

KEEGAN WATCHED ERIK KISS JULES, all the while trying to get his unruly cock to stand down. He wanted to suggest they all return to Erik's and continue like nothing had come between them.

Which wasn't what Jules wanted.

He knew she wanted to see if they could make this relationship work in the real world.

And as much as he wanted it to, he knew she had legitimate concerns. There'd always be people who'd say stupid shit and look down on them. It'd never be easy, but he'd make damn sure that, when it was just the three of them together, nothing would get in their way.

Now, they just had to make her believe they could.

So... "Are we ready?"

Jules gave them each a bright smile then looped her arm though Erik's. "I am. My friend's house is only a few minutes away. We work together. For Carol. He's a great guy. You'll love him."

Erik exchanged a look with Keegan over Jules's head. Yeah, he wanted to know who this person was that Jules thought they'd "love."

But neither of them was stupid enough to ask her if she'd ever been involved with this "great guy."

She wasn't kidding about the drive. It literally only took minutes to get where they were going. Not even long enough to start a conversation because she was giving directions.

The closer they got, the more tension he felt from the backseat, where Erik sat staring steadily out the front window.

He was hiding it well but Keegan knew Erik was seriously stressing this. Their previous date at the restaurant had been easier for him because those people were anonymous faces in a crowd.

These were Jules's friends. People she worked with. People

she liked to spend time with.

And Erik knew his personality lacked tact these days.

Hell, Keegan should be worrying about his own reclusive personality. He tended to want to sit in a corner and watch everyone else. But, he realized, after these past few years when he'd been forced to be the face of the company, he'd become a little more comfortable in social settings.

Maybe he'd finally learned enough to make small talk with strangers. He'd never been good at it, but knowing Jules, he figured her friends would be just as open and easy to talk to as she was.

Christ, I hope so.

When he parked where Jules told him to, he was pretty sure he knew which house they wanted. The one that still had the Christmas lights blazing and the open curtains. Inside, he saw a crowd of people, most of them laughing or smiling.

You can do this.

Since Erik had helped Jules out of the car and was holding her hand, Keegan motioned for them to head across the street as he followed close behind.

Jules didn't bother knocking on the door. She just turned the knob and walked into the mass of people and sound.

Erik had slipped behind her as they entered so Keegan saw his back go rigid.

He wanted to put his hand on his friend's shoulder, let him know he was there, but Erik knew Keegan had his back. Would always have his back.

"Hey, Jules! You made it."

A tall man with dark hair and a face that must have women flocking gave Jules a bear hug.

"Thanks for having us. Jon." She turned to smile at Erik. "This is Erik and Keegan."

The man's attention turned to Erik and his gaze narrowed in

shock before quickly dissolving into matter-of-fact sympathy. "Jon Petrius." He stuck out his hand. "Erik Riley, right?"

It was Erik's turn to be surprised and he took Jon's hand by habit. "That's right. Have we met?"

"No, but I've worked for Carol for a lot of years. I've worked your Christmas party several times. I recognized your face. Nice to meet you."

The shock made Erik go slack-jawed. Keegan could almost hear his gears grinding in confusion. No one had ever taken a picture of Erik's face after the explosion. So that could only mean that Erik was still recognizable, even with the scars. "Nice to meet you, too."

Jon turned to Keegan and he realized he remembered this man's face, probably from their parties.

"Keegan Malone." He stuck out his hand and Jon took it with a firm grip. "Nice to meet you."

"Glad you could come." Jon smiled. "And if you don't mind, I'm going to introduce you to my partner, Gary, before we start with all these other miscreants. I warn you now, though, he loves to talk shop. He's an engineer, too. Mechanical. Once you get him going, he doesn't tend to stop. Follow me. We'll get you set up with drinks then I'll let Gary loose on you. Trust me, you'll need the drink first."

As they moved through the small house, Jules stopped to talk to a few people. Not all of them hid their shock and Keegan heard a few whispered conversations behind them, but Erik seemed to be handling himself better than Keegan had ever expected. Or dared to hope for.

Keegan released the breath he was holding and made a conscious effort to relax his shoulders.

But he couldn't stop watching Erik.

Jules must have known every person in the house because

she greeted everyone she passed with a stunning smile or a few words.

They all smiled back and gave hugs. And she never failed to introduce Erik and Keegan. A few of them did double takes at Erik, but none of them turned away in disgust or froze up and stared at him like he was a circus freak.

When they finally made it to the kitchen, Erik was visibly more relaxed than he had been when they walked in.

Jon walked into the kitchen first, wrapping his arm around another man who turned slowly to face them.

Gary was at least ten years older than Jon, so he was probably thirty-five, maybe forty.

And obviously ill. So thin, he looked like a prison camp survivor.

Jules threw her arms around the man's shoulders for a big hug. "Hey, Gary. You're looking so much better than last time. Did you like the soup I sent home with Jon?"

"The soup was wonderful, sweetheart."

"Good, then I'll make sure to send more next time."

"And if you sneak in a loaf of white bread, I will love you for all eternity."

Jules laughed and the sound made Keegan's heart skip a beat. Damn, he just wanted to wrap his arms around her, grab Erik, and go the hell home.

Instead, he put on a smile and shook the guy's hand when Jules introduced him. Gary's hand felt so frail, he was afraid he'd squeeze too hard and crush his bones.

Gary raised an eyebrow at him, as if he knew what he was thinking, then he turned to Erik, looked him straight in the eyes, and said, "Afghanistan?"

Keegan had absolutely no idea what the hell the guy was thinking. Erik did, though.

"No. Explosion in the lab. Mostly fire damage."

"My apologies for being so blunt. My nephew came back from his third tour with similar scarring and I thought—"

"No need for apologies," Erik cut in, his tone downright gentle. "Your nephew is a brave man."

"Yes, he is. He's still going through tough times but his wife's stuck by him. They'll be fine. Maybe you'll get to meet him tonight. I've invited him several times but he's not comfortable among other people yet. Someday I hope..."

Jon gave his partner a hug and kept his arm around the slightly shorter man. "One of these days, I'm just going to drive over there and shove him in the car."

Gary laughed. "I'd like to see you try, you scarecrow. Jimmy's got about fifty pounds of muscle on you."

"True, but he likes me." Jon waved at the fridge. "Anyway, we've got beer and liquor and pretty much anything you could want. Pick your poison and hurry up. The good seats go fast. You've gotta stake your claim early."

Keegan and Erik opted for beer, Jules had a whiskey sour.

When Jules started to head back to the living room, she snaked her arm through Keegan's and held out her hand to Erik.

Who took it and squeezed but didn't move.

"I'm gonna talk to Gary for a few minutes. I'll be right out."

Jules' smile got wider then she leaned forward and went on her toes so she could kiss Erik. "Don't be too long."

When she turned, Erik's gaze met Keegan's. And for the first time in a long time, Erik grinned at him and nodded. At that moment, he looked so much like the old Erik, Keegan actually blinked in surprise.

Then Erik turned back to Gary.

"So, your nephew." Erik leaned back against the counter. "How's he handling his recovery?"

Keegan didn't hear any more because Jules pulled him back

to the front room, where twenty or so people were debating the merits of the Capitals over the Flyers.

Jules joined the conversation easily. Keegan wasn't familiar enough with the game to add anything. Which was just as well. Between his unwavering attraction to Jules and his concern for Erik, his concentration was fractured.

He just hoped this night would go a long way to fixing the fractures in their relationship.

"THANKS FOR ASKING us to come along with you tonight."

"I'm glad you were both able to come."

Jules turned in the front seat so she could see Erik. She tried not to smile too widely but she couldn't help herself.

Tonight had gone better than she'd dared to hope. Erik had actually looked like he was having a good time. He'd spent a lot of time talking to Gary. Keegan had been a little quiet but she'd realized that was his normal state of being. When he had something to say, he said it. Otherwise, he listened. And he didn't miss much. She figured she talked enough for all three of them.

From the few winks she'd gotten, her friends had been sufficiently impressed with her guys and no one had said anything stupid to Erik.

Win.

At least, a cautiously optimistic win.

Erik wore a slight grin that widened when she smiled back. In that instant, the shadows covered him at just the right angles that only the unscarred side of his face was visible and she had a brief flash of what he'd looked like before.

Startled, she blinked because he didn't look like the man she'd grown so fond of.

Oh, just admit it. You love him.

Keegan slid her a quick look. "Jules? You okay?"

And you love him too. What the hell are you going to do?

She nodded and smiled. "I'm fine. Just a little tired."

Maybe a little drunk? Maybe just a little.

But she'd been in such a good mood, especially because she was with her guys. She'd been celebrating.

And trying not to notice that Keegan and Erik weren't saying much to each other.

Damn it. She didn't want them to be pissed off at each other. She wanted everything to be perfect.

Which was stupid, because she knew nothing ever would be. Life was messy and dirty and fucked up.

And sometimes you just had to push ahead and get to the next good thing while living through the last bad thing.

Huh. Maybe she wasn't as drunk as she'd thought because that actually sounded profound.

Which made her giggle because, yeah, she'd had a little too much to drink. Or maybe just enough.

Erik leaned forward and now the lights from oncoming cars showed him so clearly, and he was the man she knew again. His lopsided smile made her hot. Hot enough that she wanted to crawl into the backseat with him and ride him while Keegan drove.

"Hell, Jules, you keep giving me that look and I will pull you back here and fuck you."

Beside her, Keegan sucked in a deep breath.

She pouted, giving Erik a look she knew he'd correctly interpret as permission. Because, oh wow, did she want him to do it. "But what about Keegan?"

"Keegan can fucking wait until we get back to my place." Erik looked into the rearview mirror. "Can't you?"

"I can wait." Keegan's voice sounded almost strangled. "But

not for long."

Erik's grin widened. "Then you better get back here, babe."

She thought about it for all of a second. Then she unclipped her seatbelt.

The rest wasn't easy and it certainly wasn't pretty but Jules managed to contort her body until she landed on Erik's lap in the backseat.

She was still laughing when Erik shoved her skirt up her thighs, grabbed her panties, and tore them down her legs.

Erik leaned forward to kiss her, cutting off her laughter and making her moan instead.

"There you go, babe. I've been dying to get inside you all night."

"Nice to know I have that effect on you." Her heart thudded almost painfully as she unbuttoned his jeans and pulled down his zipper.

Erik shoved his hands in her hair, holding her mouth at just the right angle to give her long, slow, deep kisses that made her toes curl.

The emotion she tasted on his lips went to her head, more potent than any liquor.

When she pulled back to finish what she'd started, she looked into Erik's eyes as she helped him move his jeans low enough to free his cock. She saw the same heat she felt burning in her gut.

The car's powerful engine gave a muted roar. Keegan must have stepped on the gas.

She didn't know how far they were from Erik's house but she wanted Keegan back here as well.

"How long until we get to Erik's?"

She didn't bother to look over her shoulder, kept her eyes locked with Erik's as she slid her hand slowly down his chest.

"Five minutes."

Keegan sounded out of breath.

She liked that.

She also liked the way Erik's chest rose and fell and the heat of his breath on her cheek.

"Drive faster because I want you back here too."

"Fuck."

She barely heard Keegan's response but it made her shiver all the same.

And when she wrapped her fingers around Erik's shaft, he said the exact same word in the exact same way.

Yes. This is what I want.

Erik began to thrust into her hand, loving the feel of her fingers gripping him tight.

He took her lips again as she tightened her grip, moaning when she felt the slickness leaking from his cock.

"Jesus Christ. You two are going to get us killed."

Keegan took a turn a little too sharply and Erik put his arms around her so she wouldn't hit the door.

"Keegan, man, be careful."

"I'm trying but it's a little tough when I know where she's got her hands."

"Don't worry," she threw the words over her shoulder. "Your turn's coming."

"I might not last that long."

Erik barely heard Keegan but Jules's laugh told him she had, loud and clear.

"Yes, you will. Because Erik's going to wait too. Aren't you?"

"No, I don't want to wait."

"Tough." She smiled to take the sting out of the word. "I'll make it worth your while."

"Honey, you make every damn thing worthwhile." Erik was still smiling but intensity burned in his eyes. "Haven't you figured that out yet?"

Her gaze collided with Erik's and she sucked in a sharp breath at the emotion there. Raw and vivid and bone-shaking.

She squeezed his cock and brought her pelvis forward so the tip brushed against her clit.

Ohmygod.

She moaned, unable to keep it locked inside.

He felt so damn good. She wanted to move into position and slam down on him. Take him all the way, fuck him hard and fast.

But she wanted Keegan here too.

As if he'd read her mind, he muttered, "Almost there."

Yes.

Her head fell back as the car turned again, this time at a slower speed. But it was still enough to jostle her, lodging the head of Erik's cock right at her entrance.

The temptation was too much.

She took him in, making them both groan.

Oh god, she didn't want to wait any more.

She started to move, Erik's hands on her hips encouraging her. Leaning forward, she let her forehead rest against Erik's as he started a slow, slow rhythm that made her burn from the inside out.

He wouldn't let her move any faster, the pace glacier-slow. He helped her sink down on him then pushed up to get even deeper.

His kiss was just as languid, as if they had all the time in the world. She felt he should be going faster, keeping pace with the speed Keegan was pushing the car.

Then the car began to slow until it finally came to a smooth stop, followed by the sound of a car door slamming and, seconds later, the back passenger door opening.

Cold night air drifted over her overheated skin for the few seconds it took for Keegan to slide in.

"Jesus, we're gonna be pretzels after this."

She smiled at Keegan's observation but couldn't think of anything to say because Erik rubbed his cock against that spot inside that made her shiver and shake.

"Then I guess you can wait your turn." Erik sounded almost out of breath.

"Fuck you." Keegan's tone lacked heat. "Move."

Apparently they'd done this before. In a couple of moves, Jules was on her back across the bench seat, Erik's cock still wedged inside her as Keegan knelt over her, pushing his cock down so she could suck him.

Yes, this was exactly what she wanted.

Mine. Both of them. Mine.

Erik slowed his thrusts as she took Keegan in. The angle was a challenge but she was up to it. She sucked on the head, swiping her tongue around and making Keegan groan. He put one hand under her head to support her. The other he used to keep his cock in her mouth. He couldn't really move without being dislodged and she felt his restraint in the slight tremble of his fingers.

Erik had stopped moving altogether, his cock as deep as he could get it, his hands on her hips gripping her tight.

She wanted Erik to move, so she rolled her hips. When he groaned, she smiled around Keegan's shaft, causing Keegan to suck in a hard breath.

"Christ, Jules. You feel so damn good." Erik began to retreat, hitting every point of pleasure on his way out.

So do you.

With one hand, she reached for Keegan, her fingers brushing against the naked skin of his flank. He'd pushed his jeans to just below his ass, baring the tight muscle. With her other hand, she reached for Erik, laying her hand over his.

Breathing through her nose, she sucked and tormented Keegan, rolling her hips like a wave against Erik.

She tried to set a faster pace but the guys wouldn't give up control. Which was just fine by her. She wanted them to dominate her. Wanted to feel cherished. Loved.

These two men loved her. They gave her what she needed and what she wanted and so very much more. She wanted to give them the same. To make them understand that she cherished them. Loved them.

But she couldn't right now because she couldn't speak. Couldn't string two words together because each man was setting his own pace, not allowing her to get into a rhythm. It scrambled her senses but made her hyperaware of everything around her.

The heat of Keegan's cock against her tongue, the fullness of Erik's cock in her pussy. The taut muscle of Keegan's thigh and the slickness of the scar tissue on Erik's hand.

Heat flushed her body from each point of contact. She heard the men's labored breathing, felt her own lungs straining.

With a groan, Erik's hips slammed forward, sinking his cock as deep as he could go. Her pussy clamped down on him, her orgasm still out of reach.

"Keegan."

"Yeah. Almost."

"Hurry."

No. Not yet. I'm not—

Erik slid his hand to her mound, his thumb finding the exact spot on her clit that made her body zing. Moaning, she tightened her lips around Keegan's shaft and sucked even harder.

"That's it, baby." Erik's low, raspy words pushed her closer. Combined with the taste of Keegan's slick skin and the way Erik's cock rubbed against that spot...

Another flick of Erik's thumb and she felt that tug low in her body that rippled even lower and became her orgasm.

"Oh *fuck*."

Keegan's harsh exclamation was followed by the jerk of his cock in her mouth then the hot sweetness of his cum.

Erik thrust another couple of times into her spasming pussy then he joined them with a shudder.

Seconds went by with their heavy breathing the one sound to be heard.

Then Keegan withdrew and maneuvered himself so he was sitting with her head on his thigh. Erik pulled out and quickly shrugged out of his shirt so he could pull his undershirt over his head and clean her up.

She would've been happy to curl into a little ball right then and sleep.

But Erik had other ideas.

"Come on. Let's get inside before we freeze out here."

With a sigh, she sat up, fixing her clothes before she slid across the seat to let Erik help her out of the car.

She must have been more tired than she realized because her knees almost gave out. Before she could right herself, Erik swept her into his arms and headed for the front door.

Over his shoulder, she saw Keegan click his remote to lock the car before he hurried to catch up.

And all was right with her world.

"SO." Erik looked at Keegan, who nodded. "We need to talk."

Erik watched Jules turn her head on the pillow, eyes half open, lips red and puffy from their kisses.

Neither he nor Keegan had been satisfied completely by the episode in the car. And Jules had been more than happy to let them hold her between them and make her come again.

Frankly, Erik didn't think he'd ever be satisfied. He'd always want more of her. And he'd never get tired of having her in this bed or any other bed, as long as she was between him and Keegan.

Keegan felt the same.

Now, they needed to know what she wanted.

Please let it be us.

Her nose crinkled even as her lips curved in a smile. "And what do we need to talk about?"

"Us."

Her eyes opened a little more. "So there is an us?"

Keegan and Erik exchanged a glance. "If you want there to be."

Her nose scrunched up. "Do you think I'd be here if I didn't?"

Erik's heart started to pound and he couldn't exactly catch his breath. "Honestly...no. I don't think you would. But we," he exchanged another glance with Keegan, "know you've been talking about going away to school."

She blinked. "And you're worried about that?"

"In a way." Erik held up a hand when her lips parted. "We're worried that we'll stand in your way of what you want to do."

She gave him a look that quickly put him in his place. "Do you really think that if I wanted to do something, I wouldn't because you told me not to?"

As both he and Keegan sighed, he saw her bite her lip, trying to hide a smile.

His eyes started to narrow and she sat up against the head-board, crossing her legs under the sheet, her hair falling over her shoulders to mostly cover her breasts.

Erik's brain momentarily stuttered to a stop at the sexy vision. Then he blinked and forced himself to look into her eyes.

"Okay, yes, I've thought about going back to school. I've been thinking about it a lot lately. But I talked to Carol on

Friday and I realized something. I would rather work to build a business of my own here than spend two years giving money to someone to teach me what I could be learning by doing. And I dare anyone to try to make me feel like I can't do what I want where I want. They can all go pound sand. I've got friends who believe in me. I've got a mother who loves me. And..."

She stopped as she looked at them. Keegan smiled as Erik nodded. "You have two guys who aren't going to let anyone tear you down. Ever."

Her smile brightened the dark room. "And you are exactly what I want. What I need."

"And you're what we need," Keegan added when Jules tried to speak. "You're what we were missing between us."

"The crap coming between us was my fault. We'd much rather have you there." Erik reached for her hand. "And I'm pretty sure I solved my other problem this morning."

She frowned. "I don't—"

"Keegan and I had a talk with the guy who sabotaged our lab this morning."

Her eyes widened. "Seriously? What happened?"

"I told him to turn himself in or I would. Actually, I said a little more than that and I may have used a few more four-letter words, but when I left his office, I felt like some of that weight on my shoulders was gone."

"Is he going to confess?" Jules sounded almost breathless and it made Erik's cock twitch.

"We don't know," Keegan answered when Erik didn't, shrugging.

"And we don't care," Erik added. "We gave him a week to make his decision and if he doesn't come clean, I give the file to the police and let them handle it."

"Oh, Erik."

Jules practically beamed and Erik knew he'd made the right

decision. For Keegan and TinMan. For himself. And for the three of them.

"I realized that holding on to that anger was toxic. And I didn't want to poison you or Keegan anymore. So..."

He trailed off, his gaze anchored to her smile.

"So..." Jules sat up on her knees and wrapped her arms around Erik's neck. "Would this be a good time to tell you I love you? Both of you?" She turned to include Keegan in her smile. "And I'm hoping like hell that you and Keegan let me stay here?"

Keegan plastered himself to her back, hands on her hips as Jules pressed herself against Erik.

"We wouldn't want you to be anywhere else.," Keegan spoke with his lips pressed against the curve of her neck, making her shiver. "Always here. Always between us."

Erik bent to take her lips for a soul-searing kiss, leaving her breathless and panting. "So that's our proposition. Do you accept?"

Jules smiled. "Absolutely."

―――――

ERIK'S SISTER, Kat, gets her happily ever after. Check out An Indecent Affair

ALSO BY STEPHANIE JULIAN

INDECENT
An Indecent Proposition

An Indecent Affair

An Indecent Arrangement

An Indecent Longing

An Indecent Desire

FAST ICE
Bylines & Blue Lines

Hard Lines & Goal Lines

Deadlines & Red Lines

REDTAILS HOCKEY
The Brick Wall

The Grinder

The Enforcer

The Instigator

The Playboy

The D-Man

The Machine

SALON GAMES
Invite Me In

Reserve My Nights

ABOUT THE AUTHOR

Stephanie Julian is a USA Today and New York Times best-selling author of contemporary and paranormal romance.

Stay in touch for all new releases and sales. Sign up here.

An Indecent Proposition

Stephanie Julian

Published by Stephanie Julian

Copyright 2013. Stephanie Julian.

CPSIA information can be obtained
at www.ICGtesting.com
Printed in the USA
LVHW081548190422
716634LV00016B/629